VINTAGE VINYL PLAYLIST

by

John Michael Flynn

Fomite
Burlington, VT

ISBN-13: 978-1-959984-16-0
Library of Congress Control Number: 2023938674

Fomite
58 Peru Street
Burlington, VT 05401
www.fomitepress.com
06/02/2023

Contents

ALBUM THREE
Forget You Knew Me
Novella Capriccioso In E
On Coral Records

The following tracks appeared in these juke boxes in slightly different forms, some with different titles, some written under the pen name Basil Rosa.

A Question Of Execution in *Retreats From Oblivion: The Journal of Noircom*

A Sea Of Blurred Light in *Fiction On The Web, UK*

Scarlet Leonard in *Fleas On The Dog*

Why The Good Are Needed in *Italian Americana Review*

The Millbury Street Legend in *Red Earth Review*

Water Towers in *Litro Magazine New York*

Not Your House in *Call Me [Stranger] Literary Journal*

Shoulda Seen Me Up There In Mississauga in *The Wrong Quarterly*
The Meatloaf Sighting in *Rue Scribe*

Glass Nails Shower Back Into The Sea, published as The Basking Shark, in *Prime Number Magazine Editors' Selections Anthology, Volume 1*

ALBUM ONE
Quintet Fortuna
A Jazz-Blues Jam In C
On Bluenote

We have to make ourselves as perfect as we can.
— Sonny Rollins, in a *Downbeat* interview

Melodia: A Sea Of Blurred Light

THE SHAMROCKS ON EACH corner of my cocktail napkin have changed into leprechauns and jigged away. New customers have barkeep Newton Smalls jumping. Most of 'em are travelers with small Gladstone bags who sit on the bench along the far wall in the darkness under a dart board nobody ever uses. I fix my numbed senses on the sot Dooley Mullhaven whistling as he explains to pal Elton Dimmer his technique for grooming his mustache. Dooley Mullhaven refers to the mustache as his pussy pleaser and this gets a guffaw from a beefy working stiff seated elbows-up over a mug of draft to Mullhaven's right. I don't know this working stiff and don't care to. I'm kinda in a compromised position since I'm sandwiched between the working stiff and Elton Dimmer. We're what you could call Dooley Mullhaven's peanut gallery.

That ain't a good thing these days on account of Dooley's been laid off, but the man is heroically, tragically upbeat. He holds to a romantic, and what I interpret as a soon to be obsolete form of charm. He's kinda like the boxer, Jim Braddock, with dreams to play football for the Fighting Irish that never really materialized. Another thing is that Dooley will shovel Shinola with his face before accepting a dole from Uncle Sam. The man's got moxie. He knows how to listen and make a person feel welcomed. As a clown, he'd be as appealing as Emmet Kelly. Maybe the best word is compassionate.

Exudes a sense of caring for others. In my book, gotta like that about any man.

Tired of talking about his mustache, Dooley turns to me from his end position at the small bar and asks if I know why this city we live in sinks three inches a year.

Dooley got the bum's rush and I feel sorry for him, but I can't answer his question. It's the first I've heard of this. Not Elton Dimmer. Seething, slurring, Elton pipes in with his two pennies: "Built on a swamp, Dooley, that's why. Whole country's nothing but a picnic for mosquitoes. Beyond me how any crackpot can measure such a fact to begin with."

Dooley Mullhaven rolls those citrine eyes of his as if he's had it with rubber-lips Dimmer. He says to me, "What else you hear of all the flap-doodle about Mayor Grifasi reinventing the city?"

Again, Elton Dimmer cuts in, sounding stentorian like he's a puffed-up Victor Mature out of one of those sword-and-sandals epics in VistaVision. "Now that, Mister Mullhaven, is worthy badinage. It's no secret this bunghole, this pit, this naked excuse for a bad-mannered Metropole is going the way of the wrecking ball. Which maybe it should be. For instance, have you heard that this bus station, including this dive we're now imbibing in, is moving out to Rainy Falls? That's right. This turf we're on is soon to be prime real estate, and all the Good Housekeeping couples will soon be buying new abodes in Rainy Falls because it will be such an easy place to leave behind by bus. Next will go the train station, of course, until the city's downtown is gutted, nothing but office space. All connected to Greasy Grifasi's allegations of a renaissance. Am I right or am I right?"

Elton Dimmer's smile, his teeth like milky kernels of corn, reminds me of a word my wife Polly once used to describe him. Polly's a nut for crossword puzzles, so she's got a vocabulary like Roget's. She called him rugose. I still ain't sure I know what Polly's descriptor means, but the word's sound, what it suggests, it's Dimmer in a nutshell.

Scratching tufted white hair at his crown, Dimmer gawks at the drink in front of him as if he's surprised it's still there. Everything about him is down tempo, a little seedy but smooth, like Johnny Hartman signing "Lush Life." Natch. With Dimmer, lush is the operative word. Maybe not rugose. The veins in his neck swell against his starched shirt collar, buttoned to the top. His wrist trembles as he holds his *Lark* cigarette, its snug red pack out on the bar. That filterless coffin nail jumps as he remarks, "We are all genuine rumors of no consequence."

"Don't bother our boy Paxton with that babble," says Mullhaven. This is a reference to me, Kent Paxton. "He's still smarting over Danny Rice." Mullhaven leans toward me and nods. "Aren't you, Kent? Nobody saw it coming. Danny was a stand-up fellow. I'm not buying the suicide line. Not after what he did in the war."

"All the more reason to buy it," I tell Mullhaven. "They call it shell-shock. I know a thing or two about it, but I'm inclined to agree. His young wife, a baby on the way, that'll keep most men in control of their demons."

"Maybe Danny wasn't most men," says Dimmer. "And maybe those demons didn't live inside of him. But outside. On the streets." Dimmer has a point. Danny had seen some brutal combat in Okinawa. He was a survivor, a churchgoer. This is how I want to remember him, but I know better. Before the war, Danny ran numbers and clean-up errands as part of a dues-paying member of a neighborhood watch managed by The Ear. Maybe he still owed some dues. Danny's wife, Anita, wouldn't know. Polly might. She'd dated Danny before he'd put on a uniform, but when I'd asked Polly about him, she'd played it coy. She didn't want to revisit her past. When I asked why, she'd said, "Because if the truth came out, it would destroy Anita. And you too, Kent. You know that behind that tough exterior, you're nothing but an egg-cream."

Natch. Maybe Polly is right. I'm lucky to share my life with her. She's still a bombshell and she and Danny had been an item once. I can speculate further, but I don't want to hurt myself or any people I'm close to. Polly has given me enough to chew on. The Ear is dead. That whole scene he ran is dead. What I need is a link, a particular favor, an IOU, or the wronged man who needed to exact revenge and terminate Danny's dance at the party.

The phone rings behind the bar. Newton answers, croaking, "A half-dozen. Andrea's Bakery. Right. I'll get 'em tomorrow morning after mass and bring 'em over. No problem."

Newton hangs up, winks at Dimmer. "My mother. She knows I live here."

A Trailways bus driver enters the lounge, complete with jacket and red and white oval patch. A colored man, sweating profusely, his eyes rimmed in scarlet, he fills the place, has the attention of everyone at the bar. After looking at us, seeing he's probably okay, but not really sure in that way that coloreds can never really be sure among whites no matter what city they're in, I think he gets the gist we aren't about to pull anything on a working man, least of all a hard-working bus driver. We're tippling in a bus station dive, after all.

The man asks Newton for a shot of bourbon and a short beer. The slacks of his uniform are wrinkled enough to prove he's been on the road a long time. He keeps his hat tucked under one arm while he runs a kerchief over the sweat glazing his forehead. His wary eyes shift toward Newton, who works up a smile for him.

Dooley Mullhaven perks up, asking Newton the barkeep, "You know this man?"

Newton nods and shoots Dooley a look as if to warn him no

monkey business. "I do. He's new on this beat. This is Baltimore, fellows. It's Saturday, so he's in from Cleveland, ain't that right Baltimore?"

"PFC Newton, my man." Baltimore looks and sounds relieved. He adds in a deeply resonant and syrupy musical way, with a slightly southern lilt that expands his vowels, "That is so right. And how is it going with you, my good Sir?"

"No need to be formal. I'm very good," says Newton. "What's new in Trailways world?"

Baltimore keeps dabbing sweat off his neck with a handkerchief. His voice matches his size. I feel puny next to him. "I did blacktop a fine lady the other day, since I thought they was bad roads on her that needed improvin', but I been wrong before."

There's a delay among us all before his stab at humor sinks in. Then we each begin chuckling until we're all in stitches. Baltimore, seeing he's landed among friendlies, beams and says, "Yeah, it's going to be fine, just fine."

Newton places both drinks on the bar. Baltimore knocks back the bourbon with ease. He drains half the short beer. "Please, one more." He wipes his lips with a napkin. Removes his wallet and lays a fin on the bar. Drains the short beer and then the second bourbon. Sighing through his nose, he yanks up his trousers with two hands and checks his shirt to make sure he hasn't spilled anything. He belches into his fist and then puts on his hat, adjusting it to look neat. He motions toward the fin. "You keep the change, PFC Newton."

Newton takes the crumpled fiver. "I thank you much, Sir."

"Now you're being the formal one," says Baltimore. He grins, his teeth large and bright and even. He has that wise sidelong look about him, no doubt a former soldier and a survivor, one accustomed to taking it on the chin. "We is off to Philadelphia."

I feel sad to see him go and hope I'll see him again. We seldom get coloreds in this bar and none of us, except maybe Dooley who is wholly unpredictable, has anything against them. In fact, we've all talked more than once of how we approved of Truman's desegregating the military services. I'd known some tough and dedicated colored boys during my time in the service during the war and I think it would have done me good to have shared a barracks with some of them, gotten to know them better. They're Americans just like the rest of us, and they put their lives on the line, but some ignorant jokers just don't see it that way.

The silence in Baltimore's wake lingers and for a moment I think the man never happened, that I'd dreamt him up. I say to Newton Smalls, "He looks like a real pro."

Newton checks his watch. "And I'm guessing he'll pull into The City of Brotherly Love about midnight. Right on time. He'll down a few more short beers before he rolls back to Cleveland, though he won't stop by again here to visit. If I understand his timetable these days, I think I'll see him once a month on a Saturday."

"A little too regular perhaps and probably why there's talk of closing down this establishment," says Dimmer. "They say drinkin' and drivin' don't mix."

"No," says Mullhaven. "They say a lot of things. Most of 'em wrong. If they close Newton down, it'll be to punish you. Nobody else."

Dimmer smirks at Mullhaven and silence settles in again. I'm getting nowhere. Like Baltimore, I can roll with a Saturday drink or two in me. Unlike Dimmer, I can't make it a habit. I tell the boys "See ya soon" and to keep their ears to the ground regarding Danny Rice news.

How much is enough? I once heard a man joke on the radio that enough is a little more than what you already have. Probably the smartest thing that fellow ever said. What I have is the wherewithal to get *that far*, you know, to that place I think of as *out there*. It's where everyone else is really whooping it up, making all sorts of dough, having the time of their lives. Each day, I'm getting to the core, am I not? That's good. I wish I could do more of it. But I can't. Not now with the way my work is going. Not a single lead on the Danny Rice case.

I'm feeling blue, restless, like a lost wanderer. I need something to cling to. Who knows what will be the bedrock that a person uses to get through life? We'd all like to know that. I relish the idea of being anyone's bedrock. It cures me of loneliness. I'll do anything for loved ones, for my Polly, but I've got cases to solve. Eventually, Polly will want kids. At least two of them. If I don't solve a few high profile cases I'll have to take down my shingle and go back to the kind of piece work I was doing before the war. I'm not an optimist. Second chances are one thing, but wishful thinking needs a category of its own. It's a sucker's bet.

What puzzles, as always, is motive. Why would a man not yet middle-aged leave his existence behind? Nobody wants to be forgotten. The poet in Danny Rice, if such a creature existed, had to crave immortality. The more I learn, the more I doubt that Danny died by his own mitts. I remember Polly saying — and it's one of many reasons why I'm so fond of her, "Your work, Kent, is an affirmation of your worth." She said I should feel free to overreact, to live like there's no tomorrow. That's what I'm trying to do, but I feel like I'm spinning my wheels. She called it "existential angst." Work distracts me from it.

Two weeks later out with Polly on a Friday night and stopping at The Heritage for a late dinner after drinks and a movie, I run into Elton Dimmer, who looks every bit a corruptible slow-burning fuse and is sitting in a booth with Dooley Mullhaven. It's like those two can't get enough of each other. They invite us to join them. There's plenty of room in their booth. They'd been out on the town and are each wiping up remains of minute steak, mashed and green beans.

"We're talking City Hall," says Dimmer. "A topic, no doubt, of some interest to you."

"To bloody hell with them," says Mullhaven. He sips from a glass of beer. Judging by his speech, it's one of many he's emptied that night. "I think Grifasi is a Commie. In the old days, they would have lynched him in the square. Drove him out on a rail."

Dimmer strikes a note of melancholy. "Not in this city. He's a hero."

"Who asked you?" says Mullhaven.

I lean over the table toward Dimmer. "I think what Grifasi needs is a good lawyer."

Dimmer nods. "I'm sure he's got more than one. Any news on Danny Rice?"

Dooley Mullhaven butts in. "If you ask me, this so-called Grifasi controversy is gonna die down soon enough. Go to the courts and get lost in the shuffle. The public's got a short memory."

Dimmer winks at Polly before he turns to Mullhaven. "But you forget. Scandal sheets entertain the working folk. It's the judge that matters. Not just the right lawyers. But the judge. That's where the difference is made."

"Are you saying threaten the judge?" asks Mullhaven.

"We all have our price," says Dimmer. "As it turns out, Danny Rice used to date the judge's daughter. I bet none of you geniuses knew that."

"And me too," says Polly. "When I was a size four, of course."

Dimmer shrugs, baffled. "I love you Polly. You're a doll at any size."

I say to Dimmer, "You really think one of the circuit judges had something to do with Danny's death?"

"No proof of suicide," says Dimmer. "He was strangled. The

suicide story was a diversion. And we have a judge in Mirko Vivian, first circuit, who has a daughter that was in *Photoplay* once, a real corker. Gams to die for."

"I think I read about her in the papers," says Polly.

"Yes." Dimmer eyes her. "You're as bright as you are pretty. See, this daughter went out to Hollywood and played some small roles in pictures. I guess she knew Norma Shearer out there. I don't think her Daddy Mirko wanted her to keep playing footsie with the likes of Danny Rice. But Danny, maybe feeling jilted, didn't listen. Then he went off to war with the rest of us. But he came back. And guess who got knocked-up out there in Hollywoodland?"

Mullhaven, looking stunned, brushes sweat off his forehead as he remarks to Dimmer, "That's the first smart thing you've said all night. Christ almighty on a pancake, do I hate politics and murder. Let's talk something else."

"You brought it up," says Dimmer. "You're always talking scandal and murder."

"I think I'm gonna scream," says Mullhaven. He then buckles as if speared in the ribs.

"Here we go again," says Dimmer. He leaps into action, hurries to help me. We both help Mullhaven stand. Polly helps too. Dooley Mullhaven groans as his head falls to her shoulder.

A phlegmatic Dimmer says to me, "You two sing him a lullaby and keep him calm. I'll phone a hack."

When the taxi arrives, we walk Dooley Mullhaven out and seat him in the back. Dimmer gives the driver Dooley's address, pays the man knowing a sawbuck will cover a generous tip.

The three of us return to our booth. Polly, looking glum, asks, "Why do you think Dooley's doing so bad?"

I shrug. "Shell shock? I don't know. The man survived the D-Day launch."

A melancholic note from Dimmer. "He was fond of Danny Rice."

"We all were," I say. "Dooley's like anybody else. Look around. All these people, they're a little mad. That guy there lost his wife. Another one, his daughter got pregnant too soon. That woman there, she just got old too soon. That other poor sap he got injured on the job and now he drinks whatever pittance on the dole that the state pays him each month."

I look at Polly, work up a sour grin. "The good thing, Polly, is that at least most injured souls are still smart enough to know our politicians are bought off and there's nothing they can do about it. Dooley Mullhaven knows this, but it's what you call hurtful knowledge."

"The pain of living," says Dimmer. "A little bit of knowing is a dangerous thing. I hate to say this, but if you ask me, Dooley's problem is he pays too much attention. He's like me. Stays inebriated in order to stomach it."

I look Dimmer in the eyes. "You choose. You have to. I feel sorry for Dooley, but he's been a wet firecracker since he lost his job. My sympathy won't change a thing."

"Tell me something," says Dimmer. "Will I get so callous? Is it inevitable?"

"You already are," says Polly.

Dimmer's stunned reaction is priceless. Polly had levelled him. I have to smirk. Polly knows the likes of Dimmer cold. No flies on her. "How many choices has that man suffered through?" she asks. "How many winds of fate and losses? I suspect that for those you call calloused, the losses are more numerous than any of us can imagine."

"With each year," I say, sounding wistful, "hope has to die in everyone, I suppose."

"You suppose all you want," says Dimmer. "Me. I need some air."

"I'll join you." I want to smoke outside. I tell Polly to order both of us pie and Sanka.

I step out to the street. The darkness feels too cold for November. I believe it's going to snow. I sense such things. Rubbing my hands together to keep warm, I watch my breath spread like a wave dissolving on a beach. I begin to float into the dank air, rising higher until I'm above the city rooftops. I walk across the sky, climbing in long strides upward through the night, tilting and dipping, my body weightless, the city shrinking beneath me like a sea of blurred light.

Big changes are coming. It will snow, doping the city, killing people left to starve in alleys. Dimmer, next to me, is unusually solemn. Silence from him, of all people, isn't something I'm accustomed to. I remember him telling me once that we're all rumors, that reality is a matter of perception. The city sinks more than three inches a year, but who knew?

I'm walking across the sky. I see the ghost of Danny Rice and take his hand. He nods as if to suggest I'm on to something. I say to Dimmer, "Mullhaven's idea that Mirko Vivian could be implicated, since he was the judge due to pass sentence on Danny before he was murdered, I gotta tell you, it's given me a new angle on this case."

"It's the only angle," says Dimmer. "But can you go after a circuit judge? The answer is no. You can't go after his corker of a daughter either."

"Why not?"

"The woman has a boy who I think looks a lot like Danny. And the judge, well, like me and like our man Baltimore that we met the other day, he knows how to survive. And sometimes that means protecting secrets."

Dimmer is in the wrong line of work. I tell him not to hang a P.I. shingle. I don't want the competition. Nor do I want to keep Polly waiting. I wish him goodnight.

For as long as I've been able, I've kept climbing between clouds, but the climbing ends with this Danny Rice case. Judge Mirko

Vivian and his daughter are off limits. One more boy in Hollywood won't know who his real father is.

Polly and I commiserate over pie and hot Sanka. "I know when I'm licked."

"Sweetheart, if you want to keep living," she says, "any time is a good time to clam up and grow invisible."

More hurtful knowledge. Call it wisdom. I bet that driver, Baltimore, could lecture me.

Harmonia: Scarlet Leonard

I NEED TO REACH WAY back decades ago into the cobwebs to share this number about my old man Burton and his partner Ray Panama. They'd counted the cash and locked their safe. Bartenders, wait staff, dancers and drunks had gone home. With the lights out, The Blue Danube Supper Club felt cavernous.

"So, you were saying," remarked Burton to Ray.

"Still don't got no weapon. Just a cadaver."

"But why Leonard? Something personal here I ain't getting?"

Ray paused a moment. "Burton, you know our man Phillip at the G-Clef? He told me Leonard has a nephew living here in Fortuna."

"Ring him up. Get him to spill. And all this time, I thought I knew the man."

"You never know, Burton. Not really. You got a thirst?"

"Not tonight. I'll lock up and set the alarm. See you on the flip side."

It was four a.m. by the time Burton got home. Over soft-boiled eggs, he confessed to his wife Avis, my Ma, that he was afraid Leonard Zion's death was going to ruin them.

"But you didn't do nothing wrong," said Avis.

"FPD will shut us down. A supper club can't be the last place a respected member of the community was seen before being killed. The river's just a walk from our place. That's where they found him."

"I know. It's in *The Standard* already. What you wanna do, Baby?" Avis wiped egg yolk off her lips. Such luscious lips they were, too. One of my pals once said he'd like to "bone her," those were his words, and I knocked him out with a left hook. We later made up when he admitted he had it coming.

"Beats me," said my old man. "I feel naïve when these things happen."

"You still got FPD friends and nothing to be afraid of."

"But look at me."

"I'm looking," said Avis, who still liked what she saw, though at 38, developing a paunch, Burton had lost a step and there were nights when bullet scars screamed out of both his legs. He was neither the soldier fighting Nazis nor the handsome bachelor that Avis, eight years younger, a brunette with disarming blue eyes, had married.

Avis didn't mind. She was still his Ava and he was her Frank, even though he fretted she'd tire of him. Once a cocktail waitress and before that a cigarette girl, Avis had finished night school classes to become a certified bookkeeper for The Blue Danube. She no longer looked exactly like bombshell Rita Hayworth in *Gloria*, but her curves and her smile still complemented a glittering gown and heels as she met couples at the door when they arrived to confirm their reservations.

Before the war, when Burton, just a skinny shaver, had frequented The Blue Danube with my grandfather, it was a first-class snort run by gangsters. When he became part owner and also a full-time detective, he'd labored to keep it first class and remove the gangster element. Having Avis and Ray on board helped make that possible. They'd known Leonard Zion as a genteel and respected Fortuna attorney who usually arrived alone to the club and drank Brandy Alexanders. Avis had known him the longest, from her days growing up on the city's east side where a Jewish diaspora had begun to develop post-war in some of the newer neighborhoods being built there.

Burton put down his cup of mud. "Tell me, Baby. Why the boosterism? Should I start smoking again? I miss my *Old Golds* and my slacks don't fit like they used to."

"Do some reducing with me at the Y pool, one lap at a time."

"I dunno. I'm all over creation with my emotions. Like a tidal wave."

"Take on Leonard's case. Help out the FPD. You need a challenge."

"Sugar, the man got eighty-sixed in our joint. Ain't that a conflict of interest?"

Avis smirked. Burton reminded her who they had to look out for, the same ruthless Albanians and their network who'd owned The Blue Danube before Burton and Ray had bought it from them. With Ike as president, those Albanians, once denigrated, had gelled and joined forces with some local Sicilians to form a well-organized influence on the cops and city government.

"Burton. You got moxie and ideals. Stand up for what's right."

"But Leonard wasn't a criminal."

Avis nodded while chewing. "But he was bent. As scarlet as they come. Always tidy. Dined in them fancy places like the Town and Country."

"Love their Cobb Salad."

"So did his male lover."

"How come I didn't know this?"

"Because I kept it from you. It's one more of my charms that you never notice."

"I feel a lousy taste coming on," said Burton.

"All those years a regular and I bet you didn't know Leonard was married."

"I just knew he was a lawyer in the Jewish community. Reliable."

"He projected that," said Avis, "but his law partner and his lover, the same man, lived in the Copper Lake neighborhood. Stan Vinovich."

"Sugar, you're giving me the heebie-jeebies."

"Don't look so shocked. Didn't make the connection, did you?"

"How could I?" asked Burton.

"Vinovich had a son and daughter," said Avis. "Like you, he was in the war."

"I remember that case. A bullet to the head and found naked in that new Howard Johnson's hotel on Route Thirty."

"What's your detective instinct tell you?"

"Maybe the same hired gun killed them both."

"Great minds think alike."

"Contracts, jealous spouses," said Burton. "Other lawyers in the firm who can't let on they work with those who make like Sodom while posing as upright Republicans."

"You're getting the bird's eye just like I thought you would."

The next day, Burton arrived at his usual time to the supper club, where he found Ray Panama admiring the cut of Avis's jib. Ray was his friend, but he showed no inclination to respect a certain decorum when it came to undressing Avis with his eyes. Not that Burton couldn't blame his friend, since Avis was in a pencil skirt and tight yellow blouse over one of those bullet-tip brassieres that Jane Russell had made famous. Burton cleared his throat to get Ray's attention and he pulled his partner away and they pow-wowed in a back room that no other employees were allowed to visit.

"The bigger question," said Burton as he sat with Ray, "is who we trust. Vinovich and Zion were members of the same firm. Everyone employed there, Jewish or scarlet or not, is a suspect."

"Including Zion's nephew. You know, Phil at G Clef was right. He's here."

Just then, Avis, excusing herself, popped in to ask if either of them would like a martini. "Not now," said Ray. Burton seconded the polite refusal and Avis left.

Ray said, "His name is Malachi. Had the keys to his uncle's apartment downtown."

"A love nest?"

"Righto. Keys to his car, too. That's all we got right now. I'm gonna look into whether he had access to certain accounts. He works in a bank."

"You think he was skimming from his uncle?"

"Not sure. He's just a teller, but if you mean, did he help secure loans and signatures on the legit, that sort of thing? Yeah, it's possible."

"He can't be trusted. No one can."

"We'll figure it out, Burton. We always do."

"Invite him here for supper. Champagne, the works. We'll make him feel welcomed."

Ray followed through and Malachi was treated to five-star hospitality. He feasted on Chicken Cordon Bleu and drank bottle after bottle of imported beer while revealing, among other facts, that his uncle Leonard kept journals.

"Can you get them, the journals, do you know where they are?" asked Burton.

"They're in his apartment."

"Why did he give you a key and not anybody else?"

"To look after the place, I guess."

Ray interjected, "What did he use the apartment for?"

"What do you think?"

"But not women?" asked Burton. "You did know that, right?"

"Do I need to go into those details?" asked Malachi.

"It would help," said Burton, who thought Malachi a handsome devil in a gray satin shirt, a silk black tie and seersucker jacket, his hair oiled in a D-A, his pointed shoes perfect. "Tell me about that last night you were here with him."

"I was here in a booth like this one." Malachi slapped padded lavender vinyl. "Uncle Leonard was sitting where you are. He loved to hear the live music."

"That, we know. He was on friendly terms with most of the cats in our house band."

"But I remember your club was quiet that night, too. A weeknight. Kind of early. The house band wasn't playing. And me," said Malachi, "I was marveling at a woman across the room and that's when I heard one of your doormen shouting 'Excuse me, anybody here with a Chevy Bel Air, license plate 401 DOI. Your headlights are on.'"

"You got a good memory, Kid. Was that Leonard's plate number?"

"I didn't recognize it. Uncle Leonard did right away. He was a bit tipsy already. He said 'That's me' and then he staggered out to the parking lot."

"Front door?"

"No. He took the back way."

"So, that's why I don't remember seeing him," said Ray.

"Me neither," added Burton.

Ray pointed toward the club's curved bar, lit from below and framed along its edges in bright beveled chrome. Behind it in one corner hung a long black velvet curtain. He said, "You're not supposed to. That curtain is an employee entrance that leads to the hall past our office and dressing rooms. The kitchen entrance is behind the saloon doors on the other side of the bar. It can get crowded back there. That's why customers go in and out the front. Eventually, we're getting valets. We'll have them park cars for our clientele. Nobody uses that back way except us and some of our staff, usually the musicians and our girls."

"You ever use it?" asked Burton.

"No. Never. All I know," said Malachi, "is Uncle Leonard thought of this place as his oasis. He felt comfortable here, like he had free rein."

"And he did," said Ray. "We all liked him. A real swell."

"Look, Malachi," said Burton. "Was there anyone here that night, maybe another lawyer or someone your uncle prosecuted that wanted to hurt him?"

Malachi rubbed his chin.

Ray said, "What we know is that no blood was found in the parking lot that night. No gasoline or oil spilled. Just his car, lights still on."

"So what's that tell you?" asked Burton. He stared hard at Malachi.

"I'm thinking that my uncle never made it back to his car."

Burton clapped his hands together. "Makes sense, doesn't it?" He smacked his lips together too. "Why else the rear exit?"

Ray said, "But what gets me is how would they know it was *his* car?"

"His killers knew him, set him up," said Malachi.

"Exactly," said Burton.

"He services his car at the Gregorian Brothers Garage," said Malachi. "I've taken it there for him in the past. You know their garage? It's up on Judas Hill behind City Hall."

"We do," said Ray. "And we know those brothers."

"One of them has a son, Armen," said Malachi. "He works as a desk clerk at the Continental Hotel. Uncle Leonard used to eat in the dining room there. He'd meet his friends, other lawyers, people like that."

"Upright honest folk," said Burton.

"But Armen," said Ray. "I know that boy. He don't fit that description."

"You do?" Burton couldn't hide his surprise. "Is there anybody in this city you don't know?"

Ray Panama puffed himself up and chuckled. "Probably not. Unfortunately."

"What kind of kid is this Armen?" asked Burton.

"Eh, you know," said Ray, "he got into trouble with two colored boys who were taken in for selling handguns out of the trunk of a Buick in South Fortuna. It was Armen's car, but he wasn't in it. Armen testified in court that the colored boys had stolen it. Leonard defended Armen, got him acquitted. It turns out that Armen had loaned the colored boys one of his Dad's cars. That they were all in it together."

"What happened to the two boys?"

"Well, they're coloreds," said Ray. He paused a moment, swallowing dryly. "They're in prison now."

"That's not right," said Malachi.

"Of course, it isn't," said Ray.

"So, Armen goes free thanks to my uncle?"

"Sounds like it," said Burton. "Unless my partner here is lying."

"Which I'm not," said Ray. "Nobody knows where those two boys got those guns from in the first place. I bet Armen knows. We need to talk to him."

"Don't be hasty," said Burton. "I'm sure Leonard saw a lot of cases like this one."

Malachi chipped in, faltering a little as he spoke. "It's like he had a secret life."

"What do you drive?" Burton asked. "Just for the record."

"I can't afford a car right now," said Malachi. "I ride the city bus. Take the trolley, too. I'm working, saving for college. Take after my father, I guess. He's a dentist."

"Nothing wrong with that. But look, Malachi, I'm tired and my legs are acting up. Get me those journals. Let's meet at Leonard's apartment tomorrow at ten?"

"I'll be there," said Malachi.

Ray and Burton left the young man alone to finish his supper, on the house. They sent over a call girl to keep him company while he ate dessert.

After closing time, Ray and his girl Eva joined Avis and Burton as Tony Martin sang his hit "Walk Hand In Hand" on the club's new juke box, the two men sipping highballs and the women sipping martinis while all four played Hearts. It was one of their mid-week routines.

Avis could talk a blue streak once she started drinking and she didn't mind hitting Burton below the belt now and then. "Leonard was a fair lawyer, don't forget that. He worked pro bono all the time, took a lot of cases for those who couldn't pay him."

"Yeah, he had a highly evolved sense of moral imperatives," said Burton, "but you should have seen the look of disappointment on his nephew's face."

"It's a rotten world out there," said Eva.

Burton said to her, "His people came from nothing. Some were gassed during the war. Those that survived, they worked hard. He knew what it was like to go hungry and he cared about the little guy, but I think somewhere it all went wrong."

In heels and crinoline that night, Avis sat a few inches taller but not bustier than Eva. Not hardly. She rested a hand on one of Ray's shoulders as she wobbled while rising and walking to the bar to refresh her drink. Ray didn't hesitate to swivel his head around to check out Avis's mincing gait one step at a time. To this day, I wonder if Ray and my mother didn't, eventually, have a secret tryst together. I hate to think of my father of getting played like that, but it could have happened. Ray was no saint. Neither was my mother.

When Avis returned, she added to the ongoing conversation as if she'd never left it, saying, "I'm of the mind our man Leonard probably had his share of enemies in high places. Dirty places."

"I think Avis is right," said Eva. "Never doubt women's intuition."

"And it's going to take you," said Avis, nodding at Burton, "and the rest of the police force a long time to interview all those who knew and trusted and even hated him."

My Dad Burton sounded defensive. "What I know of Leonard Zion, personally speaking, is that after my mother died, he helped me get through the legal red tape with her so-called estate and all the money she owed others. I put everything in his hands and he didn't let me down. I never knew he was scarlet or that he was married."

"So, who has a motive then?" asked Ray.

"Malachi," said Burton. "He's too fearless. I bet he knew all along that his uncle was a gunsel and he was probably blackmailing him."

Gunsel, by the way, is the kind of old-school slang my father used. At that time, it was still a safe way to refer to someone as homosexual. Gotta remember the times. If you were gay, you were in the closet.

"But I can't link Malachi to the murder of Stan Vinovich, the lover," said Ray. "And to be honest, that boy doesn't strike me as a murderer. He's an Eagle Scout."

"I think you're right as usual, my Darling," said Eva.

"Still, he was in on part of it, I'm sure," said Burton. "Too much to gain. The dirt on his uncle, the key to his love nest. He could provide evidence to Leonard's wife and legal partners. I think Armen is in, too. Armen's bad news."

"Those poor colored boys," said Ray. "They're in jail. Armen should be there with them. It's not right. It's just not right at all."

"A lot's not right, Ray," remarked Burton. "You should know that by now."

"But he don't," said Eva. She laughed bitterly. She dabbed some spittle from her lips that left the imprint of a red kiss on her white napkin. "That's why we love him."

Burton eyed his partner Ray, a short man balding, also running to fat, and he told himself he couldn't be sure of anything anymore, that he'd never been sure. What would be the next surprise? He needed to be better prepared. He suspected something; its hammering left a sting in his left knee he hoped Avis would massage later and make go away.

❧

A dream started Leonard Zion's journal. Burton held the small spiral notebook, *Fortuna Nocturna* written in black ink on its beige cover. Zion had written in pencil, relying on a gift for penmanship, recording with care and delicacy chapters, moods and conflicts from his life, spelling them out in vivid detail.

Seated, a Gin Rickey in hand, Burton continued to read pages and Zion's vision of the Clepsydra Lounge on Fortuna's Raven Street. Leonard wrote how he remembered one of its stalwarts, describing the man as contentious, reedy, a flannel-puss, hemorrhoidal, opinionated and dyspeptic. Not to mention a lush. Leonard had also scribbled in the margins that a reader who didn't know the meaning of dyspeptic had to look it up and that like all dreams this one, too, was more real than reality itself. Such margin notes convinced Burton that Leonard Zion had suffered, at one time, literary aspirations. It was a point he should not overlook.

Perhaps now Burton had all he needed. He dialed Ray and asked him to invite their journalist friend from *The Standard*, Stacy Onus, to ask if she was free for lunch at Café Agonistes. Ray called back to say she most certainly was, as long as they were footing the bill. They met her there.

Stacy looked comely in her lipstick, a long blue overcoat with a fur pelt at the collar and bone-white buttons, an accordion skirt with a floral pattern, synthetic pearls and an orange blouse with a bow top that matched her beige cardigan. It was winter, a bit breezier than usual, the sun out and the temperature just a tad above freezing. They sat near the window, a drafty spot, but they wanted the afternoon sunshine.

Ray and Burton treated themselves to broiled scallops with mashed potatoes and leek soup, while Stacy, prone to bubbly chuckles and long-winded stories, devoured a Monte Christo sandwich with hand-cut fries and told the waiter to keep the Bloody Marys coming. She explained to the boys she didn't care about her figure and how little work she'd get done that day. She'd had it, she said, with efficiency and restraint. Ray and Burton were eager familiar companions and as a threesome they found it easy to erase the hours that bridged afternoon into evening.

Stacy's chatter as she got increasingly drunk and smoked her Benson and Hedges took Burton's mind off varying states of insecurity about his work, his age, his growing obsession with an increasingly blurry past. He faded in and out of her racy stories glad that, unlike Ray who'd slept with Stacy more than once, and who'd slept with everyone it seemed, he'd never been the sort to even consider adultery. He sipped a Schlitz draft in a short glass. Ray sipped a Rob Roy. Stacy got into details she had on the Stan Vinovich murder. "This is our man."

"How do you figure?" asked Burton. "In what way?"

"I covered that murder. If I want the past, I go back to it," said Stacy. "Sometimes, you know how sometimes you believe you've experienced an event, long ago, but then you try to remember it and you can't. You go back to the place, maybe it's a neighborhood here in the city and it's gone, the whole neighborhood, everything. As if it never happened."

"I know what you mean," said Ray. "What's that got to do with our case?"

"Everything," said Stacy. "It's connected."

"I think I get it," said Burton. "Vinovich had a few years on Zion and he'd already burned in hell with guilt regarding his family and community standing as a closet case and maybe he decided he'd gone too far down that blind alley with his secret life."

"His real nature," said Stacy. "So he decided if he was to burn, then he'd do it like he was breathing in and out."

"Right," said Tiny. "In and out. But I still don't understand."

"Zion killed Vinovich," said Burton. "It was a ruse. He paid Malachi to pay Armen to drive him to the Howard Johnson's. The two were supposed to meet there. As lovers. A usual thing. The only difference was that Vinovich wasn't expecting to get shot."

"But why would Leonard do that?" asked Ray. "It's too extreme."

"Because they were done." said Stacy. She looked at Burton. "Go on. I totally follow."

"Just a matter of time," said Burton. "All they'd worked for would go down the drain. That part of the city has been changing for a long time now. The Jewish community is growing. It's close-knit. Word travels fast. The family names, in both cases, would be disgraced."

"So, Zion suddenly becomes a killer?" asked Ray. "Doesn't add up."

"No," said Burton. "They agreed to it. And I think Zion dreamed it up. He had, what you could say, a romantic imagination. See, I met with Malachi at the bank. He was able to show me transfers of funds into his uncle's account. From Vinovich. The boy Armen, that whole situation, it was a favor. Unfortunately, they treated the colored boys as collateral damage. Zion was using them to earn extra money. The important thing was that Armen got paid and got off because Vinovich owed money to the Gregorian Brothers. How much, I can't say. A lot of green stamps and dinners at The

Continental maybe. Blackmail money that Vinovich was supposed to pay the Gregorians or else they'd spill the whole story."

"Zion knew all this, arranged it all, too?" asked Ray.

"That's right," said Stacy. She was glowing. "It makes its own sick sense, in its way."

"But Ray, listen, there's more," said Burton. "I read Zion's journals. Pored through them. And no, Stacy, you can't have them for your story. He describes Vinovich as a gold digger. Vinovich had children and his wife, but he'd been married once before and still had unresolved issues with that first wife from over fifteen years ago. She knew he was in the closet and she was blackmailing him, too."

"So Vinovich owed everybody money," said Ray. "It's always money, isn't it?"

"And so did Zion, I bet," said Stacy. "Oh, what a doozy for *The Standard*."

"There's a line in the journal that explains it," said Burton. "Zion wrote 'If only for myself. It's always about someone else. All this money.' Zion at least could assess where he'd been and where he was going. Make sense of it. He was at the end with Vinovich. Sick and tired of him. True, they were lovers, but Vinovich was threatening to tell Zion's wife and, so to keep him quiet, Zion paid him blackmail money. This helped Vinovich keep making blackmail payments to his first wife. All very underhanded, tit for tat and secret."

"How on earth did you find this out?" asked Stacy.

"It's all in the journals. I just had to read between the lines. And then I had to stop reading. Malachi helped too. You were right, Ray. The kid's a Boy Scout. When we were at the downtown apartment, I thought it too spic and span, that there had to be another meeting place."

"Again, in the journals?" asked Stacy.

"Righto. A bar. The Clepsydra Lounge on Raven Street," said Burton.

"I know that bunghole," said Ray.

"Sure, you do. But Malachi didn't. And he didn't know his uncle held practically all his client meetings there at odd hours. That's where he met Vinovich sometimes, too. I didn't bother you about it, Ray, because it was a hunch, but when I stopped by there and talked to the bartender and some regulars, it was confirmed for me. The place was Zion's hideout."

"Not like our club," said Ray. "Like day and night."

"Naturally, he used our Danube here to be social," said Burton. "Put up a good front. But you have to admit it was strange he never hired a babysitter or brought his wife. The difference with The Clepsydra was that he'd have his meetings there during the daytime, at off hours, when it was empty. There's a back room there that he used. And his journals suggest his obsession wasn't with the past so much as it was about him learning how to see. He liked this thought and he goes back to it lots of times in his journal, one agonizing description at a time."

"Spoken like a poet," said Ray. He grinned, impressed, at Burton. "What would I do without you, partner?"

Stacy had to laugh. "Solve a lot fewer cases."

Burton said, "At the age of fifty-five, Zion was coming to realize he'd never really thought about anything in his life, so he decided to compensate by taking action. He orchestrated the murder of his lover and then he murdered himself. He never went to the car. He walked to the river, fast as possible, from our back entrance. Shot himself along the shore and fell in. Consider how FPD found the body. Afloat. Gunshot wound in the chest. Nobody took pains to make sure it sank to the bottom. The way I see it, if anything, it was a form of release for Zion. He'd had enough of the charade."

"Physician, heal thyself," said Stacy. "He was tormented by love."

"It's all in the journals. Leonard left clues. He wanted us to catch on."

"Hopeless," said Ray. "Must be tough these days being so scarlet."

"I wouldn't know," added Burton. "I liked the man. I'm not here to judge.

Clavis: All Roads Lead To Gravity

His morning meditation session finished, ready to begin, Caleb Lincoln Barnhart, as always, rendered a small indigo X in the center of his canvas. Where his brushes would take him was anyone's guess. He'd had enough of representation and the actual. What his meditations had been telling him of late was that he should continue to hope for a fusion of Pollock's energy, Hopper's control, and Utrillo's sense of color, all of it becoming a distillation of the essence that had been seeping from his lungs, breath by breath, during the past few months. This was maybe ambitious and unrealistic, but this was his way. All art, after all, he thought, is only a pretense.

What stopped him from summoning that X and starting a new painting was the thought that he would one day never be able to show or explain any of them to his daughter Tyesha, even if the girl summoned the courage to visit him, an act Caleb felt comfortable assuming she'd never perform. Why should she? Her mother, Trini, had remarried and trooped Tyesha off to the west, to Eudonie. Nothing there for the likes of a gimp like him, that was for damned sure.

Then best he get on with it, Caleb thought, so in a tight sleeve-less T-shirt and loose gym shorts, he dragged his bulky upper torso across the wooden floor of his work room. Both ends of his stumps were covered in thin cotton. They weren't raw and aching, for a change, even though he'd done a lot of walking in his prosthetic legs the day before, getting more comfortable now in them with each passing day.

He liked his new pair of pins. With loose trousers on and the help of his cane, he could pass for an average guy looking a little worse for wear. When he went to church, or shopping, or to Fortuna Park to watch the Settlers play baseball, there were challenges he had to face that other people never even thought about. The hardest was waiting in long lines, but that was also where he'd met Marilyn Cross, a woman he'd seen in church on more than one occasion, and who shopped at the same market that he usually went to.

It turned out that Marilyn lived in his neighborhood. He'd asked her out. She'd stunned him by accepting. They'd kept it simple, having lunch together on a weekday near the office where she worked. Though Marilyn was younger than he was, they were both too seasoned to get too keyed up about the potential of a late-in-life romance. At the same time, it had been such a pleasure to talk to her. A University of Fortuna grad and an assistant manager in the accounting department of a software design firm, she too was divorced and yet still hopeful, not angry, didn't like to call attention to herself. She'd confessed that, like him, she preferred to fit in and look unobtrusive, part of the scenery.

Just like those legs of his standing like a pair of giant toothpicks in one corner.

Thinking of Marilyn, Caleb knew he'd be fine. He'd keep getting around. They'd had only one date, and they'd chatted a number of times during the coffee and doughnuts hour after mass. Like his new prosthetic legs, Marilyn didn't chafe and burn and impede his sense of locomotion. And that, in essence, was the main thing for a loner like him.

She didn't talk about his stumps either. People often looked so shocked, so uncomfortable, when he referred to them in that way. What else call them? The looked like fish heads without eyes, the flesh so slick and smooth and calloused there now. He kept those stumps fixed squarely on his blanket with its Navaho Indian pattern, leaning forward to help propel the blanket in its glide across the varnished wooden floorboards. When Caleb reached his wheelchair, he felt relieved. He hugged it and stayed still and caught his breath.

My reliable friend, my chariot, he thought. The Caleb Express. Electra-glide in stainless. Ironsides. He'd thought of them all for possible nicknames but none had stuck.

He was ready now. With care, he rolled his chair backwards until it was pinned against a section of one wall that had already been scarred many times due to this process. He locked the chair's wheels. Gripping its padded arm rests, veins bulging in his forearms, Caleb shoved himself forward and upward at the same time, controlling and raising his truncated body as if a gymnast on parallel bars, twisting his torso enough so that he could drop his bottom into the chair's seat.

What was cold there against his bottom? He drove one hand under his buttocks. It was a book. He pulled it free and looked at it. *Zen in the Art of Archery*. Right, Mr. Herrigel. He'd been reading that enlightened German night before last before he'd nodded off.

He missed archery. He wondered if Marilyn would be interested in it, or in Zen or meditation. Probably not, which was fine, but one never knew. He liked knowing she was a devout Catholic, as he was, and that she came across as open-minded. He also liked knowing that she was a pragmatist in her ways, avoiding eccentricity and, as she'd told him, she preferred the conventional, which he did not. In this way, they might balance each other.

Balance. How he missed easy balance. There was no such thing, of course, but a pursuit such as archery might get him back to the life-sustaining illusion that he could find some of it. Not like he had to move around much. Just stand still and breathe and let the arrow fly.

Sighing, Caleb reached around to the back of his chair and slid the book into a wide sleeve, a catch-all where he kept a bottle of water, some prescription bottles, his eyeglasses, a Settlers baseball cap, a few pencils and a Word Search puzzle book, among other small sometimes necessary things. He should really go through his catch-all back there. Well, he would, one of these days. Time was one thing he had plenty of.

After nearly a minute of collecting his breath and feeling the sweat dry around his eyes, Caleb unlocked his wheels. He released a sustained exhalation and rolled himself away from the wall. When he reached his standing easel, with its companion table on one side for his portable stereo and a stack of compact discs, and a second table on the other side for his palettes, knives, coffee cans full of brushes, new, old and even dried-up tubes of paint, bundles of rags and a stack of sketch pads waiting there for him, all of it littering chaotically the paint-splotched surface of the table, Caleb closed his eyes and waited to see what he would paint. It would come to him. Always did. He shouldn't rush it, and he should remember he'd change it many times.

He saw an arrow pierce the sky, and his face was on the head of the arrow.

He'd work in oils this time, not acrylics. He wanted to go slowly. He'd been feeling wintry, still locked into the colder weather and its demands. Though it was early March, he still kept the heat on, had to, and it was windier outside than usual. Out like a lion, in like a lamb. The ides of March. He remembered that phrase, having learned it at Fortuna High School. Mrs. Poulin's English class. It was from Shakespeare. He couldn't remember which play.

Was it the ides? No, that day had passed. It was later in the month now, past Saint Patrick's day, as well, which was always a noisy bit of hoo-hah in a city like Fortuna with so many mostly third and fourth generation Irish who drank their green beer and munched down their boiled potatoes and corned beef as if they'd just danced a jig across the sea from County Mayo. Unless he had an appointment with a doctor or a therapist, the day itself, its number, wasn't important. Nothing was important, not really. Except maybe the arrow. Except flight.

In mind. One velvet Jesus after another began firing out of the darkness, each one bearded and cloaked and with one hand raised in the air to form a symbol of peace. Some wore haloes, some didn't. As Caleb watched them, eyes still closed, he breathed through flared nostrils. He remembered the first time his mother, God rest her soul, rushed him to the hospital because he'd been trying to gouge out his eyes with yellow crayons. Not green or red or black. Yellow. Don't ask me why yellow, he thought.

Life abided in all the unknowing. This was the value of meditation. It brought him closer to eternal truths, most of which were open-ended tunnels into darkness. What sustained him now were his attempts not to understand but to accept beyond what religion taught him, the deeper lasting mysteries. Where did one's soul begin and come to an end? Nobody really knew. One fired off into the dark wishing for the best.

It's here, too, on this blank canvas, he thought. The first and last answer. Darkness. The void. Home. He'd returned again. He'd never left. He was ready for another journey. That journey never ended. Didn't matter if he'd sell the painting or not. What mattered was that he remained a warrior by making a new painting that was better than the last one he'd finished.

He hadn't shown Marilyn his paintings. He hadn't shown her his home. Hadn't mentioned his daughter. Maybe he would, little by little. There was no reason to hurry. Not as if he could run off anywhere. He chuckled inwardly at his little joke: him *running* off. Fat chance of that.

Why had he thought he'd ever really left home? Why, why, why? Because he had.

Fortuna for a long time had been his, long ago, part of him, part of another life. Maybe it still was, but he couldn't say any longer because now it felt as if he'd never really been there. Sure, there was the house on Emporia Street, though it was gone now, along with the neighborhood he'd grown up in, all of it razed to make room for the expansion of a newer larger freeway cloverleaf and all sorts of exit ramps. Fortuna had once been a city port, defined by the two rivers that ran through it and joined at its center. Now, the rivers were dead things and smelled like sewage and a freeway blistered through the center, always jammed with cars. One suffered it on the way to another city, such as Avalon, or else to one of those growing grid towns like Rebar.

Could he remember the girls he'd kissed and Fortuna as the city where he'd reached puberty and played baseball and practiced archery and earned high marks in school and had first broke out into acne? He could. Maybe he'd tell Marilyn about it.

Yet even though he'd left and returned and lived there now, Fortuna had never been home. He'd always felt, had known deeply within that there'd never be home, that he'd never fit in anywhere. Because he'd never felt as if he belonged. On the plus side, he hadn't missed Fortuna when he was away. Now that he was back, and often went to visit his mother's grave, he took comfort not in a hero's welcome, but in his long periods of isolation.

He'd endured. He wasn't any damn hero. The hero had been his brave tireless and generous mother. Such a warm heart she'd been.

Not that his father had been a bad man either, though Caleb, being the baby, had never really known him. At least, unlike so many other fathers, his old man hadn't run off. He'd been killed on the job in an accident. It happened sometimes, especially with steel workers. Or so Caleb had been told. Not he nor any of his brothers had ever worked in construction. Not like the old man had. Made sense now, of course, but they'd hungered as boys for adventure and getting out and his mother had constantly told them, "There'll be time enough for that, you'll see."

It had been a blessing she hadn't lived long enough to see him lose both his pins, to become reduced to Stumpy Caleb, half a man. Both had been blown off by the detonation of a pair of IUDs on the road into Fallujah.

Sometimes, fighting Dick Cheney's war had felt perhaps stupid, but maybe not. Maybe he'd been brave (some had told him), to have signed up for the Army reserves back in '92 when he'd tired of watching Operation Desert Storm unfold on television and had felt as if his life meant nothing, that he could do more, be more. He'd agreed to twenty years as a reservist, seemed a square deal at the time, all those years ago. It had meant job security, a pension, some respect from those he worked with and knew at church. At first, the time commitment had never been too much of an imposition, and the salary was a big help considering he'd gotten Trini pregnant and she, Haitian-born, a true immigrant and a pious Catholic, would not consent to an abortion.

What he couldn't have predicted was 9-11 and Rumsfeld and W. Bush and all their babble about weapons of mass destruction fueling the argument that so many reservists had to be mobilized to Iraq to bring down Sadam, or else sent to Afghanistan to fight the Taliban. Hell, he wasn't gonna start thinking about all that again, was he? Feeling sorry for himself. Regretting what he'd lost.

Trini, Tyesha, natural mobility — for what? Freedom. Liberty. To be a hero?

Maybe it was all a crock, but he wasn't gonna dwell on it. He'd dream of archery and paint his sorrow out of his system because in the end his life didn't mean squat. He'd leave something more honorable than his sawed-off stumps behind. In the end, his life was about straining every muscle in his body to lift himself into his chair, where he'd sometimes sit and pretend to stand, not too wobbly, holding a sill, looking out, reducing all the marinades, potions and visitations within.

His prosthetic legs were working just fine, giving him the illusion of a normal life. To all those who'd helped him in the long process of adapting to them, he was grateful. It wasn't the same, of course. He didn't like getting used to the illusion that he was normal. He wore them when he had to go out and engage with the public, get to the pharmacy and fill his prescriptions, though such trips continued to decrease, which was fine with him.

There were the anti-depressants still, and the blood thinners, and the pain killers and they all helped, but he liked thinking he didn't always need them, which was true. He used them per his doctor's orders, discriminately, like he used his other legal forms of evasions such as his medical marijuana card.

He meditated. He painted. He got high and listened to music. He'd had his fill of reality, after all. He liked to imagine that none of his life had happened. He'd put on his prosthetics and go out for a jog. He'd skip rope. He'd take the stairs two at a time instead of the elevator.

On some days he did use stairs and his hips didn't churn and wrench as much as they used to. His wind was good. He had his weights and his upper body workouts, his own little gym space. He had a house on Bland Avenue bigger than anything his parents had ever known. A full ranch, all one level, with a wide front door and a ramp and a flat paved path to his drive.

He still had all his archery and fishing equipment stored away. A pistol and a shotgun, both legal, just in case. No hills to contend with. His street just a few blocks from the high school where none other than Early Stephens, one of those great 1930s-era jazz saxophonists only aficionados knew about, had once been a student. Early had died young and all doped up. That was a tempting choice, but not the way Caleb would go. He knew that now. Tyesha was in her twenties, and he in his late fifties. He might like to go to her wedding one day. Maybe bring Marilyn with him. That is, if he was invited, and if Marilyn was interested.

Caleb picked up one of his paint brushes. As he did so, he blew a sigh, hearing the crackle of flames from each of the minor supporting players he'd been in his life. Son, brother, soldier, husband, father, archer, baseball player, private first class, assistant squadron leader, legless cripple, amateur painter, and gimp. Each man still inside peeling off his make-up to tell him that the current play was over and that soon another one would begin.

He was what could be called a character actor. Not a lead. He didn't star in anything. He walked on to the stage and found the warmest spot and dried up thirsting for new forms of hell to release him from the old ones. Didn't make him, he supposed, any different from other men.

The air inside his work space, rife with the fumes of solvents, paints and dirty rags, lay heavy. Its hue, infused by mid-day sun through a pair of windows, reminded him of his mother's chrome yellow wool coat, the one she was wearing the night she'd been killed. She'd been dying of kidney failure. Yellow, again. Her jaundiced skin. But what killed her was a delivery truck on a summer night that creamed her tiny body. A few who'd been at the scene had said it was suicide, that she'd stepped out in front of that truck. Others had sworn that the truck driver was speeding and his mother had been waiting patiently to cross the street.

Nobody every learned the truth. No, hell, they did. His mother was dead. That was the truth. Yellow chrome coat. Like that Leonard Cohen song about the blue raincoat. Maybe that's what he'd paint.

He closed his eyes again and saw a flash of orange as he imagined a scorch that rose with the sun to blunt the edges of his body. He saw a flamenco dancer's red silk sash. He'd had something once. Fearless, he'd been. Not a leader. One that the others could trust. What had happened to that version of Caleb? He'd either lost him or gave him up.

Like the man in that song "Creep" from The Stone Temple Pilots…*take time with a wounded hand*…Caleb could feel it and he wanted to reach it, though he didn't know what it was…*I'm half the man I used to be*…he opened his eyes and looked around. He stuck his paintbrush sideways into his mouth as if he was a horse chomping at a bit. He wheeled himself away from the canvas. When he reached his favorite windowsill in the room, he stopped and let his body bake in the high March sun. Spring was coming. This would be his day, his first of the year, no more quarantine, life slowly returning to normal. Something about the sun proved it. Again, yellow.

What was *this thing* he was trying to imagine? Whatever it was, whatever its color, he knew it was there. Like the certainty of heat, even within the chill of night in the desert. How that heat had brought sweat that had beetled and itched and muttered like a pair of whispery crones plotting murder in a corner at a party. Heat, sun and sweat coaxing a storm of memories and fears. Mother's yellow coat. All that sand. A blinding yellow flash. The deafening sound.

He closed his eyes and lived it again.

Lived it over and over.…

There he rode, in the moment, slumped in his saddle like a tired cowboy on horseback. His handicapped parking placard. The looks he got as he moved step by step without his cane. He couldn't fake it, no matter how skilled he got with his fabricated pins. The nurses no longer came to help change his bandages and clothes, to make sure his set-up was working for him. No, those days were behind him now. He wasn't a patient any longer. He was a survivor. Maybe Marilyn would understand that. Maybe she wouldn't pity him. Only time would tell. If she was interested, he'd give her a chance.

If anyone came, it was a therapist, one paid for through the V.A., which he felt he rightly deserved, though they didn't come as often now. He usually went to see them once or twice a month to review his exercise regimen and to practice walking. Many of them were male nurses, not the sultry, gentle-eyed babes that peopled his fantasies. Marilyn was sultry. She was easy on the eyes. Maybe his pins were false, but the rest of his anatomy functioned and maybe she wouldn't cringe at the sight of him in bed. If that happened, she'd be his first since his return. The first and, he hoped, the last.

Just to have a regular companion. Just to wake in the morning and know he wasn't alone.

He was trying to keep pace with Don Quixote, the old man who'd seen more windmills than anyone else. Caleb had him beaten when it came to each velvet Jesus. He saw more of them than he could count, blowing out of a roseate light beyond the sun, an accretion of fury, the promise of future torrents out of an airbrushed sky.

There was a time when Caleb couldn't have slid across the floor on his blanket or climbed into his chair to wheel over to this blazing windowsill. A time when he couldn't sleep or stay awake without painkillers and tranquilizers. Without morphine. Without an IV bag. Without constant rehab and counseling, not as part of his life, but the whole of it.

Now, alone, he realized yet again how fortunate he was. He was nothing, a nobody, but so many people had worked so hard to keep him alive, to get him back to a sense of dignity and self-respect.

He hadn't liked who he'd once been, back when he'd first accepted that he hadn't been killed, that he was a civilian and would have to start over. When he'd realized the journey wasn't finished, not yet, and he had to grasp this truth and claim it, and praise God not denounce him. And that he, not God, was the only one who could answer the question: why me?

Why me? He was so little of so many nothings.

He could laugh at this. It was funny. If he could laugh, then he'd be okay. That was his message to himself. One he'd bring to others through his paintings. Not that he had to, but because he wanted to. He'd always had a knack for painting, so why not pursue it. He'd always been able to laugh at himself too.

Pulling his hand away, Caleb wavered at the sill, woozy, stunned, restless with the prickly grease from his pores. He'd been forty-four in 2006. Kaboom. He'd stayed alive, though in dire need for constant care. As those early years had passed, he'd tried to love his Trini and Tyesha, but the nightmare of what had happened had been too hard for both of those women to accept. How, for so long, he'd hated this weakness in them. Especially Trini, taking her various lovers, abandoning her Catholicism, or so it seemed, along with any sense of loyalty.

Tyesha hadn't decided to join the military. Or to go to college. She'd mulled them both over. She had some kind of fighting gene in her, no doubt about that. She was an MMA fighter now, a killer in a cage where women beat the living vinegar out of each other. He'd never been to one of her fights. Nor would he attend one, ever, but he'd support her from a distance. As if that mattered. As if Tyesha really cared.

He'd seen clips of her online in various bouts. Cage matches. Blood sport. She wasn't a dainty petit demure young creature. Not hardly. She was all fists, scowls, corn rows, sharpened elbows, lethal strangleholds, dart-like punches and roundhouse kicks. She loved and excelled in it, but it didn't pay that well, not yet, so she still had to wait tables. So young she still was, with her fair cocoa-cinnamon skin, and her mother's forgiving brown eyes. A girl like her inside a cage of all places, travelling the country to compete and earn trophies and a small purse — he'd never imagined such a development.

MMA for women, despite all its popularity among men savaging each other, didn't draw the same kind of crowds. He hoped she'd retire before seriously injuring herself. It would probably be an injury that would force her to retire. As long as it wasn't too damaging. Could be worse, he supposed. To think of what she could have gotten into — lap-dancing for drug-dealing scumbags, for one. Nothing her or her new Daddy could do about it. Her new Daddy. Maybe he was an alright guy, and maybe not.

Caleb didn't know. He'd never met the man. Never would.

It was important that Tyesha felt complete, and that new father of hers, a black man, along with her beautiful black mother, take care of her. Tyesha was fair enough to look odd when with them, as white as her real Daddy. What did that any of that matter? Tyesha was excelling in a pursuit she really liked. She was still his daughter. She'd live her own dreams and she'd always be far from him, and it wasn't unrealistic to think he might never see her again.

He loved her. He prayed for her as his own mother had prayed for him. That's what mattered.

For a while, when still hopeful and naive, he'd liked being a father. Trini had, in her own way, done him a favor. He was maybe better off alone, left behind to pray. Of what value was a man hacked off above the knees? Sometimes had to piss in a bag he kept on an IV rack next to his bed, for those super-fast needs to empty his bladder. The worst were soft and rapid bowel movements, the ones that came on without a warning. Had to get to the toilet and fast. His special toilet. Handicapped access bars and all that. Like his special shower with its bars and seat. But he ate so lightly now, no meat, very little dairy, practically a vegan so his trips to the throne didn't happen that often and he could usually control himself, though there'd been more than a few messes early on. Amazing what the body could be taught to do.

He kept his arms muscular, trim, though sagging shorelines of flesh ran across the front of his neck. Flesh that had once been so smooth. Happened to one and all, he knew that, but like anyone else he didn't much like accepting it. Most of his wardrobe was comprised of shorts that, like his T-shirts, hugged his frame. He liked underwear, long or short, that athletes wore. His slacks were baggy and fit with ease. No jeans or any tight trousers. Always loose clothes and a sun hat too, since he'd lost so much hair.

Just get him out of this body. If only he knew how.

Behind him, somewhere, was that tiny house in the wind-burnt shallows of Fortuna. Gone now. There'd been one bed and he and his two brothers, Dale and Brodie, sleeping in it. All three of them were tiny enough to wheeze without waking each other. How grave his memory of that bedroom felt. How silent the afternoons it poached in. Dale went off to Alaska to work in logging. He was the oldest. Sent money home. Had a son now who had joined the Navy. Caleb hadn't seen Dale in over ten years. They'd never been all that close.

Hadn't seen Brodie in a decade either. Might never see him again. Brodie could never shut up long enough to keep himself out of trouble. He was in a state prison. Repeated felonies and narcotics trafficking charges guaranteed to keep him in for at least five more years, if he behaved, which was unlikely knowing Brodie's temper.

God-damned Brodie couldn't keep away from the meth and the fantasy of easy money. Wasted life, really, and Caleb didn't feel sorry for him. Brodie had always thought himself too good for Fortuna and maybe he was. He'd never find out. He was a con now, nothing more. Once he was out, he'd start using meth again and find himself back behind bars. Caleb didn't care about Brodie anymore. Why should he?

Caleb had watched him, as he'd watched Dale, while growing up. As the baby of the family, the one who had no memory of Daddy, he'd decided to do well in school. He'd played baseball, had been a pitcher, threw a mean slider and curve and had even made the team at Fortuna State the one year he'd spent there, though he hadn't pitched much, just a few relief appearances. He'd dropped out of Fortuna State and had chosen to travel, see some of the world. After some mostly uneventful years in various dead-end jobs, the best of them when he was working steady in Avalon as a warehouse manager, doing what he thought he was supposed to do, meeting Tyesha there, getting her pregnant, going all in, playing the hero of a man that he'd thought she'd been hoping to find.

Tyesha had never been shy about despising winters in Avalon, and maybe the novelty of being married to a white man wore off because one night she didn't come home. Then another night. It became evident to Caleb that she was out with other men. Tyesha was about six years old the year Trini just up and left him and moved in with a truck driver, an older black man. They'd lived together a while, but that hadn't worked out.

Then Trini had moved south for a while, far away, where she'd dated various men, and Caleb had made his payments, both in alimony and child support and he hadn't fought her over anything. He'd just let her go. He'd ditched Avalon too, taking another warehouse management job back on home turf in Fortuna. When he got bored with that job, feeling dried up and useless and lonely, he'd enlisted as a reservist. Years passed, his payments were made, he dated other women, he paid his bills and got to work on time. It all changed in April of '05 when he was put on active duty and deployed as part of the Third Infantry Division.

Remembering, getting rest, sleeping without the pain of his ghost legs trying to run, the idea of living as one under constant re-invention, it had all become so unappealing. Yet what else could he do other than to try? There had to be a way to live, without fear, so that he could inspire others. He knew he was no hero, but that didn't matter. People wanted inspiration from him. They needed their heroes.

One of his counselors had been right when she'd suggested he reach out to others who might be hurting in his neighborhood, to start small, locally, and just be himself. The reality of his situation, seeing both his fake pins, would always be a shock to others. He had to keep reminding himself of this, and of how sheltered most people were. He also had to keep his eyes open, regardless of how stunted he felt by his needs, his failures with painting, his wheelchair and his windmills. Feeling uncertain half the time if he was looking forward or back.

It was a puny world, ultimately, just as puny as his work room, still not very dark and yet sealed off, all blinds drawn. His sanctuary, he had to admit, and it was here he'd allowed some stunning work to bleed out of his mind and onto a canvas.

He thought of his past life that was so far…far…away….

He thought of Trini when she was carrying Tyesha. Grumpy, angry, aching, volatile and tired all the time. Trini struggling to sleep.

Pregnant. The word died on his lips when he said it. Everything was pregnant all the time. Air and water, all basic elements, presented to him each day possibilities, newborn life, whatever he chose to accept and pursue. This positive, constructive outlook was the only one left to him. Anything else, whether driven by emotions or self-destructive impulses, would hasten his end.

He could admit it now. He wanted to live, to accept his fate.

He heard a snort from his brother. Which one? *Brodie is that you?*

Wheeling around away from the window, he stared into the room. He could see that Brodie's forehead was oily, with a scarlet flush and shine to it. Caleb watched Brodie squirm in his sleep. He didn't think about how Brodie, so very different from him, had been born out of the same womb, from the same giver of seed. Instead, he thought of the scarlet in Brodie's forehead, how hot it looked, how it boiled damp with Brodie's own juices.

Somewhere in a prison cell, Brodie, his brother, the middle son, was suffering and dying. There was little that Caleb could do to help him. Why should he? How many times did he have to tell himself that he didn't care about Brodie? But he did care. They were brothers. The bond was deep and lasting.

How little they'd known way back during that time as boys when they'd thought of the particulars of what they would become. Successful Brodie, a tycoon, rich and powerful. Caleb had always felt grounded and at ease with life. No big money for him. He wanted to travel, to see the world. Getting married, having a daughter to raise, had always felt right. His problem was that he'd never earned enough to become a homeowner. A kind of player of a husband, a dandy, what Trini wanted him to be and not what he was. Yet she'd run off to live with a truck driver.

Made no sense. None at all.

Trini had complained about the size of their apartment, the limitations on their finances due to his job, and why couldn't he find something better? He was a white man, after all. He'd tried. He'd lacked the education and training. Hence he'd joined the US Army

Reserve. As one friend had told him, "Don't matter what you do. Some women just grow bored easy."

Brodie, what will I become now?

He could say, at least, that he didn't know the answer. Fractured, he was. A wounded soldier. Somebody's hero. More than a dabbler in life, but one who gave his all, who didn't back down, who'd served, who'd never opened or closed any doors unless he was told to.

He heard a number called. He was no longer in his work room. He was seated in a church basement with Trini at a Wednesday night bingo game. This was his limit when it came to gambling, but not Trini's. She loved to gamble, and to party at casinos. He, like a fool, would let her go. He'd even given her money to gamble with and she'd lost it all. He'd done his best to help make her feel happy. He didn't like confrontation. Let her have her fun.

While he'd been at work all day, she'd stayed home to take care of Tyesha. Once Tyesha got older, she'd wanted time to play. Usually, it was the other way around, with men running from women. Not in his case.

Dear God, he thought. Please confirm my status as *a number*. One pawing at windmills.

Caleb heard his throat create a little wheeze and he thought himself pitiful, but this was nothing new. Few people suffered an excess of self-love. Once — at least in his own mind — he had been a somebody. Maybe he'd even known and understood love. Who could say? All the choices he'd made had rendered him back to this blob in a chair, staring into the darkness with his back to a window sill. What he could do, and what always helped him feel better, was to spin his arms in circles, letting them whack at fetid, indifferent air.

He stopped whirling his arms. He was breathing harder now, but he felt better. He felt looser, even though he hadn't painted anything. Not even his initiating X.

Not a worry. It was tobacco time. He wheeled his way to his little smoking table in one corner and found his pack of coffin nails and lit one up. He didn't open the window. He watched the room fill slowly with smoke.

One of his brothers, again Brodie, rolled over and sounded a tiny sniffle as if he were repressing a wail of pain. Brodie was still asleep in that bed and so small, basting in feverish sweat. Brodie was in prison. He'd been stabbed there. A shiv to his groin. These things happened all the time in prisons. Brodie was dying now.

Caleb went to him. He saw blood rise into Brodie's face, a long look of anguish and confusion there as Brodie gasped and choked, his body twitching. That shiv, it had cut a main artery. By the time the guards found him he would be dead.

Caleb then stood from his chair and he walked to the bed and he lifted Brodie out of it and held him up in two hands so that little Brodie could let his feet and arms dangle as he giggled and drooled. He must like, thought Caleb, this weightlessness. Caleb liked it too. Both of them, in the air, free of gravity and restraints.

"There now, Brodie, don't be afraid. Everything is going to be okay."

As Caleb walked little Brodie to a darker cooler place away from that bed, he held him up and he look into Brodie's eyes. *Blue skies, nothing but blue skies from now on.*

Caleb was looking into mirrors, Not windows. He was no longer at the sill. He had both his legs. He had his childhood and his brother Brodie in both his hands.

Don't die on me now.

He thought they looked at each other as if they knew they were one.

———

To be with a woman again. Just once more. To feel that wonderment and a sense of magical possibility. To go way back before the accident.

In all his darkness now, with his reticence and wisdom, Caleb spoke back to the silence of how he'd bring his birthday into light. He'd let the corners of simmering arguments unfold. This day was his birthday.

Some gift. He had the news. It was official. Brodie's obituary was online. He'd found it. There'd been no wake or funeral. Dale had called from Alaska at a weird hour and he'd sounded drunk. They didn't say they should have seen it coming. Nor did they say that Brodie had wasted his life. "Damn crying shame" was what Dale had said. "And you, Caleb, you holding up?"

As well, Dale, as can be expected. Thanks for calling with the crummy news.

He'd end up like Brodie, just ashes in an urn after cremation. Caleb had told Dale he didn't wanted those ashes. Not that they had been offered, which had been a relief. One less decision to make. They'd gone to Brodie's woman friend named Shirley who'd early on given Brodie a son out of wedlock. A grown boy now who Caleb had known nothing about. Didn't want to know. According to Dale, Shirley and that boy were Brodie's family now. They'd taken care of all details. Caleb had never met them. He hadn't wanted to. Brodie had flushed his life down the toilet. Caleb would not waste his own. He could always find Brodie's obit online, with its stupid lie: died of natural causes.

A shiv to the groin. That's what had killed Brodie. He'd probably done something to earn it too. Stolen from another inmate one time too many. If a shiv was an arrow, Brodie's death proved it took only one arrow to change everything.

In the dream Caleb had awakened with, prior to his meditation, everyone he'd ever loved was standing around him at an archery range. He'd drawn back the bow string and let the arrow fly and they'd all applauded when it had pierced the red bull's eye at its center.

His meditation had gone well. The house felt full but, as usual, nobody in it. Nobody except him had ever been there. Right. It was his birthday. He must not forget this. Time to prepare, allow — using his bow like the warrior Ulysses, and his trusty quiver of arrows.

Caleb leaned on his cane and trudged along on his pins. The less he was, the less he did, the better he did it. One mistake and one correction at a time. Take each shrug and shuffle with patience and an acceptance of gravity.

He paused a moment and imagined Tyler the neighbor boy. Tyler was getting ready for school, but first he'd come visit him. Tyler had a young boy's enthusiasm for soldiers and the Army. Many a boy did. Some outgrew it. Others, like him, hadn't until they'd lived it out. What would he and Tyler talk about today? How Tyler's alarm clock went off and he hadn't heard it? Caleb imagined Tyler gargling and spitting. His mother breaking eggs for breakfast. Kettle whistling. Kettle emptied. Tyler's mother setting it with a clunk back on the stove.

Tyler always smelled so young. Like any boy, wanting so much, he was both amalgamation and innocent response to the iron and twill that bled its milk into the din. Tyler without a Daddy. Tyler's mother out there, sleeping around, bringing home various lovers. Her name was Dana and she'd struck Caleb as the type who didn't watch life from the sidelines with one ear against a wall. She got under the covers and went all the way.

Tyler would visit. Yes, okay. Dana, most likely, would be with him. Caleb knew this because of the way Ragu, his orange and ginger tabby, was looking at him. Ragu only shared that look when expecting a visitor. He was a strange cat in that he liked visitors too.

Caleb remembered again that the older he got, the longer it took him to complete once simple and comforting tasks. Still, he decided to avoid his easel this morning and make himself coffee, determined to have it ready before Tyler arrived. There was his potted coleus to water too, and on his way to it he should stop to breathe at a partially opened window.

It was April now. Even with nearly all the other windows closed, he could hear bird's singing from the dwarf trees and shrubbery in his little yard.

As he watered the coleus, Caleb thought of how powdery its leaves felt as he touched them. He thought of Marilyn's flesh. Her face. The easy grace there. The hunger. They'd seen each other again. A dinner this time. She'd had wine. A lot of it. He didn't drink anymore and, being the sober one, was able to get them home.

They'd kissed each other goodnight. A long kiss. More than one of them. They'd held each other for so long on the front steps of her house that his stumps had begun to throb and ache. He couldn't remember when he'd last stood in one place on his pins for so long. Yet just thinking of that night, he felt better.

The wrinkles of sleep still trapped and folded in his mind began freeing themselves and he allowed himself to talk to his coleus, asking, "So you think you know look by smell?"

No answer. Ragu on the table next to the coleus was giving him one of his classic looks of disapproval, as if to say: Really? Talking to a plant. Reverting to *that* again? *Why don't you talk to me?*

In the fumes of each coleus leaf, Caleb found pictures and auras, each one testing his memory, bringing him closer to a vegetal essence, a kindness, the sandstorm of doubt within his peppery heart. There were no trips to the embankments of a pond aglow at twilight. If possible, he'd sit through his birthday afternoon in one of Fortuna's parks, rain or shine, letting the wavelengths pass through and challenge him. He thought of the song, "Wavelength" by Van Morrison. Maybe he'd listen to some Van later on. It was a comforting thought.

He could be an agent of change; he would probably need to be in order to keep going. Locomotion, now, was all. He was no landed shipwreck to be dismantled, no riddle to be solved. He was a grown man and spare him pity. He would never surrender to the way others saw him.

Infirmity. How he despised the courtesy in such a word. Cripple was so much harsher and yet more accurate.

The coleus plant began to speak. Caleb listened. He didn't know what any plant knew. Ah, the trickiness of silence, with its firing of cannons that offered no promises. To the flesh, then, of each sunrise, he must set out as if a boat leaving port — his sea a tumble of motives and re-defining notions. Each soft burr up a stem assuring him growth had occurred. If growth was there, so was pain. If pain was there, so was growth.

One day, Tyler would enlist in the Army and know this. Mom Dana already knew about pain, but what she'd learned about growth hadn't guaranteed her anything. Certainly not happiness. Let Tyler remain a boy and Dana his protective matron, regardless of her wanton proclivities. There was in them an innocence, a trust developed through routines. Consistency. Mutual concern. Those essential elements of an examined life that Caleb felt, at times, he had lost. All because of aging, he supposed, and his compromising affliction.

Time waited for no one. Call it bad luck or an unfortunate turn of events. Call it genetic disposition. Call it karma, or the beginning of the end, or the start of a new beginning. It was all in one's head, ultimately. Then again, maybe Marilyn in his life would change all that. Maybe he'd discover his body again, but in a new much slower and more lasting way.

Returning the coleus to its stand near his bedroom, Caleb thought he could smell the bacon grease on Tyler's fingers as he licked them in front of Mom Dana and told her how tasty the bacon was this morning. Breath of the young. Unwavering and clean.

Caleb waited. He listened. Beginner's mind. The archer greets the sunrise. Tyler, as always, was punctual, but maybe his mother was asking him why so sullen this morning?

She was not getting an answer.

Caleb felt sad about this. He wanted their life next door to be the picture of perfection that his own would never be. He heard Ragu scratch across the floor and when Ragu looked up at him with his usual "I'm hungry" look, Caleb said to him, "Do I smell sad this morning?"

Ragu sat on his haunches and waited. It was his feeding time. It was *always* his feeding time. "Shut up, you Garfield clone," he told the cat. Nothing else but food concerned that animal. Caleb labored to pick him up, so wily, so warm and it surprised him the way Ragu didn't squirm free but rather licked at Caleb's face.

There came a knock at his door. Tyler. Two more raps. Not Tyler. The boy never knocked twice. Then who?

Caleb put Ragu down and the cat scurried away. Caleb reminded himself not to appear as if he'd been expecting the boy's visit. Without a word, using his cane, he moved one uneven step at a time into the kitchen.

He opened the door, as habit, acting like he wasn't expecting Tyler to be standing there, backpack on, his cheeks freshly scrubbed and pink, with Mom Dana behind him, arms crossed, looking concerned and as if lacking sleep, her hair still damp but perfect, no make-up on yet, but smiling because her latest suitor had been satisfying certain needs. But Tyler wasn't there. Nor was Dana.

Marilyn was there, in a spring windbreaker, a yellow one, and standing in front of her was a tall girl with blue eyes, teeth in braces, dirty-blond hair in pigtails, partly like a pencil-drawing of an innocent girl, maybe about twelve or thirteen, and partly like a young woman on the verge of developing breasts and hips and learning some painful lessons about womanhood. Caleb, startled, felt his mouth go dry and did not know what to say.

Marilyn, in her dulcet yet confident voice, asked, "How are you today, Caleb?"

Because a boy is impatient, he breathes without thought. Like other boys, he demands his extractions from sun and water. Caleb still couldn't speak. Archer, draw thy bow.

Closer to you, strange Marilyn Cross, than you think.

Caleb looked beyond Marilyn, with her hair combed neatly and long, her blue eyes wide and alluring, and he welcomed the fresh blush of morning light and air with its consistent bird song. Off in the distance he heard tree branches shake under a gentle wind.

Ragu appeared at his feet on the kitchen floor and Caleb looked down at him and told him to wait. Ragu was having none of that. He sprinted out into the yard.

The girl let out a shriek of delight. Then she looked up at Caleb, too serious and concerned, as if she'd done something wrong. She knows, thought Caleb. Marilyn must have told her. And she looks like Marilyn. *What's going on here?*

"Let him go," said Caleb. "He'll come back."

"What's its name?" asked the girl.

"Ragu," said Caleb. "Like the tomato sauce. Because of his color, I guess. Or it's easy to say. I dunno."

Caleb looked at Marilyn. Her eyes were shining. She looked so eager. For what? He felt —what did he feel? Aroused, thrilled, shocked? So many emotions at once had begun to boil within.

"Come in, come in," he said automatically. "If you want, of course."

"We can't," said Marilyn. "On my way to work. And Manda is going to school."

Caleb heard a delivery truck downshift on Bland Avenue about a block away. Seldom was anything as difficult as one thought it might be — not *where*, but *how* to walk and keep pace with unanticipated vibrations. His life was that crude now, a question of walking and not wanting to be alone.

He insisted Marilyn and Manda at least step into his kitchen. And after some hesitation they agreed to this, though stayed close to the door, both looking guarded and nervous. Manda leaned backwards against her mother as if she were a supporting wall. Caleb had to sit. He did so slowly, as usual, but didn't need struggle to bend his prosthetic legs into place, Manda all the while keeping her eyes glued to his every move.

Caleb didn't mind the staring. He was used to it, but who was this girl? "Where do you go to school, Amanda?"

"It's Manda. No A," she said.

Caleb sounded a snort. Whatever. Spoiled and demanding like all children. "Sorry. Manda. I won't forget."

Marilyn, one hand on her daughter's shoulder, stopped Manda before she could answer any further. "Saint Agnes," she said. "Amanda is her birth name, but she prefers Manda, which is fine with me. She's my daughter, Caleb. I wanted you to meet her."

He had assumed as much. He appreciated the show of seriousness from Marilyn about their meeting. Marilyn wasn't one to play games. She was direct too, which he respected and liked.

"Let's try again, then," said Caleb. "Hello Manda, pleased to meet you."

Manda grinned, liking the show of courtliness from Caleb. "Hello, Mr. Barnhart, pleased to meet you." Manda offered her hand, all of it a piece of what appeared to Caleb as a performance, what she was supposed to do in such a situation. Caleb told her to call him by his first name. He took her hand and without any show of fear, drew Manda closer to him and said softly, "Please sit down with me. And maybe your mother will sit too. Just for a minute." He wanted to add that he spent a lot of time alone, but that would be tiresome and self-pitying.

Manda frowned in fear and turned and looked with anxiety toward her mother, who nodded to give permission, and both of them sat at the kitchen table. This surprised Caleb, but he liked that the two would stay for a minute.

"I won't offer you anything," said Caleb. "It's too much work for me, you know, spur of the moment. And besides, you're not staying long."

"We understand," said Manda. "It's no problem."

No you don't, he thought. But that was okay. She was just trying to be nice, to show pity. "Besides, you're in a hurry," he said. "I don't want to keep you."

He then looked squarely at Marilyn. "But I didn't know you had a daughter. You didn't tell me. You're not ashamed of her are you? Just look at her, she's beautiful."

"You don't pull any punches, do you?" said Marilyn.

Caleb shook his head no. "I've nothing to lose by being direct. And neither do you."

"I live with my Dad," said Manda. "In case you were wondering."

"I see." He smiled at the girl. He couldn't tell if she liked him, but he liked her immediately. She looked like her mother, and she was one to listen, fiercely attentive. All sorts of information and impressions were getting categorized and assorted rapidly in that active young brain of hers.

Marilyn leaned over the table, keeping her purse there, one hand on it. She said to Caleb, "Manda's father is an orthodontist in town here. She stays with me now and then. Per our arrangement. Since her father remarried, you see."

"Then that explains the railroad tracks," said Caleb. He motioned toward Manda's mouth. The girl blushed.

"Yes, they're expensive," said Marilyn.

"I know. But she deserves the best," said Caleb.

"She does and she thought, when I told her about you," said Marilyn, "that you might help her with some suggestions for a project she could tackle for her school's science fair."

Caleb thought Marilyn had spoken too formally, as if wanting to impress not only him, but her daughter. Clearly, the stakes were high for her. This, too, he respected. No, he loved Marilyn for it. The woman had lost full custody of her daughter in the legal sense, but was no doubt in every other way doing what she could to be there for Manda, a loving, upstanding and responsible mother.

What warmed him most was the thought that she'd brought her daughter to see him, of all people. What did that say about how she felt about them possibly having a long-term relationship? It spoke volumes, didn't it?

For the first time, he could imagine himself taking on the challenge of being part of a couple. It felt like a proper next step. It felt like keeping in motion. It felt too good to be true.

Looking at Marilyn, pausing before he spoke, Caleb began to understand just how much their first kiss had meant. To Marilyn, they'd already started a relationship. She probably hadn't been with many men since her divorce. If she had, she'd likely behaved carefully. She wasn't the type to just make out on the front steps with a candidate she'd found through an online dating site. She couldn't be. Not with a girl like Manda to be concerned about. And there was no telling what kind of woman Manda's step-mother was, as well as

Marilyn's ex-husband. No telling, at all, with people. They could be such monsters.

For the time being, Caleb couldn't allow himself to get too close. All fine. A woman had to know that a man understood his place. Best he remain cautious and a little aloof. There would be time to loosen up.

Caleb looked at Marilyn. He made sure there was eye contact. He liked what he saw there. "Yes, I do know a little about science, I suppose. But not too much."

"Mommy told me to ask you, that maybe you could help. That you've been through a lot. And your condition."

Marilyn stopped her. She glared at her daughter, who started to blush and pout. "His condition? Really?"

"But I don't know," said Manda.

"Of course you don't," said Caleb. He spoke to put her at ease. He was gentle. "And it's not important. And it's nothing to do with science. Not really. Not for your purposes, at least."

"She's sorry," said Marilyn. She'd begun wringing her hands. Caleb didn't understand why. Did she really think he was so fragile? "Manda didn't mean it that way."

"Which way?" asked Caleb.

"You know. Insulting."

"No insult. She's just being Amanda. I mean, Manda."

"Is that bad?" asked the girl. "You don't even know me."

"And you don't know me," said Caleb. "So, we're even. No harm either way. Right?"

Manda, brightening, nodded, showing that ability in the young to bounce away from one issue to the next without any harmful or lasting residual effect. "Okay."

"Good," said Caleb. "So, science fair." The adult in Caleb expected nothing and hence was seldom disappointed. The child in him wanted to make light of the moment and sustain it and maybe crack a joke. Caleb chose neutral ground. "I'd like to help you," he said. "I've got the time. It would be my pleasure. Do you like dinosaurs?"

"Now, what girl her age doesn't like dinosaurs?" asked Marilyn. She sounded pointed and sarcastic.

"Mommy means no," said Manda. Her eyes implored Marilyn to stay out of this. She then faced Caleb, looking disappointed and a little apologetic but not afraid. "I'm sorry, Mr. Barnhart. Maybe this wasn't a good idea."

"Remember, call me Caleb. And we could start this afternoon after school." Caleb paused. Did he sound too eager? He worked up a grin for Manda. If he won her over, he'd win Marilyn, perhaps, in the process, really secure something between them.

It was a gamble worth taking. Wasn't this why Marilyn had brought her? She was using her daughter to get closer to him. He understood this. He'd use his daughter, as well, eventually. Both daughters were common ground to share. He'd never expected anything like this, and certainly it wouldn't be easy, but he felt lucky for a change. He couldn't recall the last time he'd felt lucky.

Manda smiled at Caleb and stood earnestly with her hair combed and her face so clean and pink.

"Wait. I have a better idea," said Caleb. "Forget dinosaurs. Let's start right now."

Manda, still seated, thought a moment. She watched Marilyn stand, keeping her purse pressed close to her stomach, as if protecting herself with it. They didn't speak. Caleb sensed that both of them were still a bit afraid. He couldn't be angry about this. He just had to be patient. He wanted to help now. The talk about dinosaurs had been only that: a cheap suggestion. He saw in Marilyn's face a yearning for this to work out. He saw in Manda's face a look of guilt.

Manda turned to him. "What's your idea?"

"Make it a good one this time," said Marilyn.

I'll try, he thought. *I want this.* "These ideas," said Caleb. He stressed the plural. "Not just one, a few of them. They're connected to science. I want you to think about them all day."

"I can do that," said Manda. "For starters."

"Okay. I want you to think about seeing, for one. And then about aiming. And then about gravity. And then about learning that there are always other ways to see and to aim. Just as there is always gravity. We adjust to it. The whole space mission, for example, was never about going to the moon. It was about the hubris of man proving he could defy gravity."

"What's a hubris of man?"

"I'll explain later," said Marilyn. She looked at Caleb, who smiled at her, forcing her to let out a small gasp. As Manda watched this wordless exchange, her face deepened to a soft crimson. She appeared intrigued. Caleb liked seeing this. He knew he was looking at a very bright young flower soon to be fully into adolescence and all the painful confusions that came with it. Marilyn had brought him a gift, the opportunity to share some of his time and to test the merits of his wisdom.

"That's all?" asked Manda. "But how does that lead into a project?"

"We'll figure that out. I'm mulling over the use of archery. Bow and arrow. Crossbow. Velocity and weight and physics and trajectory. Delivery systems. Drones, maybe. I don't know. But for now, I think it's enough just to mull over these relationships, especially if you really think about them and their practical applications in our daily lives."

"But Manda has a point. What's it got to do with science?" asked Marilyn.

"No, Mom, I get it now," said Manda. "Practical applications. I love that. Maybe we could make something related to archery. Something that flies."

"That's what I mean," said Caleb. "The physics is the science part. What holds up the arrow or the plane and for how long and why? It's not so simple. It's all physics. That can be your goal. To define and show some of these principles at work."

"Use the bow and arrow as my experiments for proof," said Manda.

"I have crossbows too. I was pretty good with them before my accident."

Another little gasp from Marilyn, this one more like an expression of fear. Caleb looked at her. He grinned. "Don't worry. I wouldn't mind getting them out of mothballs. There's a shooting range out near Rebar. We could go out there and practice and do some experiments."

Marilyn looked at her daughter who had clasped her hands together and raised them to her breasts and was beaming from ear to ear. "Really, you'd do that for me?"

"We can do it together. Your Mom can come too, if she wants."

"It all depends on her father, so we'll see," said Marilyn. She sounded blunt and icy. "Honestly Caleb, I was thinking test tubes and lab coats. Maybe petri dishes."

"Oh Mommy, that's so boring. I never shot a crossbow before."

"I'll teach you. I'd love to," said Caleb. He looked at Marilyn again. He shouldn't appear too hungry, regardless of how much he wanted this. "But only if your mother agrees to it."

"And your father and your step-mother," said Marilyn. Shrugging, looking at Caleb, wilting a little, she said, "It's complicated."

"I get that," said Caleb. "Doesn't mean we can't try."

Manda began imploring her, "Please Mommy, please, I know Daddy wouldn't mind. He already said he was too busy. And it's about school, at least."

"And what about Elizabeth," said Marilyn, dryly.

"What about her?" said Manda. She sounded bitter. "She's not my mother. You are."

Caleb balked at this. Then he smiled. Manda was at least clear regarding her loyalty.

"Well, all this was my idea in the first place," said Marilyn.

"Was it now?" said Caleb. "That's interesting." There was no innocence, but there was fear in Marilyn for certain, but he thought there should be. Her concerns weren't wrong. Convincing Manda's father would probably not be the challenge. It would be the jealous irrational step-mother, but maybe Manda could handle it on her own.

Caleb, smiling at the girl, began to feel twinges of the loneliness that would set in after both of them left. What a shock to learn Marilyn had a daughter. Next, it would be his turn to shock her with news of Tyesha. He might now need to justify having waited to tell her. Marilyn might not understand his qualms and hesitancy. Then again, she might, since they were equal to her own. He'd have a chance to thank her, too, for bringing Manda to him, for helping him see that he could still relate to a young person. He'd told Marilyn that he'd begun to fear that he'd lost the ability to do this.

Observing Manda, Caleb began to laugh. He couldn't help himself. Changes and omens and the answers to prayers always came in such surprising forms. The laughter lightened the weight of his body and he surrendered to it, carried along.

"What's so funny?" asked Marilyn.

Caleb, sighing, didn't bother to reply. There was no logic at play here. No explanation. It was just gravity. Just relief. Just being alive.

He laughed once more, overjoyed by being able to do it, to hear the sound of his own laughter, pleased that it had come spontaneously and without effort. There was no explanation for it nor should there be.

It was his birthday, after all.

Metrum: Our Blowout

WHEN I FIRST MET Troy Marquis Callahan he defined his life as two sides of a coin. Tails meant preparing for the next football season. Heads was when all those collisions and third-down conversions were underway. Like the enthusiast in his favorite book, Roderick Chucky's Nuggets From The Iron Mine, Troy needed his sports fix to avoid miring himself in lamentations. These days, having moved away from Fortuna to start my own family, I don't see him. I miss him. I'll hazard the assumption that Troy misses me, as well, but not as much as he misses our mutual friend Devin Murray.

Devin and Troy couldn't have been more different. They'd met in Fortuna while working at the same club that eventually hired me. Devin and I were waiters. Troy, one of the bouncers. Devin was gay. Troy and I were not. Troy was black. Devin and I were not. These differences among us were never an issue.

We shared many common interests, one of them a passion for pro football. A younger third wheel between them, I started graduate school at Fortuna State and quit waiting tables just as Devin's career as head accountant for an independent film company began to take off.

Troy, at the same time, was married and hoping to start a family. He was fired as a bouncer because the club owner chose to hire one of his nephews. Troy could have taken legal action citing racism as the reason for his dismissal, but he wasn't that petty. He saw the move for what it was: pure nepotism. Devin, instead, took action. Since Devin's tight-knit company had been founded by Fortuna natives, they shot many films throughout the region. This allowed Devin to put Troy on payroll at a non-union salary in a variety of behind-the-scene positions. I believed Devin when he told me that everybody in the company loved Troy.

In 2008 while working on a movie about a special dog, Troy was employed as Devin's driver, on call. Devin paid Troy $100 per day cash, plus meals, to pick him up at the Hotel Wellington in downtown Fortuna and bring him back each night. Troy rode Devin to the movie set in the town of Colony. On Fridays, he chauffeured Devin from Colony to a second set in Valentine, where Devin distributed payroll checks to the second unit filming there. I stayed connected due to Devin's phone calls insisting I join those two to either watch football, *Queer Babysitter,* or reruns of *Deranged Companions.*

It was a frigid winter that year. Devin was indulging in a debilitating personal ritual, guzzling more beer than ever, nearly a twelve-pack each night. He'd invite me, on occasion to join him and Troy for a late and always heavy dinner at ten p.m. at a restaurant called Sur Le Table. There, Devin would indulge himself, asking the waiter to bring two beers at a time and sucking them down. Troy and I watched with dismay, neither of us drinking. We ate lightly, as well. We didn't know how to tell Devin that he should consider changing his lifestyle.

One of Troy's tasks was to make daily beer runs, paying cash one case at a time at a discount emporium. Devin, overweight, unhealthy, on statins such as Lipitor, suffered from gout. Troy, always fit and clean-shaven, put Devin to bed drunk many an evening before hurrying home to his wife. Troy, a gentleman, prided himself on his loyalty to family and friends. I have no doubt that it was a struggle for him to balance those two important elements in his life.

One January night, we three sat at the O'Leary & Shock's restaurant bar in the Hotel Wellington and watched the championship game between the Avalon Racers and the Fortuna Yahoos. Every fan in the place, which was packed, appeared to be rooting for those Racers. Yet we were in Fortuna, in one of her more renowned hotels. Troy would later say that he sat there feeling like a foreigner in the city he'd been raised in.

It was trendy in those days to be big on Avalon. The Racers won in what's now touted as an historical upset. They robbed our Yahoos of a perfect season, due to a "miraculous" play by DeCoriolanus Saint-Vasquez. To this day, I find that Racers victory difficult to accept. Troy does, as well. It felt too good to be true and fit a narrative that Avalon was continuing to regain its confidence in the wake of an economic downturn, really a national issue and still fresh in public memory, but all we heard about through media outlets was how it had devastated great unholy Avalon.

I joined Troy after the game to help guide a besotted Devin to his room. Devin, incoherent, had pissed on himself, his gout making it impossible for him to walk without support. He kept slurring, trying to sound black, I guess, as he said to Troy, "I'm on the righteous path, I am, but it's a real mother."

These were not moments to savor as we helped a wheezing groaning Devin take off his shoes before sliding him under a blanket with his jeans, socks and shirt still on. Devin had to be on set the next day at 7 a.m. Troy had to get him there.

I rented on the city's South Side, which had been considered the tough part of town during the time when Troy had grown up there. It was slowly getting gentrified as outsiders like myself moved in, and people of color, many of them Spanish speakers, moved out of the city and re-populated what were once considered down-at-heels suburban communities.

Troy was exceptional in that he lived in Rebar, which was a tonier up-and-coming suburb. He was married to a white woman with a college education and deep local ties. Not the stereotypical gangster of a black man, not Troy. We talked about this often, and the challenges he faced, in general. Since I was earning an advanced degree in Sociology, I was fascinated by his take on racism. "I have to let them speak first. They just don't know anyone like me," he'd say. "They have to feel like I respect them, even if I don't. I always have to remember that it's like they're afraid. I'm used to be the zoo animal they ain't talked to before. I don't even think about it much."

I took a taxi home that night to my place on Bland Avenue. Fortuna was deflated. Troy told me later that driving alone he had to stop twice to clear his head, clouded as it was with a debate over whether he was bitter about a Fortuna team losing yet again to an Avalon one, paranoid the game had been rigged, or whether it was the best thing that could have happened to Avalon, to the country, in general. Troy would have been arrested if stopped by a cop. He wasn't. He got lucky. I ascribe this to karma because he'd been helping Devin, who wasn't the only diehard fan who'd gone to bed wasted and disappointed.

Troy, muscle-bound and with a disarming smile, was not to be messed with, had starred in high-school football as a lineman. He'd grown up a fan admiring Fortuna players such as Rivetgun Hayes and Antoine Ballast. He'd invested 45 years into being loyal to the Yahoos. It fascinated him that black men from warmer climes were willing to confront Fortuna weather to play for a team which throughout his teenage years was considered fourth-rate. He admired the work ethic of former players Jigsaw Jones and Mac "Flash" Dunlap, both of them transplants to the region. He'd seen the team play live before the current ownership changed its logo from the ax-wielding Pilgrim to the Flying Yahoo, back when they were the Fortuna Pilgrims and their home "stadium" was the old Pilgrim Field, known today as New Normal Field at Fortuna University, a school esteemed more for its hockey program than for football. It was also once home to the Fortuna baseball franchise before it moved to the mid-west, changing its name to become the Whistlers of the Eastern Grainbelt League.

A neck injury during his senior year ended Troy's aspirations to play any more football. Though he'd received scholarship offers from both Krown, and Prince, he did not attend those local universities. Maybe because I was an ardent listener, tried really hard not to be racist or homophobic, and was also an outsider to Fortuna who'd moved there to further my education, Troy took a liking to me. We seldom discussed this. Troy talked, though, loved to commiserate. He enjoyed delving into examinations of the society as a whole, an area that I was well-versed in. Self-taught, having worked a variety of jobs, Troy never tired of asking me about books and perspectives on various social theories, or discussing his belief in what he called "loyalty to God and the consolations and consequences of ritual."

When it came to sports, in Troy's opinion they possessed an intrinsic value beyond entertainment. They offered structure. Athletes could be used as tools to help define national imperatives. He brought up Joe Louis and Jesse Owens as examples. To Troy, sports were a sub-culture defined by demarcated limits on space and time that helped individuals define and profit by a sense of self-respect as they fit into a team model. In football, for one, the only built-in serendipity that existed in its rule book was the coin-toss that started each game. Unlike many vicissitudes in his life, the sporting rituals he'd known had helped him build confidence toward achievable goals, allowing a measurable sense of accomplishment. While growing up an only child with a father in prison, and a mother who worked long hours in two jobs to make ends meet, he'd always been hungry for structure and guidance and a feeling of acceptance. A football game made sense to him. It was brutal, unpredictable, yet finite, its actions controlled by severe regulations. So was one's life, generally, but with one primary difference. In football, he could be part of a winning team. In life, there was no end. The game went on and on and on. People like him, like his parents, maybe worked hard but still ended up losing.

According to Troy, a select few in Fortuna followed the football ritual during the era he was in high school. One of his English teachers had played for the team when they were the Cannibals under coach Bunk Worthy. He told Troy to read Eddy Berry's classic, *Slo-Mo He Don't Play*. Troy earned his first A for a book report. Like many fans in the 70s, Troy followed the Headhunters, and the Girders, stellar squads in the Unity Football Association. That same teacher gave him *Become The Citadel* by Lance Person. Reading sports books became Troy's ritual. Athletes and coaches became role models, their stories pushing him to read for pleasure.

Though Devin had never played football, he loved the sport. I think this was because as a gay man who'd attended high school in the 70s, he lived to defy stereotypes and prove that men of any orientation could enjoy conventional macho pursuits with other men. I also think Troy admired him for this. Like Devin, Troy also defied stereotypes. He talked with erudition about fans who followed the local Fortuna State versus University of Fortuna rivalry, the venerable Krown versus Prince game, though he knew these rivalries couldn't match the national level of, say, the Wings And Waffles Bowl. He felt the Fortuna sports of his boyhood were provincial in many respects. Though Tattoo Reynolds, and Benny Hatchet before him, were local legends, Fortuna Park, home to the city's baseball team, the Settlers, had rarely sold out. The same ran true for the old Fortuna Arena and Rollie Bing's Pumas in basketball, along with hockey's Rapiers of the Henri Cheval era. Tickets for sports events were cheap and easy to come by.

I didn't know. I hailed from the rural southern Mid-West, where when I grew up segregation was an unstated norm and I hadn't seen black and gay men support each other as if they were brothers. The baseball team I'd followed with fervor, the Rock Horses, was based in a city far away. They'd beaten the Fortuna Settlers in the '67 national championship, an event, Troy admitted, that had made him cry when a little boy.

Though Troy assured me many a Fortuna-area kid could recite the Rapiers or Pumas rosters by heart, baseball was the region's game. Troy played for me the vintage record album that he owned, *Dare To Conquer*, and we listened to famed broadcaster Harry Grampus who for decades had done play by play from Fortuna Park. Generally, the Settlers of Troy's boyhood were defined by losing. His pro football team, back then an upstart, boasted one major player: Rigoberto Manuel Alvarez-Guarino, known to fans as Manny G. One of the few Latinos, at that time, to leave a mark on popular culture in Fortuna.

Still, Troy stayed loyal. He'd even met Rod Dowell, the Yahoo's first mascot. As a life-sized version of the team's original logo, Rod was a beefy white fellow who wore silver wings above each ear and a long black cloak. He'd stand by a cannon and each time the team scored, which in that era wasn't often, he got to fire it once.

In 1986, having been loyal to the Yahoos through some miserable seasons, Troy suffered through their drubbing in the championship against the Riatas, an expansion team from Texas. So did Rod. In that match, poor old Rod hadn't been allowed on the field as mascot. He'd been forced to pay for his hotel room and plane ticket and he'd sat sweating with his binoculars in nose-bleed seats, dusty desert winds swirling around him. Troy told me how Rod had described it as one of the worst sports experiences he'd endured.

There was Troy's father-in-law, too, Lou Sheehan, one of the construction foremen who'd built what in 1971 became the Yahoos' stadium in the suburb of Boysenberry when the team and the Sectarian Football Association merged with the Unity Football Association. Custer Armstrong, founder of the Yahoos and the Sectarian Football Association, still owned the franchise at that time. Mr. Sheehan, decrying how corners were cut that sacrificed safety to ensure profit, described Custer Armstrong as a crook and his Boysenberry venue as a "tinhorn's gutbucket," whatever that meant. He didn't think it deserved its commemorative plaque in the parking lot of present-day state-of-the-art JoyRamCo Stadium.

So, Custer Armstrong's SFA and his Yahoos joined the UFA the same year that Troy was born and his father was sentenced to a thirty-year hitch for first-degree murder. Devin had also been born that same year; he, too, without a father figure. Many personal similarities and emotions were tied to their fealty to each other, to the Yahoos, and to defying stereotypes. I think for both of them, sharing a team to root for extended their sense of family and belonging to a place. It helped ease painfully complex and less conspicuous issues regarding self-acceptance, masculinity and the need for companionship.

Troy told me that while driving full of drunken angst that January night, he couldn't stop punishing himself, asking if the Avalon Racers had won fairly. Was there something wrong with him as a fan? Had his ritual betrayed him? Had the "miracle" catch been staged? He felt badly for Devin and all his slurring about the righteous path. Sure, it was a mother, all right, but it appeared their salad days together were starting to vanish. What could Troy do to stop this?

The next day, conditions were frigid on the movie set. Troy dropped Devin off an hour late at the temporary film office, one floor of an empty commercial building on Colony's Main Street. He picked him up at six. Devin, unshaven, limping, jittery, needed help getting into Troy's car. His face was crab-pink, bloated, and he slouched and wheezed next to Troy at the wheel. He was unable to buckle his seat belt. Troy helped him. When Devin began to twitch in spasms, reeking of beer that sweated from his pores, Troy asked if he was okay. Devin sounded a mournful, "I just don't know, man. It's not supposed to be this way."

They rode back to Fortuna in silence until Devin apologized. Troy absorbed the apology, asking, "But what is it, Devin? What's going on with you?"

Unwilling to face Troy, Devin opened and closed his fists. He stared into the night, remarking distantly, sounding frightened as he repeated, "It's not supposed to happen like this. Not this way, Troy. This isn't, it wasn't…what I planned."

Later, unable to sleep, Troy tried to fathom what Devin had meant. Who could plan anything if they didn't follow through on those plans? God just laughed at people like Devin. What more could he do to help his friend?

A phone call from Memorial Hospital woke Troy at three a.m. He knew the woman on the phone, one of the producers of the dog movie. She wanted Troy to know that Devin was alive, but he'd suffered a massive stroke.

"I'll be right there."

No, Troy couldn't visit him. Maybe in a week. Regarding the movie, Troy's services would no longer be needed. They were already over-budget. Devin's two office assistants would double their workloads to compensate for his absence.

Troy later phoned one of those assistants. He'd gotten to know them well. He liked them and he struggled to hold back tears. "This is Troy. This can't be happening," he said.

The assistant replied gently, calmly, that she understood, but Devin hadn't been taking very good care of himself. They all knew that. Of course, it was horrible, but the movie had to get made. She asked Troy if he would pick up Devin's personal belongings and take them to an address where Devin would stay temporarily once out of the hospital. Later, she explained, Devin would be moved to a group home closer to family members.

Troy said, with regret of course, he was glad to help. He'd pick up the belongings. No one had to pay him for it either. He told the assistant he felt guilty, as if he could have done more, could have seen it coming. She said to him, sounding genuine, "You didn't do anything wrong. You were always there for him. We all saw that. It's a trajectory with some people."

A trajectory, thought Troy. What a cold word to describe a person's life.

Three weeks after Devin's stroke, weary of pitying and doubting himself and leaning on his wife for support, Troy met me for lunch. We talked about how Devin would often tell us never to trust any movie business connections and, whenever possible, to get on with our lives in our own ways.

"Our own trajectories," I told Troy.

"I guess," he said. "But I don't like that word. It's not like we're missiles."

As I sat with him, it occurred to me that we were no longer young. That a door had slammed in our faces. We needed to make adjustments, create new rituals, stay on the so-called righteous path. We talked about how Devin had understood that he'd been playing with fire, destroying himself with alcohol, and wasn't the type to take anyone's advice.

"He kept telling me," said Troy, "that it wasn't supposed to be like this."

"But isn't it?" I asked. "Truth is, we're not supposed to drink ourselves to death. You saw him. Two beers at a time at Sur Le Table."

"I know," said Troy. "We didn't love him enough. Is that it?"

I had no answer for that question. Poor, surprisingly innocent Troy. His life had been tied to Devin's and it, too, was falling apart. I didn't see him for a couple weeks and as football season got into its full swing, I learned later that he'd phoned one of the people whose number Devin had given him, the set construction chief of a film with A-list actors scheduled to begin in Fortuna very soon. Using Devin's name, Troy got the chief to call him back. "Crewed-up," said the chief. "Too bad, really. If you'd called some days ago, I could have used you. But I'm crewed-up now. And tell Devin I said hi."

Troy, dismayed, hadn't been able to muster the nerve to tell the set-crew chief that Devin wasn't in the game any longer.

As another few weeks passed, and football season really heated up, both Troy and I took little comfort in what became an increasingly fatalistic outlook. Troy's so-called movie career wasn't meant to be. He began new rituals, though he continued reading, rising early, doing his gym workouts. He told me that at least he would stay on the righteous path. He was going to church regularly, spending more quality time with his wife and child.

I did what I could to help, connecting him to a friend in the athletic department at the university where Troy was hired as a weight training assistant for the men's hockey team. Troy was perfect for such a job. He quit drinking and changed his diet to vegetarian-only. Yet he couldn't stem the depression that overcame him whenever he thought about Devin, the times they'd shared, what might have been if he'd intervened more aggressively to stop his drinking.

When Troy talked to his wife about how this troubled him, she insisted that he let Devin go, that his loyalty wasn't going to move Devin away from his group home, obsessive self-destructive behavior and his dependency on medications. Troy led a clean simple life in Rebar and he should be happy with that. He didn't need Devin or work in movies to complete himself. Troy listened to his wife, thought her advice practical, but he never felt sure of comfortable that she really understood the profound depth of the friendship that he and Devin had shared.

Months later, long after football season was over, and as the first forsythia buds started to open, I visited members of Devin's family for the first time. They struck me as entirely suspicious of my concern for Devin's well-being. Apparently, Devin hadn't told them about my friendship, or Troy's, with him. I think Devin's family members believed I'd been sponging off him, and that Troy's long time with Devin and the rituals it entailed had enabled Devin's self-destructive tendencies. That I was lying when speaking about Troy's and my own concerns.

Devin's alcoholism, never Troy's fault, had been so advanced that without Troy's help on that dog movie, Devin would have lost his job. How many mornings had Troy shouted Devin out of bed, helping him dress, hurrying him to the set and pumping him full of coffee? All of it becoming dysfunctional and increasingly ritualized between them. Did that make Troy a friend or an enabler? He and I discussed how such thin margins separated these distinctions.

Some of Devin's family members used a cruel rationale for their rejection of Troy's claim, and my own, of abiding friendship. They weren't meek when boasting that Devin worked in the movie business, knew "real stars" and because of this tended to attract "leeches and outsiders." I was no "star." Neither was Troy. They didn't use the N-word, at least, though they called Troy things like "lyin' eye-candy, a jock," and asked me what kind of twisted career advancement he was after.

As for me, I was "a calendar boy, a hick know-it-all from some Fortuna college." Troy was seen in a worse light because he was a local, "a sponge, a driver with delusions of grandeur." That phrase sounds even more bone-chilling when spoken in a Fortuna accent.

I found all this disheartening. It disgusted me. Anyone would take offense at such people, such language. Not Troy. He took it in stride, confessing to me, "Remember who you're talking to. I grew up in Fortuna. Welcome to my world. I've been called a whole lot worse. I know this region and I know how these people can be."

Whenever we visited Devin, we found him sedated into a nearly vegetal state. He couldn't comprehend the situation or defend our loyalty. Early on, when proper treatment might have made a difference, Devin hadn't heeded his therapists and doctors. He'd chosen not to follow prescribed exercise regimens, and hadn't shown enough improvement to justify reductions in his dosages.

With each visit, I saw how steadily his body was atrophying. When I joined Troy on what I decided would be my last painful visit to that group home, I winced seeing Devin in his wheelchair, shockingly pale, inert, a sagging and empty look about him due mostly to his Lithium prescription. He drooled and mumbled and didn't even recognize us.

On the way home, Troy went inward and said little. If our relationship with Devin had been a game, we'd not only lost it, we'd been blown out.

I've never seen that dog movie. I refuse to. I'm sure Troy hasn't seen it either. We've stayed in touch, but he long ago stopped talking about movies as if they were important or interesting. I watch football sometimes, though rarely, and I wonder if all the incredible success Fortuna sports teams have earned in recent decades brings Troy any pleasure.

Before leaving Fortuna to move west and take a university

teaching position, I stopped by the university athletic complex to visit him. I'd gotten engaged. Troy was thrilled to hear this. He talked to me about fatherhood and how it consistently brought him a renewed sense of purpose and some new consoling rituals that were keeping him on the righteous path. Though he was no longer on Facebook, he'd been emailing me many pictures of his daughter.

The big news was that he had a son. I hadn't known this. Could I guess his name? I was right. It was Devin. Troy showed me a photo. The adorable infant had Troy's deep caramel skin-tone and his mother's piercing green eyes. We didn't gush and tell each other that the boy would do great things one day. We hoped this, of course, but our blowout had taught us to be skeptical and restrained.

Modum: A Question of Execution

I'D HEARD TINY ARIA say a million times that in Fortuna if you scratched beneath the surface, you'd only find more surface. He laid this on me again when he phoned about the Reno Morelli kidnapping. Reno owned The Gutterball, a dive where mooks, con-men and low-level operatives met to figure out which cops weren't on the take and which ones had to be. Cops drank there on the sly all the time.

The Gutterball was sometimes lucrative, but Reno's real breadwinner was the Blue Moon, a joint where I once worked. This glitz-palace was perfect for wedding receptions, reunions, Christmas parties and always booked six months in advance. A couple of cast-concrete lions bookended the entrance steps. In the middle of the front parking lot stood a massive fountain with a pair of cherubs lit from under the water with colored floodlights. The lobby featured a red carpet and a huge chandelier. All that was missing were a couple of slot machines. Many a made-guy had earned bones while still a parking valet there. I had, too, but that was eons ago. I've since gone the other way and though I still work the Blue Moon, I also track down criminals and help to lock them up.

Cherry, my girl, was the featured dancer at the Blue Moon on the night Reno disappeared. One minute, Reno was there sipping Dewar's, the next he was gone. According to Tiny, Fortuna cops were called in and they found in the Blue Moon office a ransom note in lipstick, with a number, a time to phone and the words *one cool million.*

I managed the Blue Moon with my partner, Tiny Aria, another convert to the law and order brigade. We ran our own PI operation on the side. We'd been out that night at a Fortuna State basketball game watching my nephew pull down rebounds. Tiny, along with Cherry and a new dancer named Vera, had been taken into FPD custody and hammered with questions. What time had they last seen Reno, for how long in his employ, did they recall anything suspicious before his disappearance?

They ID'd his car, a white Lexus with gold trim, still in the parking lot. Cops phoned his wife. She said he wasn't home. For a professional mobster, Reno was known as a straight-up operator, had very few enemies, so this was a surprise. Of course, it was all a lie. Half the cops in Fortuna were on the take.

Reno was a sly silver worm, a capo. Not untouchable, however. Nobody is. Tiny feared he'd been whacked. What happened between those in the upper echelons was seldom the business of those like Tiny and me who served them alcohol and an old-school floor show. Vera spoke of Reno as a "giving soul." Yeah, right.

Some cops I knew described him as a "charitable enough," a man who contributed to the policeman's benevolent fund and the fireman's ball and offered regular bonuses to his kitchen staff. I asked around and learned he threw parties for certain individuals with clout, treated them to prime rib and lobster and all the Asti they could drink.

Vera's dopy line was priceless: "Why would anyone want to hurt such a kind man?"

For all his allegedly admirable qualities, I could have given a dozen reasons, but nobody was asking me. So, after hearing from

Tiny, I started snooping and learned Reno had recently gotten involved in a new enterprise, a neo-food restaurant called Kut that he was managing for an ace named Taka and that the place was funded by both Yakuza and maybe Russian interests. Fat chance of that. In short, Reno's capo status meant nothing to them.

For the most part, Reno played the gentleman in public, looked the part, but he was both a lecher and a lady's man, like a lot of those guys of his ilk. He got along well with players from other mobs. His secret, he once told me, was respect, of course. It's a stale, tired Mafia line. His other secret was that he stayed away from narcotics and guns. Maybe that was true, but I doubted it. Owning a dive and a banquet hall and other so-called concerns, along with paying off cops was old-school diplomacy that didn't carry enough cred to make the likes of Reno be feared. This gave me one more reason to wonder why anyone would even bother with Reno. It also cast a powerful doubt in my mind that I could trust anything I'd heard from or about the man, no matter the source.

And remember this: I worked for him. I wore a mask too, earning my keep in both worlds. Neither of us was all that original.

Kut featured a nouveau-styled cuisine that attorneys on diets tended to like. When I asked Cherry if she'd eaten there — and she had — she told me her drizzled-with-miso and Asian-inspired steak entree had looked like an angle Picasso might have used for one of his cubist renderings. Gotta love Cherry's esoteric humor.

I went to Kut to poke around. I spoke to Taka directly and got his permission to speak to his staff about Reno. None of his doormen, kitchen or wait staff knew anything out of the ordinary. I phoned or else visited some of Reno's alleged friends and associates, including his wife by his second marriage (he was on his third), and then I dropped in on my old friend Budgie Weld of the Fortuna police. Budgie suspected that Reno owed money to people from out of town. Who didn't? Related to the Kut operation? Probably, thought Budgie. Yet he, too, was surprised this had happened.

Budgie was a sweetheart. A cop on the take, but he had mouths to feed. "Reno tended to keep a low profile. Makes no sense. He was keeping the right people happy."

"But he's had his share of enemies," I said. "Maybe someone's back in town."

From what I could glean from Budgie, the FPD had no plans to assign a detective to the case. The file on Reno would stay open and leads would be gathered and assessed. All par for the course. This was seen as a mob kidnapping. Let the mob handle it. Why waste tax-payer dollars?

Was it the mob? I didn't think so. It just didn't add up.

I then phoned another cop-crone from days gone by, one Sergeant Marvin Dino Marvin; we'd bowled in a league together at Fortune Star Lanes, one of only three remaining alleys in the city. Marvin was a heck of a bowler and headed up the Fortune Hill precinct house. He told me, "Don't take this the wrong way, my friend. I know Reno wasn't always exemplary in his business dealings, a real scumbag, but you got crummier fish to fry."

"What you trying to tell me? Take matters into my own hands? I still work for the guy."

"How you do it is your business. All I know is they found some new evidence. Randy Zane's sentence got reduced. There's just no evidence. He's out on parole."

A blessing from Marvin. Randy Zane had been in stir for at least a nickel and I'd forgotten about him. He was the brother of Reno's second wife. He'd botched a warehouse heist for Reno in which a young cop, a black man with a wife and three kids had been shot dead in the chest. There'd been a huge outcry for justice, but nobody knew the perp and there was no way Reno would take the fall. Since

Randy Zane had been there and essentially in charge, Reno snitched on him. By doing so, Reno cleared his name and made the cops look good. What I knew about that warehouse job was that three men, including Randy, had been hired. I didn't know the names or whereabouts of the other two. One of them had been the perp. Not Randy.

I started on the phone with Reno's second wife, Brigid, Randy's sister. I begged Brigid, explaining that her brother was in deep trouble and I could maybe help him. She agreed, with reluctance, to meet me at Scarlet O'Hara's.

"He wanted out, he got out," she said. She didn't want to order a drink, or to stay long.

"I know about Reno. It's your brother I want. You think he's around? Who's he run with? He got a girl?"

She said Randy was always wild and even the likes of Reno couldn't keep up with him. "He likes the high drama."

"So, then a kidnapping does fit. Doesn't it?"

She shrugged. "What kidnapping? It's your stinkin' world, not mine. You got five more minutes with me. You do know, how much I despise you, right?"

I used those minutes wisely, describing what had happened. Brigid admitted that she genuinely doubted her brother Randy's sanity.

"Randy never grew up. He thought working for Reno was the be-all and end-all. It was sordid stuff. I'm glad Reno dumped me for some tramp. That man was never faithful. I have no idea what Randy saw in him. Or what I did, either."

"Money, that's what. You got a nice house out of the divorce settlement, didn't you?"

"Bet your ass, I did. Had it coming to me. But the smartest thing was that Reno and I never had no kids together. Maybe he learned his lesson from his first marriage."

"You think they got something to do with this?"

"His kids? No. He took care of them. Money-wise, anyways. Domenic, his son, he's still around Fortuna. His daughter, I don't know. She's long gone. I never got that close to them."

"You sure you ain't seen your brother Randy around?"

"Even if I had, you think I'd tell you?"

I got the picture. She wasn't stupid. Brigid rose and started to leave. Then she stopped. "But Randy, he was the one Reno was closest to. They had a real almost father-son bond."

"I didn't know that."

"I was even a little jealous of it. Kinda gay almost. But not gay. You know, Randy and me, we lost our father early. Maybe Reno fit that role for him."

"But why kidnapping?"

"Why else? You said so yourself. Money. Randy was locked up, took the blame for killing a poor black kid, made it sound like he was one of those white supremacists, had his name smeared all over the city as a possible cop killer, even though there wasn't any evidence of any of it. His friendship with Reno was something he valued. How much now I can't say. I just know for sure that Randy didn't kill anybody and he loved Reno very much."

"At one time, anyway, right?"

Brigid nodded. "Always. Randy's just out of his league."

She'd been very generous with her time. I thanked Brigid and asked if I could speak with her again, if necessary. She said not a chance. She was leaving town for a while. "Sordid stuff," she said again. "I've had it up to here with everything sordid."

Many a cop in Fortuna was now on the hunt for Randy Zane. He had to be our man. I phoned Fortuna Plumbing Supply where he'd worked as a clerk before getting entangled with Reno. I got lucky and showed up before any cops. There was one fat old coot in overalls, a manager who'd been there with Randy years ago and after I pitched him face to face, he agreed to give me five minutes. His name was Arthur Brand.

"When Randy was here working with you, did he have a girl?" I asked.

"He had a few, I suppose, but there was one, yeah, she'd even come by now and then."

That girl's name was Nina Dart, a former model now a buyer for a clothing boutique on the city's tony west side. Arthur Brand's guess was that they'd been together about eight years, maybe more. He was a savvy old duff, that Arthur, he found Nina's Facebook page for me, complete with her address and current status — single. She still looked hot to trot, too. I kissed old Arthur on his bald head as I thanked him, adding, "I only took five minutes. A deal's a deal."

I beat it out of there before old Arthur could even reply. I was no genius, but I knew where I'd find Randy Zane. I did more searching online and found it obvious that Nina spent lavishly on clothes and visits to fashion shows. I phoned Budgie Weld, calling in a favor, asking if he'd dig up her record and give it a close look. Budgie got back to me pronto and I learned Nina had been busted once for possession of a controlled substance. Budgie guessed if not cocaine then amphetamines, common enough among models. I shared with Budgie what I knew. It wasn't much, but it was more than he had and he was grateful.

"Get you the bust on this," I told him. "Might even merit you a promotion."

Budgie liked hearing that, but he knew it was just me blowing hot air. I told him to phone Marvin, Dino Marvin at the Fortune Hill precinct house, as well, to fill him in, but not to use my name. Then I tracked down Reno's son, Domenic, who owned a dry-cleaning business. Conveniently enough for me, it wasn't far from Nina's west side address.

I'd met Domenic a few times and so he recognized me when I walked in. He'd put on weight and lost some hair and he balked, at first, until I told Domenic his old man Reno was still alive and that I was determined to find him. I think Domenic liked hearing that, but he looked justly skeptical and suspicious.

"I didn't know there was so much honor among thieves," he said.

"There isn't, Dom. It's why Reno was nipped. I think he's tied up in an apartment just down the street from here."

I told him about Randy Zane and Nina and this put Domenic at ease because he knew as much about them as I did, if not more. He'd been closer to his mother, who'd died of cancer, and it was her death that had kept him in Fortuna and helped him grow closer to his father Reno, and to Brigid. He explained that when Reno, along with Randy Zane, were first starting out in cahoots together, Randy was dating Nina, but Nina wanted Randy to move to the west coast so she could get into television. Randy had convinced her to stay in Fortuna, promising her he'd be owning at least one lucrative local restaurant and a fancy bar and maybe a modeling agency once he and Reno finalized a few more lucrative transactions together.

"Randy was smart," said Domenic.

"No, he wasn't. But go on. Let's hear your side."

"What I mean," said Domenic, "is no strip-tease-dump and drug-dealing tycoon in a suit. Randy wanted no part of that whole scene. He wanted to marry Nina. I think she wanted that, too. There was a time when I went out with all of them, me and my wife and Brigid and Dad. It was good for a while."

"But I think your old Dad got in the way, didn't he?"

Domenic shrugged. "If you mean, was Reno sleeping with Nina, yeah, probably. I mean, it's twisted, but not beyond the realm."

"Hate to say it, but I'm afraid your old man couldn't keep it in his pants. My guess is that Randy didn't even learn that until after he went to prison."

"What's the word?" asked Domenic. "Motive? My Dad was never stupid. He got his way, usually. He screwed over Randy and then he just let Nina go. Threw her out like she was rancid meat."

"Nice, Domenic. Real nice. He was her Sugar Daddy, nothing Randy could be."

"Nina was a piece of work, a handful. And expensive. Still, Dad was generous to her maybe just to keep her quiet. I don't know. I think she was probably ungrateful and got bored with him like she did with all her men."

"And Randy, young and ambitious, must have been furious when he learned that about your father and Nina."

"Yeah, you said it. But if you sleep with canines," said Domenic, "you wake up with fleas. Maybe you're right about Randy too. Maybe he was never all that bright."

—⁓—

A kidnapping. A high-stakes gambit. Not a choice any amateur should make. All a question of execution. Too many steps are required. Snare the hostage. Pick up the ransom. They're better for TV cop programs and yet they're more common than they should be. I think this is because they speak to the lust and ignorance of many a two-bit criminal mind. At least with a hit, you know a pro is getting paid handsomely. Because of this, the job usually gets done. How well and when and for how much money are other questions. But it gets done.

I shared these ruminations with Tiny and Cherry over Moo Shi Chicken at the Dragon Lantern House. Budgie Weld had received another call from me and I convinced him to send over boots to watch Nina's place. Sure enough, after a week of surveillance they saw Randy Zane open the front door one night to pay for a pizza delivery order. What a stupid move. Budgie didn't hesitate. He sent in a team to storm the place and while Nina screamed, Randy went for his Glock and was killed immediately. Three shots fired in self-defense from an officer just doing his job. Those boys found Reno in the basement, allegedly kidnapped, sitting in an easy chair, drinking Dewar's and watching ESPN highlights.

Turned out, Reno was in on the ruse from the start. He owed money, with interest, to Taka and the Yakuza interests for services related to running Cut, which was not turning its expected profit. Most likely, Reno had been skimming from the so-called operations budget. Reno, in true-blue dirt-bag fashion, also owed big to other interests, none of which he could pay back, so he had hatched a plan. He understood that Randy was livid with him over his long-ago fling with Nina. Randy could forgive Nina, he loved her, but he couldn't forgive Reno, who he felt had twice betrayed him. Reno, always smooth and sly, convinced Randy he'd make it up to him and that they'd all get fat on ransom money. Randy, being one twig shy of a total moron tree, went along with it. But kidnappings are too complex and rarely go as planned, even for someone with Reno's experience, connections and cunning.

"Who'd they intend to get the ransom from? That's the problem," said Tiny. "I mean, I know Reno's made, a player, but he was in free-fall and there's a lot of little spokes on one big wheel that keeps on turning and turning, you know? And besides, even with inflation, a cool million don't come easy. Reno's like all of us. Disposable."

"Tiny, you're a regular Shakespeare. I couldn't have said it better myself."

I watched Tiny curse, having spilled soy sauce on his new tie.

"Just take it off," Cherry told him. "Loosen up. Relax. You solved another case."

"Do that," I said. "I'll get it dry-cleaned for you. I know a good place."

Tiny took our advice. Then he ordered another round of Mai Tais. The three of us continued eating. Reno would do time, but thanks to lawyers and mobbed-up connections, it would most likely be in a country-club style at a minimum security farm. Nina was now a widow and one cop's murder remained unsolved, though the press and the people of Fortuna would accept Randy had been guilty, after all. Call it closure for them, I guess.

Cherry leaned against me and ran her hand along my thigh. She offered a penny for my thoughts and I told her I was just glad to still be alive on the food chain. For March in Fortuna, the night felt warm.

ALBUM TWO

Purse ~ Conscience

Galliards And Pavanes

In 12 Polyphonous Movements

On Mercury Living Presence

"The humblest composer will not find true humility in aiming low…."
— Charles Ives from *Essays Before A Sonata*

Why The Good Are Needed

I GOT NO IDEA what love is, not really, but what I do knows is that when I'm hungry I gotta eat and I'm just a kid and I'm hungry all the time. At least that's what my old Papa tells me. He calls me all kinds of names in Italian and they ain't worth repeating. He drinks a lot, especially when the weather's changing and it's another fall day, which means it's getting colder and it's been about two weeks of my old Papa being M-I-A and when Papa goes without working he wanders all over the city and drinks in the different bars and me, I don't drink, I never will, because I see how it makes Papa get vicious toward Mama and I don't like that. None of us kids do. But we put up with it. We gotta. How else we gonna live? See, you put up with things, that's what life is. I believe this, though sometimes I have my doubts.

I'm figuring I'll wander toward Giaconda's Pharmacy, away from traffic, move down the side streets and once I get there I can hear the clucking of chickens and the smell of their poop. I know there's a man that keeps 'em alive and sells 'em outta wooden cages in a run-down building in his backyard. I know he ain't supposed to do this, but he keeps quiet and nobody bothers him and he sells enough chickens to the old women, you know, the ones like Mama from the old country and he don't need to keep no sign above no door. He just sells his chickens and some fresh eggs and the old women sometimes they trade with him, sometimes they buy on credit, you know, it's a neighborhood and we all look out for one another, but me I don't go near no chickens. I don't wanna step in that poop, but the old man there he never runs me off. I think he likes seeing me watching him.

I change my mind. I need to find old Papa. I get to the first bar. It's a room with no sign above its door. I hear music. Sounds like Caruso singing from *Tosca*. I know this cuz Mama listens to opera any time it's on the radio. Mama told me about Caruso and *Tosca* and Verdi. I kinda like opera, but I don't tell nobody.

I peek in and I see dark in there and the room almost empty and there's a man he's a bartender washing glasses and putting 'em away. He's got a red apron on. I think I know this man. He's Dolan. Lots of guys named Dolan, Dooley and Duffy in these neighborhoods. He ain't Italian, of course, but he's seen me at mass at Saint Agatha's and he knows about old Papa and I think he likes me because he's seen me more than once bringing Papa home in the little red wagon. You try pulling a grown man home in a boy's red wagon. It ain't easy, especially when he's so drunk he can't walk or talk and he pees all over himself.

"Hey Duffy," I say all saucy like. "What's up, Duffy? How you doing today, Duffy?"

He says, "It's Dolan to you, kid. Where you getting Duffy?"

I feel stupid. I made a mistake. I say I'm sorry.

Dolan says, "Don't sweat it, kid, it's okay, you lookin' for your old man?"

I nod and for some reason I want to cry. It don't seem like I got any friends and why does Papa have to drink so much and why do I always gotta drag him home in the wagon?

Dolan's older than Papa, with hair the color of orangeade, so after his first words he don't say nothing more. He ain't in any kind of hurry, but he knows me, knows why I'm there and he keeps it simple when he decides to open his mouth. My name is Togo. It's a funny name from the old country, at least that's what Mama tells me, but it's mine and I kinda like it.

"So how is Togo doing today?" Dolan says in his harsh kinda accent that I been told ain't like anything heard outside this neighborhood. Then he grins because he knows why I'm there, he sees I'm about to cry because I feel so bad and don't know the reason.

"I ain't seen him," he tells me. "Sorry."

My face reddens and I feel shame and I think about Papa's drinking and how he makes such misery for the rest of us and sometimes I just want to smack him, just let him have it, because I seen him smack my brothers more than once and even Mama a couple times before he slammed the door to his bedroom. You know how it is in our place, it ain't like one of them big houses that the president lives in and it ain't like what a lot of the other people have who don't live in the city and are getting out now that the war is gonna end soon. We're always falling on top of each other and it's the worst time when Papa is home and drunk and he's got no work and he's beating everything in sight, including me. That's why I turn red in front of Dolan. It's a lot to think about. It don't seem right.

I don't linger. I say *ciao see ya later alligator* to Dolan and for some reason he don't say nothing back, don't even smile. Maybe because he don't have to, because he knows I'm sad even though I'm putting on a brave face. I gotta do it. I'm doing it for Mama, my sisters and brothers. We want Papa home. We're *la famiglia*. Can't have the old man out drunk and carousing all the time even though that's all he ever does and we're sick of it.

I start wheeling toward a furniture store and then I hurry past a liquor store where I know my older brothers sometimes buy their Lucky Strikes. I don't know the clerk in there, so after peeking into the window a minute, I scoot along and slip down an alley and head toward a light coming from the open door of a room where smoke is leaking out in flat clouds that spread on the air and leave a pleasing smell. It's sweetish cigar smoke and I know Papa smokes a cigar now and then so I figure he might be in there.

I keep peeking in and see a handful of men sitting around a table. They're wearing hats and suspenders and drinking Dago Red out of small glasses and smoking them cigars that smell like cherries and wood chips and one of them is eating prosciutto sliced thin and this is how it is in the neighborhood even though there's coloreds and Latins and all them Irish ones. We all pretty much know our place and get along. It's the war. We gotta do it to beat the Nazis.

These men are like brothers to each other and they sit and play cards, mostly bridge but some play poker because it makes them feel more American, and they're older so some of them wear not only hats but also neckties and jackets. Mama tells me a man should dress up and someday I'm gonna have enough swag that I can wear a suit and leather shoes and a Stetson hat and not look like poor Togo from the other side of the tracks. Nobody's gonna call me names and get away with it. I'm gonna puff my own cigars, live large, but in an honest way and make my future wife and my Mama happy without any liquor and carousing.

Some of my brothers, they're already into this. They're home from the war and they've seen bad things and they're living clean and I can't blame them, but even them, even my brothers Aldo and Carmine, they was both in Germany fighting and now they got plans and they tell me it's almost over there in Germany and Italy and Japan, but we still got lots of boys dying in Japan and I got two brothers still there near Osaka fighting like Sergeant Fury and His Howling Commandos. Mama's so nervous about all my brothers. I got one brother in Alaska and I keep telling Mama that even a war can't last forever and my brothers are heroes, but they want nothing to do with old Papa the drunk, so that's why I'm stuck with running around the neighborhood with a wagon trying to find him all the time.

All my sisters are working in the factories making shoes and my brothers that are home are working construction and earning good money, but nobody's got plans to stick around this neighborhood. They don't have to. My brothers are gonna get houses out in the suburbs. My sisters are gonna find husbands. They're gonna have the American dream. That's what freedom is for, ain't it? That's why we're fighting. Get a house of your own. Get out of the neighborhood. Make yourself a garden, grow some tomatoes and basil and have your own big family. Make Mama proud.

～

The light is thick with smoke and the air is licorice sweet with the Sambuca some of the men are sipping, but most of them sip Dago Red and this Social Club it's for men, these are good men who had pretty good lives back in *Italia* where they went to school and had professions. They aren't like my Papa, who never had no school and can't even read in Italian so forget about English. Sometimes they let Papa drink and play cards with them, but I'm turning beet-red with shame — it's what the priest, Father Raymond, calls original sin.

Again I'm realizing these men they don't want nothing to do with Papa because he's useless and just thinking these words makes me sad beyond belief and so I sulk out of there and I don't even say *ciao* and it's not like the old men care. They ignore me because they know I'm not the only neighborhood kid trying to find his old Papa and bring him home. A lot of my friends lost their Papas and their brothers in the war. It's a hard time. Nobody wants to talk about it.

Out of the alley and on to the avenue I make my way along and hear all kinds of shouts, noises, car horns and screeching brakes. They all seem far away, part of another city, the one I'm not old enough to live in and understand yet. I see one of the neighborhood women out front of her house and she's in her robe, curlers and slippers and talking to another of the neighborhood ladies who, listening to her, keeps a cigarette in her mouth, nodding up and down. I don't' know what they're yapping about, but I'm guessing it's their husbands and how they wished they'd get home soon from the war and how, at last, they'll all feel glad the war is over. Everybody will feel peachy keen about that. I know I will. My brother, Rico, he didn't make it. He was fighting out there in the Pacific. You should have seen Mama crying when my sisters said Rico was lost at sea. Mama don't read English, so the military man he just left the letter with my sisters and they read it to her.

They say my brother Rico is the biggest of heroes. I'm too young, being the twelfth of fourteen, to really know my big brother Rico, but he'll always be a hero to me and one day I'm gonna be a soldier and maybe I won't be a hero, but I'm not gonna die. I'm gonna show Rico and all my brothers I learned from them. What that is I don't know yet, but I'll find out.

I hear somebody laughing at me. I just ignore it. Maybe cuz my pants are torn. I gotta get Mama to sew 'em up again. I fell yesterday and they got caught on something. I didn't tell Mama. She gets mad when I do this because I ain't big enough yet to fit into my brother's pants.

I watch cars for a while as they move along in a heavy stream. I'm on the quiet side of the street where all the apartment houses are and so I'm out of harm from cars that are out this time of day. People are coming home from jobs mostly, but it's the trolley that really confuses the cars in this neighborhood. We're just far enough out from the last stop on the city line, and there's the buses of course, but out here they all kind of swarm together at the different circles and it can be dangerous at this hour, even I know this, so I'm careful.

I'm coming on to a restaurant with a green canopy that most of the time is flapping in the wind, but not this time and I won't go in there because I know it's too expensive for the likes of Papa to be drinking in. Just as I'm walking past the front door, out comes a man with a toothpick in his mouth and he looks up and down the street, his silver hair trimmed neatly. He's wearing a black double-breasted with pin-stripes that looks real quality. I like his brown leather shoes. I turn red again as I envy this fat guy. I even follow him a while, since he's walking alone and this is my neighborhood, not just his, and I know if I don't bother him he won't bother me.

I follow him just long enough before he's on to me and my timing is perfect because I'm on the corner and I pop into Valenti's Corner where sometimes Mama picks up bananas and I know Valenti will be there and he's the kind of man that's always smiling and he knows me and says hello to me and Mama every time we stop in. Valenti knows everybody in the neighborhood so I ask him if he's seen my old Papa and he says he has, that he came in earlier today for cigarettes and, yeah, he didn't look sober and he said something about heading up the street toward Strega Bar so I best head there, but I should look after myself, be careful while I keep trying to chase him down.

Valenti asks about Mama and I don't tell him the truth, I never speak truth about Mama, I just say that she's fine and I thank Valenti for asking because that's what good boys do and in the end, even though people don't always like me, I'm a good boy. Valenti's impressed by my manners and tosses me a free Bazooka Joe bubble-gum, which I promptly unwrap and pop into my mouth and start chewing on hard as I walk toward Strega Bar and unroll the little comic that smells of sugar dust and read about Bazooka Joe fighting in the war.

On my way, I pass one bakery that's closed, and so is the bank next to it and the little store that always has dolls on display in the window. My sisters all love this store and dream about owning dolls one day. I make the sign of the cross, blessing myself, snapping my bubblegum between my teeth as I pass a ceramic statue of the Virgin Mary on a little piece of grass behind a fence in front of a porch and then I pass a few more little lawns with fences and some patios and then Pompeii Pizzeria, and another bakery, but this one is open and I get real hungry with the smell of hot bread and *amoretti* and *cannoli* and I'm shaking with hunger as I chew my bubblegum so much that my jaw hurts and I know Mama won't yell at me but my sisters will because chewing gum rots your teeth and my sisters they never had chewing gum, they chewed balls of tar off the street, so I shouldn't talk, but I think they're just jealous. It's not like I bought it for a penny. Valenti gave it to me and when that happens, you know that you're doing good in your own neighborhood.

When I get to Strega Bar, I get a bad feeling, but I push open the door just the same and right away I smell beer and cigarettes and darkness and I can hardly breathe and start tugging on the pants of the men at the bar asking if they've seen my old Papa, but they aren't having any of it, calling me names like greasy kid, telling me to buzz off and using the kind of language that Father Raymond says gets you a one-way ticket to hell. They ain't debating if they like my kind. They're sure they don't and that makes me think that Papa wasn't here, and if he was he didn't stay long. I don't like this place and all the smudged faces of the men at the bar, and they don't like me either and when the bartender sees me he raises his fist so I get outta there.

Back on the street with my wagon I don't know what to do. It's dark now and I'm pooped and hungry.

When I get home and climb the last flight up to my place, my mouth is dry and I beg Mama for some seltzer but we don't got any. She lets me have some still water out of the ice box. I find Mama where I always do at this time of evening. With my sisters in the kitchen over the gas stove making spaghetti and sauce, but no meatballs. I'm so hungry, I tell her, I want some and she says not until I bring Papa home.

"But I tried," I tell her. "I looked everywhere, I can't find him."

My oldest sister, Connie, she translates my words into snappy Italian. Connie lives on the second floor with her new husband Angelo who's just back from the war. Connie's got a baby inside of her and she's growing quite round and so she usually doesn't help Mama on the third floor, but she's helping tonight because one of the bars phoned and told Mama where Papa is located. Connie tells me all this in English. Papa's at the Anchor Bar. It's in a different part of the neighborhood that I'm used to. I'll have to be extra care-ful after dark, but if I keep quiet no one will bother me. My wagon wheels are oiled so they won't squeak and call attention to me. I just have to look in both directions crossing the streets.

No doubt they'll be waiting for me there and Connie tells me Papa's been sleeping in a room above Anchor Bar and he's been drunk for a week. I have to bring him home. I've left my red wagon on the first floor, in the back by the laundry racks and the wringer.

I tell Connie I'm ready and that I don't like doing this. Papa's heavy to carry.

"But you gotta do it," says Connie. "You're the only one around."

This is true. My brothers are at jobs. My sisters are at jobs. Mama and Connie need each other and they're busy at home all day, too. Nobody works harder than Mama. This is my task. Each of us has at least one. It's how families work.

I can't help it, but even though I know all this I start to cry in front of Mama. I'm so hungry that I can taste metal in my stomach that burble up to my mouth and I start to gag as I choke on tears and out pops the bubblegum. When Mama sees it she launches into shouts and calls me bad names in Italian until Connie steps in and says, "Togo, now, go get your father and then you can eat all the macaroni you want when you come back."

—◆—

The hardest part is pulling the wagon over ruts and train tracks and Papa lies squeezed into it like he's a mashed doughnut. He's so drunk he doesn't know who I am. When I get to our apartment house, my sister Fanny's home and so isn't my brother who insists everyone call Henry now, even though his real name is Luigi. Henry's a really big guy and he fought in the Battle of the Bulge and was shot in the ribs, but he's better now. He helps me carry Papa up the stairs to the third floor. What a load! I know this is a lot for Henry because after he got shot he lost some parts of his insides and he's put back together again, and still he's strong man, but he knows he ain't the same and so we work together, brother and brother, and he pats me on the head and says, "Togo, don't be mad at Ma for this and don't be mad at Papa either. Just do your part and keep doing it. It's what good soldiers do."

I really like it when Henry talks to me this way. It makes it easier for me to tell him I'm mad, that I feel ashamed, that this isn't right. Henry doesn't like hearing this. He frowns at me. He raises his hand to strike me, but then he stops. He looks at me. He sighs.

I run off. I know Papa is in his bed. I know I've done my task. I don't need no beating for it.

—◆—

At the table, when all my tired noisy sisters are home and out of their work clothes and smelling like soap, complaining about their jobs and aching backs, they all tell me I'm a good boy. My old Papa is locked in his room, door closed, and he'll stay there alone for many days and the room will stink of his pee, but Mama will clean the sheets with ammonia and lye and she'll go to work and come home and cook more spaghetti and she'll cry when she's alone. I know this because I spy on her and I see her crying and I think that I understand how she feels. On these nights when I bring Papa home, I have to cry, too. I can't say why, but I feel it like a big hole inside even after my belly is full after eating so much spaghetti.

I don't tell anyone about my crying. I go off alone up to the roof of our building, where I have my corner and it's safe and I won't fall off. I look out over the neighborhood and the sky and I can smell the bay and hear the seagulls and the foghorns and the trolleys and cars and the shouts of so many tiny people below. I tell myself I do this task because I love my family and not everyone is good, not even my old Papa, and that's why the good are needed.

The Millbury Street Legend

Look, Thomas, you're my nephew and believe it or not what your mother has told you about your Uncle Karchi is true. She hasn't told you a thing? She said I'd fill you in if you asked? Okay. Why don't you sit? This may take a while.

The thing with Uncle Karchi is that he said he wanted to make good, but he didn't. Not really. Actions speak loudest. I never believed a word he said. Your Mom, being the youngest with three brothers, didn't know him the way I did.

No. Sorry. Let me start again. He was my brother. I was supposed to love him unconditionally. Damn it, I did. When he let me.

You really want to hear your Uncle Karchi's story? Really? We can go back into the reception hall and I'll buy you a drink. Your sister is a beautiful bride. Okay, okay, we'll stay here.

So first thing is don't be hard on your uncle. Forgiveness is an underrated virtue. Things have changed. Here in Worcester alone, half the Catholic churches I grew up with are closed. You should have heard your grandmother complain about the new storefront churches popping up in pod malls. As you know, she was a devout Catholic, bless her soul, but after that scandal back in the 90s and the way it finally broke, she never again had the same — how can I say it? — *naïve* devotion.

But you want me to talk about Uncle Karchi and me growing up together on Union Hill, on Dorchester Street, not far from Vale Street and Worcester Academy. Nowadays, that neighborhood's a mess, but even back then it was touch-and-go and always changing. Immigrants and newcomers gotta start somewhere, I suppose.

Your Uncle Karchi wasn't wicked bad, but he never went to mass or to school, for starters. He was raised like the rest of us by your grandfather, Theodore. Your other uncle, my oldest brother Dean, as you know, was killed in Vietnam. Theodore seldom talked about Dean. Neither did my Ma. She kept one framed picture of him above the TV in the living room. There was Dean, the Pope, and JFK. Growing up, me and your Mom knew Dean was a hero. To this day, nobody knows what happened to his body. He was what they called M-I-A. Missing in action. If that don't break a family's heart, I don't know what does.

So anyways, when Uncle Karchi dropped out of Voke High, he needed money. He moved in with some guys and started selling weed full-time. I graduated from Voke. For a while, I got him a job with me stocking shelves at Zayres in Webster Square. We lifted weights at the Y, and drank cheap beers in Monahan's, Lord Vasil's 333, The Blarney Stone, and Mulcahey's pub. Most of them dives are long gone and nobody misses 'em. We had fake IDs but nobody carded us. Remember, this was the late 70s and the drinking age was still eighteen.

Karchi and I we'd torch a joint with friends in the parking lot of Ralph's Diner and then go inside to hear live bands. We'd get hot dogs at Coney Island. Sometimes, we'd take our meals at Herbie's, which is still there. Great soup, by the way. In Leitrim's pub we'd pick up freshman girls from Assumption College. For a while, we went out every night and tossed darts, shot pool, or got into fights — from Grafton Hill to Chandler to South Main, the city was ours.

But we always ended our nights in the Hotel Vernon.

See, we played flag football for The Ship. That team, those were my boys. Hotel Vernon was our sponsor. What a team, too. There was Doug Normandin at quarterback. He drove a truck for American Linens. Jamie Duran, our half-back, worked a Teamster gig with UPS. Armen Gregorian played middle linebacker and sold cars at Harr Ford on Goldstar Boulevard. I looked up to these guys.

Not Karchi. He sold dime bags of third-rate weed to most of 'em.

The Ship: second family. Hotel Vernon: second home. You roll on through Worcester on the 290 Expressway and at the Kelly Square exit on one side you'll see it on the corner plain as day. Way back when Babe Ruth pitched for the Boston *Braves*, he lived on nearby Vernon Hill and he'd walk to the Hotel to buy a plate of raw hamburg. He'd eat it with his fingers while standing at the bar.

Babe once said this. He said, "Never let the fear of striking out keep you from playing the game."

You gotta love that. It's fearless and it's how Karchi rolled.

So you haven't been inside the Hotel? Of course not. My sister would never allow it and that ain't necessarily a bad thing. Quick description: first-floor lounge lined with reddish slats of wood that curve like the interior walls of a schooner. Behind the bar there's a model ship that's a centerpiece for the shelves that hold liquor bottles. This ship is a three-masted clipper too large to fit in a bottle, and it's lit from below so it looks haunted. It's handmade. Full sails and riggings detailed down to each knot. Thing is, no one knows who built it or how it got there.

Was it a good place to stay? Hell, no. Basically, it was a flea-bag dump and an eyesore, but it still anchors that one corner where Kelly Square melts into Millbury Street. A lotta history there.

See, Millbury Street was once a canal linked Venice-style to the Blackstone River, back when Tommie Heinsohn and Bob Cousy played hoops at Holy Cross before making their names with the Celtics. All my life that's been an immigrant neighborhood crowded with dives.

What do you mean, Wormtown? You don't think Worcester's loaded with history? I refuse to call my home city by that name.

Wormtown. It's disrespectful. I look like a worm to you?

One thing, though, I always wondered about was why we called the traffic circles squares. Lincoln, and Newton Square, for example — those are traffic *rotaries* on the city's dashboard. What the Brits call roundabouts. Is it any surprise the Boston snobs think we're chowderheads.

Back to the Hotel. On the outside, it's still sheathed in yellow brick. Red brick everywhere else. There's a *Miller* neon above its door that faces one-way Millbury. It's a quick walk from Vernon Hill and Monahan's package store, the Emerald Isle Diner, and the Golemo *Polska* Sausage mural you can see from 290. No windows on the first floor, just a pair of rectangular slits. Sandstone sills frame the higher windows where troubled residents have more than once nose-dived into oblivion.

Troubled, yeah, we're all troubled, ain't we?

Growing up, your uncle and me, see, we'd tool down Union Hill, cross a bridge over 290 and with Kelly Square spread out before us we'd watch cars speed-dodge each other like they were in a game of chicken. Horns blaring, drivers shouting, it was a confusing juncture of six streets, some one-way, some without stop signs, all of them forming a cockeyed hub accessible from lucky Exit 13.

Chaos. Your grandfather Theodore liked to say that the Boston-Hibernian politicos inflicted it on the city. Since in his prime he was a bruiser and a card-carrying member of the steamfitter's union, he could get away with those wisecracks. Me, I never joined no union. Don't mean what it used to, especially now.

On the other side of Kelly Square, narrow Water Street wobbled through mostly Jewish-owned businesses. Widoff's Bakery, for one. Charlie's Surplus used to be there. Charlie Boulanger kept a mountain of damaged *Chuck Taylors* on the floor under a low-swinging bulb. Yeah, those old-school high-top basketball sneakers, that's right. They were all we wore back then. Weren't no Jordan *Nikes* to tempt us. Karch and me we'd rummage through 'em looking to make matching pairs. Charlie B gave Ma a family rate: five pairs for ten bucks.

Weintraub's Deli is still there. It's a classic and you should go because one day they'll just tear it down like they've done to so much of the city. Every year on your grandfather's birthday, we'd take him there and treat him to his favorite: liverwurst on rye with a bottle of their homemade cream soda. Karchi, me and some friends we'd hang around that neighborhood in the warehouses that stored truck frames, suspension coils and gigantic rolls of upholstery fabric. The original Saint John's High was there. You had ironmonger shops, gear works, cold storage buildings — the air always smelling of creosote from the nearby rail yards. There was Sir Morgan's Cove as a place to go hear live music. A tough place. The Stones played there one time. Never announced it. Just showed up. Wished I'd been there. You could say Gilrein's picked up where Sir Morgan's left off. I mean, Worcester's the kind of city that needs a dive where you can hear live blues, but I don't think Gilrein's is even what it used to be. Then again, what is?

All these places are gone. You think that's sad? Maybe so. But it's life.

So Karch and me we'd share a grinder fifty-fifty bought on credit from Kelly Square Pizza And Grinders. We'd meet everybody there. Nicky Renard clerked at Old Colony Paint and Wallpaper. Eunice Renny was a tailor at Maurice the Pants Man. She played Bingo with Ma at Holy Name on Friday nights. Fat Luciano was always munching down a slice with pepperoni. He drove delivery for Table Talk. Luciano was a trip. He'd stop on our street early Sunday mornings and leave cartons of week-old pies for Mrs. Lopez and some of the other ladies on the street with a lot of kids. We all knew it was illegal and Luciano was risking his job, but nobody ever said a word about it. For me, Union Hill was more than a neighborhood then. It was mixed, too, not all one race or ethnic group. All the neighbors were like family. We kids were all born at Memorial Hospital and were told to speak English, though most of our parents didn't. We went to Union Hill Elementary. We knew everybody's business. We looked after each other. Nowadays, I can't say the same. Some three-deckers are boarded up, others have been made into condos. Some streets and yards are clean. Others, there's trash everywhere and who knows what the hell language they're speaking. Last I heard the city's largest new immigrant population is from Bhutan. What they speak there? I got no clue.

At Goldstein Scrap, Uncle Karch and I knew Zeph, a retired plumber who fought in World War II. He'd tell us the coolest hero stories. We knew guys at Foley Aluminum and anyone who shopped at Chevalier Furniture knew your grandmother cuz she worked there so long. Grandpa Theodore worked close-by at Wyman Gordon along with the Dads and uncles of a lotta Voke classmates. He didn't want me at Wyman. "Get a real skill," he'd say. "That place won't last."

Turned out he was right. Thirty years he worked there. Dropped dead a year into his retirement. What they do? They made airplane parts and sold most of them to Israel. Even today, that's big business. It just don't happen around here, that's all. Broke my heart when they leveled that factory. It's an empty lot now.

Me? I got a skill. Baking. Yeah, some guys called me a sissy. I didn't care. I started at Automatic Rolls on Southbridge Street in Auburn from six a.m. to three. Mostly, I cleaned and changed baking racks. McDonald's was our biggest client — 50 million buns served meant job security. I wore my hairnet and apron with pride. I even got Uncle Karchi hired there, but all he did was complain.

After work, I'd take Karch to D'Amico's on Shrewsbury Street, which in those days was an Italian neighborhood. We'd fill up on a meatball the size of Jupiter. We'd drive off to meet his dope connections in Green Hill Park, where we'd drink beers and smoke some grass, but when it came to hard stuff I drew the line.

So this, my good nephew, is the message in my story. Don't do drugs. Keep away from 'em, especially the hard stuff.

Your Uncle Karchi always had drugs on him. Not me. I kept saying no while he kept zipping down a freeway toward hell. He'd make fun of me, saying, "I make more selling crack in one day than you do in a month of washing flour out of your pubes."

You think that's funny? Maybe it is now, but not then. I hated him for saying that.

Still, no matter how drunk or sly, your Uncle Karchi was hard to resist. At six-four, a beanpole, he always had scraggly hair in his eyes. Muscle-wise, I could cream him, but I respected his speed. He had excellent hands, too, but serious guys didn't like him, especially Augie Cooper and Jose Molina. They'd both been high school football stars. Augie at Burncoat. Jose at South. They stomached Karchi because The Ship was usually short of guys.

It came as no surprise when Karchi quit Automatic Rolls. Why? Because he started selling weapons with Lizard — real name Gary Monitor — a cretin from May Street who'd done time. Lizard would shadow Karchi, promising him salad days were around the corner. Whenever Lizard approached, Augie Cooper made a show of walking away. I wish to this day Karchi had done the same.

No, I take that back. I wish I had stepped in. That's what I'd confess in front of a priest. Not my actions. My *inaction*.

Let me share an average night in the Hotel. Picture the air like it's strata of marine layers of cigarette smoke trapped under a low ceiling of stamped tin squares peppered with holes. More than once while shooting pool, I'd see a mouse drop from one of them holes and scamper across the slate.

Not the night I'm thinking about, though, no, I was feeling no pain that night— we all were pain-free — cuz our team, The Ship, won against Sweet Life Foods due to practicing one night a week at Gaskell Park. We played our games on Sunday mornings and Tuesday nights, either at Crompton Park or a grass panel near the fire station at Chadwick Square. Our schedule was set, but locations changed at the last minute and someone would phone to update us. Sometimes I drove a half-hour out to Leicester to pick up teammates, especially on Sundays because guys knew if they got hammered after the game they'd risk a DUI.

Claude Boudreaux, our sponsor and coach, covered a player's cab fare. No crashes were gonna be linked to rides home from his dive. Fed us, too. Each game-day, win or lose, a sheet of plywood went over the pool table for a post-game feast. From Widoff's, he bought every bulkie they had. From Weintraub's, piles of cold cuts, deli salads and half-sours. He filled big bowls of chips. Sometimes, he cooked a pot of chili.

I'd get to work the next morning, but I was usually late and reeking of beer.

So this one night, your Uncle Karchi approached me. His eyes bloodshot, making the rounds, he was apologizing to everyone. He and Lizard had shown up late to our game, wasted, in a Buick *LeSabre*. Without them, we would have needed to forfeit due to a lack of players. During half-time, they'd brought members of the opposing team over to the Buick, where Lizard opened its trunk to show off some guns. Neither one knew that a guy on that other team was a part-time cop in the town of West Boylston. Yep, out in the burbs where you live now.

Augie Cooper knew. He huddled us up on the field while Lizard and Karchi strutted around the Buick. He told us about the cop, and with that we agreed to lose. This pleased the cop, but the loss made us one win shy of making the playoffs.

Sure, guys were ticked off. Me, I ignored Uncle Karchi's apologies. He offered to buy me rounds. Big deal. I kept refusing. He insisted I join him at The Lamplighter to meet strippers. As if that would make everything better. I said no. It was just an excuse for him to keep dealing drugs. Those girls there were his best coke clients. At that point, losing my temper, I told him to fuck off and get his shit together.

Sorry, I know that's strong language, but those were my *exact* words. You know, brothers can be really mean to each other and I can't lie to you or to God, can I? It was the only time I point-blank hit my brother with truth. If he wanted a fight, I was ready. I'd kick his butt and he knew it. I also knew, deep down, I was sending the right message.

I felt satisfied I'd taken enough action, but nothing changed. Karchi started dressing flashier and throwing money around. I caught him smoking crack in my car. He'd snort lines in the toilets of every dive we drank in. A full-time pharmacy and gun shop, he looked seedy, twitching all the time.

I started to get worried, but I did nothing to help him. Your mother was too young to know what was really going on. Ma tended to shield her, and even Ma had no clue, not really. But I did. I just kept my mouth shut. Again, inaction. I had no plans for my future, just a greater awareness of possibilities brought on by a raise

I'd earned at Automatic Rolls. I started saving. Not for season tickets to Bruins games, but a better life, a way out. I told Ma and all she said was, "Sooner you get out the better. One less mouth to feed."

I bought a nicer car. Nothing great, but it was reliable. When I told Karchi about my raise, he blew me off. "Donkey work," he said. "You're looking at a tycoon."

I asked Jose Molina to talk sense into him. Jose tried. Karchi blew him off. I talked to Augie Cooper about my future and how I believed things were going to improve. Augie confirmed what I'd been thinking — my brother Karchi was living in fantasyland.

I couldn't live there. I had to be ready to adapt because change comes whether you want it or not.

One night, I told Theodore about my issues with Karchi. "Dad, he never listens. All he wants to do is get high."

My old man whacked me in the head. "You really so stupid? That road goes one way."

"Then why don't you tell Karchi? Don't tell me. I already know that."

It was a time when I needed my old man and he was there, but he wasn't there for Karchi. For some reason, it was different with him. Maybe because he was the middle son. Or maybe because of Dean getting killed. To this day, I don't know.

I felt sorry for your Uncle Karchi. I believed he'd turn the corner, but Sunday night's party at Hotel Vernon became an extension of Saturday night's, with flag football in between to keep his blood pumping. Sunday morning games were the worst. They started at nine and we were hung-over for all of 'em. After one night with Karchi and this redheaded stripper who drank me under the table, I was hit so hard from my blind side that I landed ten feet out of bounds, my head slamming against the side of a Johnny-On-The-Spot. The collision knocked me out. Coach Claude snapped me awake with ammonia pellets.

As a way to tame headaches before Sunday morning games, Karchi convinced me to smoke bong hits with him. He always had coke and coke whores, or he was tripping on acid, but he chose me first — never anyone else — to join him. Was I flattered? Yeah, to some extent. You ask why? Because this meant sex as long as I used a condom and agreed to toot with him down Millbury Street, where the legend still held — no man alive had made it from end to end while stopping for one drink in each of its bars.

It was never one drink and I never said no. I became an enabler. That's what they'd call it now. We'd start at the Hotel and stagger south against traffic, hitting a bar every fifty yards. I can list a few: Stoney O'Brien's, 3G's, Green Pub, Emerald Island, Green Island Diner, The Pit, and The Harding, which was Karchi's favorite. Down at the end past Riley's Engineering, there was Madigan's Again, and then the Irish House. Some were on a corner; some had bands and a cover to get in. The beer was cheap, the regulars as tough and loyal as they were friendly.

Karchi-the-drugstore was a magnet. I was his muscle, and I admit to liking how his customers bought us rounds. He'd snort coke. I'd down shots. Because of him, I became popular, and popularity became my drug of choice.

Blitzed at four a.m. we'd sit with two pole dancers in a booth at the Acapulco on Highland Ave, bleary-eyed over nachos and *huevos rancheros*. Having sold his crack and coke, his pockets would be stuffed with cash. I'd down coffee, sober up and drive us out of the city to the Redwood Motel in Charlton. He'd pay for two rooms, we'd each get laid and I'd drive the dancers back to The Lamplighter. Next, we'd change into our jerseys with *The Ship* in fuzzy felt letters. I kept all football stuff in my trunk. The letters had started to peel after machine washings, but the uniform didn't matter. Nor did the game. Nor anything else. I got more and more careless and at

Automatic Rolls I showed up late one time too many with a hangover and they fired me.

Theodore gave me two weeks. "You pissant, find something new or move your ass out."

The Ship lost our season's final game to Morgan Industries and it was party on at the Hotel. Nobody heard the thugs enter. They slipped in wearing jeans and sweatshirts like the rest of us. The music was loud, cigarette smoke fogged the air, and the crowd was a wall in front of the bar. The old-time regulars that lived upstairs had long ago turned in.

Those thugs knew Lizard and before anyone could stop them, they were dragging him out to Millbury Street and Lizard was shouting "You got it wrong. It ain't me."

I started toward the door. Augie Cooper stopped me. "Don't be stupid," he said.

Someone shouted behind me, "Hey, Lizard!"

It was Karchi squirming through the crowd and out to the street.

I followed him. Augie horse-collared me from behind.

Jose Molina grabbed Karchi and shouted, "*Pendejo*, they will kill you."

Karchi didn't stop. Neither did I. Karchi was my brother. He was standing by Lizard and I was gonna stand by him. Karchi fought with Jose until Jose released his hold. Augie let me go, too. I got to the sidewalk in time to see Lizard on the ground in an alley across from the bar. Thugs were kicking him in the ribs. He was spitting up blood.

Karchi bolted across Millbury, yelling slurred nonsense. He made it easy for those thugs. They left Lizard moaning, seized Karchi and slammed him against a brick wall. Karchi crumbled. One thug propped him up, pinning his arms behind his back. The other thug drove steady punches into his stomach until Karchi was slumped over and gasping. A black car drove up. Doors opened.

Tires squealed. The car was gone and so were Karchi and Lizard.

Drunk, dazed, I'd watched with the others from across the street under the *Miller* neon's red glow, Led Zeppelin blasting "Whole Lotta Love" through the Hotel's open door. Looking back, it's one thing to say it happened so fast, but nobody called the cops or lifted a finger to help.

I moped back inside and found Augie Cooper and shouted at him that it was wrong, that Karchi was family, that I should have done something.

Augie's pained look proved he got my gist. He shouted back, "But it don't work that way. Not for me. I got kids to look after and a wife."

"They wanna play, they gotta pay," shouted Jose. "Even if he is your brother."

I'd heard enough. I ran to my car and drove the city, looking for that car, for my brother, all the while listening to the radio and thinking about fearless Babe Ruth eating his raw pound of hamburg. I had to do something, but all I did was drive around until I was so tired I could barely get myself home.

Next day, I got the news while nursing a coffee in the Kenmore Diner and reading Help Wanted ads in the *Telegram*. It was Theodore, of all people. He'd left work early to tell me cops had phoned him. They had ID's for two bodies found in a trash dumpster near the Great Brook Valley housing project. Their mouths were stuffed with baggies that had once held drugs. They'd been shot somewhere else, dragged there and left to rot.

All Theodore said was, "Get in bed with dogs, what you gonna catch?"

Both my father and I had failed Karchi. A good brother, a good father *makes* you listen. I couldn't blame Theodore. Truth was, he'd tried with Karchi, but they'd fought all the time and eventually Theodore just gave up. Can't say I blame him. The man worked hard. He lost one son to a stupid war. Eventually, he just got tired.

I felt so guilty, as if it had been my fault. I took long walks to Gaskell Park at the top of Vernon Hill. Three-deckers lined the streets like canyon walls. I walked past the blue panels and white marble of Saint Vincent's Hospital. Night after night this was my journey alone. A turning point in my life. I never felt safe during those walks and I never found answers.

The funeral was held at what some guys used to call The Polack Church, you know, Our Lady of Czestochowa on Ward Street. Theodore and Ma went there every Sunday because Father Krzysztof said the 7 and 11:30 a.m. in Polish. Not this time. Father Krzysztof said Karchi's funeral in English and kept the sermon super-short. Wasn't like my brother had been a model citizen.

Of course I've relived that night and those times over and over and I still feel heavy regret. It's still hard for me to breathe when I think about what I could have done, could have said — anything to change the path he was on.

No, your mother isn't avoiding the issue. She knew little about this stuff and Karchi's death came as a shock. Me, I keep telling myself I could've grabbed Karchi and shook him out of his stupidity. Shook him hard. Made him listen.

I'm sick with guilt. My doing wrong was that I did *nothing*. I let my brother's death happen. I knew better, but I didn't act like I loved Karchi. Mostly, I loved his worst qualities and I think a part of me was afraid I'd be rejected if I challenged them.

Yeah, you're right, it's a form of purgatory, I hear you on that. Sure, I've said a few thousand Hail Marys. You can say a couple more for me, for all the good they'll do.

Karchi in a better place? Maybe. But I sure ain't.

C'mon, Thomas, let's get back to the reception. They'll be cutting the cake soon.

Water Towers

SLENDER, WITH LONG FINE hands and arms, Garland Desjardin looked younger than his age, 33, and had once told Moxine Mason Shelby he didn't feel "powerful enough to be a ghost" and that when she married him, she'd learn that even with his music he was an "invisible type, prone to being stepped on."

Garland paused and listened. Moxine again. She was telling him it wasn't his time to join her on the other side; there were other forms of love he should consider, maybe truer more dangerous forms. Some were meant to live longer. Some just briefly. And some, if not all, must suffer as they live.

But what does all this suffering amount to?

Receiving no answer, Garland waited to hear Moxine again out of a darkness that peeled away to reveal dawn and then late morning light while he went through his motions, getting himself to work. He'd made it to the restaurant and he was standing there as if transported while remembering one of his nocturnal Moxine conversations. Was it really the best choice just to continue on with his life as if nothing traumatic had happened? Though he, no one else, had chosen this path, he couldn't say with certainty that he'd chosen correctly.

He backed away from the restaurant's commotion toward the window where he'd thought he'd seen Moxine earlier. He had. There she floated again behind the drapes and lacy panels reminding him to stay true to the musical talents he'd developed.

"Don't worry, Mox, getting by, haven't forgotten you. Can't. Wouldn't know how."

He was talking to himself again. No, to Moxine. Why was it taking the woman at Table Four so long to order? It was a one-page menu, not the Old Testament in Hebrew.

A draft sliced in through a gap between window curtains. He mumbled, "Moxine, I'm here for you. I won't leave."

But I want you to leave me. To start fresh on your own. Some dreams simply aren't realized.

Garland felt a chill from the window, but he stayed close to it. He liked it best because he knew that Moxine did, too, though neither of them had said why. In their shared knowledge of each other, without explanations, there existed a mystifying charm and unity.

There were four windows along one wall in the restaurant's main dining room that reminded him of stained-glass windows, back before he left the Catholic Church when he attended masses with his mother and prayed for the father he'd lost as a boy, a man he remembered vaguely for his rough cheek and unfiltered cigarettes and blue after-shave in a bottle. This was their window. Like an altar. Like the eye atop each pyramid on a dollar bill. It was from here that he could see out and keep his back to the lousy workaday routine.

He could hear Moxine whispering that everything would be okay. As if that life had never happened, fragments of it returning while Garland saw his face reflected in the window pane as *that other me.* Before Moxine's death. Back when he'd linger at the piano and toy with some Chopin through slow afternoons, Moxine in a flowing flower-print cotton skirt drinking sweet tea on a bench under a camellia that shaded the fieldstone courtyard in back of his mother's narrow three-story brick house. She liked to hum little ditties close to his ear, pausing now and then in her soft voice to assure him he that this latest thunderstorm of emotions and insecurities like all the others would pass, so he should keep practicing and master the piano.

Her Gar she called him. *Sleep, sleep, let another dream come.*

What was up with the woman at Table Four? Not today of all days; he had no patience. She was throwing him dirty looks. On her phone, too. Pushing little buttons. Everyone was, all their answers and their happiness residing elsewhere.

What he wanted was to make a scene, lie there on the restaurant's carpet and wait for the day to pass. Of course, he couldn't. If he wasn't careful, another waiter would nab Table Four. It had happened in the past and he'd been warned if it happened too often, he'd be fired. No shortage of waiters in this city and he needed this job, saw it as continuing on, coping, needing at least one show of stability and consistency in his life after Moxine. It was a small price to pay in order to call himself a musician and to live in such a place. The job offered benefits and consolations, as well. He seldom bought food, finding it easy to live on one free meal a day. It kept him out of his apartment, where if not careful he'd disintegrate into self-pity.

Calling him. The woman at Table Four. Signaling him as if he were a small plane approaching a runway. Not by name, of course. She used the word "Waiter" but she could have easily called him Robot. No smell of courtesy in this urbane air, but he was getting used to it. She wasn't the kind who liked to wait. None of them were.

An adult, acting as such, his grief a private matter, Garland nodded as if he understood, as if about to hurry to her side. He didn't. He ignored her and stayed at his special window with Moxine. Along the street below in this charming old part of the city, a breeze stirred trimmed lindens along both sidewalks. He looked in both directions. Moxine had adored this neighborhood. This was to be her city as an adult, too, with a new zip code that would prove status and self-actualization.

How she'd stood with him in his mother's living room, saying one day they'd live in Manhattan together and her Gar would perform Rachmaninoff as well as jazz, vamping it up like he was mother's favorite, Van Cliburn, and with all the finesse of one of his heroes, Claudio Arrau. He could become more than a piano player. He had his degree and talent, but if he put in the practice, he'd become another Glenn Gould perhaps. Such divine achievement was possible. All his recitals, his teachers, had said so.

Moxine would work for a management team in digital advertising and sales. Perhaps pursue an advanced diploma. Do all these things before having children. They'd have three, name them Ludwig, Wolfgang and Frederic. A joke, of course, their private one.

Do you remember that joke?

I do, he thought. He smiled. Had those moments really happened or were they sugar-coated renditions from a past he wanted too much to believe in? This was his reality now, this window, this uncertainty, Moxine's voice, and he alone burdened by the lancing shadow of a tree branch that speared through the window to bisect the room into varying degrees of murkiness. Separation between the physical and ephemeral, gently fused into a force that told him he was still his mother's boy, must keep quiet and do his job, try not to get lost in foggy ruminations.

At Table Four, the woman, standing now, raised open arms to another middle-aged Botox queen and then a third, all with their hair dyed blond, their cheeks shiny and their lips plump — like a trio of guppies freed from different aquariums. They were ugly enough to be stars of their own reality TV show. That's what one had to be these days in order to survive: inconsiderate, on the attack. Garland watched the trio hug in that careful and practiced New York City way, sizing each other up as they exchanged subtle jibes amid pleasantries. Women, indeed, could be mean swimmers.

They were drinkers, no doubt, and they'd lived more than a few episodes of *Sex and the City*, or any TV series about the despair of professional women spun perhaps from a hit movie or novel. What was that Prada one with Meryl Streep? Moxine had liked it. All part of the kiddie drool on television that now counted for literature and Moxine had sometimes followed certain programs in marathon doses as a pleasurable guilt-soaked sojourn from reality.

None of that for him: too banal, mind-numbing and cultish. Better to discover somnambulant moments, so splendid in this room. The smell of coffee on a hot plate in the corner, one far brick wall lacquered so thickly that it shined when the sun reached it. Varnished grains in the coffered panels that covered the lower half of the other walls and spoke of parlor drawing rooms from an era when all was built by hand to last.

Little was new here in this room, which was why he liked it. Time distinguished any surface in the way it defined and distinguished music. He not only believed this; he'd devoted his life to studying it.

The women were beckoning him. They demanded he hobble on over like he was a lanky Charlie Chaplin, with alacrity, hungering for their approval and to lean over their powdered shoulders dazzled by the mingling scents of their unguents while reciting, as if deliriously turned on, the soup of the day, the three specials and the two desserts he was paid to memorize. He was to flirt with them, to feel satisfied sucking up to their whimsical shows of entitlement, bringing them sweet fruit-colored libations laced with near toxic quantities of white alcohol and the momentary promise of blissful escape they craved.

He heard Moxine again at the window. He'd been afraid of these sightings, at first, but he'd gotten used to them and now took time to really grasp what she was telling him. This time, her message was that everything had to change.

Garland nodded toward one of the women at Table Four. His facial expression was designed to express that he was on his way and that their happiness was what he lived for. When he moved toward them, his gait was methodical, with a sullenly composed aura, but he paused in the center of the large room, making sure he had their attention. He could see them around their table, watching, appraising him, their chins and their hungers rising. They leaned forward to say come, come, we own your body and soul, you must pamper us.

Sorry, ladies. In the middle of that room, certain all at Table Four could see him, Garland placed his round tray on the carpeted floor and then began to lie down. It was a sea-blue carpet, vacuumed thoroughly each night by professional cleaners. He liked its stony blue that reminded him of a crab shell before being cooked. A cold inviting cerulean tint with a comforting chilliness, his bed for the time being.

Once supine, he rested his hands across his sternum and he sighed while looking up at the ceiling. He listened to the ebbing of conversation in the room, the sudden gasps and little questions such as "What on earth?" He spread his arms out to his sides and he thought, I'm doing the back stroke now the way I learned it as a boy in a river named after an extinct Indian tribe. There were no mosquitoes or water moccasins or any other natural dangers. The sun was shining, the water flowed swiftly, with purpose, carrying him along.

He heard a flurry of questions: What's he doing? What's wrong? What's happening?

"I'm Bartleby," he said to the ceiling. "And today, I would prefer not to."

Of course, they didn't know what he was referring to. It had been one of Moxine's favorite stories by one of those American novelists that Europeans more than Americans honor and appreciate and see distinctly as American. Poor Bartleby. He'd had enough. Poor me, thought Gar. No, not poor. I still have Moxine.

"Please get off the floor, Gar. What is this? Have you lost your mind?"

Possibly. It was a man asking the question, his floor manager, boss-man, all Brooklynese in his manner and his expectations of servitude from lesser employees.

Perhaps he had, indeed, gone off the rails. It was a wonderful thought.

~⁓~

A subtle radiance, as if from a candle, brightened the quiet. It was, Gar supposed, an earned sense of self-actualization that had made his stunt, no, his *choice* so satisfying. Recovery, after all, was part of loss. To progress was to age, deteriorate, to take risks and to learn. It was the reducing of that insecure person he once saw himself as. Moxine understood this. She wanted him to progress, to live on without her and to fully realize not who he was, but who he was going to become.

It occurred to Gar that, of late, when he spoke to people, it was from a gentler, firmer and more distant perch, a place in his mind with a unique solidity, one that resembled an object he'd found as a boy during a walk, either a polished arrowhead stone, or a dirty Indian-head nickel, anything that kept the patina of time and helped him to observe himself pensively, to think of the stoicism of an Indian chief, of all the bloodshed that the American empire had been built on.

Objects like various chord progressions helped him feel the weight of time passing. It never ended. Time just went on and on.

Anybody could comment on time, but who really understood it? He heard Moxine better now and this was a mark of time having passed. She kept telling him to keep enduring the silences, to keep listening, to sharpen all his filters and membranes. There was no escape from them. If they were developed as tools, they'd bring him profound moments of tutelage that both deserved his attention and would improve him. All part of mastery, which was a process.

Finally, he was free. His work day had ended with the floor manager calling him into his office. Gar had rather liked sitting there, not far from the clamor of the kitchen, as if a truant who'd been dragged in by the police, little more than an accessory to ameliorate the boredom that the other waiters and the kitchen staff contended with each day. It was hardly a decorous affair with the floor manager. Gar had been upbraided, questioned, sent home not with any declaration but rather with a tacit and rather gentle admission. "You know, Gar, I'm going to have to fire you."

"I know, Sir. I think I want that."

Not with a bang, but with a whimper. Rather poetic. He'd always have memories of counting tips, assessing doubts, urges and hungers, despising those Botox queens especially, the way they sipped and cackled and gossiped.

Now, he could step outside at will to walk the Manhattan his Moxine had so revered. Knowing this remained a comfort. All was in the present tense. No such state as the past. Okay my lover, he heard Moxine say. Let's move on.

They were walking together and hadn't gotten far before Garland had to pause to admire hand-chiseled granite steps, three of them, each so scarred and unevenly formed and yet solid and supported by black wrought-iron railings that led to a door painted glossy cranberry red, a polished brass monkey for a knocker. On the building's face, the bricks were painted pale blue, chipped and scarred in places, as well. Garland knew such bricks could be tuck-pointed and sandblasted to look uniform and new. One of his Charleston uncles, an architect, had once been immersed in such work and had often talked to him about construction from this period.

Here, some brick fronts were painted tangerine, dusty rose, curry yellow. Signs of renewal and re-gentrification. Gayness, he thought, chuckling. How nice. Windows trimmed in a satiny yet durable white.

Moxine took his arm, held him close by her side and together they studied a turquoise door that gleamed when a bar of sunlight peeped across it from behind low thin clouds. Its cast-iron knocker resembled a small cannonball. The doorway was framed by windows on each side, each with louvered shutters and a short box planter at their sills. They wore an air of battered elegance.

This feels so Belle Epoque. The French respect time's inevitable cruelty.

Knowing Moxine did not expect a reply, Garland remained silent. He agreed with her. Why not? After all, she liked having the last word regarding such nuances. He also knew he could no longer embrace the city without her. She reminded him how much she liked knowing gas lanterns were still part of the architecture in that neighborhood, but she wanted to keep going, and so they strolled a block further along until reaching a lane cobbled in round stones. This neighborhood, so cozy, so close to her heart, its lanes rife with subtle personal touches, was a world apart and yet not all that remote from the thundering metropolis just blocks away of a more chromatic and prosaic Big Apple with its steel tubing and mirrored glass, its parking garages, standardized offices, condos and eateries.

She confessed that this was where she first fell in love with him. This was where now she would continue to visit. He could always find her there. No other place she'd rather be.

Garland stood a moment on the sidewalk of that lane and waited as if he were letting the air speak to him. Moxine was no longer there. Warmth flooded his body as he smiled with a memory of Ingrid Bergman's face in one of Moxine's favorite classic films, *Saratoga Trunk* and how Moxine, Southern-born like him, had often said she'd been conceived in the wrong era.

What did it really mean to comprehend death? Did he want to cry? He couldn't, not here.

He kept waiting for Moxine to speak, knowing it was futile as he looked toward a window where a sliver of light filled a gap between ochre drapes. One more nuance.

She'd called him, "My Gar."

He didn't hear her voice. That window would have to be enough and he spent a long time, or so it seemed, studying the color of a small flower of light in it, and in bloom. Stop and smell. Daylight has a scent. *I am a flower in bloom.* Wasn't everything? In its way, yes.

Garland looked away from the window up at trees that lined the sidewalk, pruned, cared for, as if there had to be in order to complete the appeal of the cityscape's character. He savored the smell of cleanliness, uniformity. Pedestrians passed him, unhurried, strolling the way he and Moxine once strolled in a relaxed almost regal way. The insistent clamor and fumes of traffic remained a distant intrusion, easy to ignore.

He looked to the sky. Not much of it exposed. He wanted to see himself there. Her Gar being reborn and perhaps that was what her dying had been for.

He walked for another hour until dusk began to settle in. He stopped at a café Moxine had often frequented. He'd been there with her a few times and knew the manager, Becca, an attractive young woman, his age, single, someone he'd gotten along with well. She and Moxine had been friends, mostly due to Moxine's regular visits.

She'd flown to Atlanta to the funeral. She'd said if there was anything she could do, please don't hesitate to call.

There he was. Hadn't phoned, he'd stopped by in person. He wondered if he looked as forlorn and anguished as he felt. He could tell by the cautious optimism in her smile that he did.

Becca wore her hair long, pulled back off her forehead and tied in a bun at the back, rather old-fashioned for one whose energy was loose and up-tempo. She had a disarming smile, ginger-colored eyebrows, a pug nose, a girlish look about her, softness that didn't intimidate, not in the least. And those eyes — she was the only person he knew with green eyes.

After a close-lipped hello, avoiding small talk, he asked her how she was. She spared him the embarrassment of having to react to any expression of her condolences. What a relief. But she did ask, slowly, with sincerity, "How are you?"

"I don't know. Out of a job. Yet again."

"You're a musician. It happens."

He told her a joke, asking, "What do you call a musician without a girlfriend?"

"I don't know, Garland. What?"

"Homeless."

It was apt. She knew it, but she didn't sound a laugh. She didn't have to, he supposed. He could tell she liked it.

"I'm seeking comfort this time. Not caffeine."

"Tea, right?" she said.

"Russian caravan. You're the only place in the city that has it."

"With milk."

"You remembered," he said.

"Just tea, then?"

"And sympathy. Do you know that old play?"

"I don't."

"I could tell you about it sometime."

Becca also hailed from another place, but had lived in Manhattan a long time. She had a flair for design, had worked briefly in the fashion industry, had burned out and was in a re-defining phase of her life. She'd even been to the apartment one evening to help Moxine price wedding planners. He'd met her that night for the first time. They'd clicked. He'd played the piano while she and Moxine drank wine together and laughed over catalogs and web sites.

She brought him his tea and left him alone, somehow knowing he preferred that. Also knowing, as he did, that she would call, that Moxine approved, that they'd get together.

After leaving Becca, walking north, he thought Belinda must become his, re-forged in his mind to meet his needs, not Moxine's and her dreamscape of lassitude from bygone days. What he liked as a counter to her horse and carriage romanticism were the outsized and sometimes lurid and vulgar shows of graffiti, the surreal blocks of mirrored glass towers. Symmetrical, in rows, flashing sunlight at pedestrians below. He must *become* this city, the one he lived in now. Not what it had been for him. Not what Moxine had fancied it might embody. Not who he thought he used to be.

He stopped and studied himself in a massive mirrored pane of bronze-colored glass. Each face looked inside for its soul, each second of time elbowed past him as it did all the others with the same unanswerable questions. He felt a disarming sexual charge as he imagined Becca's face dirtied by the gritty fumes from a slithering asp of traffic. *Re-born constantly as long as I'm here.* No amount of counseling would cure him. He just had to accept it. *There was no reason. These things just happen.* There was Becca now. She was a bridge to cross.

He could not forget Moxine's statement that love brought miraculous resilience. At times, he had forgotten this. He promised himself not a day would pass without him thinking about and acting on her words. Never once had he doubted their veracity. The key now was in moving, taking action, trusting she would approve.

—❧—

The morning windless, its unseen edges growing sharper as if preparing to cauterize from him all thought of his third eye, that place where one bears witness from. Bodies flew upwards off the street and dissolved in a magenta sky. He didn't have enough money, couldn't afford this life and would need to move, but where?

It was while shaving and listening to Takemitsu's "A Flock Descends Into The Pentagonal Garden" that he began to feel calmer. He had his savings, his mother's support, his piano, a possibility with Becca, and time. Lots of time. If careful and persistent, he'd be fine. He'd prepare a recital program and try to find help booking a performance.

Gar, my Gar, we all get better. I'm with you now, as always.

He was surprised not to see his new roommate, had expected him for company at breakfast. It wasn't until Garland started eating his toast that he remembered Drake had left with his girlfriend to attend a conference in California on new trends in computer gaming. Drake had friends out there and he'd be gone at least two weeks.

Garland realized at that moment just how much he hungered to speak with someone, to share the fringes of his dreams, particularly how he'd seen Moxine swimming to him in a river while he was bathing naked. He'd felt such a strong voltage in that dream, powerful enough to wake him. Why not phone Becca? Well, for one, he'd told her ever so coolly, perhaps foolishly, to call him.

While sipping coffee, he sat in front of his apartment's one big window and turned on his laptop. He began searching for psychiatrists. Earlier in the week, he had lied to his mother that he was seeing a therapist. Not to deceive but to console her.

His craving had changed. Now he wanted more than just professional support. His dreams, evaluated, could help: anything to move closer to harmonious mergers with the city's gargantuan pulse. Anything to understand who he'd become. Death changes a person. It had changed him. But how?

This was when he turned and saw Moxine's face in the apartment window. He felt so startled that it angered him. "What are you doing?"

She didn't answer. Her face, nothing more, and so large, filled the window. "Talk to me."

As he'd seen it in her coffin. Too perfect. A face that made him cringe as he broke into a sweat. He wanted to smash that face to pieces, drive his fist through that window. This wasn't his Moxine. This was a death mask looking at him as if it knew all his lies and insecurities.

A phone call interrupted Garland's nightmarish tussle. It was Becca. She sounded excited. Would he like to join her this afternoon? She and her friend Jade were going to the city's Metropolitan Museum of Art.

Garland listened, astonished. This was not how he'd expected his day to transpire. He hadn't been to that museum in over a year. Did Becca mean Jade the waitress at Le Gambol Cafe? Hadn't she been one of Moxine's acquaintances? Hadn't they met her as a couple?

"Yes, Garland, the same Jade."

He heard in Becca's voice an effervescence and an energy he wanted to be around. He told her he'd love to go, but unfortunately, he had a time-slot reserved in a practice room.

"Oh, sorry to hear that." Her disappointment sounded genuine.

"But some other time. Promise."

Becca said of course. "But Garland, are you okay? Really?"

He paused. He listened. This was a gift. He heard Moxine give him the answer he was looking for and he decided against telling Becca that he was searching the Internet for shrinks.

"No, wait. I'm going. I can cancel and get other slots. I can practice here at home, too. I just like working my chops in other spaces sometimes. Can we have lunch together, too? I remember they have a cafe there."

"That would be great, Garland," said Becca. "You'll like Jade. We'll have fun. A blast."

Could Becca be too eager? At once, he began to have reservations. The words "a blast" were what set off his doubts. Were they teenagers? He shouldn't judge prematurely. He should consider himself wise and lucid enough to have at least realized he needed to use his new freedom and break out of his maudlin routine.

⚬⚬⚬

Jade hadn't come. It was just the two of them. Strike one. He felt deceived. He might have believed her if Becca had said Jade needed to work, or she was having her period, or she just didn't want to be a third wheel, but instead Becca had prattled on about Jade's building Super being sick and Jade needing to fix a leaky faucet. Baloney, all of it. He knew a lie when he heard one. Becca had set him up, most likely assuming he'd say yes to a trio instead of them as a couple and the possible succumbing to a confusing physical attraction.

Did he have confused feelings toward Becca? Was she deep enough to grasp what he was going through? Despite her optimism and cheerful girl-next-door vibe, there was a shallowness about her that he couldn't see beyond. None of the women he'd been close to, including his mother, had been shallow. He understood women and felt like one of them much of the time. It was a phenomenon he couldn't explain, one that had often led him to question his sexual orientation. Much of it had ended when he met Moxine, who'd liked that he tended to take a back seat and let the women in his life monitor the machinations so that he could keep his head immersed in music.

As they walked along, both noticed the words painted in smaller white letters on the glossy green door of a truck stopped in traffic. AMERICAN CASKET COMPANY. She said nothing. He laughed out loud.

Becca just didn't get his laugh. Didn't grasp that life was an ironic road movie. If he were to write it as a chamber piece, he'd title it: Some of My Most Dignified Friends And Loved Ones Now Live In Boxes. It was a title John Zorn or Frank Zappa might appreciate. Could he even bring up those composer's names with Becca? Maybe. But he wouldn't try. If she didn't know them, she'd likely feel he was condescending to her.

Moxine, on the other hand, had introduced him to obscure composers and artists, such as Tan Dun, and Harry Partch. She loved learning about new composers so much that there had developed between them an unspoken acceptance that his ability to perform, understand and appreciate music, not so much his physical prowess and manliness, was what really turned her on. The first time he'd taken her north was to show her the city where he'd studied for his Master's, Philadelphia, where his mother's side of the family hailed from. They'd driven first to visit his sister and her husband and two children through Delaware Water Gap as it opened into Pennsylvania, hazy, a little warmer, sluggish, but not too slow since they'd been driving an interstate. In New Jersey they'd seen townships, not towns or parishes, and the sign-makers used the abbreviation, TWP.

He lost himself in a memory of how softer light had begun to rise off the silver-glazed shoulders of hills, like rounded walls of trees rising above the wider lethargic expanses of the Delaware River. Wherever he had visited with Moxine, she would engage him and stun him with her knowledge of history, talking for hours about English and Dutch colonial settlers, Native Delaware, Algonquin and Mohawk tribes, outcast fur trappers from Quebec and Ottawa, remarking on what they must have felt finding the wealth, beauty, dangers and promise in the land they believed would become New France. Garland remembered how sleepy the warmth had been in the air, soothing and expansive, a terrain that napped with its eyes open, the hills like green waves that peeled all the way down into Moxine's native state.

Those past trips had been for him an understanding of his mother's urban childhood, so much different from his father's Tennessee boyhood. He'd seen himself better, too, an uninitiated lad from hill country who was in his mid-twenties before he'd seen row houses, sectioned off neighborhoods, overt street violence and poverty. Before he'd seen Memphis and understood the value of living fully in the present tense, without fear — and all those seasons of his innocence when highway dreams ran like satin ribbons through his sleep. Back when his father was alive. Back when as a family they'd take Sunday drives to scenic overlooks and riverside picnic areas, and his parents would talk to him and his sister about pioneers and gold-rushers who'd crossed the Atlantic from Europe and then by wagon to the prairie states, curious, desperate, itching for the Western Star.

Becca looked at him. "We're almost there. You look bored."

He offered her a weak smile. What to say? He should be polite. Should have stayed home. They'd barely started their day together, but he knew, without question, they had little in common that mattered.

Garland kept walking, how he loved to walk in this city and remembered what it had felt like to ride with Moxine through regions where the people had been dressed in flannels and suspenders even though it had been hot. One woman in a walker had exited a diner with her daughter at her side, and the daughter had that really scary countrified look to her. Muscular and overfed in jeans and boots and a denim shirt worn untucked.

He had to speak, to get it out. "I was thinking, Becca, that there's nothing like cheesy tourist roadside archeology to lift one's spirits. I wonder if they have anything like that in the museum."

Becca eyed him sideways. She shrugged.

"I remember this one time," Garland continued, "when Moxine and I saw this kid's trolley and mini-golf course. It had a giant plywood hot dog atop the roof of the trolley ticket booth. We just laughed and laughed at that."

"But why is that funny?"

"You'd have to ask Moxine that."

"She's not here, Garland."

"Oh, but you're wrong. She is. She's always here."

Becca eyed him sideways again. She was chewing gum. She took a pack from her purse and offered him a piece. He refused kindly.

"I think Americans," he said, "were simpler folk once, a lot less ironic, unaccustomed to being entertained. Maybe that's why the hot dog amused. And I'm sure many a little girl and boy have terrific memories of that trolley ride and why not? It was beautiful green country there."

"I don't always like the city either," said Becca. "Just look at all these people, this traffic. I have to pee, too. When I have my house one day, it's going to have four bathrooms. Two on the first floor, two on the second. My mother always said you can never have enough bathrooms. That's one thing I don't like about this city."

Bathrooms? Who was this girl? "Don't worry, Becca. I'm sure the museum has toilets."

Once inside The Met, they'd agreed that if separated, they could phone each other. Instead of staying together, he followed his instincts with such intensity that he forgot about her as he languished among the American landscape painters, allowing his eye for color and composition to discern the masterful hand behind each image. At one point, while backing up to get a longer perspective on a painting, he bumped into Becca. He felt like a heel and apologized, but she appeared not to mind and asked if she could stay with him for a while.

Together, they found a painting, "Landscape with Church Spire." They both liked it. By Jan Matulka, an American artist, Czech-born, it was new to them and Garland spent a long time absorbing it, leaning to one side as if to sway with Matulka's trees. During that time, Becca wandered off, saying she needed to keep moving. They agreed to meet at the café for lunch.

After the Matulka, Garland wanted to return to Marsden Hartley's painting, "Blueberry Highway, Dogtown." He saw similarities between Hartley's and Matulka's respective approaches, from the use of bolder more modern colors, to the Cezanne and Matisse influences, to the slightly larger than real evocation of small-town life and a quality that Garland thought of as uniquely American, though he couldn't put his finger on how to define it.

As he studied the Hartley, he lost himself in the thought that America was a place in his mind, and he traveled there with other vagabonds. One just kept going. One absorbed, selected, changed or was altered by impressions long after a piece of the ride, for the time being, ended. Essentially, that's what his book of life was starting to be about. Catching up with who he really was, trusting that no one got there completely because that destination in the mind was the mind itself. He was already there.

Could he compose pieces of music or songs that expressed such profound ideas? If only he knew a composer or a writer who could help him. The Gershwins had collaborated. So had Lennon and McCartney. Playing music was one thing, but composing classical pieces or a pop song was quite another.

In the café, struggling to control his excitement about what he'd seen and absorbed, he hummed little melodies as he ate his salad. Becca ate slowly, slumped in her chair, a sandwich in one hand. She drank coffee, telling him, "I always think I'm going to like museums and then I come and realize after an hour I've seen enough."

"You're bored?"

She nodded while she chewed her big sandwich. She'd bought not one but two big cookies. She should be more careful about what she ate, but it would be rude of him to tell her.

"Becca, just out of curiosity, what do you think about when you look at a painting?"

"I like fashion. I look at what they wear. The colors, I guess."

"That's how we're different. I explore and look for what's missing. There are so many good artists nobody has ever heard of. Lately, I've been hung up on what it means to be an American and to be a man, to have lost someone I loved. Moxine, of course."

"Of course." She sounded disappointed.

"I still feel like I'm on the verge of starting my life and I want to leave my various rooms, and to examine the quadrants of memory, to piece together and pull apart the drives and the flights and the walks I've made. It's all non-linear, you know?"

Becca just stared glumly at him while chewing.

"They're not about destinations so much, though destinations matter," he said. "They're more about the speed traps and the security cameras and how I've dealt with them."

"Moxine always said that about you. I can see it now."

See what? Why was she so evasive? "What do you want?" he asked. "Other than four bathrooms."

"I kinda like working at the café. Free meals. Maybe some security."

"Not for me. How can that be for *any* artist?"

Becca, looking at him, resumed chewing her sandwich. Mechanically, he thought. Swinishly. He waited for a sign to show him she understood what he was driving at. How had she and Moxine shared anything in common?

"What I like about these places," he said. "I mean museums in general, is that they remind me that we have only our imaginations to fear."

She shrugged indifferently. "I just get tired of it too fast. It's not reality."

"But it reflects our reality. Gives us a common understanding."

"Whatever." Having finished her sandwich, she began unwrapping one of her cookies. "You just think you're original, Garland. I suppose musicians are like that."

"Colorado makes sense, too." He'd passed the remark coyly. He raised his eyebrows.

"I don't get it."

He leaned back and frowned. What had he been thinking? He began talking as if to himself. "Art itself creates the hunger. The more people see it, the more it changes and fulfills them, and the more of it they want."

"Like a drug," said Becca.

He silenced himself, startled. She'd actually been listening. Somewhere, certainly across the city, cars, taxis and trucks were wiping their carbon smears across the air, he thought. Somewhere, bombs were dropping. And he was seated suffering the delusion of safety with a girl he didn't much like. He listened to Becca slurp her soda. Moxine had counted each calorie and she'd waxed on and on about art and she'd been the only woman who understood him.

Looking at Becca, not sure of what to say next, he still felt grateful. She had, after all, wrenched him out of hiding to show him he could still love art, though he preferred to be alone with his thoughts and his piano.

Come night time, he would sit and focus and play brilliantly. The twilight, with its suggestions of winter coming on soon, would bronze fires in the glass panes of city buildings he could see from his apartment. The concrete and asphalt would glow.

He thought of Copland's pieces about American cities. Overall, it was turning into a good day, wasn't it? Becca couldn't help being who she was. Nor could he. It would be a better night, and this is what he told Becca when they parted ways.

He thought himself a gentleman and made a point to thank and to compliment her. Lastly, he surprised her with a gift, a little ceramic lapel pin of a pink turtle that he'd bought at the museum gift shop. A token of their day together. She appeared to like it, but he couldn't really tell. No matter. He understood now that she wasn't the type he cared to read.

❧❧❧

Glad to be home alone, Garland sat at his Baldwin, recently tuned, and sipped a cup of hot tea with milk and thought about which sonata or etude he might lose himself in, because once he started, he was not going to stop. He'd play until exhausted, fully expending the twisted-up energy inside of him.

He thought of all the people he might call. He decided not to contact any of them. He thought about ordering Chinese food, but changed his mind. Did he want to go out again? Wasn't sure. The room didn't feel right. Too warm, a warmer than usual night. He got up and took off his sweater. Maybe he'd go out somewhere, after all.

He paused, turned to the window, thinking that he'd heard a woman's voice. He had. It was Moxine telling him to open all the windows to air out the apartment. Moxine said one thing more. He should go up and breathe new air.

Go up? What did she mean? Go up where?

There was no answer. He waited. The silence deepened. He opened all the windows. Then he sat at his piano. Night air streamed in and normally he didn't like such air because of its humidity and the risk it could damage his piano, but it wasn't humid. The night was dry, crisp, comfortably tepid.

What to play? Liszt's *Sonata in B Minor*? Not now. He'd start comparing himself to Arrau and he lost all confidence whenever he did that, as much as he revered that Argentine master. Who was he fooling? There were many masters to learn from, to ravage his confidence whenever he thought of how skillfully they executed certain pieces. Barenboim, Grimaud, Argerich, Pollini, Gilels, Richter, the cacophony of names ran endlessly in his head. He had for years been studying their music.

He stretched his fingers, slowed his breathing. He thought of Alicia de Larrocha playing Albeniz. Brigitte Engerer's recording, in her prime, of Tchaikovsky's *The Seasons*. Why had Tchaikovsky named his twelve pieces that way? He should have called them *The Months*. Never too much rubato in Engerer's playing. Like Lazar Berman performing Liszt, or Marie-Catherine Girod's versions of "Songs Without Words."

That's what he'd play! The Mendelssohn. He had the sheet music handy.

He began by falling into the music, losing his body, seeing nothing but his fingers and the keys and the area of balance between his yes to the music and his no to his ability to master it. What was in him that made his style closer to Girod's, a woman's, than to, say, Gieseking's, or Bolet's? He couldn't say, in the same fashion he couldn't explain why so many female players were appealing to him. It was as if he misunderstood their sensibilities at a deeper level, opting for the arduous task of achieving their languidness and delicacy. As Moxine would have said, he preferred always the greater more impossible challenge. And why not?

Playing like he'd never seen the piece before, discovering it, Garland recalled how Mendelssohn in a letter had written that he wanted to "make the piano sing." How had Mendelssohn put it? *Music alone can awaken the same ideas and feelings in one mind on another.*

Garland was paraphrasing, of course, letting thoughts and energy cascade out of him while playing. He shouldn't worry about being accurate when it came to trivialities such as remembering a quotation he'd read somewhere. What mattered was his posture, poise, stamina, concentration and once more how he was learning to play the piano as if for the first time. The instrument was so much larger and more powerful than he was. And always would be.

On and on he played, one Mendelssohn Opus after another until he began to tire, to overcompensate, to hear voices within arguing over just how gently or slowly to render certain progressions. He felt the burn in his lower back that assured him he was nearing his time to stop. He had to. He was done. Mendelssohn was such a workout.

Garland raised both his hands and, feeling uncomfortably stiff, he stood just as a warm breeze gusted through one of the windows. He looked around the room and imagined an audience was there with him, applauding.

He took a bow. He smiled. The roof! That's what Moxine had meant when she'd said *go up*. He'd gone there with her on a few occasions, sometimes with Carlos and Donna who lived in 6-F down the hall. The Super didn't mind. Only one rule. Pot was okay but no alcohol. Fine, fine. He'd bring his soul up to Moxine to be alone with her in just the right intimate way.

He swore he could feel and smell Moxine leaning against him. There was no way she'd let him destroy anything. He closed the piano, found his apartment keys, and stepped out into the corridor. He locked the apartment door.

The roof, Gar. The roof. Just go.

A little chillier and windier than he'd expected. He thought these were minor discomforts as he sat near a raised steel ventilation duct and held on to one of its supportive pipe stanchions. He couldn't see much because his building stood lower than most of those around it. If willing to move to one corner and lean out, he'd see a slice of the skyline aglow at night. He didn't want slices. He wanted wind-lashed zones that fed his imagination. He wanted memories of Moxine and maybe he'd say a prayer or two.

A sudden fume of marijuana. *Someone else is here.* He heard footsteps. Whispers between two male voices. Should he run? This could be a dangerous place at such an hour.

The steps grew louder, closer. The pot fume strengthened. He'd been hoping for the Super, but it wasn't him. There were two of them, one pimply with long hair, skinny and holding a guitar. The other taller, older, alarmingly handsome in a leather jacket, and he looked stoned as he offered a lit joint and said, "You alone?"

"I am," said Garland.

"Not a cop?"

Garland shook his head no. "The Super smokes up here. I'm not a cop."

The younger one in his jeans jacket, with his long hair and rodent-like features, didn't speak. He had eyelashes that struck Garland as girlish. The older one, with his shingles of hair and rigid jaw, made Garland feel safer, as if he could be trusted. Garland moved closer to him.

"I'm Tanner," said the older one. "New in the building." Tanner didn't shake hands. A fist bump instead. "This is Felton."

Felton didn't shake hands either. He just nodded.

"You brought your guitar," said Garland to Felton. "Were you playing?"

"He was," said Tanner.

Garland said no to the marijuana. Tanner, shrugging, carefully put out the joint. "Pulsing, blinding, flashing energy," he said. "What is it about rooftops? And water towers? They promise something, don't they?"

Garland, pleasantly surprised by Tanner's show of linguistic facility, offered a guarded shrug.

"It's so cool you're not a cop," said Felton. He looked troubled.

"Actually, I'm a pianist."

"Wait, man, was that you?" asked Felton.

"We heard," said Tanner. "We've been up here a while smoking out and jamming."

Felton's eyes lit up. "That *was* you, wasn't it?"

"Piano?" asked Garland. "Probably. My windows were open."

Felton raised his guitar. "Man, I wish I could play this thing the way you were playing those keys. I thought it was, maybe, a recording. Blew my mind."

"Nope. In the flesh," said Garland. He felt tickled, overjoyed by their curiosity. This sort of thing didn't happen to him. "Come to think of it, maybe I will take a hit. If you don't mind."

"Knock yourself out," said Tanner.

While Garland puffed on the joint, Tanner got busy pulling from his jacket a wrinkled sheet of paper with writing on both sides. After sharing the joint with Felton, Garland offered it to Tanner. The three smoked together.

"Should I?" Tanner asked Felton, waving the piece of paper.

"Why you asking me?" said Felton. "Ask him."

Tanner shrugged. He turned to Garland. "Wanna see? I was writing a poem about them, you know, the rooftops. I stopped, but I kept going when I heard your music. Felton played along with his guitar. It inspired us."

"It's not my music. It's Mendelssohn."

"You're the real thing," said Tanner. "Frickin' sublime."

"Sublime?"

"Like manna from the Gods."

"Tanner's a poet," said Felton. "For real."

Garland thought a moment. "I see. Why don't you read it then, Tanner? I'm a little tired. I'd prefer to listen."

"And I'll play," said Felton. "Like paying you back for your piano."

"It was just practice, but I appreciate the thought."

"You won't make fun of me?" asked Felton.

"Why would he do that?" asked Tanner.

"I don't know, Tanner. Cuz, you know. Just cuz."

Garland felt a twinge of sympathy. Felton was still just a kid and felt vulnerable playing in front of others. Garland had known the feeling well for a long time, but he'd long ago gotten over it. He was tempted to share this with Felton, but he might come across as superior and ruin the easy camaraderie that was developing between them.

He eyed Felton. "You play. Tanner reads. I listen."

Felton looked toward Tanner, who said, "You're on."

Sitting on the peat-stones and tar, Felton began to strum his student guitar, ever so sweetly, finding different rhythms. Garland sat, too. He watched Felton's long fingers move smoothly, naturally along the fret board. Mostly open chords that placed his status as a high-level beginner who if he kept practicing would one day be quite skilled.

Tanner, standing, held his paper in two hands and began to read in dramatic surges, pausing now and then to let Felton fill in gaps.

"And tasting like his blood and mucus
and the wormy stink of failed ambitions
and boots denting his skull until he blacks out,
his wings clipped and his body slumped on the ground
with a paperback masterpiece in his rear pocket.
Oh, Momma send me back into my amniotic cocoon
where I hear soft waves from heaven."

Tanner paused. Felton went into a solo, showing dexterity and a touch of Spanish flamenco influence. Garland thought Tanner looked embarrassed. Why? He thought Tanner had a practiced feel for compelling language.

Felton was the true beginner among them. He paused. There was silence. Were they both finished?

"That was nice," said Garland. He wasn't sure he understood the poem, but it had shown an appealing sensual energy, much like Tanner himself.

"No, there's more," said Tanner.

"I like your line about 'I hear soft waves.' You could use that in a song," said Garland.

"Like riding a wave," said Tanner.

"Go ahead, Tanner, read on, I'd like to hear the rest."

Tanner said okay. Felton resumed playing.

"All the dreams are not his fault.
They come. They will not be understood.
Nor can they be the source of inspiration or blame.
He still craves experience and it has made him
through the small moments, through fear.
He knows one day, he will lengthen

> *like a late afternoon shadow*
> *and give shade and disappear."*

Another silence.

"That's it? That's the end?" asked Garland. He still wasn't sure about meaning, but he didn't care.

"Not yet, but mostly, yeah."

"It does feel like there's more to come."

"How can you tell?" asked Tanner. "I mean, there is. But do you like it so far?"

"It's about death, I think. I have dreams about death all the time."

"Mind-blowing," said Felton. "I had the same thought when I first read it."

"Kind of right," said Tanner. "You kinda get me."

"Rooftops," said Felton. He was so stoned that he giggled. "Water towers. Like that one there." He motioned toward the water tower rising above them, casting its shadow. Wooden, like an old barrel on stilts. Such towers could be seen on the lower rooftops of the older buildings throughout this part of the city.

Garland giggled too. He couldn't remember when he'd had so much simple fun. Water towers did possess a certain poetry, didn't they?

"And death?" he asked. As he looked at Felton a swelling heat rippled throughout his body so powerfully that it brought a scarlet rush into his face. It was the pot, had to be. "Water Towers And Death. Maybe that's what we should call it."

"We?" asked Tanner. "What you mean?"

"I don't know." Garland rose and leaned toward Tanner, unable to control the grin on his face and showing not an ounce of caution. He kept moving around Tanner and he studied his face from different angles until he could see it clearly in the hard wash from a flood light. He was one handsome creature. "Tanner, you're not from around here, are you?"

"I kind of ended up here. I could run off, but I want to stay. I live here with my Dad. He works on Wall Street."

"I live in Queens," said Felton. "Rent a place with a couple of other guys. It's a hole and I get the urge to run somewhere else, but it don't feel right. Not yet."

"Run where? From what?" said Garland. "You're here. Make music. Or else move to Nashville or something."

"What's your name, by the way?" asked Tanner.

"I didn't say?" Garland paused. He was really stoned. He sounded a nervous laugh. "Sorry, I think I'm high."

"We all are," said Tanner. He laughed. "That's kind of the point, ain't it?"

"Garland. My name's Garland."

His face brightening, Tanner stood straighter. "Garland. Nice name. I can tell you're from down South. Not some kind of racist jerk-off, are you?"

"No, Tanner. I'm not. At least I try not to be."

"What was that music you were playing again? Sometimes, I write my poems to music."

"Mendelssohn. They're called *Songs Without Words*. I'm sure it's on Spotify."

"What isn't?" said Felton. He snickered.

"Read some more for me, would you?" asked Garland. "To the end."

Tanner said "Okay." He cleared his throat and eased into his poem. Felton followed, strumming lightly.

> *"No matter how I feel in this maze,*
> *I'm still in motion and intact.*
> *Messengers share what's been said a million*

> *times and none of it matters when I lie*
> *here with you and we drift to sleep*
> *and all needs for definitions blur.*
> *I lose skepticism and fear. I discover flowing*
> *inside of myself a colossal city, not an eroding*
> *iron lung, but a sense of beauty about myself,*
> *my ability to define a life, a dream I must share.*
> *Tell me, is this love?"*

Garland knew Tanner had reached the end. He couldn't say why, but he knew. Maybe it was Tanner's body language. Maybe he'd grasped the poem, after all.

"When I lie here with you," said Garland in a loud whisper. Eyes blooming, he looked off into the night sky as if his body was emptied and he remained there like an empty vessel letting the wind caress his face and fill him through his pores as he saw small soft pulses and tracers of light, each a different color. He knew they weren't there, just the products of his imagination, but there were hundreds of them, all too large to be stars, each an amorphous and throbbing source of energy in metallic and silky blues and reds and yellows, floating and arcing and bursting through a milky haze across the night.

"Hey, you okay?" asked Felton.

"I'm fine," said Garland. He didn't turn to face Felton. "Just a little dazed."

"Hell yeah, aren't we all."

Garland remained aloof, evasive. He looked up at the water tower. It would frighten a small boy, wouldn't it? Then he looked out in a westwardly direction toward the Hudson, a thin gleaming worm pooling the stars reflecting down from the night sky. What was going on? It was wonderful. The lights had stopped bursting and shooting and now they were spreading and drifting slowly like vaporous bodies. Now and then, one would expand and rise and propel itself along like a bird of prey in flight, but there was nothing in any of them that felt intimidating. They were there, the three of them, Garland thought, to enchant, to help him remember beauty and hope and that he was still very much alive.

"Tanner, 'When Stars Explode.' How's that for a title?" he said.

"No title, not yet. Besides, that would be every night," said Tanner. "Scientifically speaking. But why not something about roof-tops like you said earlier?"

Garland frowned and then grinned and frowned again. Then he turned to Tanner and said, "I've got it. Water Towers. And I've got a better idea about that poem of yours. Would you care to hear it?"

"Water Towers, trashy and rough, I know," said Tanner. "But I like it. You know, this poems just blasted out of me. I couldn't control it."

"Maybe that's as it should be, and it's not trashy at all. I think we should make it a song. Maybe two songs. Maybe a kind of tone poem. We can pull out some of the stronger lines and riff on them, you know, improvise and adapt the language to a melody and go back and forth and maybe repeat until we get a chorus and a through-line. We can do all the work in my apartment at the piano. I'll even order Chinese take-out and some beer, if you like."

"Are you serious?" said Felton. He was beaming. "Yeah, man, let's jam."

"So, you'd like that, Felton?" asked Garland. "What about you, Tanner?"

"Right now?"

Fortune favors the brave, thought Garland. A tart explosion burst inside his mouth as he imagined the three of them around his piano, working together in harmonious comprehension of their various talents. To join so casually at what seemed the perfect time. To create something new. They would work until they collapsed and it wouldn't for one moment feel like work. It would be pure joy, a communion meant to be, but he shouldn't hurry them to decide.

"Yes," said Garland. "Right now."

Tanner glanced at Felton briefly before he clapped his hands. "Let's go."

This gorgeous wild-eyed poet, thought Garland, and his pony-sized guitar-playing pal — what a stroke of fate to have met them. And to meet himself, Garland Desjardin, at last, a widower feeling no longer abandoned, lost and muttering to a ghost. They'd be more than collaborators. They'd be family. He couldn't explain it, but he knew Moxine approved.

Not Your House

S HE'S IN FRONT OF me with the blade tipped against my stomach, one of those French knives to mince, dice, and julienne vegetables. I drove her to such a rage, copping my attitude of adolescent diffidence and forcing her to desperately lunge towards her utensils drawer that she frantically dug through until she found the weapon she needed and, wielding it, flung herself around, its blade a foot long and nearly catching me across the cheek.

I'm not seething, I'm cool, restrained, but she's fuming and as a bead of sweat hangs off her nose she faces me, there, in *her* kitchen and she screams, showing no control, "This is my house, my house, not yours and what I say is what goes in my house! Do you understand me?"

I don't nod. I say nothing. I'm her son, her blood, she wouldn't dare use that blade on me. This is a joke, right? I'm chuckling inside, not really scared of her emotions but puzzled by them and I show, in return, an unearned confidence and boldness as I sneer at her, which I've done many times before. It says that nobody pushes me around.

She screams again, letting fly the curses I've learned from her, that I'm now so proud to know. Few of her words make sense, popping and hissing off her wet lips, spit flying to prove her raw emotion and the bile that matches the crimson splotching across her face.

"You son of a bitch I'll kill you, I swear."

She glares and lunges forward, nudging the knife towards me until she sees me react, just a twitch, but it's enough to know that she's scared me, at last, having pinned my back against the kitchen door. I expect her to hesitate, compose herself and back down, but she keeps thrusting the knife in short jabs into my stomach. It begins to hurt and I flinch. She's drawing power from this and raises the knife as she leans in to press the blade against my throat and that's when I see and understand that she doesn't know what she's doing. She's capable of anything and I'm dumb enough to not be afraid.

I watch as she continues to seethe. We may be staring each other in the eyes, but I know she doesn't see anything. We sweat and glare, furious. I don't know how the fight started or why.

It's not a dream. This is happening. This is my life and all I can think is that it sucks.

She keeps threatening with the knife until, for reasons unknown to me, fatigue perhaps, the tension inside her collapses. This isn't the first time I've seen her angry, but I've never seen her this hysterical and violent, and it's the most scared I've ever felt, realizing she might actually do it, make it my last day, carve me up and leave me in a stew of blood on her kitchen floor.

But I don't care and so I shout at her. "Go ahead! I wanna die. At least it'll get me out of this fucking house."

She bursts into a sob and slams the knife to the floor. She howls and bawls and staggers crookedly, dazed and without control, away from me out of the kitchen and around a corner toward her bedroom. Once she's out of sight, I hear her bedroom door slammed behind her. I stand, sweat raining down my sides and I'm not sure I can think reasonably but I'm able to ask myself if I feel as much guilt as I do fear and shock. Why have I brought this out of her? What am I trying to prove? It started because I'm sick of school, of harassment on the bus, in the locker room, in corridors between classes. I'm sick of what my brother calls "the mentality," where the same bullies we knew in Little League are now dominant in the school parking lot and bathrooms and in wood shop, where one of them smashed a project I was working on, meant to be a gift for my mother. He thought nothing of it, cackled and sneered with his woodshop clique behind him, a posse of supportive thugs. Smashed that wooden magazine rack, still in its infancy, a replica of a cranberry bog rake made of white pine that shattered with ease against a glazed cinderblock wall. The shop teacher wasn't around. All I did was stand there frozen, pimpled, fat and not menacing enough to take any of them on, and not a single ally to back me up.

I've never told this to my mother and I never will, even though a few days after the knife incident, she leaves my brother and sister to watch the house while she takes me for a long walk at twilight in our neighborhood, the crickets chirping around us, the air smelling green and sharp. We don't hug. We don't discuss our kitchen fight or apologize. It's there, but it's buried, which means I'm supposed to forget about it, as she will, though I suspect we both know we can't. We must live with it as one more disturbing memory, add it to a growing list of spats and quarrels and confrontations, all of them painful to recall. So, I won't. I see them as acts of recrimination and spite. To be filed away in layers that harden inside me one upon the other like the skin forming calluses on my feet.

Why do we hate each other so much? I don't think we do. I refuse to believe it. Yet we always fight. She tells me she's still angry with me, but that she's still my mother. She knows I'm still angry with her. She can live with this, she says, because she also knows my anger will pass. Just as hers will. Our talk doesn't go much beyond this. I don't know if she's right. I don't know what to think. What starts to settle in eventually is this feeling of doubt about my ability to understand anything, and I suspect that it will take a long time for this doubt to change and develop into something else and become a constant and worthy of my trust.

During our walk, I don't feel this doubt because I believe nothing will change between us and that that my thoughts really don't matter. She will dictate all terms for as long as I am around. Things will be different once I'm gone. I'll be away from here soon, and once I graduate I'll run away and never look back. Where I'll go is anyone's guess, but I'll know the place when I see it. This is about the only thing I'm sure of.

There are two months left and as the school year goes on, I become increasingly a loner, isolated, moody. I begin a journey inward through a series of charts that I use to record, in words, various measures between emotional highs and lows. One chart begins with the heading: *Moments of Stupor Awareness*. I find that I like toying with words and how they connect to my emotions. Another chart is headed: *Attempts to Codify-Modify*. This is followed by: *More Frustration Rooms*. All these are drenched in what I deem a sense of new release and understanding. I collect the charts in one three-ring binder titled: *Repetition X of Drama Dream*. This binder feels like the only thing in my life that is my own, without religion or rules or anyone else's approval, a guide to who I am crafted during quiet hours of privacy to help me comprehend my hunger for a question, not an answer, because I don't know what's wrong. Not with me, not with my mother, not with any of the culture of school. I just don't know. When my father was alive, I might have gone to him. I can't say. I've tried talking to teachers and guidance counselors, but it's like they've seen too many others like me before. They don't want any part of whatever future I must represent to them.

I write furiously, rendering crazed erratic passages that fill one page after another. I draw sketches of all sorts, many of them picturing naked women with large breasts. I write some poems that are epically long, some tiny and nasty. The key is that no one knows about them. They define themselves in my mind and hence draw their own lines of separation to fill different pages, producing their own logic. I never once write that I hate my mother. I try to, at times, but I can't. Nor am I sure that I love her — isn't a son bound by duty to love their mother? What is wrong with me? I don't know. I resolve that, in time, I will weaken the thread of loneliness that holds my days together, but I don't know how to do it.

I need a better job than the one I have at the doughnut shop. My mother, of all people, suggests I quit and see a man she knows who runs a construction business. He's an old acquaintance of my father's, actually attended his funeral. The man offers me a job at ten dollars an hour on Saturdays with a few hours each day after school. At school, I withdraw further, quit the baseball team, as much as I love baseball. I quit the drama club and chorus — two other pursuits that have brought steady joys as well as harassments. Everything school-related becomes secondary, of no importance, a question of time served until I graduate. I walk the corridors there as if I'm a ghost, seeing nothing, seen by none. I only visit the men's room when I know it's empty. I'm failing at least two classes I need to graduate, so I concentrate on them at home a little more and my little brother, who's smart, my opposite, helps me. I mean, I actually study for the first time in my life, hoping I'll learn enough to merit D grades. Thing is, if I hate my mother so much, why am I concerned about shaming her if I don't graduate?

I bolt from classes early each day, cutting out an hour after lunch. I have work-study status now and this allows me to nourish a new heat within, to forget about the nightmares I have of acting out one fantasy after another, whether burning down the school or copy-catting one of the mass-killing shooters that keep popping up all over the country. I understand those kids. I get why they feel so lost, so dried-up, teeming with a desire to terrorize. But I couldn't go that far. I talked to my brother about this and he said deep down that I want to be positive. I said he was wrong, but after some thought and a lot of scribbling, I began to see how wise he is for his age. I need a change of scene. I do for my construction boss whatever I'm told, no matter how dull or dirty, in order to earn my pay. This I really like. If asked, I can show others how, in my own way, without "the mentality," I have a knack for the ability to live well.

Still, I feel so alone. Though I believe, one day, I'll get the life I'm destined to have with love that isn't doubted and show them all they were wrong for shutting me out. In short, I'll get my revenge.

Shoulda Seen Me Up There In Mississauga

IF THE GRAVEL STREET I lived on had a name, I didn't know it because there wasn't a sign. It wasn't far from the Grotta Azzurra restaurant, and Mae's Old Flame boutique. On foot, I could get to DePasquale in two minutes. Shura and I didn't walk. We veered, sliced and cantered down alleys and streets as if chased by imaginary demons. The forecast had called for three more days of rain. It had been wrong. Weak sun behind thin clouds meant street puddles wouldn't last long, but it was chilly enough so that they might freeze overnight. We hurried down narrow shortcuts between the bubbling clapboards of three-decker units that keened and swelled so closely together that, at one point, I stopped to marvel that I could stand still, reach out and touch them both. I laughed. "Reminds me of a mother sticking her arm out the kitchen window to borrow a cup of sugar from the mother next door."

"But don't touch those clapboards," said Shura. "See that loose paint. It's got lead in it. So, keep your fingers out of your mouth."

I wiped my hands against my thighs. I looked up between three-decker units, their gutters and rooflines uneven, as if each was about to collapse on the other. I kept walking and came to a street where on both sides the units were painted in either faded yellow, pea-green, and robin's egg blue. One of them was purple. All the paint was blistered and flaking off.

I picked up a large curled chip of paint. "Think kids live around here? This is poison."

Shura sounded a note of sarcasm. "Leave it to Mayor Cianci. He's gonna fix 'em up."

"Yeah, our guy Buddy's a saint."

Shura hurried me along and we took one shortcut after another across The Hill's mazes of one-way streets and alleys lined with three-deckers packed in tightly side-to-side and back-to-back, most of them thrown up at the same time without planning. Here and there, slouched gargantuan multi-families filled two lots on a corner. Clotheslines and phone wires linked them. They hung in low arcs frosted white by sea air. Sway-backed and bulging, the three-deckers created canyon-like walls, their porches leaning a little in one direction, looking older than their years. We moved down one lumpy squiggle of a street after another.

"Who owns these places?" I asked.

"The mayor, for one," she said. "And landlords that never step foot in the neighborhood."

"The mayor? But the people up here love him."

She smirked. "What's that tell you about the people?"

A car passed us. Shouts were heard. The sounds carried. I looked down a street at stacked porches, round corner posts, missing pickets, busted railings. I saw flat roofs at the same height. I felt hemmed in and I felt dread. There was never enough sky. I started to think about Los Angeles and I imagined how open the sky was there, with palm trees and beaches and sunny weather year-round. I thought about Manhattan. Wouldn't be much sky there.

"Wait." Shura stopped me. She looked afraid. "I think we're being followed. I always get this feeling when I'm over here."

"I know what you mean. You get used to it. Look up there. What do you bet a single mother lives on the second floor, and I bet that Spa on the first floor was used as a bookie's parlor for running numbers before the state took over with the Lottery. Trust me, I'm getting to know these neighborhoods. You have to be careful. The windows have eyes."

Shura laughed out loud. "And you really think you're going to like Manhattan? You think you're the first person to ever walk around over here? I lived here myself. Not far from this street. You see that place on the first floor over there." She pointed up the street. "I remember when that was a small jewelry polishing operation. It was run by a fishmonger. He had his Nana living on the second floor. She'd sweep off a neighbor's porch for extra money. She and the fishmonger had a daughter who got pregnant by a man who went to prison and died there. They kept her and her daughter in a dark room on the third floor with the blinds drawn. They even made her take care of a stowaway sick aunt who had just arrived and was outliving her welcome."

I looked at her. Where was this coming from?

"Nah, that can't be true," I said. "You're just making it up."

Shura beamed. She kissed me on the cheek. "Babycakes, you are still so green. You need to learn about these places. They all have stories."

"Catholic families," I said. "I should know. I'm from one of them."

"It's not just Gangland here. It's where people live. They just happen to be poor."

"I do know one thing," I said. "Packs of kids romp these streets. When I first moved up here it was hot enough for me to sleep with the windows open. I heard them. They kept me up all night. They were screaming at each other and sometimes these fights would break out and everybody would empty out into the streets. Those kids, they'd fight with whatever they could find. Rocks, chains, knives, you name it."

"Don't romanticize, Chandler. It's not *West Side Story.*"

"Nobody gets used to it," I said. "Do they?"

"You tell me. You're the expert who lives here."

A fear began to gnaw at me as if something was about to go wrong. I struggled not to show it, but I suspected Shura could sense it in me. I sounded a note of a false bravado. "A pair of buffoons, that's what we are."

"Speak for yourself," she said.

"Just head for that huge bug KJ was telling us about."

"I'm following you," said Shura.

"That's a switch."

We laughed together and I felt a moment of happiness I promised myself not to forget. Church bells rang. Not an uncommon sound on The Hill. The timing of them couldn't have been better suited to my mood.

We were on our way to KJ's new apartment. It would be a surprise visit and our way of showing support with our Iranian friend, an actor and a mime and thanks to Orbit's guidance he was studying at the Conservatory. KJ still didn't have a visa or any legal status, the war still raged in his native Iran and he was still dating Bree and holding on to his intentions to marry her. As Shura and I walked, we chatted about KJ's life and all the uncertainties in it and how amazing it was that he could endure so much risk, loneliness and alienation and still make his way toward a new life.

Shura talked about how Orbit had lived briefly with Gail and Kevin on Vail Street. KJ had lived briefly on Rico. He'd run with some shady mob-connected characters and had befriended Leland, whom I'd met and who had helped KJ quite a bit until one day Leland had just vanished.

Shura also confessed that she had lied. She'd never lived on The Hill. This surprised me. Judging by her knowledge of the streets, I'd assumed she'd lived there at one point. She said she'd lived *near* it, not far from the YMCA building and the *Harry Cast In Spot Lite* mural on the wall of the Mohican Hotel, and then later near the old Jacob Licht lighting store block. She'd worked as an exotic dancer in a club not far from The Hill and Interstate 95 called The Gemini. She also used to dance at the Mohican Hotel. I found this hard to believe, but she insisted on it.

"I was the brainy stripper." She sounded proud of herself. "I read Shakespeare in the dressing room between my performances. The girls were rough, believe me, but they liked me okay. The money wasn't too shabby, either."

"How long you do that for?"

"A little over a year," she said.

"And you didn't get into drugs or get come-ons from mob guys?"

"I never liked coke. I'd bend over and snort it and then ask myself, 'Now what?' And there was plenty of coke, certainly. The mob guys, I don't know. They left me alone. I wasn't flashy. I danced and I went home. Most of them knew I wasn't their type, but the types you're thinking about, they drank at the Civic View, and The Peppermint Lounge. The Gemini never really got that crowded."

"But how did you get along? You're so different from that."

She shrugged. "I don't know, really. I liked the girls there. They'd seen some very hard living. I showed them respect. And I minded my own business."

"I bet you did, and I'm sure it was dangerous."

"I wouldn't do it now. I was young. I was hot enough, I guess. And I was a good dancer. It kept me in shape. I'm glad I did it."

"And I'm glad you stopped."

She smiled to show she liked that I'd said that. We laughed again and hugged in the street. We made out for a while, not caring if we were seen. As we started again to walk along, I saw a glow in her face as she said to me, "This is really fun, Chandler. I'm shocked by how much fun. I haven't been over here in ages."

——✳——

KJ's bug turned out to be a broken TV antenna of colossal proportions that dangled over the front edge of the flat roof of his three-decker. Like a radiated crippled insect from a sci-fi movie, it could drop at any moment and eclipse us. It reminded me of the big blue bug on the rooftop of an exterminator's business that anyone passing through Providence on Route 95 could spot from about half a mile away.

Shura appeared to like it. She stood in the middle of KJ's narrow street, hands in the pockets of her loose slacks, observing the antenna as if it were a modern art installation.

"Pretty cool, isn't it?" I said. "Like a set piece or something out of a sci-fi movie."

"Maybe," she said. "Maybe not. But it is oddly alluring, I'll give you that much."

I hurried her around to the back, explaining that KJ had told me not to use the front door because the third-floor doorbell didn't work. We could knock all day long, but the widow and her daughter who lived on the first floor would never answer.

"Third floor, I think it's this way," I said.

A sliver of an alley between three-deckers led to a rear yard outlined by a rusty rolled-over length of chain-link fence that anyone could step over. The rear view of the three-deckers, much like the front one, showed that side by side they created urban canyon walls. Each backyard had a fence either of broken chain-link or broken wooden pickets. The yards were a series of flag-sized plots of mostly dirt beneath clotheslines that sagged. Here, weak fences butted against each other, as did the streets and buildings. All too claustrophobic for me.

KJ's yard was a patch of packed dirt and occasional clumps of grass that smelled like dog shit. A mangy yellow cat eyeballed me from atop a beached washing machine that had been stripped of its best parts. The chewed-up haunch of a rat dangled between the cat's teeth.

Treads were missing on the back wooden stairs. Lengths of railing were gone. I led the way, warning Shura which treads were weak and to be avoided. As we climbed higher, I heard pumping bass notes under Grace Jones singing "Warm Leatherette."

The third-floor landing was rickety and it wobbled with each careful step I took. Nail heads stuck out of boards that had warped in the sun and long ago lost their paint. I felt I had to protect Shura, look out for her safety. I liked this feeling. At the back door, I kept her close to me as I knocked loudly, waited, knocked again.

I assumed it was Derek who opened the door. It was hard to tell the brothers apart. He spoke loudly, almost shouting over Grace Jones from the boom box on the kitchen table behind him. Something was said, but I hadn't understood any of it. I just assumed he was Derek because he recognized Shura straight away, beamed at her, and I recalled Shura telling me that she and Derek had taken an acting seminar together with Orbit at Trinity.

Shura shadowed me as I stepped into the kitchen. She kept her backside pressed against the rear door, closing it behind us. Derek hadn't shaken my hand, but he pecked a small kiss on both of Shura's cheeks, perhaps knowing she appreciated a more European style of greeting.

Water-stained wallpaper peeled from the kitchen walls and gave off fumes of leaky plumbing. Scarred dirty wainscoting and cabinetry, long ago painted beige, matched the dingy white of a ceramic sink full of dirty dishes. The stove top needed a scrubbing.

Derek shut off the music. Shura remarked that Grace Jones was a genius. He agreed with her, saying she was his favorite these days along with Roxy Music. Derek moved in a strangely effeminate way. I'd learned from Orbit that he'd been a Marine. Yet with one glance, anyone's first assumption would be that he was gay. I also recalled Orbit telling me that Derek went both ways, but this was not the reason his career as a Marine hadn't worked out. When I'd asked Orbit why Derek had been discharged, early and honorably, he'd said he didn't know and that Derek hated to talk about it.

Derek's tight black leotard announced in detail the shape and size of his genitalia. He wore his sleeveless satin gold-dust shirt, just as tightly. Fake pearl shirt buttons ran across the top of his shoulders, and an open triangle flap revealed chest hair. The shirt had the look of an Atomic Age costume, a touch of Ziggy Stardust that I thought out of sync with his pink leg warmers and clog shoes.

Sweating, breathing hard, Derek's reptilian eyes judged me. For a moment, it seemed he might leap for my throat, but he simmered, standing still, rubbing a hand up his forehead as if wiping himself dry.

"They don't go," Shura said. She had changed her voice, made it harder, more street. She seemed comfortable in the milieu — and with Derek.

"As if you'd know," he said.

A sneer from Shura. "From my dancing days," she said. "Never underestimate a woman's taste in clothes."

"No kidding." He seemed to like her snappy comeback. Bronze touches highlighted each gelled wave in his hair. When Derek folded his arms, the *Semper Fi* tattoo on one hairless arm covered the *No Guts No Glory* on the other.

"And your clogs." Shura motioned toward Derek's wooden shoes that added six inches to his height. "They don't match your shirt."

Derek seemed to warm up to the criticism. As he caught his breath, his small eyes remained fixed on Shura. "How do you mean?"

"I don't know, you tell me." Shura sounded sincere. "I think you're trying to spice up your bad-boy image, aren't you? But I can't be sure."

"So, you're calling me half-queer?" asked Derek. "Aren't you?"

"Take it as a compliment."

"You're the queer." He shoved Shura, playfully so. He grinned at her. Shura shoved him back, with force.

Derek wasn't offended. He laughed. "Take it easy," he said. "I ain't fighting with you."

"Because you know better," she said.

Derek padded sweat off his neck with a purple bandanna. He seemed loose now, relaxed. Shura hadn't backed down. She'd shown strength. He respected this. He looked at me and asked, "You here for KJ?"

"No," said Shura. "He's here for a blow job."

I blanched at this, but Derek burst out laughing. Shura knew exactly how to handle him. She was about to offer up another edgy quip when someone shouted, "Hey, what's going on here?"

It was Doughie, Derek's twin brother. The resemblance startled me. They were each like dolls or specimens cooked up in a lab. It was eerie and unsettling to watch Doughie as he stormed through the doorway at the opposite end of the kitchen that led to the other rooms of the apartment. His eyelids were painted purple to match purple cotton sweatpants with red leg warmers. He filled the kitchen, languidly so, sidling toward us in a black *Bay City Rollers* T-shirt that hugged the high prow of his sternum. A wide headband made of red silk kept hair off his forehead.

Doughie then stopped before he reached us; he bear-hugged Derek, lifting him off the floor, and with no small effort drove him against the wainscoting. The kitchen shook when they thudded against the wall, calcimine dust like a spray of snow from the ceiling. Derek broke free and swung a wild uppercut that grazed the wall as Doughie avoided it.

Barefoot, his eyebrows shaved, Doughie snickered at his brother. The same height as Derek, not an ounce of fat padded his frame. "Careful, Hercules," said Doughie, "You'll knock this whole slum right over."

Derek, cursing, studied his fist as he opened and closed it.

"You are way serious, my brother, ain't you?" said Doughie. "Now let's knock off the attitude and get along here."

"We came by to see KJ," I said. "That's all."

Doughie looked at me. His nostrils flared. "Who are you?"

"A friend," I said. "He asked me to come by."

"Oh, you're the restaurant cook," he said. "That's cool. I think I met you that one time at a party at Orbit's."

"That's right," I said.

"You did," said Shura.

Doughie laughed as he nodded at me, offering his approval. He then looked at Shura. He appraised her as if considering his chances with her in bed. "And just who do we have here?"

"Shura," said Derek. "She and I go back. They're both of them friends of KJ's."

"KJ ain't here," said Doughie. He was all smiles as he approached me and wrapped me in a hug, slapping me on the back with two hands. "But any friend of KJ's is a friend of mine."

Doughie faced Shura as if they were old friends. Shura blurted out, "Don't hug me. And don't slap me on the back."

Backing off, his voice conciliatory, Doughie said, "No problem, Sweetheart. I aim to please."

Derek grinned, winking at Shura. She didn't wink back at him.

"Now don't you listen to my brother Derek here," said Doughie. He bore down on Shura. "If you're here for the nostril icebergs, all I can say is the less Peruvian gunpowder he snorts, the better. It was a blizzard, man, at this club in Ontario. Quebec wasn't any better. We were both dancing for all these sluts up there and one of them kept talking to me in French while inhaling the blow right off the stage in front of me. I swear they'd suck it off my pecker if I let 'em."

Shura looked at Derek as if to ask if his brother always spoke this way in front of women. Derek shrugged and made a face to tell her not to worry.

"Yeah, maybe you should put it in your act," said Shura. She'd dropped a bomb of sarcasm that Doughie seemed to have missed since he kept on talking as if he couldn't stop.

He said, "You know what this girl up there told me? She said the French word for 'biggest dick in Canada' was the same as my first and last name. So maybe you're right."

Only Shura laughed, forcing out a snide cackle at his stupid remark. Doughie liked this and shot a salacious eyeball Shura's way and then, as if percolating, beamed at her. On a roll — amusing himself — he turned to me and slapped me a high five. "Hey, how's it hanging, brother? Sorry, KJ ain't here. He didn't tell us you might be coming by."

I asked the obvious regarding KJ's whereabouts. Neither brother knew.

"He's his own man," said Derek.

"That little Iranian dude has got it rough," said Doughie. "We like him. He looks after our place while we're on the road."

"What are you guys, the next Chippendales or something?" I asked.

"That ain't funny," said Derek.

"Don't say that," said Doughie. "Like breaking a mirror. Ten years of bad luck."

"He didn't mean it," said Shura. Again, she was sticking up for me.

"What? My brother here can't speak for himself?" asked Doughie.

"Sorry, man," I said. I worked up an uneasy smile. Derek and Doughie were eccentric, mercurial and potentially violent to be sure and they probably snorted a lot of coke and sucked down a lot of speed as they made their living as peacocks dancing naked, but according to KJ they weren't charging him rent. KJ could sleep on a mattress in their spare room for as long as he needed. Here was Shura's venerated genteel poverty in its purest form. I wondered if she saw it that way.

Doughie grinned at me, a kind of lunatic's piercing sickle of a smile that set my teeth on edge. Then he turned to Derek as if exploding. "I ain't enabling you. You don't need no more coke. That shit fucks you up."

Derek shouted back as if bored, "You're a cunt. Go practice. Your routines suck."

Doughie motioned with one hand as if masturbating. "*Semper Fi* my ass. I should make you apologize."

"For what?" said Derek. "What's the matter with you, anyways? Talking like that in front of Shura."

Shura butted in. "We have to go. Just tell KJ we stopped by."

"Sure, sure," said Derek. "KJ needs all the friends he can get. We're hitting the road tomorrow. Hartford, Buffalo, and then Pittsburgh. I'm sure he'll be around."

"You do a circuit?" I was genuinely curious and it showed.

"Yeah, a circuit," said Derek. He laughed. "Truck-stop dives and coke-whore hellholes."

"Wait, wait," said a breathless Doughie. "You wanna see something cool?" He pointed to a cabinet above the stove with a Playboy center-fold of Cheryl Tiegs tacked to it. "In there," he said. "Check this out."

His stride long, Doughie loped to the cabinet but couldn't open it. He rapped the side of his fist against the door. It popped open.

Reaching up, he pulled out a shoe box and he sniffed it. "Smells empty. But what's this?" He removed a black nine-millimeter Ruger from the box. "I just got this. Might come in handy on the road."

He pointed it at me, affecting the snarl of a gangster. "You still want in on this deal? Or maybe I'll cap your ass first."

I raised both my hands, playing along. It was the first time anyone had ever pointed a gun at me. It was strange, but I didn't feel nervous. I felt like laughing. This was one big joke. Let Doughie shoot at me. He'd probably miss.

"Doughie, c'mon, knock that shit off," said Derek.

"What, you think I'm stupid?" said Doughie. "It ain't loaded." He lowered the gun.

That's when I realized how scared I'd been. It was a delayed bodily reaction, proven by the roiling inside my bowels. Nothing went on inside my head. I was blank there. Tight. The rest of me felt loose, as if exhausted.

"Nice little heater, ain't it?" Doughie faced Shura, towered over her. I could imagine him sending more than one female into fits of passion. "You like a man with a gun? Feast your eyes on the hottest male stripper east of Harrisburg, P-A. Shoulda seen me up there in Mississauga with them girls tossing bills at me like they were tickets to Nirvana. I did my "Brick House" number and by the end of the night they were throwing themselves at me. That's why Derek's acting like such a pussy. He's jealous."

"I'd be jealous too." Shura had said it ever so coolly.

Doughie's salacious smile proved he liked this from Shura. "Would you now?" He slid his hips forward against her pelvis and kept flirting. "You just name the time and the place."

That's when the gun went off. I've come to learn they're always loud, but in that box of a kitchen, under that ceiling, it stunned me and, I swear, I heard my eardrums sizzling.

There was the smell, the shock, the silence as we looked at each other. Doughie had nearly blown his and Shura's feet off. The action that had caused him to trigger the Ruger had been a swinging out of his arm. The bullet had fired at an angle, away from their bodies, leaving a splintery hole in the wainscoting.

"That's it," I said. I sounded nervous. "We're out of here."

Derek laughed at my attempt to protect Shura.

"I'm fine," said Shura.

"Yeah, she can handle herself," said Derek. "Don't you worry."

"You should worry," said Doughie. He turned to me. He turned back to Shura and smiled again. "See," he said. He was gloating. "I even got your boyfriend all worked up into a lather."

"When you got it, you got it," said Shura.

It was the perfect response, leaving that sickle spreading across Doughie's face as we bolted the hell out of there.

Rainlight

I park in rainlight
I run out of rhymes
— Al Young

MARCUS YOU'RE STILL FOR real in me. Not a Dawg. *My* Dawg. What can I say…what does it all mean?

I was thinking of you on the night they finally elected a black man. No, not they. *We* elected him. I'm thinking of you now as the streets, once again, have erupted. You'd be telling me to say it proud-like, puffing out your chest, "A black man. A brother. For real."

Rest in peace, Marcus. LA homeboy cruising in your ride, I see you absorb the city's pain as you read her signs: Pena's Used Trucks, Yin Wah Furniture Appliance, and Bagel Bodega. You may not have trusted what you saw, but you felt it. You had sensuous light in your eyes and you drank it all in and you reserved judgment. For so long, Marcus, I wanted to be you.

Now I stand here with flowers. It's not right that I'm alone. There should be others here to mark this anniversary. The rain, however, feels right. It's gentle, the way you were. It's steady. It's ignored.

Fifteen years, Marcus, can you believe it? I can't. Just as I can't believe the shit that is *still* going down. Fifteen years. It don't mean jack in the big picture.

Remember the time you showed me that Pentecostal church in that little house you said had been imported from Alabama? You showed me Madonna statuaries in front yards, introduced me to corner fruit sellers, friends in mobile estates and maxed-out made-it canyon-side cribs with Star-of-David-shaped swimming pools. We went to so many parties together, from gay enclaves in West Hollywood with S and M saunas, to *Vato* junky hovels, to A-list baby showers joined by whoever we were dating at the time.

Today, I feel as dismal and dried-up as one of the gang-tagged palms thirsting along Hoover. On the way to your grave, I stopped at the Milagros market *fruitas y verdures* and I asked for Jose, but they told me he hadn't worked there for years.

I went to see Juwahn, the blind KC Smog junkyard maven and he came out and he looked rough. Looked old and heavy, but he said hello to me and the more I talked, the more he said he thought he recognized my scent and voice. It had been lots of years, but Juwahn still had his shepherd with him on a chain. Even that shepherd looked old.

Juwahn showed me an *Astro* van that he was working on. Peppered with bullet holes, it smelled of mud from the Rio Grande.

Juwahn says hello, Marcus. He misses you. Remembers you. Said he wished you hadn't gone there that night. Hadn't tried to score. Hadn't believed all those rumors about Yolanda. Hadn't bought so deeply into the game.

I look around the cemetery and I see new graves. I wish the game would end. I wish there'd be no need for protest. I remember you asking: Why can't people just get along?

I get back in my car and drive away.

I'm not like you, Marcus. I never was. Opposites attract, I think, even though I still like your old-school music and listen to George Duke on vinyl, one of your favorites. I remember the time you told me you were getting out at last, going back into the machine for a GED and you were adamant, saying: My posse can wait and they be waiting a long time now for me in my full-blown changes.

We were high and grooving to Power 101 and feeling bigger than Disneyland and I was telling you I'd be a d-j someday, make a fool of that Rick Dees, but you just laughed and told me to stick to what I knew, which in those days wasn't much. Of course, if I'd really known what I thought I'd known, man, I'd have put Einstein to shame.

When I got the news, I didn't cry. I didn't believe it. When weeks passed and the reality sunk in, I retreated. I changed my face, my clothes, my attitude, my city. It no longer mattered what I thought. I was no player with a juke. You were. You had always been.

I kept to myself, studious, employed. I wasn't about posters of raging self-promotion all over T-phone poles in Inglewood. There were plenty of others that had that game going on. I stopped wearing my *Dodgers* cap backwards and my eyes veered away from bling. I hit the road for a while, figured why not. I worked odd jobs, took it all in. Didn't have much to complain about and I thought about you every day. I figured I'd earn as far as my wits would take me. When I got tired, I came back.

Now, I've got a regular gig driving a tow truck. I like it because I help people out of jams. No shortage of jammed-up people, Marcus.

You knew, you always knew. You were the seer among us, the wise one. You were about avoiding minefields along Crenshaw and Florence in the glowing echoes of homes in those neighborhoods where early Hollywood Mabels once made it big playing maids to the likes of Clark Gable.

How all our fathers and their fathers took it so hard from the racist establishment. You once told me you were a child of misunderstandings, but you were wiser for it, weren't you? Change is going on, Marcus. I'm not sure what to call it. I won't call it freedom. There never really was freedom, not really. It's the will to freedom that matters. To my mind, it's a concept, it's relative, it's scented bait in the fight to live with dignity that never ends.

There are signs going on now, good omens. Hope is not dead. With each passing day, I see hope drive rooted flowers. Amazing what the youngbloods can do now. Nothing we'd ever dream of attempting. That has got to be a good thing.

Nowhere-near-enough was what you lived with all your life. It was too short. Flamed out like a comet. You know, I was never sick as a child until you started to teach me about what made those barons rich on plantations. Bunker Hill and Central Ave meant a glorious time for your God-linked Grandma who, bless her heart, raised you. When a strange man told you he was his father, and when your sister confessed who your mother really was — why she was in prison and why your father never came around — it was a heavy dose of opened eyes. Surprise, surprise. But it didn't kill you.

Greed killed you, Marcus. I hate to say it, but you know I speak the truth.

As I drive along, I feel you within me like a power, a spiritual progress erasing all the past perspectives I learned while playing the fool. Nowadays, I go with my guiding voices wherever I please and I'm hearing you tell me I should roll to *Roscoe's* for a Lord Harvey. Back to one of our old haunts for more memories. I'm no movie star wannabe, no stud with too many women, no militant crying bring 'em on, but I didn't forget you, Marcus and I never will.

I'm not *it* in these parts, never was. I'm just another aspirant seeking righteous paths to something better, melting like a popsicle under California sunshine. All the Mex-Asian vibes and aromas are still here and I still get hungry when I sniff *carne de pollo* on a hot grill, and I love those *muchachas* like Yolanda with their big easy smiles. I wonder where Yolanda is these days. She sure did soften your days out of LA county prison.

You vowed you'd never go back there, no matter the urges and the vast despair that sometimes wrenched your heart. You didn't. I respected you for that. You checked them out, all the girls, and that's why Yolanda got tired of you, but you didn't see it that way. We never see ourselves, Marcus, not from the outside in the way others see us, until something goes wrong and it's too late.

It was all about Yolanda that night. She was never anyone's property, but she was beautiful, man, and worth fighting for. My guess is that she has a few kids now and I hope she's happy. Where were they today, Marcus, all your fly brothers, your friends, your posse? Most of them are gone too, or else locked up, or else protesting. To think how stupid and vain we were, cruising, peddling just enough to buy a little more to get a little higher. Like a snake eating its tail, Marcus, until it ate yours. It wasn't really a fight about Yolanda. It was about the business. It was about ego. Give a fool a gun and he'll do foolish things.

Some days, I ride to work by bus and I think about those words: *drive by*. I think of how crime leads to mourning the dead — and how precious it is to know love.

Perfect Posture

IN A MATCHING BLACK skirt and jacket bought for the occasion, Jill Kaiser smiles to impress and at the same time to relax herself. If asked, she'll say she feels like a switchblade in a nasty fantasy in which she slices to ribbons the lot of them propped like wax museum figures around that boardroom table. She won't be asked and she takes pleasure in knowing this. Such gorillas and dinosaurs they are. Still, MBA in hand, her inner cop also knows she can work for them and once in, she'll work even harder for her own selfish aims.

The stares come, the appraising of her figure as if she's a mannequin, a polite show of lust dreaded yet prepared for. Jill at the far end of the table hasn't fully caught her questioner's name. She thinks it Kirk, but had trouble hearing because there is traffic below the room's open windows. She'd been told Ben would be conducting the interview. Apparently, plans have changed. Her inner cop asks if this is a test. If so, it's unseemly but appropriate and nothing she can't handle. She'll just avoid addressing any of them by first name.

Jill hears her mother telling her long ago, "In that world among those troglodytes, make sure your breath is clean. But more than anything, it's posture that counts."

Seated now, Jill eases a breath mint between her teeth and then offers to share. Each man refuses kindly. Well, it isn't as if they haven't already reviewed her file. She lets her cop speak slowly, assuming that her experience for a woman her age isn't unusual. It's not her gender that matters here. Nor her cunning. It's her will to power.

One of them, a Dave, says, "Your CV is interesting, Ms. Kaiser, but really, why should we hire you?"

At least Dave called her *Ms.* Hope springs eternal, but Jill feels herself melting inside as she slides down an imaginary chute into chlorinated water and a tale unfolds, all of it true as she expounds on some of the legal moves she made to increase her last company's bottom line. She doesn't mention the employee layoffs or the reductions in salaries or the encouraged early retirements. There's no reason to, since these simians know only too well about the bloodletting required to remain profitable in an increasingly competitive market.

Nor does she speak of Inez Garcia. That would be too personal. Inez, an immigration attorney, is the one. Some of these men must have an understanding of what it means to be happy in love and Jill hungers to share this, but at the same time her cop knows it's wise to hold back. This is business, though a tiny insecure part of her wants to boast that she and Inez have just celebrated the anniversary of their fifth year together.

If she were a man, such an admission would be interpreted as showing character and commitment. Inez had told her, "Don't go there. Remember, those cutthroats know an iron pony when they see one. Show them your soul and they'll crush you. You're made of Teflon and brass tacks. That's what they're looking for."

This, she thinks, is what's required at the moment: a healthy dose of Inez's cold persistence. At 85-grand a year she'll be starting with more than at her last position, though that salary had grown slightly. And that, they all know, is why she jumped ship. Her salary with this company will grow, as well, significantly and more rapidly, without any ceiling other than the proverbial glass one.

Her life with Inez will never be the same. If all goes well, it might mean a home away from the city in a tony burb. An expense account. Plenty of new shoes and clothes. Enough certainly for restaurant meals, but forget about weekend excursions. They'll both be too busy.

What she really wants, but what her cop won't allow her to express, is to feel pride over not only chasing a dream but achieving it. Not her mother's dream. Never hers. Her mother had likened Jill to Uma Thurman's character in the *Kill Bill* movies, saying, "If that's what you want to do, chop them all up with your mighty Ginsu, then go for it. Just leave me to my gardening and don't you even think of voting Republican."

Opposites, that's what they'd become. Not that Jill had done poorly by any standards as a girl raised by a stoner lush hippie who'd done little with her Liberal Arts diploma except work as an assistant manager for an organic food co-op while more than once admitting that she wasn't really sure which of her lovers was Jill's Daddy.

Redemptive transformation is possible, isn't it? One has to believe first. This, Jill thinks, remains her affliction. For too long, craving her mother's acceptance, she'd bought into her secular anti-establishment cant. She hadn't believed. Inez, a pious Catholic, was helping her accept that it wasn't too late to start.

She hears her cop talking, but what she imagines across fields of dream snow under glass is how she hiked as a girl from point to point, tested and seeking to orient her path through blizzards with only a tampon and the glass of water she kept at her bedside table throughout childhood. These stodgy mercenaries know nothing of what she's lived through. Her cop asks: Why should they? It isn't as if they'd care even if they knew. Nobody cares. Find your own God or drug or habit. The flame under one's own frying pan is the only heat that matters.

"Do you consider yourself a team player?" This is from Jim. He appears harmless, doughy. Jill admires him because he doesn't smile, though she knows she could mop him up in his own drool if necessary. She suspects he knows this too. His simmering look of disdain, at least, is honest, though utterly ridiculous. On first glance, he'd undressed her and threw her on a bed in a Daisy Chain on the edge of town.

The others just sit gathering cobwebs. What kind of story would they and Jim like to hear? Of course, she plays as part of a team, especially when the team needs her. Should she relate to Jim how she used to hunt with Mother for psilocybin mushrooms on state-protected woodlands? How they'd rest and smoke a joint together while seated on stone outcroppings covered with moss? Jim would be horrified by such yarns, but he might be led to understand that such time together had helped Jill learn the differences a mother and daughter could define themselves by.

How profoundly she and her mother, Queen Patchouli of the Tie-dye, had connected in those days. They'd come to an understanding that they'd never really comprehend each other. To her credit, Mother is still trying. Still getting high to the Grateful Dead after all these years. On Facebook too much for her own good and forever bickering about its connections to Russian spies. Yet she accepted Inez. Loves Inez in her own way, as she loves her Jill.

Next comes a question regarding whether Jill can endure the amount of travel this position demands. So many corporate accounts. Growth in Singapore and Dubai. This is from the only black man in the room. His name is Herb and he wears a bowtie and bears a resemblance to the actor, Morgan Freeman. Jill likes him, feels she can work with him. Still, she doesn't smile when she remarks that travel is one of the appealing elements of the job.

Now, who is this Cliff character with the horsy bicuspids asking about her home life? Only a Dad and a churchgoer would ask such a question. She could work with such a Dad, but she'd have to force herself to stomach his insufferably square morality. Not a problem. She was becoming a believer, after all. Sadly, such men don't live their jobs, putting family first, and because of this they're usually the first to get axed during layoffs.

Jill shrugs at Cliff, showing an indifference which startles him. He'd expected total obeisance. Her cop face makes it clear: No, Cliff, sorry. Not from *this* girl believer. Doesn't he understand that a woman cannot miss what never existed for her, that the fear of missing out is another form of entitlement?

Her cop could have been more forthcoming and detailed about her hobbies, but like many of her generation Jill really doesn't have any. She won't dare use the phrase "side hustles." Nor will she delve into the notion of home in the traditional sense as a ball of sticky ramen she finds difficult to unseat from inside her craw. She lived in a trailer park for a while, back when Mom's coke habit nearly destroyed her. She'll say one thing in defense of her mother. The woman knows how to pull back in order to survive.

"If we take you on, you will be welcomed here." This is Kirk speaking. All listen as they're supposed to, enraptured. "We encourage those who see their job as a mission."

Albeit frightening, Kirk's honesty is real. He knows the worst any of them can do is to lie. They're all so closed. Each day at the office will mean another new form of darkness. But her position isn't about honesty. Not yet anyway. It's about money, status, power and the potential for more money. Make the company richer. Inez had been so right when she'd said the bitch in her had to murder the cop, find traction and start bulldozing obsolete naive versions of herself. "This is what believers do," she'd said. "They take an eye for an eye. Without guilt."

They're all believers. All men. So what? Jill doesn't even vaguely have to be interested in any of them. She's not. She'll act as one of their colleagues. She'll let them be avuncular if they so desire. She'll learn from and use them, but she will not sleep with any of them. Each of their foreheads will act as the rung of a ladder. She'll outlast them too.

Just control me, she thinks. Bring on the manacles. What they don't yet understand, but what makes her perfect for this job is that she can't stomach the thought of freedom.

Her cop helps her gin up a radiant smile and share it with them, one at a time, finding it easy to move from one to the other in an appropriately paced manner. She feels their sexual hunger and their heavy contempt and their doubt and she loves it all. This is how men operate. They have to be conquered, shown up, impressed. Otherwise, she doesn't matter to them.

She can be as much a male beast as any of them and she feels a flutter of gratification when Kirk's leer, ever so false and manipulative, beams her way. Naughty Kirk didn't get to the top by accident. He'll be the first to try probing into her panties. No problem there. She'll shut him down and make it clear just how damaging to him, and how profitable for her, any harassment lawsuit can be. Me Too helped bake this into the pie. Not that Kirk doesn't realize this. He isn't stupid, not hardly, but he's still a man.

Jill begins to feel herself overheating into one of the flash-dreams she often has when under stress. In this one, she hears herself confessing that she knew she was a lesbian at the age of 12 when she'd get wet while poring over Wonder Woman comic books. She uncrosses and then crosses her legs. They all notice as if on cue. Do they like what they see? They should. Years of gym workouts have not been a waste of time. But look, Boys, don't even think you can touch.

How on earth can such a large corporate enterprise not have a single woman among their executives? Stone-age, all of them. She should just walk out. Maybe her mother had also been right about there not being a point to any of this lust for achievement. Just wear sandals and stretch pants and start her own cupcake bakery near a beach somewhere. Lots of other content and accomplished women had done it.

Herb appears impressed and maybe feels some comforting identification with her as a minority. He wants to know what Jill will "bring" to the company. She's done her homework on the company's plans to expand into India and she'd even prepared a longwinded reply to this question, one designed to highlight her achievements.

Jill's inner cop doesn't bother with any of it. She sees in Herb suffrage, an endurance and a candidness that she respects. She won't bore him with lessons she's learned. She tells Herb and the others very little. Let them guess and feel intrigued. This job, like all others, will become eventually a routine, another step, an exercise in forming relationships.

Her cop is right. She doesn't need to explain. Herb, she can sense, has enough gaydar to grasp how she rolls. Herb probably understands only too well that every pig in the sty isn't that interesting if they're all the same. Those who intrigue come across as just a tad different. In the name of generous sincerity, she doesn't want Herb to accept her. She's no victim, or oppressed, or deserving of sympathy. She believes Herb wouldn't want to be thought of this way either.

"I'm not your equal," says Jill's cop. "I'm not less than any of you either. I'm not only teachable, I'm ruthless. It's not that I like to win. It's that I despise losing."

Not all of this is macho cop bluster. What she's done correctly is to avoid telling them anything about her real feelings, and how to run their operation. She's shown the correct posture too. Ever so erect, so rigid. Near phallic. What's that old song? *It's a man's world.* Lying isn't the only method but often the most expedient one, but one can't lie to professional liars. If she accepts this job, she'll be their puppet. They're all puppets, but there's dignity in knowing this.

She spots dampness starting to shine on Puppet Master Kirk's lips. It's decided; she has the job. Kirk's easy to see through. He'll teach her and boast that he likes "different" and "her fresh energy." As Inez had said, "Just let them think they run you. Don't make the leash harder on you than it has to be. You can always say no. And you always have me to come home to."

Does she? She hopes so, but maybe Inez is a little too fond of her own confidence.

Jill hears her cop again, that mighty sheriff with her shield who begins to tell the Boys she's grateful for this opportunity. She knows her cop will have to accept a steady fade from any contract with freedom. Amen, Sister Cop. Freedom is exhausting. Just say yes to fourteen-hour work days, seven days a week, keeping pace with the heartless monotony and the robots and monomaniacs that characterize "business as usual."

She wants her cop to say she believes that with dutiful effort and consistency that Jill Kaiser will transcend past definitions of limits and grow beyond them to help this new company, this new parent, thrive. Her cop doesn't express any of this. Such insipid optimism is beneath her. Instead, shield high, she dishes out inspired looks of guileless enthusiasm. She has to show these boy cops that, in her thirties and young enough to be nearly a daughter to some of them, she can spin and cajole with the best of them. She still exudes a restless longing to cast off the burdens of liberty. So be it. This is why their prison is a perfect fit.

An awkward silence. Taboo in an interview usually, but not this time. Jill likes how they continue to gawk and maybe want her to cross and uncross her legs again. Kirk, that mustache of sweat still pearly on his upper lip, leans over the table and thanks her for coming.

She pushes her breasts forward. Any obsessive bondage to a desire defines what most people view as the road to success. She wants to be flogged on that road and sent to bed whining. Next up is her monogrammed ball and chain. She can taste the heartburn already.

Again out with her breasts, in time with her deep breathing, only this time while standing and with a stony look at Kirk to let him know once more it will never pay to dare even ask for a taste. They'll be a team. She'll slay them with her deceitful kindness to get each day a little more of what she already has.

It's done. Out the door she breezes, knowing she'll never, not for a nanosecond, be her mother. She'll heed the cop and her army of ninjas within, no matter how ugly their deeds, and race toward the flames until she can't race any longer.

A restaurant awaits at the nearest street corner. Not a long walk. She strides in and sits up straight at the bar, her posture perfect. She orders a Caesar salad and a dry martini and tells the bartender to keep them coming. She and her cop will have what they need.

The Meatloaf Sighting

Eyes closed, head back, Yogi Mungeon rinses shampoo from his hair, so much steam in the shower making it impossible to see. The coaches and most players have gone, a few are getting dressed. Not usually one of the laggards, Yogi plans to be gone in a hurry, too much homework, but he doesn't see one much larger teammate sneak up from behind, reach around Yogi's pelvis and flick his middle finger one time, really hard, snapping it against Yogi's penis, forcing Yogi to buckle and gasp, doubling over, grabbing his privates, protecting them, shampoo burning his eyes.

Tractor again. Friggin' Tractor.

The showers keep running and steam keeps blooming. Yogi doesn't swing. He knows; he fears. Trac's sadistic impulses make him a titan on the playing field. But Yogi won't back down. Nobody's gonna call him a pussy and see him give in to Tractor. Regaining his breath, standing straighter, he shouts "Just cut it, Trac, will ya?"

Leering, Tractor sounds his trademark laugh. A sniveling cackle. He bears down on Yogi, his damp flesh scarlet and his shoulders gleaming through the steam. Someone chucks a towel with a *splat* against tiled walls. Two other players, Hart Hartigan and Grant Toma, both soaped up, appear behind Trac. Hart sounds off first. "C'mon Mungeon, nobody talks to Trac that way."

"Team captain," says Grant. "Bust your stupid head wide open."

Cory Baker's face emerges from steam. "Yeah Mungeon, didn't you hear? Trac got into Tech with a full boat. That's a D-One school. He's a frickin' god."

Tractor, still leering, starts using the shower head raining down next to Yogi's. He kneads the foaming shampoo already in his long brown hair that snakes like kelp seaweed down over his collarbone. "You heard it here, Dipshit," says Tractor.

Yogi wants to spit in his face. Trac's a skilled mechanic, a welder, a town hero, team captain, but he'll only leave Rebar if he's in a coffin. If he's lucky and doesn't end up in prison, he'll take over his father's garage.

"Just leave me alone," shouts Yogi.

Tractor mimics Yogi, repeating "leave me alone" twice and topping it off with a girlish whine that stirs Grant, Cory and Hart into laughter.

Just my stupidity, thinks Yogi. Usually be gone by now. And I got this exam tomorrow. Chemistry. Periodic tables. This is what *they* never see, the coaches and teachers and fans. The men in town who gather at the home end-zone for each game and cheer the team on. They don't love Trac. They worship him. Rebar's finest. Idiots, all of them.

Stone-faced as he showers, Yogi tells himself he'll wait Tractor out. Tractor can burn bright like a road flare, but Yogi suspects that Tractor will eventually grow bored and restless. Rather than fizzle, he'll play the heat-seeking missile and lust after another target.

For the past two years Yogi's played football and he's had nightmares of Tractor's hissing cackling face. Why doesn't he quit? No, he won't. That would be giving in. He's a fighter and those nightmares he has, he knows he shares them with many of the other average-sized kids at Rebar High. It's mostly the few black and Latino teammates that Tractor leaves alone. He's shrewd that way, knows how to avoid any racist angles, picks on those who he figures can't or, like Yogi, won't defend themselves. Those others, they don't show fear of Tractor in school hallways when they see him coming. Tractor shows them respect, his fists hooked out as if ready to swing, his hair scraggly, his eyes darting from side to side as if searching for prey. Maybe those others fear him, but if they do, they mask it and they don't engage.

Survival by avoidance, thinks Yogi. Sticking to their own, staying in their clique. It's the white kids, especially underclassmen like him, that have to stay on constant alert whether on the field when coaches aren't looking, or in halls between classes or in this shower room full of steam under low caged lights. Derek Tractor Trachtenberg, team captain, gets written about in the local newspaper, gets his way with them, playing God.

Yogi won't have it. He closes his eyes to better absorb soothing hot water that streams down his back. This is what he should focus on. He rubs more soap under his arms. Imagines Tetracycline Tractor's face as he's seen it in nightmares, as pink as an Easter ham. In one repeated nightmare, Tractor's glaring, inches away, his cheeks scarred by white-headed zits. They're horrid craters, the largest ones broken, weeping, having healed imperfectly. That acne defines Tractor's ugliness, within and without, thinks Yogi, even though Tractor's been blessed with a physique like that of a Roman statue.

Open their eyes, gouge them out, thinks Yogi. Open my own. Gouge them out too.

Having rinsed his hair and under his arms, Yogi watches as Tractor, now in the middle of the shower room, flicks both his wrists and prances while changing his voice to sound effeminate. "I'm Yogi Mungeon, part bird, queer-bait and part douchebag."

Tractor cackles at his own performance much to the delight of the others, who also cackle and Yogi thinks they're like so many hens, nothing but feathers without each other as the shower heads hiss down, steam spreading to cloud Tractor from Yogi's view, though Yogi can feel his presence and he clinches his anus, each muscle in his body knowing there's more to come, but he can't run, he won't, he's no coward, they'd just chase after him anyway and make it worse.

A bar of soap strikes Yogi in the side of the head. Yogi lashes out, swinging one fist, striking only air. Who threw that?

Hart's voice shouts out of the steam: "Just try it, Mungeon."

Hart cackles and Tractor cackles with him and their cackles become wolf howls as they start to grow fur and bare their fangs and blindside each other and bark and howl in a frenzy of shoves, Hart getting the worst of it and landing with a thud against a tiled wall. More cackles and howls and teeth shining brighter and louder and same old crap, thinks Yogi, ignore them, get out, won't get to bed until after midnight, history homework, chemistry exam, no top-tier school will give him a scholarship, he'll have to earn it and he'll show these goons and pissants one day; he'll get treated like an equal and peons like them will work for him and then he'll have the last sniveling cackle and howl while he brays at the moon.

Scalding water hits Yogi's head and he shouts, scalp burning, his face a sudden vivid pink. Lunging for the shower knob, he shuts it off with one turn and leaping away, shouts, "Who did that?"

More cackles and howls swelling around him as Yogi curses and stumbles away from steam and all their wet stinking flesh into the cooler dry air of the locker room. Yet the others follow and snap their towels at his buttocks and thighs, leaving crimson welts that sting, one snapped towel striking his scrotum from behind, forcing Yogi to plunge forward, gagging, absorbing the pain, arousing more howls and cackles.

Tractor, towel in hand, now facing Yogi, blocks his way. "What? You think you could get away from us? Think again, Yogi."

Tractor sounds a swinish snort. He strikes Yogi in the forehead, one stiff thrusting jab with a clenched fist, his knuckles striking skin an inch above Yogi's right eye. A sneaky and practiced maneuver arousing whoops and jeers as Yogi, blinded a moment, arms flailing, lurches toward his locker and falls over the wooden bench bolted to the floor in front of it, can't see them, but he can hear their taunts.

"Useless…dipshit…douchebag…."

Blocking his ears, dropping naked to the cold enameled wooden bench, Yogi bends over and fighting off head spins, locks his arms around his calves, hears the towels as they keep snapping and stinging against his back. His flesh prickles, still wet, the air growing colder. Why do they do this? Coach said he was improving, made some solid plays in practice, but he shouldn't whine, not now, not ever. Nobody likes a whiner. Then why does he feel himself falling deeper into a void, wanting to whine and shout and cry until the laughter and the towel snapping stops.

Silence blooms. Yogi can see himself falling into a soft and forgiving pool of darkness. He looks up and sees that the locker room is empty. What time is it? Did he hear them leave? Did he black out? Clenching and unclenching both fists, Yogi thinks: Animals, won't get near him again, no one will.

So quiet now. Why doesn't he just quit? What's he trying to prove?

Wood shop. Tractor spends most of his day there. A lot of dangerous equipment. He could club Trac from behind with a hammer and then shove him forward into the table saw, turn it on and with its blade whining at full speed push Trac's body into it, cutting his face vertically into two chunks, sending serious blood everywhere like in a slasher flic, do it all in front of everyone, make them witness a crime they'd never forget.

Why do they all love Tractor? Don't they see? Don't they know anything?

Yogi slips into his jeans. He's standing barefoot with socks in one hand when a janitor pushing a mop bucket into the locker room approaches. The old black janitor, Mr. Stubbens, a familiar face around school, looks lumpy and tired in a blue shirt, kinked hair gone silver, face shiny with pearls of sweat, a ring of keys jangling from his belt.

"Son, you still here? You know what time it is?" Mr. Stubbens scowls at Yogi. "This ain't no night school. Go on home now. I got cleaning to do."

The wan light in the locker room expands and shrinks and all is soundless. Mr. Stubbens, scowling, leaning on his mop handle. Yogi staring at him. Mr. Stubbens staring back at Yogi.

"What is it, Son? You got something to say?"

Yogi shakes his head no and hurries to get his socks on, doesn't bother tying his shoes.

"I fucking hate this place," he mutters.

"Join the club," says Mr. Stubbens.

Yogi grabs his coat and gym bag. Slams shut his locker, spinning the lock. "I'll blow it up."

"Don't be saying that, Son. Them are strong words. Can't meet poison with poison."

"Yeah I can," says Yogi. "I'll be on TV. National coverage. Fame."

Yogi stares at the old black man. His face curls like a sheet of paper in flames.

—⁓—

In Rebar's White Marsh Mall that Saturday afternoon, Ronald Mungeon took a second glance until certain of it. His sternum collapsed as he blew out a mournful sigh and dodged his youngest son, Justin, who was running in a circle around him, pushing at his older brother Yogi, who kept swinging at him, causing Justin to swing back and curse and create a ruckus for passing shoppers. Ronald dodged his sons. Unruly, sure enough and nothing new, but he had a larger issue to address. He couldn't believe it. He looked again. The original Bat Out of Hell was not only in front of him in the Hardware section, he was seated and looking rather nervous on a green *John Deere* riding mower.

Ronald was gawking at the rock star Meatloaf, in jeans and a denim shirt, his hair still long but graying. A young salesman was assuring Meatloaf he could drive and control the machine with ease. It was clear to Ronald, painfully so, that this tyke of a salesman had no clue regarding the identity of his customer.

Now wasn't this a soft form of misery, thought Ronald. It aroused heartburn that bubbled into his throat, forcing him to remain still and modulate his breathing while his boys still cursed and slapped at and pulled each other's hair and swung roundhouse punches at each other, calling attention to their behavior, though Ronald appeared as if unaware of it. He felt like he'd fallen into a hole, remembering the late-night cruises in his old Dodge and the make-out sessions he'd enjoyed with different girls on different nights, with only one constant, music, and one song in particular "Paradise By The Dashboard Light" playing on a cassette through the speaker system that was once his pride and joy.

Ronald remembered the many midnight showings he'd attended while drunk and stoned and in costume with his rowdy friends, shouting "Not meatloaf again" whenever the man appeared on screen as Eddie in *Rocky Horror Picture Show*.

Salad days, indeed, and now this titan of operatic teen angst and a monument within the landscape of Ronald's personal iconography was sitting a stone's throw from him and testing a machine that would cut the grass around his estate home. Didn't such a rock star have dozens of minions and serfs to manage such prosaic duties for him? Ronald was sure that he did. If so, then Ronald had to like this about Meatloaf. In spite of his fame and wealth, he was still a regular guy.

It wasn't the mighty who had fallen. It was Ronald Mungeon, just another faceless middle-aged white male, an accountant out shopping with his two hyper-rambunctious boys. Feeling battered and flabby, Ronald realized he had to sit. He felt light-headed. He hadn't shaved that morning, so he scratched at his five o'clock shadow and asked himself why on a Saturday he felt so tired. He always felt tired, didn't he?

Time to round up the boys. Where had they gone? No wonder it had gotten so quiet so sudden. He went after them, moving out of Hardware, out of that store altogether and into the mall, finding and directing the boys, shoving them along, telling them "Cut the crap" as he nudged them toward a shoe store where the clerk was dressed like a basketball referee. He told the boys to look for what they needed. He'd be right with them. He needed to sit for a moment. He had a headache.

No, it couldn't have been Meatloaf. Then again, Rebar had seen an increase in property values, and maybe his wife had been right about them moving to such an appealing zip code. It was possible that they were achieving some social mobility, he supposed. And in the right direction. Was it a sign of some kind? When was the last time he'd even listened to a Meatloaf song? He heard them on the radio and in stores now and then, but it had been years since he'd last taken the time just to listen to music of any kind, in any format, from his past. Why was this so? Perhaps because it made it easier for him to forget memories of nights on dirt roads when a new album or cassette had been added to his collection and a rock ballad on the radio kept him connected to what was deemed "the song" to keep him "cool" and "in the loop" with his friends, to keep his fervidly carnal predilections charged and actualized.

How had he grown so dumpy and old? Was he really the model for Homer Simpson and Peter Griffin and all those other white male father cartoons who were characterized as imbecilic? It seemed that no matter what he believed, or how decently he tried to live, he would be hated because he was white and a male. The trendsetters probably hated Meatloaf too, for the same reason. When had it all become about hate and division? Had it started with his generation? Perhaps so. Well, Ronald Mungeon didn't hate anyone. He and Meatloaf had aged together, and they were as far out of the loop and uncool as anyone could be — was there something wrong with that? Ronald didn't think so.

He had his two sons to raise. One more year and Yogi would have to start thinking about college. He'd played well Friday night on the football field, but he didn't seem to like football or his coaches or teammates. He'd come home after the game, pouting, no parties with the others, just straight to bed complaining he was sore. Well, things were tough at his age, changing fast. At least Yogi had come home after the game, hadn't stayed out all night getting into trouble.

Ronald had Rhea too, his wife of nearly twenty-two years, and he wouldn't dare reduce her to a cartoonish stereotype. They had a marriage that was working. Like all marriages, it was an ongoing project. Their sons were in decent public schools. Rhea had a secure job as an administrative assistant. Even though she had to work on Saturdays, it offered better insurance than his job did. They went to church each Sunday and afterwards visited her parents. Ronald's parents had passed on before their sons had been born.

Had it been so wrong to make such a simple honest life? If not, then why did he feel this guilt bubbling up, as if he'd chosen unwisely? What to tell Rhea, the boys? He decided to keep quiet. His sons linked meatloaf to ketchup, not high-school sex. They didn't link cars or Daddy to rapturous acts of connubial bliss, conception, and excessively strident pop music. Nor did they view time as a thief who sneaks into one's routine and exposes how much a faded picture in a wobbly frame a whole chapter in one's life has become.

How deranged, once, his idealism. How hungry he'd been for change. Where had that Ronald Mungeon disappeared to? How much had he missed out on? Too much. Was it too late? Probably, but too late for what? He was locked in. His life was no longer about him. He had sons to feed — they ate like draft horses — and in-laws with ailing health to worry about. He'd never dreamed he'd spend so many Saturdays shopping for sneakers and underwear and electronic gadgets he wasn't even sure boys his age were ready for.

The important questions now were about reliable dentists, long division, the Periodic Table, ways to get them home from their after-school activities. The question of his identity — who *he'd* become, who he was now — these he thought of as luxuries. At a certain point, one must answer all questions on one's own, and boy did it feel lonely and difficult, but that's what it meant to be an adult. It explained why so much of the culture around him felt so trapped in adolescent concerns. Kids weren't kids anymore. They were the targets of marketing campaigns.

Therefore, he had to do it. And fast. He just had to know for sure.

Ronald glanced at the shoe store and saw that his boys were still there, enthralled with all those sneakers they'd never own, though they appeared to be arguing, and he saw that they were pushing each other, and Justin had swung a vicious right hook at Yogi, who'd dodged it. Well, boys will be boys. He had to know. Just had to. So he hurried back toward the big anchor store and its Hardware section, pleased to see that Meatloaf was still there and in what looked like a deep discussion over perhaps the *John Deere's* motor or any warranty.

Ronald tried not to stare, but it meant everything to be certain. He felt a sense of thrill, a relief, that he had not imagined a resemblance. This was the man who represented what Ronald's past had become. Essentially, tawdry concerns for keeping grass mowed, garbage put out, taxes paid on time. This was how dull life could be. For the first time, Ronald heard himself think that it would be merciful to die. He'd heard the thought so clearly that it had shocked him to the point of staggering a moment while gawking. A clerk, a young black man, stirred him and asked if he needed anything. Ronald offered an embarrassed, "No thanks, just looking."

Rhea. The girl he'd mounted in his Dodge more than any of the others, so many late nights on deserted roads, Meatloaf crooning at full volume, "Two Out Of Three Ain't Bad."

He wouldn't tell Rhea. She disliked feeling and accepting her age even more than he did.

A message in this had been aimed at him. He should embrace it, consider if there was any value in how far he'd come — not how far back he went.

Did his sons realize he adored them? It remained hard to say. It was a constantly messy process with them and it would never end, not until Ronald Mungeon was one with those nocturnal creatures Meatloaf's tunes had long ago stirred out of his imagination.

Ronald stood there still dazed. He watched as Meatloaf nodded, getting his questions answered. Cost, maintenance, how long such an expensive machine could be expected to last.

One of his sons appeared, Justin, both his hands covering his face, blood running between his fingers and down his arms and over the front of his T-shirt. He was whining and shrieking, "Daddy, Daddy, Daddy…."

"What the hell?" Ronald grabbed his son by the shoulders. "What happened? Let me see your face. Where's your brother?"

Lowering Justin's arms, Ronald took a close look at the boy's face, streaked with blood, his nose still bleeding and swollen now and plum-colored, Justin wailing, "Yogi broke my nose, he broke my nose."

Then Yogi arrived as if he'd been summoned by the accusation and was eager to admit it. He stood there, sneering, his thumbs hooked into the belt loops of his jeans, one knee bent out, muttering, "You'll live, you big crybaby."

"Shut up, you," shouted Ronald. Without any restraint, he sounded an oversized moan. "I ought to break your God-damned nose."

"Go ahead and try," said Yogi.

"I have to pee," cried Justin.

"Then go pee," shouted Yogi. "And wipe yourself off. I didn't break your stupid nose."

"Yes you did," shouted Justin.

"Stop it, both of you." Ronald, overwhelmed by a sudden flush of anger, grabbed them both by the arms. He squeezed tightly. He shook them. Then he paused and looked at them. They were both on the cusp of becoming teens more miserable than they already were, and oh Christ, they had so far to go.

Merciful or not, did he, their father, really seek death? Had his own father experienced such moments? Of course he had, but the adult in the room didn't discuss such things.

Leaning over, Ronald told himself: cope with it. He brought his two boys together, gripping each one tightly under an arm. He was still large and strong enough to demand control and get it. "Let's get you cleaned up. Now," he said to Justin. Then he turned to Yogi, "And as for you, I'll deal with you later. Just what the hell has got into you lately?"

As he led them out of the store, he saw himself as guiding them away from his past, his era, his memories to coddle on his own time. How fortunate he was to have a past, at all. To have secrets, failures and successes and yet in the present under the surface where it really mattered, he had what his own late father had called "the basics," all he'd ever wanted.

Glass Nails Shower Back Into The Sea

THREE DORIES BOBBED IN place, framing three sides of a square net. Made of heavy aluminum pointed at both tips, they were called dories rather than longboats because they acted as cubs to their mother vessel, the 72-foot steel hag, *Iron Jane.* Low in the water and stinking of diesel, *Iron Jane* lolled and creaked alongside the fourth margin of the net and cast a moving shadow that cloaked half of one dory in darkness. Bald tires hung against her glossy green hull like a bracelet of black washers.

The men in each dory continued to pull. With the ebbing of chaotic waves the net began to rise. They stood elbow to elbow, from six to ten in a group, pulling with all their might. With every rising swell, the sea splashed their faces, shining against the bibs of their oilskins. When the Atlantic dipped, so did each dory. As more of the net was sucked under, the men released it, fearing the loss of fingers. The horizon didn't care. It sizzled white-hot under the sun.

As they started to see the catch, exclamations "Squid, yeah, squid," fired off between them. Finally, thought Vic, the effort pays off.

You ready? Is anybody?

Vic thought a moment.

No. But at least I know it and that tells me I'm making progress.

Vic watched seagulls perched in a line on *Iron Jane's* rail. Some circled in a noisy collective overhead. Though he preferred his full name, everyone called him Vic. This frustration I understood, since I was named Paul Peter Coyne, after two apostles, but Pee Wee had stuck in grammar school. I'd been massive compared to my schoolmates and as I aged, I got tired of painful associations to my adolescence. I'd assumed one day that I'd grow into being addressed as Paul, but this never happened.

Vic remembered how I'd told him all this. He was easy to talk to, didn't say much.

He watched the net begin to curve over the edge of each dory, taking the shape of a bowl. High up the bow of *Iron Jane,* it gleamed like a spider web. Just a few feet from Vic's hands, a shapeless cloud of squid and fish fogged hissing green water. The pinkish cloud expanded with each inch of the net's ascent. Breaking the water's surface, it shined with a glassy radiance. A shark fin cleaved through its surface. Vic with Pat Degnan next to him continued to eye it.

Mitch McSherry stood behind them. Scarlet-cheeked, fists on hips, green eyes flinty, Mitch was part barbed wire and mostly straight razor. Hair barbered to a coppery shine, his neck creased and sun-scorched, he wore a scowl of disapproval that defined his attitude toward life. He wore his jeans and a blue T-shirt so tightly that they looked painted to his frame. He was the only one out there not wearing oilskins. He kept a pack of cigarettes rolled atop one shoulder into one sleeve. A fillet knife in a leather sheath was fixed to his belt. His jeans were tucked into his black rubber boots. Standard gear, the boots ran up to his knees. All the men wore them.

"Harden 'em up. Let's go. Harden 'em up." Each shout came barked in a clipped cadence, a harsh local accent that flattened all R's. "Harden 'em up. Let's go."

Vic sneaked a glance over his shoulder, took a long look at Mitch's face. Wet, crimson and shining veins swelled in his neck. One blue vein gleamed down the middle of Mitch's forehead.

"What you gawking it, Silva? Turn around. Don't lean. Don't bend over. Bend with your knees and pull with your legs. C'mon, get it in gear."

Vic turned back toward the net. So much of his job meant balance and putting up with surprises like having Mitch as foreman in his dory. Vic assumed Mitch did it because he got bored standing in Sonny's shadow on the *Iron Jane* away from the action.

"You peckerheads! Together for Christ's sake. Harden 'em up. Let's go."

Mitch wouldn't back off. He clapped his hands, keeping to a rhythm while he shouted, "Harden 'em up. Let's go. Making progress. Harden 'em up…."

As the net emerged black and dripping, so did the gleaming fish inside it. Mitch had moved from the winch to the dory's tip that sat lowest in the water. He leaned over to study surges, bubbles and swirls of surface foam. Bottle-green one moment, black the next, the sea was a book Mitch could read. It fizzed in places like spilled sparkling wine marked by tiny frothing fissures and erratic whirlpools. When it darkened it looked like a polished onyx.

If the sea meant anything, thought Vic, it meant life was a show of violent change.

"What you see?" asked Pat Degnan. "See much?"

Mitch, ignoring Pat's question, scowled at him. He stood straight and waved one arm to get Sonny's attention.

Sonny stood at his usual perch at *Iron Jane's* bow, high above his dories and net, overseeing the operation. Bowlegged, gimpy, Napoleonic, the puffy swells under his brown eyes proved he hadn't been sleeping well. His face was a sun-washed map of cuts and boils, his hair a wild tangle of silver shot through with black. His flannel shirt was tattered, tails out, roomy enough to sleep in. Did he like what he saw? Never. Not Sonny. The years had made his body lumpish and he needed Thorazine to withstand a nagging back injury, but he gave off an aura of pained endurance and a tired solidity of purpose that went unquestioned.

—∞—

Baggy trousers tucked into black rubber boots, Sonny lurched along *Iron Jane's* rail, his gait reluctant, low-slung, as if unpredictable winds pushed him along. A cigarette behind his ear, he stopped a moment and rested elbows on the rail. He rubbed his jaw as he surveyed the dories. They formed a wobbling frame upon the water.

To him, thought Vic, we must look puny.

Sonny scratched and fingered the stubble of a two-day beard, mumbling vague expressions of doubt. As usual, he lacked experienced manpower. Many of his boys were unfamiliar greenhorns. Others, more seasoned, hadn't shown up as promised, forcing him to take what he was given — ex-cons, drifters, dope-smoking die-hards with hangovers, and baby-faced boys free for the summer and wet behind the ears. Some wouldn't come back the following day. Some would get so drunk that night they'd end up in jail.

A few would come back. Very few. The desperate ones. Sonny always needed reliable help. He'd make a place for any kid who didn't mind hard work. The pay was $50 per day cash and some days ran twelve hours long.

Iron Jane steamed off Bowen's Wharf each morning at 5:30. Vic could work seven days or take a day off when needed. Working for Sonny meant learning the ropes, making contacts. If Vic showed mettle, he might earn a chance to crew off-shore with a lobster, a scallop or a swordfish boat. Nothing was guaranteed.

Some guys had connections. Vic and Pat Degnan had me. I'd staked my name on them. That's how I know these intimate details. I'd started as a trap-fisherman when I was sixteen and I spent so much time at sea that while on land I had either a cot at the Seaman's Institute, a room in a boarding house lousy with winos and Newport carpetbaggers, or else I used Vic as a come-and-go roommate and stayed at his place in Bristol. Vic was generous with me. I had my own key and could park my red Volkswagen *Rabbit* in his driveway. I had to cram myself into that car but I loved it.

"What you seeing?" shouted Sonny. "Squid?"

"Up the wazoo," cried Mitch. "Like I told you. Means you owe me a hundred bucks. We're gonna have to bail."

Pat looked at Vic. "How can he tell?"

"Why now you want to talk?" said Vic. "When we shouldn't."

"So?"

"He's Mitch," shouted Vic. "He knows everything."

"Damn right I do," said Mitch. "And don't you morons forget it."

Leaning over the dory's edge, Pat took a closer look. He flinched as he heard "Shark!" from another dory.

Vic flinched, too. He saw the fin. He muttered, "Big sucker."

"Great white?" asked Pat.

Mitch cackled. "Forget the shark you guys. We got work to do."

Vic never asked me for rent money. I bought the beer, but he always offered to chip in. I wouldn't let him. Lobstering off-shore meant I was pulling in three-grand a week. Never had time to spend it. I didn't want an address, a conformist life. Stormy Weather was my registered name in the phone book. I worked hard and partied hard and liked crashing in Vic's tiny extra room with its sloped mustard-colored walls. Two such rooms made the whole of Vic's apartment. I liked that Vic got the gist that a meal ticket was nothing to sneeze at.

They're gonna be long brutal days, Vic. They never get easier. Gotta get used to that.

Vic held on and pulled the net but kept a wary eye on the shark fin. The bundled net at his feet, once a coil, had become a tangled blob. He eyed that, too, making sure his boots stayed on top without any net choking his ankles.

Loud, smelling of hot oil, the winches sputtered like lawn mowers at one end of each dory. They powered a shiny metal spool that revolved slowly. Each spool pulled a bright yellow line that was attached to the net in the water. These lines, made of a lacquered blend of polypropylene and hemp, were fixed to the net at various seam ends. They inched slowly out of the deep, littered with leafy rags of dripping seaweed. Waist-high, taut, they ran length-wise end to end down the middle of each dory, tied to over a ton of fish underwater and inside the net.

Vic stood motionless, alert, cautious in front of the yellow line, seeing it as the barrier, saw blade and danger it could be. The key in such a situation was economy of motion. Avoid jerky movements. He remembered what I'd told him about keeping his feet spread apart.

Yet he was tempted, as always, to touch the line as if he were a boy seeing flame for the first time. He didn't. He kept his hands limp at his sides. Played a game with himself and liked that he could do this. It allowed his hands to throb a while. He found it impossible to use neoprene gloves when pulling the net out of the water. The glove's fingers were too bulky for the net's small holes and didn't help him get a grip. No matter how calloused his fingers got, the net and salt water still scorched his hands and forced them to swell.

Within the net, a slow boil began to grow louder. Trapped fish slashed seawater as more of them came in contact with the air.

The shark moved closer at a steady clip.

Trappin' is one of the oldest forms of commercial fishing still practiced. It's a proving ground. Just go out there and pull up nets. Don't even think about tomorrow.

But then what?

But then nothing, Vic. A man measures his worth not by other men, or what women expect from him, but by the excellence he demands from himself. My old man used to tell me this all the time. Maybe he wasn't original, but he lived what he preached and I understand him now that I'm older and he's long gone.

Yeah, Pee Wee, I follow. You know, even my mother said she was proud I was working as a fisherman. But I don't why.

Tradition. The Portuguese are known as some of the best fishermen in the world. Think about it, Vic, you could still be washing dishes. Where's the tradition in that?

"Huge!" Pat was shouting at Vic. "Look at that thing."

Vic looked at Pat, refusing to show the fear he felt in his stomach. He saw that Pat was leaning over the water, trying to grab the fin. He saw Cliff Larch moving from the far end of the dory. Cliff was skinny, a rash of pimples across his forehead. He stood close enough to Pat to push him overboard if he wanted to.

Vic lunged toward Pat. "Hey, don't lean out like that. You nuts?"

The dory rocked. The shark had nosed under and nudged it, throwing them all off balance. Vic saw Cliff nudge Pat. Perhaps on purpose and perhaps not. Vic would never be able to say. He didn't have time; he widened his legs and did all he could to keep his balance.

Pat didn't. He paddled the air as he fell.

Vic reached and latched on to one suspender strap of Pat's oilskins. This slowed Pat's descent, didn't stop him. Gasping, flailing his arms, Pat keeled toward water. Vic tried to yank him back, holding on, grabbing Pat's oilskins with both hands, bending his knees, keeping his rear low, his weight underneath him. Waves slapped into Vic's neck, salt stinging his lips as he grunted, clenching his jaw. His elbows burned as he held on, falling with Pat's dropping weight.

A wave lifted the dory and threw Pat and Vic backward. Vic

felt no resistance. His stomach flip-flopped. All grew silent for a moment. He felt as if soaring in a dream.

The dream ended when Vic gagged and the crotch of his oilskins rode up his scrotum. He thought he'd vomit as the pain in his testicles sent a cold ripple racing through his stomach. Saltwater continued to burn his eyes.

It was Mitch who'd grabbed and yanked Vic backward. He'd grabbed Pat, too. Timed it with a wave that had lifted the dory away from the shark, saving both his underlings from spilling overboard.

Cliff, tight-lipped, had done nothing to help. He'd stepped aside to let Vic and Pat's slapstick routine play itself out.

The splashing of the sea, the flatulent sputter of the winches and the caws of the gulls returned to Vic's senses. Pain sharpened, fired another bolt through him and a cold sweat came on. Dizziness. He gagged again and fought off wrenching urges to vomit. This was comedy all right — he, Pat and Mitch soaked, ridiculous, panting and dazed.

Coarse laughter swelled, pierced by shouts and curses. Mitch, poker-faced, popped to his feet and shoved Vic aside. Slapping wet hands against wet jeans, he leered at those who'd been watching. He spit saltwater off his lips. Then he flipped them his middle finger.

All the men jeered at him and laughed.

"Very funny." Mitch cursed them, using one profane label after another, fueling laughter that grew louder when Mitch, after yanking Pat to his feet, cuffed him against the ear. "What I say about leaning over? This ain't pin-the-tail-on-the-donkey out here."

The barrage of Mitch's curses continued as Pat sulked, struggling to regain his breath.

Panting, Vic tried to make sense of what had happened. He blurted out to Pat, "You crazy, man? You hurt? What you do that for?"

"He ain't hurt," shouted Mitch. He turned to Pat. "Are you?"

Pat looked cowed, moon-eyed, unable to meet Mitch's glare. His ribcage heaving, he shook his head no.

"Just shocked," said Mitch. "Christ, Degnan, get with the program. You owe Silva here a cold one for saving your ass. And Silva you owe me one for saving yours. Back to work now, both of you. You're making me out like a clown."

Sonny shouted, "Hey Mitch, tell them boys they want a shark, the nearest aquarium's in Mystic."

Laughter erupted again at Sonny's comment. Big G, a foreman in one of the dories, used both hands to slap his stomach, sounding a bellow that Vic hated at that moment, hating them all, but he had to admit he'd have acted the same way if not involved. They were bastards, wouldn't cut him any slack for trying to save Pat. Then again, Mitch had saved him and Mitch was royalty and they were laughing at him, too.

Nobody got kid-glove treatment.

Vic decided not to wallow in self-pity or think about whether Cliff Larch had nudged Pat. He felt sorry for Pat, but sorrier for Mitch, all the egg covering his face since he was Sonny's right-hand man and owned a share of the company.

Vic clenched his teeth, squinted and fought off the heated pulsing throughout his body. Nobody cared how loudly he might curse. How miserable he felt. If only he could unwind a moment with a cigarette, find some calm, let this pulsing subside. He returned to his standing position with his hands in the net. Vomiting would feel good, rid him of nausea, but there was no way he'd humiliate himself further. Had to get his wind back, stand his ground, ignore the pain.

He should pay attention to someone else, so Vic sneaked a glance at Pat and managed the suggestion of a rueful grin. He studied Pat with what Loren described as his soulful eyes. Big like ponds, she'd said.

So fresh-faced with his pug nose, shrill blue eyes and messy curls of sand-colored hair, Pat had a sweetly clownish look about him and tended to grin when nervous. But Pat didn't even look back at him.

"You good?" Vic asked. "You gonna make it?"

Lips puffy, his face a pink pout shiny with seawater, Pat began to speak. He stopped. He stared at Vic as if begging for a way out of this misery. The dory rocked back and forth. Vic lacked an answer for Pat. The kid had no idea that Cliff might have bumped him on purpose.

Hey Pat, can I tell you something? Loren's got a bun in the oven. I found out last night.

Vic looked up from the net. Across roughly 30 yards of sea, there stood barrel-shaped Big G. Full name: Gunther Wolf. His dory looked as if it might flip over. White-haired with a high pink complexion, he pumped his arms in an effort to maintain his balance. His crew, about eight in all, most of them smaller and all younger men, did the same.

Like monkeys scratching the air, thought Vic. He spit in disgust.

Why would anyone want to bring a kid into this world?

I dunno, Pee Wee. It just happened.

Big G's dory looked more and more as if it would spill its men overboard.

Spittle flew off Big G's lips. "Sonny, we got to drop it!"

Sonny tried to shout with force. His words sounded puny. "Leave it, G. Don't drop it. Just leave it."

"But Sonny," crowed Big G. "Could capsize."

Woody Holly, another barrel-shaped foreman, cupped his hands around his mouth. Feet planted wide to maintain balance, he sounded scared as he cried, "G, what the hell is going on over there?"

Sonny was waving his arms, shouting at Big G. "No, no, no."

"Keep winching it up!"

This shout had come from Mitch. Vic had once heard a green-horn ask Mitch his position in the management structure. Mitch had told him: Just to the right-hand-side of God, the Devil and the shit-hole they both take a dump in.

Mitch added a fiery, "C'mon you guys, get a fuckin' clue."

"Listen to Mitch," shouted Sonny. "Keep them winches running."

Sonny's order answered all questions.

The shark fin continued to cleave and skitter. Trapped fish continued to gasp and splash. Overhead, a handful of gulls cawed in a flurry of commotion. One of them dropped a turd on to Vic's head. Insult to injury, Vic thought. He didn't bother to wipe it off. He'd let it dry there and wash it away after he got home.

Mitch, standing at the winch, had seen this happen. Stone-faced, he shouted, "That's about the size of it, ain't it, Silva?"

Pat brightened and shouted at Mitch, "That's good luck, right?"

"Might as well be," said Mitch.

Pleased Pat had spoken, Vic faced him and said, "Yeah, but it's for both of us, not just me, so no more shark diving."

Pat didn't reply. He looked away to where the shark fin sliced water along the jagged edge of *Iron Jane's* shadow.

She never said so, Pee Wee, but I don't think Loren wanted to get pregnant.

So what's your point?

Is it a mistake or God's will and what should I do?

You love her?

Not sure.

About time you got sure, ain't it?

He had neither time nor energy for all the darkness clouding his head. Was he a failure? They all were. The sea assured them of it. With a shrug in Pat's direction, feeling disappointed with himself, Vic kept both hands on the net and continued to pull. He felt momentum at last, helped by the labor of each winch.

As the dory tilted and the taut yellow winch line grazed his back, Vic felt uncomfortable with the net at his feet. All part of a dangerous job, but he didn't believe he'd be doing it for long. The Dekka scallop boats were up from the Carolinas. Or else he'd crew on a lobster boat six days a week, so far out he wouldn't see land. Maybe a swordfish boat. Nice dreams, but he shouldn't forget that able-bodied hands outnumbered commercial boats working out of Newport by at least ten to one. The odds were tough, even for hands with experience.

Vic paused a moment. So many diehards with experience wanted trips: sons, cousins, nephews of skippers. He couldn't let that stop him. Had to be patient, keep working. If he went all in with Loren, it meant a child, it meant pulling harder, getting fish into port, money into his pockets.

The net cut deeper into his hands. The Atlantic rose like a tilting glass table, the net and his dory rose with it. He felt a moment of weightlessness and hurried to get ahead, keep more net out of water and into the bundled slack under his boots. No time to hesitate.

He looked up. The shark fin had disappeared within *Iron Jane's* shadow. Colors had begun to emerge: pink, orange, silver, gold, chrome yellow, scarlet, emerald, and the spangled scales of fish that swarmed as they battled. They were a rainbow of blades of all sizes gone berserk upon touching the air. The fish flung their bodies, squiggling and lancing, some of them glittering as they snapped and spanked the water, zigzagging in desperate surges.

Old wild days were over. He had to start planning. He — not God — had neglected to use protection. It was meant to be. Sure, sometimes, the whole thing pissed him off. Other times, he believed in the happiness he felt with Loren. He had to think clearly, keep *making* his life.

Veins swelled in his neck. A small piercing headache throbbed behind his eyes. During the night, he'd sucked down a six-pack of beers alone. He'd phoned Loren, hadn't told her much. Couldn't remember what they'd talked about.

Vic looked across water and watched greenhorns under Big G's command still struggling to right their dory. They'd made progress. They moved as if doped, pawing the air.

He knew the fear he saw in their faces. It was how he felt whenever he couldn't roll with waves, give his body over to them, both feet planted, no matter the punishment he took. If he avoided injuries, he could fish maybe ten years. For now, what he earned per week — it would never be enough to raise a kid on.

He looked at Pat, who just couldn't focus on the work. Pat's head was bent back and he was gawking at the gulls veering through long rays of sunlight.

"Head down," said Vic. "Mitch sees you gawking like that, he'll chuck you overboard."

Pat shrugged and kept his head bent back as if he didn't care.

Loren's hot, man. Way to go. You should marry her.

Pat is not my problem, thought Vic. He looked again at Big G's dory. Finally, the men were balanced. The sea was calming down. He felt a wave of nausea due to the fumes from the winches that kept fouling the air. Their sputtering remained constant and intrusive.

Yet the winches had started to make a difference. The net was moving. Vic felt a sudden queasiness, a touch of elation, a bubble of air rising in his stomach.

Here's my advice. Push doubts aside, stay sharp, keep your head clear, do the right thing.

He watched Big G line his men up elbow to elbow. Having done this, he waved at Sonny. Mitch saw this. He whistled between two fingers to help Big G get Sonny's attention. Sonny shouted for the men to start pulling again.

As he pulled, Vic didn't feel his arms and legs. Oddly enough, he liked this numbness. He trusted it and it brought the comforting promise of a second wind.

What kind of life could he offer Loren?

A drop of sweat hung at the tip of his nose. Rivers of sweat rained down his sides. He heard his own heavy breathing — nothing more.

He'd planted a seed. A piece of him inside of her. A person.

I know what you're thinking, Vic. Don't run. You're no coward. Do what's right.

His heart beating fast, Vic ran his forearm across his face, salty sweat in his eyes.

You got what it takes.

He sucked in draughts of air, kept pulling, blocking out the noise, finding a deep silence within himself. The winches continued sputtering. The bailer appeared. Like a giant butterfly net, it hung from its stays over *Iron Jane's* side.

Glenn Lesley and Shrimpy Keefe manned the bailer's long boom from *Iron Jane's* deck. They dipped her net in a scooping motion through the fish. Shrimpy Keefe controlled a sliding mechanism on the handle that opened and closed the net. Glenn made sure the boom hung high enough so the net would pass unobstructed over the deck.

The bailer's rising net released a gleaming excess of water that sounded like glass nails showering back into the sea. A few lucky fish fell away, curling and twisting as they smacked against waves. All eyes watched as the bailer soared through the air above *Iron Jane*, bulging with fish that shined as they flapped and spit.

Swoosh. It opened. Fish spilled from its bottom, flesh spanking flesh, some bouncing with a thud against the deck.

"Harden 'em up." Mitch sounded fatigued but persistent. He didn't look at his crewmen. An inward cast hardened the crimson in his face. "Let's go. Harden 'em up."

Vic sneaked a glance at Cliff. The bastard was guilty, but it wasn't Vic's problem. It was Pat's. Vic glanced at Pat, who was making noises now like a wounded animal, mumbling under his breath, snorting through his nose.

Mitch had been right. Pat owed him, but now wasn't the time.

With each dip of the bailer, the net felt lighter and rose with less effort. Each foreman managed his winch, making sure the yellow line fed evenly as it wrapped around its spool.

A cry went up. "There goes the shark!"

Vic watched it as he kept pulling. A sign of humiliation, danger, a prehistoric predator. Got to respect it, thought Vic. Yet out of the water, the shark looked small. Its hide was the color of wet clay, its white underside pearly inside the bailer net. Small or not, it was still the largest he'd ever seen up-close.

"I was right." Mitch spat. "Some kind of nurse shark, I think. Not exactly sure, but either way it's harmless."

The bailer lifted the shark over the deck, but this time Glenn didn't release it. Instead, he and Shrimpy swung the net to the far side of *Iron Jane* where they opened it and dropped the shark out of sight.

All heard its splash.

"So much for Jaws," crowed Big G. This aroused a chuckle from a few men.

Mitch snickered as he studied Pat. "See, Degnan. Nothing to it. Now keep focused. You too, Silva."

Pat in silence stared straight ahead and kept pulling. Vic did the same.

Mitch turned to Cliff. "You with us here?"

Cliff, icy and stiff, nodded twice.

"Better be," said Mitch.

Vic felt less queasy, needed to stretch his fingers and work out cramps. The pulling had slowed. They were all too tired. When would it end? As Mitch had predicted, the net was loaded with squid. *Iron Jane's* deck held a mountain of fish and she creaked over-burdened and deep in the water. Maybe half of the net had been emptied. The other half would have to wait until tomorrow.

A new slice in Vic's palm began to sting. He flicked his hand back and forth. A small wound was the worst kind. It would annoy him for days. He thought of the sorting to come, every fish to be culled and boxed on ice. For that work, each man could wear gloves but would still need mobility in both hands. The cut would sting, filled with sweat and fish blood. If he wasn't careful, he'd get iodine poisoning.

How did the others do it? They didn't dwell on the pain; they ignored it and it went away. Vic knew he could do this. He'd put this wound out of mind until another took its place. Sure his body ached, but he couldn't complain. They were all hurting. The hurt in Pat had to be monstrous because it was dingy with shame.

Yet he'd saved Pat. Mitch had saved him. That meant they worked as a team. Had to count for something in Sonny's eyes. From another point of view, they'd provided comic relief. Yeah, eventually, had to count for something.

"Hey Pat," said Vic. "So what if they laughed. Screw 'em."

Vic waited for Pat's reply. Nothing came. Pat didn't even look at him.

A clot of resentment burned in Vic as he glanced at Cliff. In the future, if possible, he'd avoid working with him in the same dory.

Still, for all his aches, Vic saw he was in pretty good shape, more upright than many others. When the winches finally stopped running, Vic saw the greenhorns who'd acted so tough on the wharf before work had begun. They stood bent over in each dory, sucking wind, their arms dangling.

Hardly any of the men were talking and it was late now, almost seven a.m.

Anomie Among Arrivistes

FOR A FEW YEARS in my early twenties I played on a softball team, ate fresh fish and chips and drank pints of stout every Friday night in the bunghole named Gideon's Ordinary that sponsored us. Yet I'd never met anyone named Gideon until fifteen years later when, in my thirties, I joined the Peace Corps to serve in Moldova at the end of the Cold War.

Whenever I think of *my* Gideon, last name Dudley, I think of someone shouting into the void, "But I have my rights!"

He was a stocky, edgy guy from Nebraska, who the few times I'd seen him had been unshaven with ratty auburn hair and equally ratty jeans. With his leather boots and guitar, he looked like a one-man sixties-era protest movement. He exuded an overheated longing to both save the world and tell it to go to hell at the same time.

Gideon was often in the company of a less tendentious ginger-haired Ohioan named Kurt Brinkman. Kurt had earned his Bachelor's in History from the Ohio State University. I wasn't a native of the Buckeye State, but I'd earned my Master's from OSU in Columbus. Kurt was from the hamlet of Marion, home to America's 29th President, Warren Gamaliel Harding. Like Gideon in that he was earnestly bespectacled at all times, Kurt didn't talk corn dogs or cow tipping. He and Gideon spoke furtively, off to the side, as if sharing trade secrets about Schopenhauer, Spengler and visits to the

Chicago Art Institute. I took a liking to them as a pair of eccentrics, but neither was in an hurry to call me a friend.

I suppose I liked speaking with Kurt because he was versed in history and not afraid to sound educated and he'd shared a longer tolerant view in his conversations with me about Stalinism. Talking with him brought me back to more innocent student days.

Gideon was a different story. A powder keg, I first met him while we were both seated on the floor in the airport at Frankfurt. Like the rest of us volunteers that day, he looked worn out from the layover, sitting with his Ibanez guitar and waiting for his big adventure to start. Seeing that I'd been eyeing his guitar, he spoke in a condescending way, as if he already knew the answer to his question, and asked me if I played. I told him no, but that I liked music. I asked him if he'd play something for me. He wasn't flattered by this request. He made it clear — not by explaining but rather by sneering at me — that he was in the heat of inspiration and writing a song and that I shouldn't disturb him. He waved a few sheets of paper on which he'd scribbled some lyrics and asked me since I didn't play guitar, why the hell he should play for me.

Whenever I get such a flippant answer from a stranger it tells me that the stranger is insecure, opinionated. I think of the Italian word, *superbia*, for the first deadly sin of pride. Perhaps Gideon was too proud of his outsider status, his college diploma, his plans. One of those quasi working-class heroes who shows the anger of a frustrated menial, but who hasn't worked beyond the chores he did while growing up. Perhaps Gideon was raised in tough conditions on a farm. I didn't know. He'd made it clear he thought me a boorish elitist Catholic from the East and so what if I'd gone to grad school at a mid-western university. He wanted nothing to do with me.

When we arrived to Moldova, after being treated to a generous welcoming ceremony, we left the airport in Chisinau in three new mini-vans. I was seated next to Gideon as I noted in my journal to write an essay, one day, about that welcoming ceremony, and that I should call it Bread And Salt. As I kept recalling and jotting details about the ceremony, Gideon, as if annoyed, kept asking our supervisor Craig, who sat in the front seat next to Igor, our Moldovan driver, how it was possible that we were being transported in German-made mini-vans when, as volunteers, we were supposed to be living in the same poor way as the locals. "I thought this was the Peace Corps, not Club Med," he remarked sourly.

Craig joked, sounding equally as sour, that Gideon could walk if he cared to. Gideon didn't laugh. He just scowled and stewed. I thought, for a moment, that he was going to slap my notebook out of my hand.

Softening a bit, Craig then looked over his shoulder at us all and explained that the newly appointed American ambassador had made sure we had these vans at our disposal. The American embassy was still being built. The ambassador had only been in this new republic for a month. The official American presence, as such, was in its infancy. The less that went wrong at the outset, the better.

For my part, I was relieved to be riding in those mini vans. I put my journal notebook away. It appeared the others felt the same way and they voiced this relief, telling Gideon to enjoy it because he'd be walking or taking public transportation for at least the next two years. One of the rules of our service was that we wouldn't be able to drive in-country. Not that a car would be easy to find. The entire region was short on fuel of any kind. Then it made sense to me. Such a large city felt so deserted because there were so few cars in it. Hardly any. No buses or trolley cars either. From what I'd read about the situation, I'd learned that the so-called Russian mafia, along with the Chechens, were trafficking lucratively in gasoline. Jerry cans of World War II vintage were worth their weight in gold. This was all

I knew at the time, thanks to minimal research, but I didn't really believe it. How in 1992 could a country not have cars and gasoline?

Gideon didn't stop grousing. "I still don't think we should be riding in them."

Craig remained composed, explaining that the vans were for embassy staff, many of whom were arriving at the same time we were, along with US AID employees, but since we were part of a government program, we were allowed to use them to get us from the airport to the hostel. It was protocol. They wanted to assure we arrived on time and safely.

Each mini-van was driven by a native Moldovan. This was a well-paid gig for them. Apparently, none of the three Moldovan drivers could agree on how to get to the dormitory where we would be based for the initial stages of our summer training program. We had to pass three months of training and all the exams that it entailed before we would be assigned individually to our towns, cities or villages.

The drivers stopped all three vans in the city center, not far from Pushkin Park, and got out. Craig and the other American administrative chaperones left us seated in the vans where, in June, it was hot and dry and we sweated, roasting, exhausted after a 17-hour flight that had begun in Philadelphia after our week-long staging there, first leg to DC, second one to Frankfurt for an all-day layover, and the final leg to Chisinau where our Air Moldova plane had been the only one on a busted-up strip of tarmac.

We watched as the drivers gathered under a shade tree and bickered in that mix of Romanian and Russian that Moldovans often use, trying to decide how best to get us to our destination. I thought to myself: who hired these drivers that don't even know their way around their own city? Must have been an operative in DC who'd merely looked over a list of names and checked off a few. It was my first of many lessons regarding how inefficiently government agencies functioned at times.

It was frustrating to sit and wait, but I accepted this phlegmatically as part of any long transit from home to a new destination. I'd traveled enough to know that the only way to behave in such situations is patiently and without expectations. Gideon, on the other hand, was having no part of it. *Superbia*, again. He twitched and carped, "What's taking them so long?" He literally began seething as he ran both his hands up his moist forehead, thinning out the already weak line of his widow's peaks. He wanted out of that van. Didn't we all?

A bit swinish, runty, corn-fed and scarlet in the face, Gideon was too loud for such a small space, I thought. He didn't ask, he *told* me to come on and join him. "Enough of this shit, let's go find a bar," he said, as if we were old drinking buddies.

I shook my head no. Wasn't interested. Didn't speak the language. A bar? For Pete's sakes, man, this was the former USSR. A truce had been declared, but the war that allegedly ended just months ago was still happening in the Trans-Dniester region. For decades, comrades had been risking their lives to escape to the West from these climes. There was a reason Churchill called it the Iron Curtain. Hadn't Gideon heard the line about how this was the land one could always get into, but good luck getting out.

"You'd rather bake inside this box?" he asked. Another sneer. "Fine. Suit yourself."

There were eight of us in the van. As I looked around at my fellow volunteers, all of them in their twenties, I saw baffled and pasty faces dirty with dried sweat, pouty young lips that assured me this wasn't the dazzling and exotic challenge any one of them had expected.

Gideon Dudley must have seen the same. He asked another fellow from South Carolina by the name of Evan if he'd join him. Evan, tall with a pronounced Adam's apple, had an endearing innocence about him. He looked at me for support and I offered my answer, a resounding, "No, I don't think Evan's going anywhere."

"No I'm not," said Evan in his fine accent. "Sorry, Gideon. Just can't do it."

One of the other passengers, someone I'd yet to meet, helped Evan out by saying, "Nobody's going anywhere."

Gideon didn't like hearing this. As a man, he'd been placed on this planet to explore and discover, to rebel and realize his entitlements to liberty, and so he protested that we were in the middle of the capital city, for crying out loud, what was wrong with us? Let's get out, see the sights, and party. Let's find an oasis and have a few drinks. He was sick to death of all this waiting and being carted around like cattle.

It occurred to me then that Gideon's face was going up in flames, more scarlet than ever with his idea of getting, as he put it, "Shit-faced" on his first night there. He kept sweating profusely. Still seated next to him, I could smell the b.o. from his clothes. I decided to shut down. Pride was a sin. If others wanted to join Gideon on his Bacchanal, let them. I wasn't there for such reasons. I'd need some time to define what kind of a mission, if any, I was on. This was not a chance to party. Volunteer or not, it was still a government job.

Feeling both awestruck and disgusted, I watched Gideon slide open the van door, making very little noise as he hopped out. His answer to one last voice of protest from behind me, begging him to come back, was a simple one. He flipped us all his middle finger. Then he ambled off down the avenue, away from and unseen by the arguing drivers and chaperones.

He'd left all his belongings in the van. "He's screwed," said one of the girls.

Most of us shrugged. Another girl remarked, "What an idiot."

Someone else said, "I guess he's only here once and he's going to make the best of it."

This was Kurt. I asked him why he hadn't joined Gideon. "I want to," he said in his restrained Mid-Western way, "but it just doesn't feel right."

"You can say that again," I quipped. "Feels all wrong. Big mistake."

"We'll see," said Kurt. "I think he's got a good point about the vans."

None of us wanted to hear it. Nor did we want any discussion. I told Kurt in a shamefully solicitous way that he was a smart man, even though I hated myself as I said it. I then took the time to intro-duce myself to the others on the van, since I hadn't met most of them either at Philadelphia, the Frankfurt airport or on the plane. That was when I learned Kurt and I shared the Ohio connection.

What struck me as eerie while we sizzled in that van, was how silent and deserted downtown Chisinau appeared. Every door closed and locked. An old city. Dusty narrow streets with wires for trolley cars overhead but not a trolley car in sight. Sun-faded sand-colored buildings that were from the 19th century, built of chunky stone with rounded edges. Dusty-rose trim around the windows, a slouching pink quality to the light. I felt an oppressively heavy wind-tossed dustiness, as I was sinking into the earth to blend with what little I could see of one main avenue, not a whiff of anything new or vibrant in the air. Everything so still.

There wasn't one pedestrian out on the sidewalks that lined both sides of the wide avenue we were parked on. If this was a city of one million people, where were they? The air felt pregnant with doom and foreboding. The hour held an end-of-the-world aban-doned feeling. Something wasn't right. Something bad, I thought, was about to happen. I'd just arrived. I might have been crazy to have volunteered, but I wasn't stupid enough to go looking for trouble when I felt a powerful premonition that trouble would find me.

Craig, looking sweaty and tired, returned with Igor to the van. His black hair was pasted to his forehead under a wool tam that he alone must have thought looked hip. As Igor drove us off, Craig took a head count. When he asked where Gideon was, we told him he'd taken off. This made Craig furious and he yelled at us that we should have stopped him. What was wrong with us? Why had we let him go? Why hadn't we come to him with this?

Myself and another male in the group were about to speak to Craig — perhaps to tell him to shove it and to take off his pretentious *Rastafari* lid — when one of the girls bailed us out, saying that Gideon had been out of control, that we'd all been a little scared. None of us had known what to do or to say, and Gideon had basically told us to piss off. He'd also left his belongings behind.

Craig, livid, started muttering under his breath, but after so much debate with three drivers who spoke limited English, he couldn't afford the time or energy to hunt down Gideon. Igor kept his eyes straight ahead as we rolled down the avenue, deserted, nothing in sight, in search of a dorm which, apparently, had neither a name, a number or a sign.

We'd be training all summer to learn the Romanian language and the Moldovan culture. We'd do some monitored teaching, as well. To his credit, Craig didn't single anyone out or lay blame, but he looked so disappointed in us, as if we'd betrayed him. I would never forgive him for this. Nor would I forgive that he and the other administrators were never reprimanded for leaving three van loads of newcomers to blister in the sun because they hadn't worked out travel directions in advance with their drivers. Besides, we'd only known Craig for the amount of time we'd been in transit. He'd joined us in DC when we'd arrived from Philadelphia.

Frazzled and angry, Craig let his true emotions break out. He slammed the dashboard, shouting, "What a God-damned stupid thing to do."

He turned to face us, taking full-on the responsibility of his job and not mincing his words. "Listen to me. All of you. This is a foreign country we're in. They've just had a civil war. They're still fighting it. We've been invited here by a government that's no more than a year old. No Americans to speak of have been here for the past seventy years. Maybe more. Don't you people get that? Seventy years."

Of course, we got that, but we were hungry and in need of rest. Gideon had acted on his own.

Nobody said a word to Craig. I didn't know what he'd expected. He just glared at us and then gave up, turning around to slam the dashboard once more.

Three days later, around two in the morning, I sat up in my dorm room cot when I heard Craig talking. He slept next door to me. His resonant voice carried and he was shouting at Gideon, who also had a healthy pair of lungs. So, Gideon had been found and he'd returned. He and Craig were going at it. Craig was calling him out for his lack of discipline, foresight and accountability. This wasn't a vacation. He repeated the words "this is unacceptable" many times.

I didn't have to eavesdrop. The conversation passed with ease through thin walls. I lay on my cot and listened to Gideon shout that he hadn't done anything wrong. It was the other guy's fault. Craig then repeatedly asked Gideon to apologize and to explain what he was going to do to make amends. Gideon declared he had nothing to apologize for, that he'd broken no rules, and that they — the Moldovan policemen who had arrested him and thrown him in jail — were the ones who should apologize.

When I heard Gideon shout, "I have my rights" I knew the

Nebraskan with the Ibanez was finished with Uncle Sam's Peace Corps in Moldova.

The two men kept arguing and I listened until Craig, at last, calmed down enough to ask Gideon to start from the beginning and explain everything. He would have to write a report. He'd have to submit it to the government. Didn't Gideon understand how sensitive an issue this was?

Gideon did his best to relate what happened. He'd left the van alone and he'd met a man from Scotland who was a traveler and looking for a fun time. They'd become fast friends. They'd gone on the hunt for a bar and they'd found an old woman on the street with a bottle of Russian vodka for sale at an exorbitant price, and they'd made friends with the old woman until two Russian guys appeared, both of them young and a little sly but friendly and determined to show the Scotsman and the American a grand old time with a lot of cheap vodka and, sure, they knew where to find it.

They'd gotten blind drunk and they were howling out in the street at four in the morning when a man approached them and said he was a cop. The Scotsman in his drunken fury, displaying his own form of *superbia,* said no bleeding way he was a cop and threatened to fight him. The two Russians scooted off down an alley, leaving Gideon and the Scotsman with the alleged cop, and the Scotsman swung first — that was the crux of Gideon's anger, as he insisted *he* was innocent because all he'd done was watch — and before he knew it there were three other cops and they had a little car and they had guns and handcuffs and they'd arrested Gideon and the Scotsman and drove them off to a prison building and slammed the prison door behind them. There they'd sat for two days to rot and to sleep off their hangovers with nothing to eat until someone from the American embassy had tracked them down and shown up to negotiate Gideon's release. The British didn't have an embassy there yet (very few countries did), so the ornery Scotsman had been left behind to fend for himself.

Craig, having heard this story perhaps one too many times, said, "Okay. I get it. But let me make this clear to you, Gideon. You are going to have to apologize to the entire group in person, and to the drivers, and to the other chaperone administrators, and to the Moldovan language teachers. This is a government program we're running here. We're being watched very closely. We have to make an impression. A proper one. This is not the time for you or anyone else to go on a bender with some drunken madman."

Gideon would also have to pen a written apology to the ambassador and staff at the American embassy. He'd have to write out his version of the story for inclusion with Craig's official report. He'd then have to sign it. Next he'd have to meet with the program administrators and convince them he should stay in the country to work as a volunteer.

I could imagine Gideon sneering as he continued to insist his rights were being violated and he'd done nothing wrong. That drinking was not against the law. That the fighting had been instigated by the Scotsman and was his fault.

"I never swung a fist. I never yelled at those cops. It was that Scotsman."

"So you won't apologize?" asked Craig. He sounded shocked by Gideon's intransigence.

"I have my rights," said Gideon.

"But you're here as an employee of the US government. There are expectations."

"I'm not apologizing, no way. I didn't do anything wrong."

The battery on my watch had stopped working. It was around 2:45 a.m. and all this drama was just underway. Craig was losing patience. He'd given Gideon his ultimatum. Either make the public apology and be subjected to a review, or else be sent home on the next plane out.

Gideon made it easy on Craig. "Fuck it. I'm out of here. I came here to help people. Not be some government pawn. You don't know what the hell you're talking about. Fuck you and fuck this program."

Gideon slammed Craig's door on his way out. I learned later that everyone heard it.

Gideon's punishment was to stay exiled in a room on the top floor of the dormitory, at the far end and away from all contact with the rest of us. If anyone wanted to visit him, we were welcome to, but Gideon's meals would be taken to him while we were in classes and he would be watched around the clock. The expectation was that his plane would be flying out the next day, and he'd be on it.

Sadly, there was no jet fuel. Air Moldova wasn't really yet officially an airline. It was seven days before the next plane leaving Chisinau airport for Germany could be booked. This was simply how things were going in those early days at the end of the Cold War.

The summer heat was intolerable and no one wanted to spend any time indoors at the dorm other than to take a frigid rinse in a communal shower on the mornings there was water, which were rare. Or try to sleep while fighting off mosquitoes as the humid night air settled in. I spent as much time as possible outdoors, even late at night, having found a broken park bench on some packed dirt behind the dorm where I sat alone with my flashlight and studied notes I'd taken during my Romanian lessons. The only thing I feared were the wild dogs that would occasionally wander through. I never saw any people there after dark.

When I thought about Gideon, the lawless outsider in a strange land, I began to understand that the hardest lesson for many participants in the experiment called a democracy is to learn they have only one right — to behave decently and hope for a skilled attorney. Otherwise, lots of luck, Bro, when you step out of line. If I learned anything in high school, it was that justice and fairness are for dreamers.

Still, I felt badly. Some part of Gideon had ventured overseas to realize an impulse and a dream to make the world a better place. He'd already been wound up tightly, and I struggled to imagine what shape he was in, maybe furiously writing song lyrics as he stewed for over a week, forced into exile in a tiny, smelly room with his guitar, his anger and remorse.

Only Kurt went to see him. Kurt felt such pity that one morning he stood up in our language class and reminded us all that Gideon was still with us, still waiting for his flight, and that he wouldn't mind some company. "We owe it to him," said Kurt. "I think it would show solidarity if we all went up to visit with him. He really didn't do anything wrong."

Dead silence. Call it fear or the psychology of the group, but Gideon was viewed as poison. True, if his side of the story was to be believed, he hadn't done anything wrong, per se, but his pride had led him to make a regrettable choice. Nobody except Kurt wanted anything to do with him.

The day after Gideon left, Kurt stopped talking to us. I tried to remain kind to him, but Kurt blamed everyone else except Gideon for Gideon's behavior and its consequences. I was seen as one more of the oppressors. Gideon's opinions and paranoia were now Kurt's. In his mind, they (meaning us fellow volunteers) were not interested in freedom. We were elitist government pawns willing to not only exercise but to preach American imperialism. Kurt lasted two more days before meeting privately with Craig, and Dolores Grape (our nanny-like supervising administrator for training) to explain that he wanted to go home.

He, too, would have a long wait, but a flight would be arranged.

Another ten days passed and Kurt appeared more and more

hollow and aloof and by that time there were two other volunteers who also wanted to go home, but for different reasons. One of them was the only other volunteer in her thirties, a woman from Indiana who Craig touted as having the best resume among us all. Evidently, she'd found her true reason for serving overseas. She'd met a young Moldovan and he'd seen a green card and she'd seen the husband she'd been after. By the end of that summer, our group would be half the size it had been upon our arrival.

The day before Kurt left, he held a yard sale in his room, putting all the goods he'd brought with him on his cot and charging steep prices for items that his blind anger wouldn't allow him to give away. Such is the nature of thwarted idealism, I suppose. It doesn't leave room for generosity. Kurt would have the last word and he'd profit by it. He made no small talk with me about Ohio winters or football games. I looked over his belongings and tried unsuccessfully to barter for lower prices. He wouldn't budge. I paid him a $20 bill for a hardcover Riverside complete works of Shakespeare, and a few more American dollars for two other novels in paperback, a handful of D and double A batteries, and a roll of toilet paper. Others paid even higher prices in dollars for clothing items, music, a portable cd player, a radio, pens, flashlights, matches and various teaching supplies.

Kurt wasn't grateful for the cash. He'd soaked us, taking revenge in his understated yet venal way. Nowadays, when on occasion I think of those two, I'm reminded of a quotation by Eric Hoffer from his essay, *Brotherhood:* "It is easier to love humanity as a whole than to love one's neighbor."

If I feel sorry for Gideon and Kurt, and sometimes I do, it's because *superbia* has sometimes gotten the best of me too, but they were so naïve, so pitifully idealistic. Who really has any rights? For what it's worth, wherever they are, I can only hope they've grown to understand this.

One-Handed Egg

Teixeira — we never dared call him Tex — labored with me as a line cook in the kitchen of a large cafeteria. Ernie was the name we gave him because it was easier than Teixeira when we needed to shout to get his attention. He was part of a shift team with me and a hard-working slender Mexican named Miguel and a muscular black guy, Dayvon Bones, and two beefier urchins who'd both done prison time, one named Tomaso, and the other we called Spider. We were led by our myopic boss, Alfonso Four-Eyes Alameda, who was always squinting and misplacing the keys to his office. Four Eyes never really lost them. One of us would just hide them for kicks whenever he put them down on a countertop and walked away.

Boss Four Eyes was fond of Ernie. I mean, they were like brothers, and Four Eyes would have me in stitches, standing there with his coke-bottle glasses on and spouting his frustrations at Ernie in Portuguese, starting with, "*Ay-koo-deesh* Ernie, what am I *ah-gonna* do with you?"

My job was my life then. In a lot of ways, it still is. I rented a one-room cell in a boarding house named after a former president. The Polk Arms it was called, with a bathroom at the end of the hall. My neighbor was a gay appliance salesman, William, never Bill, who worked at the old Sears that once anchored the nearby mall. It's gone now. So is William. He died of AIDS when that particular pandemic was going down. I liked William, even though more than once I had to tell him to turn down his music. I'd open his door without knocking to find him jumping on his bed and sweating through air guitar sessions to Queen at full volume. I'm telling you, it's true, I can't make this up. Anyway, my needs were met. The problem was that I believed there had to be more and I didn't know what I had to do to get it. Not really. Had no clue.

Ernie often gave me advice. I was a patient listener and he liked that about me. Some of his advice was to keep it simple, find a good woman, listen good, never borrow money from friends and do something positive with whatever I learned when I listened so closely.

And to never start smoking. Ernie smoked all the time. Always at the loading dock at the back of the building, puffing away, holding court. Married, he said he'd found a solid woman in Bianca, who I'd met a couple of times in a bar Ernie would take me to after work. Bianca was hot to trot and, like Ernie, a chain-smoker.

Here's what she told me once, "See, Darling, Ernie's problem is that he don't take his own advice. He smokes like a fiend and he owes everybody money."

I think Ernie was a hustler and gambler on the side, but he liked to keep up appearances. He'd show up each day dressed perfectly in his cook's uniform of starched whites and checkered pants and black rubber-soled shoes. He stood five feet tall, usually had a five o'clock shadow, even though he shaved each day and reeked of Brut and hair oil. He wore his black hair slicked back so that it looked as if enameled to his head. I think Bianca made sure of this. She was the type who wouldn't let her husband leave the house without making certain he looked right. That was the kind of woman I was after. I knew Bianca had a sister, Iris, and I'd met her at the bar a few times and I had my sights on her, I did.

Ernie weighed no more than a hundred pounds soaking wet, but he could eat enough for ten men at each meal. Some of the larger boys on our crew gave him a hard time about his appetite, and the money he owed them. Little sums, you know, ten bucks here for some lottery tickets, another ten bucks for cigarettes and maybe a bet. Lots of little bets. This would be Ernie's downfall, all this betting, and that's what I told him each time he tried to hit me up for swag.

He'd say to me, "Just ah-five, Ostrich, I only need ah-five." Ostrich was my nickname. Ostrich Timothy Daigneault. My people's roots go back to Quebec, I guess, but I don't really know and nobody gives a hoot about that stuff so I never bring it up. The nickname Ostrich was because of my height and weight. Guys joked that I disappeared when I turned sideways, and if my neck was any longer I could rent it out as a crane. For a while I took offense and argued it wasn't my fault, that I had a high-running metabolism. Then I learned to just take it and shut up. Then I started, ever so slowly, to dish it out myself. I had nicknames for all the guys, but I didn't use them too much. Just when I really needed their attention or wanted to piss them off.

I refused to give Ernie a fiver that day, or any other day and it got so bad that I went to Four Eyes and begged him to do something about it. This put me in good with all the kitchen crew. We were sick of Ernie hitting on us. Four Eyes told me he was sick of it too, that Ernie owed him a thousand dollars. I begged him to take action, anything, he had my support and I'd get the crew to support him too.

Turns out, Four Eyes was smarter than I'd thought. He brought us together in the kitchen for an emergency meeting. Ernie wasn't there. Four Eyes wanted our help. He was sick of Ernie begging money. He understood we all were. "That true?" he asked. It was true, all right.

This was Four Eyes' plan. He created a bet. He would announce the bet to everyone in a big way, including Ernie, and the rule was that in order to play the bet you had to ante one-hundred bucks cash, which in those times was a lot of money for me, I think, for us all. I mean, we didn't have no health insurance or pension plans. It was a dead-end job and we all knew that as soon as something better came along, we'd grab it. We also knew that few of us would likely be going anywhere anytime soon, least of all guys like Spider who'd done time. The cool thing was that it was a fake bet, so the hundred bucks each would come back to us in private when Ernie wasn't around. Four Eyes vowed we had his word on that. The main thing was that Ernie saw all the money in front of him. Ultimately, it would all be just an elaborate con.

These were the rules of Four Eyes' bet. Ernie liked to boast that he could crack two dozen eggs into the Hobart's big steel mixing bowl with one hand tied behind his back, letting those raw eggs spill one at a time without so much as a single tiny jot of eggshell falling into the raw egg mix. So, Four Eyes bet Ernie a thousand bucks that he couldn't do this. If Ernie did it, then Ernie would no longer owe Four Eyes any more money.

However, Ernie also wouldn't be able to borrow a penny after that. In fact, if Ernie could do this feat, all the guys would wipe their slates clean. Ernie would be debt-free among his work colleagues. But with one catch. Ernie could never borrow anything from any worker, ever. If word got out that he did, Four Eyes would fire him. No questions asked.

Now, Ernie needed his job. If he failed at the challenge, he'd have to pay Four Eyes back double what he owed, a little over two grand. For the rest of us, he'd have to buy a round of drinks at the bar.

The genius was that, no matter the result, Ernie could no longer borrow money from us.

Was Ernie game? He was. I think he believed the risk was worth it. Crack 24 perfect eggs? No problem.

Try doing this sometime. It ain't easy. But I'd seen Ernie in action. His was no empty boast and I think Four Eyes knew it, but he didn't care.

Acting as judge, Four Eyes got each of us to sign an agreement in front of Ernie that we'd be witnesses. This would make it official. Four Eyes stood to double his money. Ernie stood to be debt free. The rest of us stood to enjoy a round of drinks.

Most of the guys said Ernie could never do it. I didn't. I'd watched Ernie in action during the three years I'd been working with him. I wanted to see those eggs, one at a time, cracked perfectly with one hand, those yolks dripping like phlegm into the mix. I also wanted to see Ernie go debt-free and never dare ask any of us to borrow a red cent again.

Four Eyes chose to do it on a Monday morning when the cafeteria was open, but business was slow, especially in the mornings. At 10:15 sharp, our morning coffee break, Four Eyes was beaming. He brought us together, including all the servers, to the middle of the kitchen space and he set up Ernie with the Hobart and a paper rack of 24 eggs and announced, "I tell you, my Ernie he's got experience and talent. This he does got. And he will prove it like he proves it every day. If Ernie, you do this, you don't pay nothing back to nobody, and you not borrow ever again. You leave us alone. No more bumming money from your co-workers. No more bully stuff from you, just because you're so little like a stinking woodpecker at my head all the time. You hear that?"

Ernie nodded solemnly at Four Eyes. He looked steely-eyed. He even had an apron on. He was breathing through his nose, an unlit cigarette behind his ear.

Every one of us, kitchen help and servers alike, gathered

around Ernie and we shrugged and nodded and wondered what would happen. We all liked knowing that no matter what, Ernie would stop borrowing from us. Four Eyes was a genius. Even if he lost, he still won, because Ernie wouldn't be allowed to play the beggar among us. Say what you want, this was entertainment, especially for a mug like Spider who washed pots and pans, and mopped the floors, ten hours a day. He worked hard, that Spider. Always in neoprene gloves. I'd help him sometimes and we'd together use steel wool pads to scrape clean the bottom insides of bay marines which were covered with caked layers of burnt mac and cheese. This kind of distraction kept the likes of Spider, Miguel and Dayvon Bones loose and easy. Otherwise, some days, Spider would get so riled he'd rip your head off before he even knew who he was speaking to. Spider was explosive, but Four Eyes couldn't fire him. He complained all the time about how hard it was to find a loyal dishwasher.

Nearly all the soft middle-aged ladies who worked out front as servers spoke Spanish or Portuguese as their first language. Those maternal ladies in their aprons and hairnets , with their big spoons and ladles, really liked me. I don't know why. Maybe because I tried to speak Spanish with them, though I was bad at it. I flirted with them and made silly jokes until Four Eyes would see me and yell at me to get back to work.

Still, those ladies fed me good too during my lunch break. I ate a lot of day-old Portuguese sweet-bread in those days, along with *bollos lovados*, a kind of dense flat Portuguese muffin with raisins in it. And spinach pies too. Handmade in the city, they were delivered to the cafeteria. Four Eyes always bought more than were sold before they started to get stale. He'd grown up eating spinach pies at home, made by his grandmother. He thought all of his workers should eat their share, so rather than toss away stale ones, he'd portion out little bags and tell us to bring them home.

Sure, I was Skinny Ostrich, but between those matronly servers and all the leftover baked goods I could take home, I feasted like a king, always taking home leftovers and sometimes sharing them with neighbor William and never paying for any of it. Four Eyes also donated extra food to some of the church pantries and the homeless shelters. It wasn't until I'd started working in a kitchen that I saw just how much edible food went to waste each day. Four Eyes knew there were many hungry families in the community and he hated to see food go to waste.

What I must add here is something that made Ernie's challenge even more difficult. Four Eyes blindfolded Ernie, who boasted, "It-ah makes-ah no difference. I no need to see nothing."

The others were laughing at cocksure Ernie. He would screw this up and embarrass himself. But they didn't know Ernie like I did. I'd have been stupid to bet against him, blindfolded or not.

Ernie proved me right. He was incredible. He stood there rigid, like he was in a trance state, with that cardboard tray of eggs at arm's length in front of him on a stainless steel table. Crack after crack, one egg, one strike, nothing more. Always in the same spot, against the steel edge of that big Hobart mixing bowl. Mechanically, in silence, surrounded by fellow workers, without pause, at a steady rhythm, and each of those glorious yokes dropped whole one by one, none of them dirtied with eggshells of any size, many of them not even pierced or fractured.

Ernie got into his zone and I heard a lot of babble in Spanish and Portuguese and big-bosomed sighs from the serving ladies as Ernie established an even pace and what amazed me was how fast he went. He never swiveled much, only just enough, using his arms and shoulders, his feet planted, and he'd pause now and then to calm his breathing, but he never moved his heavy black shoes. He reached out, lifted one egg, swung it to the bowl's edge, sounded one crack and let the yolk drop form his long thin fingers.

He repeated the process 24 times. It was beautiful, man, I'd never seen anything like it. Try this at home and see how far you get before splinters of eggshells start polluting the yolk mix. Imagine doing this with one hand and blindfolded.

After we removed Ernie's blindfold and untied his left arm, I joined the others to study the egg mixture. We found nothing dirty there. There was moaning and groaning, but those raw eggs were an unspoiled yellow. Four Eyes started hugging Ernie, praising Jesus in Portuguese, and slapping him repeatedly on the back and calling him a hero.

"But I won-ah and you lost," said Ernie. "Why-ah you hug me like a crazy man?"

"Because it is so beautiful," said Four Eyes. He was gushing. "What you do. It was so perfect. Who can do such a thing? Only my Ernie."

I had to agree. Ernie, ever humble, said it was nothing, that the others were maybe stupid not to believe in him. "Now I-ah show you," he said. "Now I-ah don't owe you nothing."

"And you don't *beg* nothing no more either," said Four Eyes. "A deal is a deal."

"Screw you and your deals," said Ernie.

Spider grabbed Ernie by the collar and shook him. "What you say, Ernie? You got my twenty dollars. Four Eyes is right. It's a deal. You don't bum no more money, you hear?"

All eyes were on Ernie. Spider was capable of anything. He had a huge spider tattooed to his neck. Hence the nickname. "I hear, I hear," said Ernie. "Now-ah get your rotten lousy hands off-ah me."

Spider let go. The challenge was over. Time to get back to work.

We were all winners. Four Eyes stayed true to his word, paid us all our money back. Ernie stayed true to his word and never again cadged a nickel off anybody, as far as I knew.

My friendship with Ernie grew. I learned just how much he liked to gamble. It was a sickness with him. It was sad. Same with his wife, Bianca. She bought lottery tickets, as many as twenty per day. He bet on horse races and greyhound races and he played poker at least two nights a week. I knew this and he invited me to the track a couple of times, but I always said no and I never asked him about gambling. I didn't think it any of my business. Call me simple, but I always thought gambling was for those who had money they could afford to lose.

Ernie and I both lived in the same neighborhood. We'd see widows every morning dressed in black who'd walk the city streets alone to the bakery or the pharmacy. They'd walk to Saint Augustine's for mass and for each saint's day and to confession. They'd mutter over rosary beads. When Ernie was with me, because sometimes we walked together after a meal, having invited me to his apartment, he'd say I was too skinny and should find a woman like Bianca to cook for me; he'd always smile at those widows and say something kind in Portuguese, but those old women were in perpetual mourning. They'd look sharply at him. They wouldn't speak.

"Widows are unhappy for life, for forever," he explained to me. "It is-ah just the rule, a tradition. If-ah we no keep it, we lose it."

He told me I should fear the widows in the same way I should fear Jesus because even though Jesus was love, Jesus was also about eternal suffering. The widows understood this and that's why they never smiled. This was also what allowed them to talk directly to god. They'd earned this privilege due to the loss of their husbands. It was a tradition of loyalty that a widow never allowed herself to get close to a new man in her life or to re-marry.

Ernie insisted Portuguese women were the best, the most loyal, and he thought I should pursue Iris. "She can cook. And I think-ah she likes you. Bianca told me. If Iris is-ah like my Bianca, she'll be *varoom* in the bedroom too."

"But I'm a nobody. What would she want with me?"

"You? Nobody?" Ernie looked flabbergasted. "You, my Ostrich, you born here. Look at me. I come here on a boat as a little boy. I still not speak-ah the good English. I am the nobody. Bianca she come too as a little girl. She the nobody too. But she-ah speak the better English than me."

"I don't make any big money," I said. "Iris would want a dentist or fireman or some lawyer or school teacher."

"Look at me," said Ernie. He was scowling now. "Who-ah you think you talking to here? Huh? I slap you. You look at me. I can crack eggs. So who cares? Bianca. She cares. She loves me good. I have it all now. I have a good woman. What you have? Huh? You got nothing. You a man or not? You get what you want in this life."

No one had ever talked to me in that way. I didn't know how to reply.

I kind of adopted Ernie as my older brother. I believed it when he said I had to stay close to him like he was my own family in the way that the Portuguese stayed close to each other. See, I'd been raised as an only child by my mother. She'd made her money in strange ways, never really telling me about it. Handsome men in suits were always involved, and she told me when I'd turned 17 that I had to get out of her apartment and make it on my own. Once that happened, my mother moved far away. I never really did learn what she did for a living. Maybe she was a call girl. I still don't know.

I don't even know where she lives. Last I heard it was some-where near Tucson, but I got no idea. Not really. We just weren't ever close. It wasn't like she cooked or something. I did all the cooking. I took care of myself. I didn't mind this, but I guess I missed her now and then. Or maybe I just missed having someone to go to. That's where Ernie came in. Ernie told me to never fear what he called "the pride of the bull" and "the love of Jesus" and he showed me how so many yards in our neighborhood had statuaries of the Madonna and where he, like other Portuguese men, tended roses and gardens that bloomed to scent the air all summer long. I ate and drank with Bianca and with Iris, too, many times. Iris was plump but in an attractive way, always smiling and glowing. Bianca would invite her over and then invite me over and she'd cook for us during these planned visits. It appeared more and more that Iris found me to her liking. Bianca told me this. I saw it too. I told Bianca the feeling was mutual. I was crazy about Bianca's *zuppa* with littleneck clams and linguini. Bianca told me Iris cooked it even better, that her food would stay warm inside of my belly long after I ate it.

"Iris can really cook like that?" I asked.

"She cook it so much better than me," said Bianca. "And even better for her man. You. Besides. You too skinny. She cook all the time for you."

It was while spending time with Bianca that I learned more and more about Iris. She was single and looking for a man. What was I waiting for? Was I interested? This second question came from Iris directly. She just asked me one night. Bianca was there too. She said we'd be good together, me and Iris. I should spend more time with her, get to know her. And so I did.

We hit it off. It was like I'd known Iris all my life. She was a lot like Bianca, super-charged with emotions, but so sweet and with such a smile and long black hair and big, I mean huge round eyes that tore me up whenever she looked at me in her kind, gentle and understanding way. As Ernie told me, "Here now, is a woman."

Iris was warm and funny and she liked me, too. That was the main thing. Wasn't like I was a Rockefeller. Didn't matter. Sure, I wasn't Portuguese, but that didn't matter either. I was Catholic, and that's what counted for a lot. Iris had Ernie's word that I was a hard worker. A good reliable one. Iris told me she liked that in a man, so I tried to live up to it.

I knew I had a future with Iris when she told me, "You don't have to be president, Tim." I loved that she didn't call me Ostrich. Just Tim. Really simple. "You just have to provide for a family. Our family. Do you want that?"

I didn't know. I was near to twenty-eight years old and maybe I should. Iris, on the other hand, wasn't going to wait around to find out. She didn't mince her words. She wanted a man for life. No pussyfooting around. Married, church, kids, the whole she-bang. Well, at least I knew where she stood on the matter.

I talked to William about it, figuring he'd be honest with me, and he was. He just blurted out, "Who do you think you are? What are you waiting for? You think your princess will just keep walking into your life one year after another? I think we get only one princess. Just one. And it sounds like she wants you as her prince."

Amazing, isn't it, where your best most useful advice comes from. A gay appliance salesman at Sears prone to dancing on his bed. Who knew?

Ernie and Bianca cared about their Portuguese kin and they suffered with them, which made it all the more startling when Ernie told me one night over *Sagres* beers at the Club Holy Ghost that he and Bianca had to get out of there. I should, too, since I was young and smart and ambitious. And I should marry Iris. I should be like his shrewd friends who had left the city and made something bigger of their lives.

"More than these blocks, this-ah neighborhood," he said.

I was floored. Not Ernie. Never him. I begged him to explain. He looked so grim, so worried, saying that it was different now, changing year after year, the older family members dying off, the traditions dying with them. Some moved back to the Azores or Brazil, others sold what they had and embraced another community where nobody spoke Portuguese. Their children mouthed English fluently and were already American with their phones and fancy cars, innocently so, many born in that land of opportunity that had taken their parents in.

"I no got nothing bad against America," he said. "What a man like-ah you gotta do here is to risk the break. The break away." He spoke, as always when serious, with an even more pronounced tendency to add a vowel, usually an *a* or an *ah*, to the end of many words. "That is-ah why they call it-ah the new world. Because-ah the people, they make it ah-new."

One week, Ernie failed to clock in for three days in a row. I went to his apartment, expecting to find Bianca. But when I knocked on the door and it opened, I saw that Bianca wasn't there. Iris was and she looked so voluptuous, so happy to see me, her hair shining and I felt the heat of passion from her immediately and though we'd talked plenty and gotten to know each other a little, we'd never done anything beyond smile at each other and percolate. As Iris laid her big dark eyes on me, I had to ask myself: Did I want her? Of course, I did.

Before I knew it, we were kissing each other in that apartment and she was taking off my pants and I tried to get her to move toward a bedroom, but Iris fought me off and said there'd be other times, that this was enough for now. We just kissed madly in the living room. "Don't push your luck," she said. I saw, in that moment, another side of her. She didn't mess around.

We smoked some reefer, which I happened to have with me, and I felt like a king as I sat there stoned on Ernie's sofa while Iris fried me some eggs and chorizo, and toasted some *bollos lovados*. She'd learned from Ernie that I liked them, so she'd bought some fresh.

"So you knew I was coming?" I asked. "What about Ernie? Was he in on this?"

She told me Ernie and Bianca had left in the middle of the night. They'd gone by bus. Took nothing with them except the clothes on their back.

"You shouldn't feel bad, My Sweet," said Iris. "They didn't say goodbye to anyone."

I liked that she called me My Sweet. This was going somewhere with us, and fast. Maybe too fast. Maybe not. Maybe Iris was just what I needed. Who did I think I was, anyway? It wasn't like girls were throwing themselves at me. William had been right. Only one princess, and only if a prince was lucky.

When I asked Iris why they'd left, she said, "Gambling. They have debts up the wazoo. Owe money to everybody around here. It's their way. They didn't tell nobody where they were going."

I must have looked crestfallen because at that moment I felt abandoned and a little betrayed. The same way I felt whenever I thought about my mother. "I'm gonna miss Ernie. He was all I had, really."

"But now you have me," said Iris. She looked at me and those glossy red lips of hers opened just a little and they were damp and I couldn't wait to kiss them again. I looked at those dreamy eyes of her, that comely softness in her flesh, all that hair and the way her breasts rose and fell with each breath. "So, My Sweet, what are we gonna do about it?"

"You really want me that bad?"

She smiled and I felt myself melting. "Didn't I make you feel good?" she asked. "There's a lot more where that came from, you know."

I moved in with my princess at the end of that month, happy to say "so long" to that boarding house, though I kept in touch with William.

Iris and I have been married now twenty years. Eventually, we bought a house. But not in that neighborhood. In a greener place where no widows walk the streets and we never hear church bells. I still work in restaurants, but I have experience now and thanks to a bank loan, I earned a two-year certificate in hospitality and kitchen management. Thanks to Iris I've learned enough Portuguese to help me over the years to manage a lot of the Brazilians who come to the U.S., some of them starting out in restaurants as they make their dream into a reality. I'm the one now who, like Ernie, can crack eggs blindfolded flawlessly with one hand.

I started a garden, complete with Madonna statuary and it gives us bags of tomatoes each year. I've grown quite fat on Iris's and my own cooking, and she loves me that way. Nobody would dare call me Ostrich any more. We go to mass every Sunday and neither of us gamble. What we know about Ernie and Bianca is that they moved to one of the suburbs near Rio in Brazil. Maybe one day we'll visit them, but for the time being, we're way too busy with our own children.

Yep, you guessed it. Our daughter's name is Bianca and our son is Ernie.

The Birds Of Panic

*A*s a playboy in *the house of the dead, I know that somewhere among one of my memories lives the evidence that all this isn't real but rather a configuration based on the confluence points where darting jetties of light meet and explode to create a kind of mundo loco, as Itzel would call it, where all we see reminds us of something we've never seen before.*

Fisher Moss paused with that thought. He'd taken the stairs, careful to remain quiet, and had made it to the last tread. Panting, he didn't see the hidden camera that filmed him opening the stairwell door and stepping outside. Nor did he see the second camera that filmed all nocturnal activity that occurred on the roof. He'd awakened from a nap earlier that evening, determined to take action once and for all. He'd remembered no dreams, no words. This wasn't typical and he'd taken it as a positive omen that meant Itzel was with him. What he'd awakened with, and he took comfort in, was a feeling of earned and slightly deranged courage.

He had his box. He carried it with him until he found an area where the slightly wavy contours of the roof, with its tiny peat stones, felt solid and dry. He crouched down and ran one hand over tar seams under the peat stones. This would be perfect. Enough light from the taller building next door that shone against the flat steel of his building's heating units and all the galvanized steel of their ventilation ducts.

First, he set up his tripod, an uncomplicated task. Next, he attached his small silver Nikon Cool Pix camera, having already set it to the video option. Standing in front of it and saying a few words, he tested the camera. He played back the digital footage. It was fine. He was ready. After pressing the Record button, he stepped quickly in front of the tiny lens and started to speak lines he'd begun mulling over in his apartment weeks ago when the lockdown had begun.

"Itzel, this is for you. It will go to the heavens with me, where we'll meet again. Without you, Itzel, vacant is what I am. A shell of my former self. Yet here on this roof, I can leave you with my soul. You know, we would have been great together, but we never even had a chance."

He paused, hurrying to turn off the camera. This was enough for now. Itzel was with him and knew what he'd been thinking. During their time together, which seemed to him now so very brief, she'd learned how to read his mind with ease.

Best now that he wait. He'd chosen this time to make his recording because it was the half-hour when the second-shift doorman was replaced by the less reliable graveyard-shift man. No one appeared to have heard him on the stairs. The doorman wouldn't use them. He'd get to the roof via the second stairwell, the one for elevator access, a few hundred feet away.

Fisher turned the camera back on.

"Itzel, I'm safe up here. I can escape the pandemic lockdown. You won't believe it, but everyone worldwide, except maybe in North Korea, has a Covid-19 story. I wear a mask and I don't care that The State is maybe impinging on my sense of liberty and freedom. Maybe The State is right. Certainly its operatives know things that I don't. But now's the time to shut up and to hide in places like this where others aren't likely to visit. Everything has changed. The streets are empty. Even the birds sound different."

Fisher checked his watch. One a.m. He stopped the recording. The new doorman, a genial young immigrant from Cameroon named Gabriel, would no doubt behave like the many that had preceded him, meaning he wouldn't last but a few months in such a lonely, low-paying job. Nor would he lose much sleep on a weeknight worrying about rooftop prowlers. Gabriel wouldn't venture up but once during his shift, around four a.m., to make a rapid uninspired check, and only if it wasn't raining.

Rain was in the forecast. Fisher could taste it under the low clouds of night sky. Not a star in sight. Even the threat of rain felt different during this pandemic. The air crisp and dank, Fisher sucked it in greedily, so pleased to have his mask off, to discover moist air again.

He needed to think about what came next in his video, so he walked the roof's perimeter, ten-stories up, protected from a fall by an enameled shoulder-high steel railing. That railing didn't mean he couldn't turn the camera back on, climb over the railing and say *hasta la vista* to it all. It was perhaps a clownish choice. . Certainly not Itzel's style. He should remember he'd come here for dignified reasons, to honor Itzel and how he loved and, of course, missed her, his Rainbow Lady. He'd cried himself out. There were no tears left. The time had come for him to say farewell first, to let go and only then move on.

Since Itzel's death in 2017, Fisher had brooded and grieved, agonizing in and out of counseling sessions and now, to add insult to injury, Covid 19, having cracked open the universe, had erased any attention in public memory that had once been paid to the death toll and the ineffectual response to Puerto Rico's Hurricane Maria. Since Maria, there had been more hurricanes, floods and fires. There had been ugly politics and Covid-19. Trump, Biden, global climate change, the greedy manipulations of humans. Aha, there was his hook. He trotted back to his camera and turned it on.

He leaned in toward the lens. "Itzel, seldom does anyone speak about what humans can do better to help each other prepare for and respond to disasters, whether its California or Australia burning up, or half of Bangladesh underwater. Whether these tragedies are caused by humans or not. Some fatal disasters just occur without provocation, and maybe they're karmic responses, God's judgment on us. As they've been occurring for eons. Why should they all devolve into a cumbersome political equation: left-leaning pro-global-warming parties versus right-leaning pro coal-and-oil parties. Yes, Itzel, *mi Corazon*, I'm so sick and tired of all the heated gasses released during debates and discussions of endlessly contentious issues."

He stopped again. Camera off. All he could say with confidence was that Iztel was gone. The facts regarding her death were sketchy at best and they'd come from Luis, a friend from college days who worked in the city's office of the CDC. Two years after the event was no longer a lead news story, Luis had been able to confirm that Itzel and her mother had died alone in a corridor on the floor in the University of Puerto Rico hospital in the industrial city of Carolina, where she'd been visiting her ill mother to arrange her move to live with them in the U.S. She and Fisher had been engaged to marry. Iztel, at 47, had been too old to have children, but she and Fisher had planned to adopt. Single for so long, she'd at last make her mother proud. Eventually, her mother would live in a comfortable affordable apartment not too far from the city and they'd visit her every weekend.

Fisher turned to the lens and said, "Who said it wasn't meant to be?"

Then he remembered the camera was off. He turned it on and repeated himself, adding, "But I refuse to accept such a fatalistic outlook. No, Itzel, it wasn't God's plan. It was indecent human malfeasance. Criminal ignorance."

Iztel and her mother hadn't been rich enough to jet off the island before the hurricane made landfall. What Fisher had learned of the Leptospirosis that had killed them was that it came on like the common cold, might evolve into dengue-like symptoms, but would surely kill a person surreptitiously within four days. With landslides, driving rain, generators burning out and interruptions in health services that the government used as excuses, both women had died neglected among many other hapless corpses. The official diagnosis had been a medical, not a political one — death due to Leptospirosis brought on by contaminated water. This had meant that no doctor could state officially that the hurricane had caused their deaths. Only politicians could. So, among many other corpses throughout the country, they weren't included on the government's official list of casualties, giving the world the impression that Hurricane Maria hadn't been all that lethal.

Turning back to the camera, aware that it was still on, Fisher stewed, saying, "The thoughtless sons of bitches. What don't they understand about Puerto Rico being an American territory? Is it because you speak Spanish there, Itzel, such a beautiful old language? I hate my country for it. I feel such shame and betrayal. I've cried for you, Itzel, and your mother, for all those forgotten ones, for so many nights. Yet nobody heeds my tears. And I come back to the question: Why should they? Because, in the end, they don't really care. If you are Puerto Rican and so very proud, then you are the Other. You're not American. Not really. And for this, for this, what's paid is such a price...."

Choking up, feeling a collapse within, Fisher buckled and lunged for the camera to shut it off. What a tragic mess, a colossal screw-up, with so many what-ifs. He could have talked Itzel out of it, made her wait until spring, but she'd argued in her feisty way that her mother needed her there, that time was running out. And he, not wanting to hurt or lose her, had relented.

Then, the unbearable realizations as he'd watched the nightmare unfold on television, unable to reach Iztel by phone, horrified by the disgusting sense of helplessness he'd felt, forced to listen to the politicians, as they'd lied after Hurricane Katrina, spin their webs, touting the arrival of the USNS Comfort in San Juan, cloaking in secrecy facts that came out later, such as only 18 of the island's 69 hospitals had even been opened.

Yet the painful truth remained that he'd be dead if he'd joined her. He should have, and now he had to face what he'd feared for so long. He would die alone.

Mother of God, amen. It was time to burn. He'd brought all the photos with him. The paper ones, having removed from them from Itzel's frames and albums. It was a little windy, but he'd brought a Zippo lighter and fluid. With the camera tilted down slightly and turned on, he sat and recorded himself in front of his pile of photos, burning them one at a time, watching their ashes spiral up into the night sky. *Cenizas a las cenizas de polvo al polvo.* Itzel had taught him that, helping him get comfortable on Sundays when they'd go to the Catholic mass in Spanish.

When the burning ritual was over, Fisher stood again and shut off the camera. He asked himself if he felt better. Perhaps. It was a step, little more. He went again to the roof's edge and looked at the avenue below and saw what was usually a busy avenue stretching out like an empty ribbon of asphalt and remembered the nights he'd come here with Iztel and how they'd watched the taxis arrive to red lights spreading against the wash of night, red changing to green and the taxis pulsing along to the next intersection. They'd just stand and watch as a couple, holding each other. She was the kind of old soul who could be happy with so little.

Nowadays, proven by the empty avenue, nobody anywhere was doing a thing. Residents of the world had to be happy with four walls and a screen. A lot less than any dream they might have thought they once had. Like the others, Fisher had to obey orders, and some wanted to gladly, but those orders came in convoluted doses and baffling narratives spoken by harried leaders, pundits and so-called experts perpetually under attack and on the defensive. The idea of living was for celebrities who could afford to hide themselves away on a yacht, or under the jacarandas of a summer escape poolside by the sea.

Only God knew when the true ritual hum would resume again. Until then, Fisher knew he'd continue to have these moments of dreaded pensive silence, with explosive eruptions that stirred all the birds of panic within him. There was only one consolation. He felt glad, at 55, that in another twenty years he'd be the same age as his father when he'd died. Yet in such a jittery and maudlin state, what was the point of living another twenty years? Maybe he should jump, after all. He began to move back to the camera. He'd turn it on. He'd film himself jumping.

He stopped. On the other hand, in the grand scheme, what remained of his life meant so little that it would pass quickly. He could hear Itzel telling him that there had to be something he should live for. That's why he should stay alive — to find that something. Oh, that was Itzel talking, all right. She was under his toenails and digging in.

What Itzel didn't know was that he really couldn't stomach the thought that when the pandemic was over, he would have to fake that he was young, full of energy and aspirations, determined to find gainful employment in a country where work, for most, had become a Zoom session online. Zoom a common verb now replacing call and text the way Skype and Google and message had replaced them. The biggest challenge of each day would be to keep enduring a sense of desolate and turgid gravity, knowing time only went forward as one stayed in gloves and tried to keep distant while accepting a pizza delivery or sipping coffee.

Why not *play* a little? With the camera on, he leaned in and he leered and said in a woman's voice, "Yes, Mr. Fisher Moss. We have reviewed your application and though we thought you interviewed well, and you really did impress us, we have decided to go, instead, with a hologram. In fact, by the year 2050, we believe all of our employees will be holograms."

He had a book with him. A virus-ridden object that reeked of another century. Just to carry it, to believe in words over images, meant he was a geezer. A gift from Itzel titled *Rat Pack Confidential* it was about the life those entertainers led night after night a long time ago. He'd read it (he'd certainly had the time) and had enjoyed learning, with shock, about the odds Sammy Davis Jr. had faced, not only as a black man but as a convert to Judaism who had married a stunner of a white European model. No black man did that sort of thing in the Jim Crow era without white allies and the payment of heavy dues.

It was time to burn that book. Facing the camera, winking at it, he stood the book upright, lit his Zippo and watched and waited. A paperback copy, it didn't take for long the pages to start curling into flames. There was a plastic smell as the cover burned blue. This was theatre, wasn't it? He could remember well the night Itzel had given it to him. His 54th birthday. He'd already proposed to her and she'd accepted. They'd decided to wait a year, not to live together yet, to make sure everything was set with her mother before they finalized their situation.

A laughable thought. To *finalize* anything. To make plans. If this lockdown had taught him anything, it was to drive both fists into the throat of anything called a plan.

Theatre. Flames. When was the last time he'd seen a live act? Fisher couldn't remember. Sammy Davis Jr. had been three years old when he'd started performing on stage. Where did boy entertainers get their start today? Fisher didn't know. Not that it mattered. Many years might pass before live theatre returned.

Though they'd used it, The Rat Pack hadn't needed television. They'd needed other people and they'd faced them each night and, in some cases, even learned their names. Don Rickles had made a living off those people by insulting them. Of late, the comics Fisher watched on Netflix, ever hopeful he'd be entertained, didn't make him laugh. They spoke with unearned rancor about scatological situations and bodily humors, the perversity of their sexual organs, using uninspired language and sharing their pathologies as if their target audience was younger than thirty, which it probably was.

"I've outlived my time," he said to the camera. "No worldliness, no grandeur, no responsibility or largesse. Wit and insight remain at a premium. Should this surprise me? Those Rat Packers made their reputations on both grand and tiny stages, a glass of booze in one hand, a cigarette in the other. Such an act now feels antiquated, so sweaty and grimy and of the flesh — with dancing, singing, sharing banter, no concerns of reprisals for telling off-color jokes in front of their equally drunk and sweaty, nicotine-addled audiences. How barbarously unhygienic, Itzel, all that seems now, when a night out among others was what we lived for. When every night was a night out, and a trip to a casino spelled a major lifetime event, not a weekend excursion to an Indian reservation in an air-conditioned bus full of senior citizens."

He paused. Shut off the camera. What time was it? Which day? It didn't even matter. The thought depressed him to no end. At least he wasn't coughing. Wasn't all that tired either. Maybe his burning ritual had provided some healing, after all. To think, regarding his job, he'd caught up on paperwork that had been plaguing him for months. The very idea of it — to be caught up — was astonishing to consider.

Itzel had worked most of her life in casino kitchens. Started here in the city at age 16 as a prep cook at a hotel, and in 1989 with only a year of experience had taken a bus west to Nevada to work at The Sands. Fisher had never been there, but he'd learned about The Sands from Itzel and from his researching of America's past back when it bloomed in his imagination. He'd always viewed those Vegas casinos as symbols of his dream of America, a wonderland that, at last, he was coming to learn really didn't exist.

For years, he'd listened to jazz records, still loved jazz and found it disheartening that many Americans didn't appreciate it. One favorite had been Nat King Cole's record of a live performance at The Sands, but the album Fisher and Itzel had loved most was one Nat had recorded with George Shearing. He could still hear Nat singing "Lost April" with strings coming up behind him while Shearing sounded a tender plink-plink on the keys, the words soft and gentle, tinged with despair: *Lost April where did you go? Like winter snow, I saw you vanish....*

Did anyone listen to or make such music anymore? It was as if the young were incapable of tenderness, depth and pathos. Or was that just the raving of a middle-aged mind? Probably a little of both. The Sands, with its Copa Room, was long gone. Now Itzel was gone, but no Disney version of Venice or Paris would replace her. The Sands had allowed Itzel in at the bottom rung, just as they'd allowed Sammy Davis Jr. to enter through the front door, not through the kitchen, and to let him use the whites-only toilets. Those rights for Sammy had come only because Frank Sinatra wouldn't perform otherwise. And this a directive straight from his mouth.

Itzel had washed dishes, worked weekends, long days and nights at a time when few Latinas labored in banquet kitchens. She'd grown up in kitchens and had developed a toughness, thick skin. Nobody messed with Itzel just as nobody had messed with Sinatra, no racist he. Who, like him, was left in the cosmos of American show business?

Were those *the days*? Itzel had never said so. A typical day had been twelve hours long for minimum wage. Maybe one day off a week. Always one female roommate. Spoke Spanish in the kitchen and was berated for it. Spoke Spanish with that roommate, living in a dumpy bungalow on the side of the tracks where, as she liked to say, "Beaners and blacks got used to pissing on each other."

Looking up at his camera, making sure it was still on, Fisher said, "Itzel, world culture remains racist, and there will always be oppressors, but one thing I loved about you, knowing how much hardship you endured, was that you were never bitter. You said to me many times that the young had to understand that there had been and would continue to be improvement. That you'd seen it with your own eyes. I want you to know that in order to never forget this, inspired by your influence on my thinking, my ethos, I try to cross lines, to talk to acquaintances and neighbors, many of whom are different than me and, like you, speak charming English with an accent. I try to learn a little about their culture and language and world-view, or else teach them a little of my own. To share, to get outside of myself helps me sedate the birds of panic and fear within. Do you know those birds? I'm sure you do."

What now, he thought. Talk about living under lockdown? Screen sharing? Spy programs embedded into his computer accounts? Thinking he lived inside a computer program? It wasn't a question of how long this pandemic would last. The holograms and robots weren't coming. They'd already arrived. This pandemic was just allowing the Technocrats a test-run worldwide.

"I will never stop loving you, Itzel. To honor you, I'll keep my life simple. No need to cross dangerous borders anywhere. To achieve. I have my basic needs. I'll continue playing by the rule that there are no rules. No one really knows what the hell is going on. No one trusts the numbers or the noise. Now, surfaces and cleanliness are everything. In the past, I used to find myself worrying that I didn't project a clever enough sauciness and elan. Why worry about that now? Without you to look after, I'm not all that necessary or useful any longer. Lost April, that's for sure. You know, all the casinos across the world are shut down. There's no work. Okay, maybe some filing and estimating and providing services from home. Some medical care, which is more dangerous now than ever. You wouldn't believe all the cads who don't wear masks and heed the realities of this pandemic and, in turn, infect and in some cases cause the deaths of medical professionals — those who work, who provide in the truest sense — who try to help those who can't help themselves."

Another pause. It was an intuition, and it didn't prove anything, but he should wrap it up. He couldn't say how he knew, but he felt that someone was coming. Who? Time to finish pronto and get back to his apartment.

"Who am I, Itzel?" he said. He took off his jacket. He began to take off his shirt, one button at a time, pulling his arms out of the sleeves before tossing it aside. Next, he stepped out of his slip-on loafers, unbuckled his belt, dropped his trousers and kicked them away. Lastly, down slid his underwear and naked in front of that camera he struck a hedonistic muscle-beach pose, knowing that Itzel liked the sight of his body, still trim and muscular for one his age.

It was while posing that the door to the far elevator stairwell entrance opened quietly, not emanating too much light from inside, and two police officers stepped expertly and without sound onto the roof. Gabriel stood behind them, phone in, in the doorway.

"I am the Rat-Face of Death," said Fisher into the camera lens. "Hemmed in by the walls of night, their stars like gouged-out eyes that spy on us all. What you, my dear Itzel always knew is that esteem is about accomplishment. Not about receptions from others. And dignity comes from maintaining one's sense of place and humility in all these various hierarchies, no matter how unfair or biased or cruel. You knew because you went from prep cook to chef to kitchen manager and then moved back east here to be closer to Puerto Rico and your ailing mother and I loved you for that and I was blessed to have met you when you were managing one of the city's top-tier restaurants. You started with nothing Itzel and you made a career. You found me. I found you. Sure, you never had time for children and a husband. Neither did I. But what does that matter? What does any of this matter?"

Another pause. What did he hear? Had those been footsteps? He inched cautiously toward the camera and was about to turn it off when he stopped and looked into the lens and said, "Governments. Bailout checks. Itzel, you come to me all the time in my dreams. Now, I'm coming to you. A widower, that's all I am. But I'm coming to you."

He stopped. What next to say, that for years he'd placidly avoided lusting after coin, having been trained by an impecunious father in the financial investments sector? That was dull stuff. He'd led a spartan bachelor's life, spending wisely and forever saving. Not that he had anything now to spend it on. Not that he had any real work. Not that anyone did, or so it seemed.

Fisher turned the camera off. Nothing to add. Naked to the world, he'd said his last words. The time had come. He'd jump, after all. With only his socks on, he bolted across the roof, not knowing that one cop, skilled in such matters, a large man, had been crouched and waiting along the perimeter. He tackled Fisher nearly knocking him out, and by the time Fisher was handcuffed and back in his trousers it had started to rain.

ALBUM THREE

Forget You Knew Me

Novella Capriccioso In E

On Coral Records

Forget You Knew Me

ALL I EVER WANTED was to sing. Maybe a little applause afterwards. And in my wildest dreams a 33 rpm recording shelved in Mother's collection with Jo Stafford, or Teresa Brewer and all those other fine lady singers who today are all but forgotten.

My tale must be told in the key of E. For entropy, after Pynchon, who just by mentioning his name proves I'm of a certain generation and attended college. Second, the E is for estrogen. My womanliness. Lastly, the cheerleader in me shouts give us an E for empathy. Brimming with it, always. Perhaps to a fault.

No, I never blamed Mother. I still don't blame anyone other than myself. You see, at the age of eighteen, decades ago, an aspiration fizzled. Maybe it was a boyfriend. Or loneliness. Or having lost my beloved Papa early. I simply stopped singing.

All our dreams fade, but there are resurrections now and then, and one of the happiest days of my life, now fifteen years ago, was that I married. As a Boomer feminist, instead of not taking my husband Dalton's family name, I followed the trend and did the stacked club-sandwich thing, calling myself Stella Luna Levestri Pierre.

Hard to believe it had been fifteen years with that name all mine in its alliterative glory. I'd really wanted to make an anti-statement, to be different, simply Stella Pierre. I didn't. I wasn't. A three-story name fit me better because, as one person with one name, I never followed through on what I really wanted for myself.

I was now in my late forties, nearly the same age as Papa when he died. I felt empty, as if I were one more vapid consumer asking herself why she hadn't followed the dictates of her conscience and rejected all the lies and noise around her.

Maybe the nightmare started during puberty. I'd have these bouts of depression, convinced life had become dreary and disappointing and would never improve and it was all due to my own cowardly neuroticism. I'd shrink into darkness, cowering away from contact with other people. And then I'd eat, swaying as if on the deck of a wonderful schooner that was gliding along glassy seas.

Eating helped me forget time and responsibilities and my fears. I'd delight in feeling myself rising into the ethers, charmed by what I saw, full of whimsy and elan. It was such a wonderfully invigorating sensation. With each bite, my vision would blur and my breathing would accelerate and I'd lose all sense of control until, my stomach swollen, my ribcage heaving, I had to stop and I'd slouch in my chair and look around and see little by little as all came back into focus. I'd then begin to count, despondently so, how many packages of cookies, pastries and microwaveable TV dinners I'd torn open and emptied. How many sandwiches I'd made, with lots of cheese and mayonnaise, the bags of potato chips, the bowls of cereal, the chocolate bars and ice cream.

Then the purging would begin. With a capital P. I had my Ipecac potion, my various laxatives and teas, as well as my trustworthy fingers. I'd feel horrible about myself, ashamed, glad I was alone, wanting to stay out of sight of people, sobbing and groaning as I vomited on my knees in front of the toilet. This was my routine, sometimes daily for weeks at a time, with trips in the mornings alone to buy more groceries and stock up in bulk, everything from pot roasts and whole chickens to all sorts of pre-packaged meals and grains and jarred preserves.

Though it was a disorder, I saw it as a habit and it stayed with me. I'd brought it into my marriage. I loved to cook and I did so for my husband Dalton and myself. That was what I told myself, at least. He and I were a family after all, yet I'd often go through an entire binge and purge cycle before he even got home from work. I kept such cycles a secret from him as much as possible.

Then I'd cook again because it was an excuse to eat again, really pack it in, and I'd leave Dalton afterwards and he had to sit puzzled in the living room while he listened to my wretched upheavals. Again and again and again. The man had been a saint.

If Dalton was my steadying hand, then I was the poetic bile in his soul. For too long I'd nurtured a delusion that by thinking myself a poet and looking the part, I'd be one. My poems began to get published around the time I abandoned the waif look, in my jeans and oversized T-shirts to hide my cringe-worthy lack of a figure, my black hair a mess, no make-up, my armpits and gimpy legs unshaved. I was not Goth she-demon, but I could be a change agent, a saving angel, a Griot moon goddess.

I had ideas jotted into notebooks, sentences written down, but did I have poems? I was seated near the little library of books I treasured, many of them signed by authors I'd met, or editors who had published me. Some of them were my own published books and seeing them on a shelf brought more pleasure than it did compared to seeing a poem or an article online. I preferred the smell and weight of books, the way they forced me to slow down. Conversely, I admitted to consolation knowing my published poems were still available and younger readers might embrace them in such a format.

It was the older readers who didn't take me seriously because, say, Random House hadn't launched a campaign to promote the way I'd added to the public consciousness.

Nobody asked me to pursue this poetry obsession. Nobody really needed my lines. I was the one with the need, battling the disorders, for too long looking like a broken broomstick. After molting out of my own exquisite corpses, what's next, when, and how would I get there? Strangers had approached, at times, to share positive honest responses to my work. These were satisfying consoling memories. The best most gratifying ones were of non-poets, many of whom felt intimidated by the experience in the same way I felt while listening to opera. I was fortunate to have experienced encouragement from such persons. I remembered that some of them hugged me afterwards. Perhaps I'd reached a point where I didn't think of myself as a fraud, though I still doubted my gifts, if they could be labeled as such.

Each poem felt like it was the last I'd experience. I could afford to question motives to live for fame, money, notoriety, when all I craved was to relax, to breathe, to feel comfortable in my skin. For a while, twice a week I was in yoga class. Then I quit. I could accept that I could not live without my meds, but I couldn't accept needing to feel so much soreness in my body. I started to like the fuller shape of my body when I studied it in the mirror. I wasn't about the physical. I craved the exceptional crystallization between the syllabic echoes in my consciousness and the language that spilled from me either into the air or on to a page. I blasted and cajoled my linguistic vituperation vinto layers above and below the ozone to help all the bullet holes there grow larger. No, the body wasn't my territory, never had been.

Pursuing one's idealized cerebral missions was a conceit, essentially. Like living in a Djuna Barnes novel. Happiness, finding one's self, these were narcissistic windmills to chase after. There was no getting *there* on the journey. There was the journey itself, an understanding of one's unrealistic expectations, teaching others, spreading goodwill, and death. One never had enough money. I would enjoy each of my days and whatever I could of personal pursuits that they offered. I lived in order to make myself into the person I thought I wanted to be, but this never happened in any consistent way. For too long, the binge-and-purge cycles were the only active measurement of progress in my life. The only thing I could really do. They'd been happening for years, off and on, sometimes in exhausting torrents and long before I met Dalton.

As you can imagine, I went to therapy sessions, first as part of a group, and later with different therapists until I found Dr. Murray. I'd often have bouts of nausea due to an inflammation in my pancreas. My nails broke easily and my blood pressure remained low, which made me feel cold most of the time, no matter the temperature. This was due to the vomiting, which screwed up my electrolytes, caused my face to swell and at my lowest point, about a year before I met Dalton, I was diagnosed with Mallory-Weiss syndrome, having seen red blood in my vomit due to a tear in my esophagus.

I found myself a physician in Dr. Klein. He recommended a therapist and nutrition specialist named Dr. Murray. She turned out to be everyone I needed rolled into one. She was expensive, but she was reliable and patient and I felt I could trust her as we began our sojourn into self-obsessed evaluations of my maladaptive behavior. Dr. Murray was a gentle and supportive beacon of hope and tenderness. She and Klein kept me on different meds. First Lexapro, which caused me to gain weight. Then Zoloft, which also added weight. At first, absolutely freaked out over the weight gain, my binging and purging got worse. Really out of control. This changed, over time, but slowly.

After about ten years of therapy with Dr. Murray, I learned to be a little more comfortable with the weight that the meds were helping me add to my body. Ten long years. Regarding my moods, I had to admit the meds were working. I knew this whenever I experimented and tried to get off them, or to decrease my dosage. Often, I was all over the map, but I did learn how to lose weight and exercise. I tried yoga again and Pilates for a while, and then Tai Chi and even went to see an acupuncturist in Washington DC, but all to no avail regarding the insistent emotional presence of the demon need to binge and purge.

I lived and worked and kept my nightmarish private life a secret. There were telltale signs such as my bloated face, but nobody knew about my mouth sores, or my irregular periods, or the constant heartburn and dehydration. Not even Mother knew. I didn't want her to. She already judged me too harshly. Her face was sharper than a scythe. She never smiled. Telling her would only generate one more reason to make me feel unworthy of calling myself her daughter.

I told myself it was all her fault. This was a lie, of course, but one that helped me get through days when I needed a reason for what was or wasn't happening in my life. Most of the time, though I looked like pink steel on the outside, I was feeling a complex stir of dreadful and bleak passions. If not bilious forms of self-loathing, then uncontrollable urges to start bawling for no reason at all. I'd follow through on those urges. I'd blame myself, citing another unrealized goal. I felt anxious and desperate and I brewed in angst constantly, thinking to hell with vanity and showing off. I just wouldn't purge. I'd love myself and just eat until I was huge and could accept myself. At least I'd feel better and maybe my esophagus would heal.

I felt so insignificant and confused. I worried I'd never amount to anything. I wasn't a real poet. There was no such animal. Every poet out there was just trying to achieve the impossible. Who read poetry anyway? It was a marginalized pursuit in an increasingly illiterate world. I began to notice that everyone was, to a degree, a poet and a performer, showing off tattoos and boasting of afflictions. The editors of magazines got younger and younger, with the requisite rings in their noses and quirky names as if they were from ethnic enclaves that didn't exist.

I could admit that I didn't like myself, that I was basically butchering my body. What I couldn't do was accept myself. I didn't mind getting older because it would bring me closer to dying. If I ate enough, I might explode. If I purged enough, I might shrivel up and vanish. It was all or nothing. Any path was fine if it lead to an extreme.

On the positive side, because my life wasn't always as bad as I preferred to view it, I loved being married and not always alone. I had mixed feelings, though, about being childless and barren. See, I was never the kind of a girl most men waited a long time for. Nor was I a decent gal who just got mixed up. Dalton Louis Pierre, my handsome and steadfast rock of a black husband, knew this when he asked for my hand in marriage. With Dalton, I never had to defend myself by quoting that Lady Gaga song, "I'm on the right track, Baby I was born this way."

Dalton accepted me for the quixotic quisling I was. He dealt with my bulimia nervosa by agreeing to help me pay for Dr. Murray's services and my regular meds. Though I earned, he was our family breadwinner, after all. I accorded him as much doting respect and shamefully obvious adoration as I could. He was a grounded sort, thoughtful and easygoing, what I needed. He seldom showed his emotions readily. He didn't often agree with my opinions, but he enjoyed hearing them. None of the people he worked with or had grown up with were like me, at all. I thought privately he got a kick out of knowing this. He'd never told me this outright; he didn't have to, I understood it. For him, I think time with me must have felt like a challenge but also a break in his routine.

It must have also felt, at varying junctures, like one of those old Dario Argento horror movies. I mean, when I binged, I tore the kitchen apart. All night long, after my purges, I suffered through bouts of diarrhea brought on by irritable bowel syndrome. I had visions of winged gryphons flying at me to claw my hair out. It wasn't pretty and I could be loud and a drama queen as I belched and farted and stunk up our house. I often burst into sobs or flew into tantrums without warning, or wailed into my pillow until falling to sleep. I wouldn't shower or shave my legs or armpits for days, and sometimes I'd sleep until the afternoon, locked into my anguish, frigidly pale in a cold sweat of depression.

If I'd been fertile, I would have probably opted for two children, a boy and a girl. I vacillated. There were stretches when I dreamed of pumping out babies, maybe six or seven. There were also stretches when I didn't think about pregnancy much. I found it easy to remind myself of what a mess the world was in. It had always been a mess. How many of the problems such as global climate change and hunger were due to alarmingly steady increases in population growth? Really, what was the point of subjecting innocents to the hollowed-out corpse that I believed America had become? Any utopian New Age fantasy should have been left on a rubbish heap where it belonged.

Some called me a rubber-faced hag behind my back. I didn't care. I approached hope and change with caution and didn't listen to all those lying politicians and their doltish followers with their fundraisers, yachts and snotty elitism. I had me a mean temper too. It came from my Papa, I suppose, who'd died when I was in my late teens and still needed him. Like Papa, I was prone to eyeing folks and warning them, "Don't you get me started on that...."

That's why I liked living off the beaten path with Dalton in Rappahannock County and enduring what some might think a prosaic life. For me, it was a blessing to live in a rambling country house hidden away off the beaten path since the essence of my being, as such, was defined mostly by perpetually cyclical acts of self-immolation. I had a knack for stepping back and being able to watch myself and make assessments, but this didn't stop me from bingeing and purging. Dalton, though, muddled along without thinking it important to show confidence in one's understanding of what life meant, if it meant anything at all.

This hadn't made us like most people. Or maybe it had. I never knew. We weren't so different in that we behaved, essentially, in an almost robotic way. We liked our days planned and predictable. I always knew what I was going to buy when I went shopping. I clipped or else downloaded coupons. I drove more than an hour one way to buy at the warehouse stores in the suburban communities outside DC. No serendipity, nor did I cater to any of those abstractions, moral absolutes and ironclad rules of behavior that my dear mother, Ruth Eustice Walker, lived by.

Rusty, as Mother was known to by girlfriends, most of them dead, was a native of Fort Royal, daughter of modest Virginia stock who started as dirt farmers outside of nearby Winchester, native home to Patsy Cline, before my great-grandfather moved to Front Royal to work in manufacturing and hit it big at the American Viscose Corporation Plant making the rayon fibers used for our parachutes during Second World War.

Like many of her ilk, my dear Rusty remained ever so unsure about everything but was unwilling to admit it. This kept her in need of religion and her prim Presbyterian Jesus in all His saving glory. Jesus guided and sustained her. Halleluiah, I'd think, if it works for you, my sweetheart-of-the-rodeo Rusty, then go with it. But count me out.

Early on, I'd learned to respect my mother for having married out of love, outside of her religion, to not only a Yankee but a lapsed Catholic originally from Pennsylvania. Like her, I had come to accept, tolerate and love others, including that devout and brittle soul known as my carp-faced Aunt Jess, who never married and lived in the house on Mosby Lane that she and Rusty grew up in, just a short ride to Front Royal Presbyterian, which she sedulously attended, cane in hand, each Sunday, with or without her sister.

Along with my Papa when he was alive, these two women, who I often thought might outlive me, taught me to tolerate everyone on this planet — I mean, let's face reality, tolerance has never been easy for anyone. We humans remain an opinionated lot. People tend to be full of it, you know, most of them downright moronic, but that didn't mean I should hate or try to kill them. Tolerance, for me, was a square with four points: observation, understanding, forgiveness and acceptance.

I remained snug, hidden in my cocoons, perfecting the art of avoidance, inflating and deflating. Better to be evasive and aloof. To have a ritual. One had to survive, after all, and like a carpenter I measured twice before cutting anything down to size, including myself. It was just as well I couldn't conceive children. I was far too selfish, too sick, too much of an oversized infant with a suppurating booboo.

The childlessness that Dalton and I grew to accept was a fact that Rusty struggled to get over. Aunt Jess blamed me for it as if I'd agreed to a pact with the devil. My first sin had been to marry a black man, but Jess and Rusty got over that one eventually, to their credit. I felt like both women would never forgive me for my barren womb. God only knew what they'd have done if a medical professional had explained my bulimia to them. For a while, there was heated talk from them both about adoption. I looked into it, just to appease them, but the process was absurdly rigid and difficult. Dalton might have wanted it, but he never said so. At rock bottom, I knew I couldn't handle it. Not what I wanted.

I wasn't silent on the subject. I told Dalton outright, many times, that I wasn't healthy, and of course he knew that. I also liked spoiling myself. I needed my distractions. My toys. I didn't need a child to complete us as husband and wife. Maybe Dalton did, but he was going to sacrifice that need for my sake. How could I not worship him for that?

Please don't get me wrong. Dalton and I were an active pair in the bedroom and we tried to conceive, but we failed time and again until I had myself examined and learned what Rusty would later bemoan as the "awful" truth. Endometriosis.

One more disorder. Basically, the cells that were supposed to line my endometrium, my uterine cavity, were homesteading outside of it. Playing hooky, you could say, from fertility school. What frightened me most was learning just how little scientists and doctors know about the causes of infertility in women with my condition. My research had shown me they had a few theories, but there was a frightening paucity of concrete reasons explaining why dear ol' Stella Luna couldn't produce no kin.

It wasn't awful. Honestly, after waking up from a purge session, doped up on an extra-high dose of Zoloft, rearing children often felt like someone else's painful ordeal. Another woman's dutifully perfect life. Mostly, my dear Rusty's or some other young Presbyterian minx in a skirt, pearls and salmon cardigan.

I doubted my late foul-mouthed and armor-coated Papa, so proud of his immigrant parents and his own tough journey from a Keystone State anthracite town to becoming a microwave electronics engineer with the Navy — may he rest in peace — ever gave all this too much thought. Like many men of his generation, he hoped for grandchildren, but the heart attack that killed him at the age of 48 — so very young — put an end to such hopes. It wasn't as if he spread his own seed all over the place, though he may have tried.

I was raised an only child, and though I had an aunt and uncle on the Pennsylvania Levestri side of the family, Papa wasn't close to them. I think they all just got through those formative years, keeping their noses clean, and as soon as possible got out of there and, like Papa, worked desperately toward a shining future as if their hardscrabble past was a hound that might catch up one day and devour them.

I was always the good little girl, the one who listened, obedient, caring, a tad unconventional. I wasn't pampered. I was taught to think for myself. "Be a tiger," Papa used to say. "Don't be a lamb because lambs get eaten whole."

Not really. Not always. But not a lie either and it helped me while growing up, especially when I realized that Papa was not just gone, but he wasn't coming back. Once I began to think for myself, I started to see there were too many zombified souls on this polluted planet of ours. Outside of my dreams, anything I produced should come into the world out of desire rather than any sense of propriety or filial or moral duty.

My offspring were my poems. Later, some students, a rare few, became like offspring too, but in a really vague and temporary sense. Unlike Dalton, who was a Southern-raised bona fide gentleman and military veteran working for Uncle Sam in that pit of secrecy, mendacity and outrageous mistrust known as Washington, DC, I found it easy to be nervy and full of sauce, indifferent, potty-mouthed and bull-headed. Dalton, on the other hand, played it shrewdly naïve and never came across as loud or well-informed, though he stayed up on history and current events. He was obedient to his own inner higher causes, very impecunious and a really natty dresser for a man of his size. I thought of him as my not so shaggy head-turner of a side-kick. My mate. My dreamboat.

When things were going smoothly, we balanced each other out. Dalton left at dark each morning and drove his long commute, nearly three hours to the Vienna red-line stop of the DC Metro, listening maybe to downloaded programs by Randall Pinkett or Van Jones or Tony Robbins. I had to give him credit. He was open-minded. He listened to so many speakers and podcasts from all walks of life, no matter their race, gender, sexuality or politics. Once he parked, he then used the Metro train to trundle himself into one of those stark honeycombs that lined the tentacled DC streets named after the various states of our more perfect union.

Me, on the other hand, I fought my dire urges and I meditated and dutifully took my meds and called Dr. Murray to make an extra appointment if I felt I needed one. I poached in the gloaming with Poe and Kafka and Baudelaire, playing my own version of a *poète maudit* in spite of the cynicism, the lies, the newsfeeds that came to me through my computer. You wouldn't find me in any Starbucks. Nor would I start downing my first cup of coffee any time before noon. You also wouldn't find me going to bed before two or three a.m.

I prided myself on not being like anyone Dalton spent his workday with and, knowing this, worn out when he arrived home to sometimes find dinner ready on the table, and his wife, for a change, not a victim of her own self-destructive behavior, Dalton and I had an agreement that we saved our sexual energy for the weekends. On workdays, he turned in early and he was asleep while I stayed locked into my cell either reading the tripe that passed for student essays or else returning to Shakespeare, Jane Austen or Christina

Rossetti for inspiration and entertainment while working on my own vers-libre compositions.

What Dalton and I shared was that we couldn't survive our jobs without absolute fealty to those slave plantations known as a cell phone and the Internet. For me, generally, it was departmental e-mails, Snapchats, Facebook posts, Tweets and gossipy confabs with various other kvetching and fetching women. Summer Rain, based in DC, a true American in that she was half Choctaw on her mother's side and half Yorkshire English on her Daddy's, was my closest poet friend. She read all my pieces, and I read all of hers, and only then did we submit them to magazines.

For Dalton, little of this was of interest. He listened to his podcasts in the car and read articles on the Internet, but much of his reading was erudite material concerned with national security that I wouldn't dare to even ask him about. That was another agreement we had. We didn't talk shop. Not at home. Not anywhere. Frankly, I hardly even knew what my Honey did for a living, but it must have been important based on his salary and our insurance plan.

Dalton had managed to survive one tour of duty in Iraq, having already earned a Bachelor's Degree in International Relations from the Virginia Military Institute. When he left the US Army, he earned an MS in Information Assurance from George Mason University. I had no idea, honestly, what such a diploma meant. I didn't really care either, and I thought Dalton found this a relief. Just as I found it refreshing that he didn't ask me to share any of my poems, or to talk about what I may have discussed in a session with Dr. Murray. He was just happy when he saw that I could go weeks at a time without succumbing to the bulimia.

"It's getting manageable," I'd tell him. "This is what I have to keep telling myself."

We resided in a rather slender and fortunate demographic category. A mixed-race couple without any of the tony Ivy league trimmings that, say, Barack Obama, brought to Washington. We didn't have children. We did have school loans, but we were able to pay them monthly, sometimes doubling up payments. I believed that this was what defined success in America. Not getting ahead but rather being able to meet one's bills and take a tiny sliver of one's earnings and put it into savings or an investment account now and then. My Papa wouldn't have been thrilled with this assessment, but he'd be pleased to see that I was exceedingly comfortable. Compared to him, I was downright soft. I mean, on my good days I slept until noon. Half my classes were in the afternoon, twice a week. The other half were online, also in the afternoon and I prepared them on Zoom, using a lot of You Tube videos while sitting in my sweatpants in the evenings after Dalton turned in.

Students watched some of my classes as recordings that they could dip into on their own time. All they needed to worry about was turning in their assignments on schedule. It was a far cry from the slender green spiral-bound attendance booklets I'd started my career with, or the slide rule and math equations that Papa used to pore over night after night while chain-smoking at his corner desk in his basement.

Before bed, I'd tip-toe down the stairs and enter that chilly smoky realm and at his insistence I'd sit on his lap. Papa never talked about what he was doing, but I'd look with him at all those sheets of graph paper and tracing paper and hastily scrawled equations and notes on his desk, those pencils and notepads full of numbers and lines and geometrical figures, and I'd get lost in them in that haze of cigarette smoke, the cup of black coffee and half a sandwich always there, always gone cold before he could finish it.

I never knew what time he went to bed. It had to be late, because he and Mother let me stay up until nine, though by the time I was finished with telling Papa a story about one misadventure or another I'd had at school, it was already ten. He'd apologize then, telling me he had to get back to work or else the bills wouldn't get paid. He'd kiss me on the cheek and say, "Don't forget to kiss your mother goodnight too."

There was always a deference to Rusty, a show of deep respect and affection for her. There were never any cheap admissions that "I love you." He never said it. He didn't have to. I think he trusted that I knew this. He was right to trust it, to show confidence in me. I was his little tiger, after all. I didn't need to hear it. I needed to know it. And I did.

Dalton was on the shy side and though tall and rangy, he didn't play basketball. He was broad-shouldered, a lot of man, but he didn't play football either. Nor did he like watermelon. I did. I loved watermelon. My point is that Dalton didn't fit any of the stereotypes. Neither did I, not really, though I had Rusty's sour Appalachian-tinged stinginess and I had Papa's gregarious appetite. I had always been the big eater in the family. The seeds of my suffering from bulimia might have been sown during my childhood. I'd discussed this with Dr. Murray, but it hadn't led me to anything conclusive.

Food solved a lot of problems. At least for a short while. I still didn't really know when or how the bulimia and all my perverse and distorted thoughts about food kicked in, because I didn't accept my emotional obsession with comestibles of all kinds, especially the fattening ones, as a disability. I loved to eat, but that love wasn't anywhere near as out of control as my obsession with poetry and romantic love. I would swoon telling Dalton: *See, Honey, I'm not just like you and that's why we get along so well.*

A born diplomat, everyone liked Dalton, except for the few hardcore racists in our neighboring hills, who we avoided, of course, at all costs. I was the opposite, what you might call a disrupter, a populist. I was a zombie too, walking wounded, always under medication. Though I was never a fan of Trump, couldn't stand the way he butchered language, especially since I often had the feeling he knew better, that it was all an act, I believed that underneath there was some devilishly scheming intelligence at work. But that's a politician for you, isn't it? "Don't buy what they sell you," Papa used to say.

I could certainly be just as biased and cocky as any politician, no matter the party affiliation. I was intrigued by the ruthless monomania in these men and women. Mostly the women. They were the worst. Such tools. Women have too much character. They can't hide their prevarications as well as men do. The deceit shows in their pretty faces.

Whether a politician or a school principal, I'd seen throughout my life in those who wielded power, their penchants for creating chaotic muddles, and their hubristic empire-mongering. Dalton argued that at least Trump and his insider operatives didn't appear to believe they knew what was best for citizens in countries such as Libya, Syria, Iraq and Afghanistan. All the talk from them, according to Dalton, had been about getting out of those places. And about oil too. Dalton liked that The Donald just came right out and blurted it, subjecting listeners to blunt force trauma. Dalton often had me in stitches with his imitation, standing so gregariously in the living room, a beer in his hand, bearing down on me with his kookiest version of Trump: "We got the oil. We're getting out of there. But we got the oil."

One reason I was still married, and happily so, was that Dalton tolerated me during relapse stretches when I gave in to my depressions, zipped off to Costco, stocked up and relapsed into a month of stuffing my face and shoving my fingers down my throat. We also avoided talking politics too seriously at home. We joked about such things. I didn't really know what his party affiliation was and I didn't want to know. For years, one of the many secrets that I kept from him and Rusty was that I'd never even voted. If asked why, I would probably say: Why should I? I never like any of the candidates. If I do, that candidate never gets past the first round of debates. Take Rand Paul, for example, or Tulsi Gabbard. Like Rodney Dangerfield, each of them, no respect at all on the national stage yet bright and brimming with ideas.

It was like I resided in a different sphere. Very few of those political suits, male or female, like mannequins wheeled out to the front display window at a high-end clothing store, appealed to my interests or needs. Their talk was what Nero Wolfe always said when speaking to his sidekick Archie: just so much "hooey." Nero was my favorite detective. I didn't care whether others still read him or not. The man had his orchids and his love for food and I adored him for his prurient pursuit of those passions.

I lived in my poems and my cozy detective novels. The USA, the world stage, neither were even news or remotely interesting for me. They never had been, I suppose. When I thought of politics I thought of looking at the water-stained pages from an old issue of *Mad* magazine. I saw the cartoon panels of a Spy Versus Spy conflict each time I heard yet another news report from some talking head on Fox or CNN, or downloaded a new app, or agreed to accept the cookies of a particular web site. All something of a joke. Freedom, liberty, c'mon, such tired-out husks of language had lost all meaning.

Speaking of cookies, the ones I took seriously came to me during weekend visits to Rusty. She never approved of my on-the-verge-of-madness appetite, and how I indulged it when given the opportunity, but she never stopped me and she always had a plate or maybe a platter of home-baked confections for me, and they were piled neatly and still warm under saran wrap. For me, food was love, though it took me many years of therapy to accept this. Once I did, I took in food gladly as if each bite was an orphan Jonah needing to journey into its whale. Namely me. I inhaled my meals as if I feared they'd disappear whenever I paused to catch my breath. For Rusty, a love equation existed, but it wasn't about accepting food. It was more about dishing it out discriminately now and then. She'd fed my father well and he'd died of a coronary due to all the extra weight he was carrying.

I didn't think this was always the case with Rusty. She learned from my father how to trust a certain amount of heated passionate abandon. Papa never met a meal he couldn't eat twice. Yet Mother told me often, even as she brought me more cookies or took me out for barbecue, that I should watch my weight. I did watch it and mostly it went up and up and then down and down. Yes, I was one of thousands of women who could identify with Oprah when she was on TV and discussing her weight struggles.

Why was my face so puffy all of a sudden? I didn't want to be like Miss Piggy, did I? No, Mother, why not? Miss Piggy was cute. And so was I, no matter how swollen my cheeks. Besides, how could I worry over calories while surrounded by cookies and cakes and knowing there were no children in my house who would gobble them up and that Dalton didn't go in for baked goods of any kind which meant more for me.

Baked goods were not a weakness. They were a path toward an orgasmic understanding of paradise. I couldn't get enough of them. I wrote a comic poem with Baked Goods as its title, in which I portrayed myself as Alice In Pastryland, falling down a hole and landing atop a huge chocolate cake. It was while on my hands and knees eating that cake, out of control, that I was visited by various scones and wedges of pie, who I promptly befriended and then betrayed, devouring them one at a time as if at an orgy. I didn't think it a very good poem. On the other hand, it said much about a part of who I was, as all my poems tended to do.

Rusty did love me, there was never any doubt about that. She could be charming, truly, arguing about how hungry she went as a girl sometimes, especially when layoffs began at American Viscose, where her father had also worked, and where she had worked briefly, all of her family profiting, including me, from a factory that dumped so much arsenic, carbon disulfide and PCB's into the lovely Shenandoah River that it became a Superfund site that required 25 years and 150 million dollars to clean up. A total disaster and much of it leveled and filled-in these days and fenced off.

No daughter or husband of Rusty Levestri would go hungry, that was the least Mother could promise. I also thought she liked giving me those plates of cookies because she knew it gave me a pretext for returning the plate, which meant I would travel to see her again. Not that I wouldn't visit. I saw her usually twice a month, every other weekend. For years, it was usually on a Saturday. It was my time. Dalton took those days for himself, either doing yard work, which was a constant and endless chore, or else visiting friends in Lexington, Warrenton, or Culpepper.

Unlike me, when he had free time, Dalton didn't like to sit home. In the fall, he tootled off every Saturday to some college football game, and sometimes I joined him and found myself drinking way too much beer afterwards. In the winter, we'd make weekend trips to visit antique shops together. Springtime we went fishing. Together. I loved fishing. I loved being in the outdoors with him. In summer, we'd take rafting trips, go camping and we'd visit his family and celebrate his birthday.

Dalton's family held an annual picnic just outside of Cartersville, Georgia. I had attended every year since we married and I'd become family. Dalton may not have liked watermelon, though he did love his fried chicken. I ate both of those foods in large quantities. I relished them. I loved potato salad too, and pass me more of that okra and mac and cheese and those black-eyed peas please.

Dalton had no father and I never knew why. Just his mother and his aunts, all of whom loved making sure my plate stayed full. They just marveled over the way the white member of their family chowed down, just as I revered and despaired and laughed over their stories and, at times, later used them in my poems.

What those ladies in the Pierre clan taught me about was another America, the one connected directly to racism, Jim Crow, outright sadistic treatment because of skin color, and yet love, forgiveness, piety and passion. Theirs was an America I had no inkling even existed back when I graduated from high school in 1990.

Dalton, though fatherless, had uncles and male cousins and nieces and nephews. Though I didn't meet them all, those whom I'd broken bread with had come to accept me because I listened and didn't judge. I genuinely loved being with them. I learned from them. Even if some of them, in turn, judged and didn't like or trust me, they could see the look of pride and happiness on Dalton's face whenever he introduced me to a cousin or a niece I was meeting for the first time. Sometimes, he was meeting them for the first time too. That was how widely some branches of his family tree tended to reach.

Mother knew so little about this part of my life. She met Dalton's mother and his three brothers and two sisters during our wedding, which was a sunny, cheerful and yet simple affair that we held in Savannah, because it was one of Dalton's favorite cities, and one of mine too. Aunt Jess came and kept Mother company, and they remained mostly stiff and pickle-faced throughout the affair and didn't stay but one night at a Motel 6, but I thought they were happy for me.

It was on my wedding day that I really understood that I'd always been Papa's girl. Not Mother's. Don't ask me why or how I knew. I just did. Something about Rusty's way of showing love wasn't fair to me. It hurt. Deep down. The eating soothed it. I just seemed incapable of doing anything right for her. Like my Aunt Jess, Rusty was one of those musty mistrustful self-righteous patriotic Americans who believed in a country that no longer existed, one that shouldn't have, especially when a citizen considered with open eyes the realities and the legacies of the slave trade and what that had meant for generations of black Americans.

For Rusty, privacy was a bigger issue than racism. She thought about black people, she prayed for them, but her actions showed me that the less she saw of them, the better. She'd rather deal with abstract transgressions or moral ambiguities and the rock-hard denial of truth than face what was happening in her neighborhood, or the pollution caused by her family's employer, or the squalor that some lived in over there on the other side of the Front Royal tracks.

What concerned Rusty was that leaders from another country had stolen her privacy, her country, her husband, her sense of security and they might steal her freedom. When she argued this with Dalton, my dear husband took a high road and let Rusty vent. He told her, as well, that she might be right, probably was, and this justified why his work in cyber security was so important. What he didn't tell her was that it also justified, in his mind, his legal ownership of weapons that he kept in our house.

That's right. Dalton had his guns, which I never saw, and he had his moments of genius. Believe me, Rusty glowed knowing that her son-in-law played a role in keeping us safe from those Russians and Chinese and rabid radicalized Muslims. More than once Rusty had told me how much Papa would have loved knowing I'd married such a man, in spite of his skin color.

She just had to add that, didn't she? In spite of — as if anyone could control the race they'd been born into. I didn't tell her how much that offended me because I didn't want any more conflict in my life. One of my tenets that had come out of years of therapy had been to avoid conflict whenever possible. At all costs, if necessary. Conflicts triggered feelings of insecurity in me, sent me running toward the freezer aisle to stock up on ice cream by the gallon.

Nor had I told Rusty that Papa knew this, even from his grave, and that he'd helped guide my decision, that I talked to him in my dreams. That I prayed to him. That he visited me sometimes. Papa was always with me. Shouldn't Rusty, such an alleged woman of faith, know this? Perhaps she did. I liked to think she did, but she wasn't the type to talk about it.

I knew it took Rusty some time, many years and Fourth of July and Christmas visits to accept Dalton, but she'd come around in her guarded way. She was lonely, after all, even with Aunt Jess's company, which was never exactly a night of waltzing at a grand soiree. Dalton had always been kind and generous to them both. Mother found no reason to be disappointed in him. If anything, she was more disappointed in me with my endometriosis and my "flabby face," as she called it, and not giving her grandchildren.

Sometimes, I thought of ways I could make her happy before she passed on. But she wasn't wired in any kind of simple way. Even if happy, she wouldn't show it. I thought more and more about adopting a child. I'd slept on the idea for the first five years of our marriage, and I'd always come back to the reality of what that meant, the demands, and my reasons for doing it. When, years later, I returned to that issue, I still understood that, as Dr. Murray had told me, I couldn't live to make Rusty happy. I had to make myself happy first.

Rusty had me, her only child, for better or worse. Wasn't I enough? Apparently not. Yet I had to be there for her. I was. Dalton and I spent far more time with her than we ever did with his mother, a booming bosomy mountain of a woman named Odelia who nobody messed with and who never complained if we didn't visit at Christmas. However, we never skipped a Thanksgiving meal at Odelia's. My bulimia be damned during that holiday. I found a way to cut loose the reins and put on the feedbag at her table, where the eating sent me into a rapturously voluptuous coma.

Odelia was more fully present than Mother. She had a sense of humor. She'd break out into song. She didn't judge. She kept filling my plate. Smiled watching me down those sweet potatoes. She filled Dalton's plate too, and never commented on how he, after about seven years of marriage, was starting to put on weight.

Odelia's life wasn't at all like mine. She'd had it so much harder and had lived through many years really chock full of disappointments. Her children probably didn't share the same father. Dalton assured me of this in private, but nobody talked about it. Why bother? They talked about who they were, blood kin, in the moment, hugging each other and listening to music and singing along to it, and going to church and behaving with all the warmth and generosity that I'd missed out on, had never seen expressed with such exuberance during holidays when growing up.

What I always purposefully neglected to tell Mother was that I wasn't so sure Papa would be thrilled with the "other race" component of his daughter's marriage. Not that Papa was a racist. Not at all. But who can say? I thought he would have been happier if I'd found an Italian man. Conversely, he would have admitted with a smile that if his Tiger, his Stella Luna was happy, then he was happy too. That's all he'd ever wanted for me. Happiness. If only life were that simple. But that was Papa. A brilliant engineer. An autodidact. Not the most sophisticated thinker when it came to emotions.

Mother stayed silent and mostly in denial on topics such as race, and I seldom pursued it. What was the point? Papa had gone to his rest long before I'd even started thinking about or looking for a husband. I'd always be his Tiger, his little girl. I liked knowing this. I could go back to that time and see myself as I was, so completely insecure, doting on him as he doted on me. One should have such pleasant memories. They were a refuge, as sweet as the creamy desserts that I sometimes over-indulge in.

If I argued what you could call issues in any way, it was with Mother and on the most basic of levels and usually over tea and a heap of brownies that I wasn't timid about plowing into my mouth one at a time until the plate was empty. I might say something to her such as, "There is no privacy, Mother, never was. It's a myth. There's no neighborhood, either. The conversations between Jack and Jill on their way uphill to the White House are just background blather that dilletantes like us labor to avoid."

Then I'd stop, having confounded her. Having showed off again, toying with language. She'd look at me as if stunned to realize such a creature, perhaps a monster (she wasn't always sure) had come from her womb. Then I'd smile at her and show her how much I loved her while I chewed on brownies and heard the echo of my own vituperative displays of arrogant linguistic gymnastics. I was a pill, no doubt about it.

We'd change the subject. We'd take a drive somewhere. She knew how much I liked to just roll with her through the countryside south of Strasburg down Winchester way into the Shenandoah Valley. We might take old Route 33 and stop at antique shops or Goodwill stores all the way into Harrisonburg just poking around looking at the views and hunting down bargains. I did this with her often when I visited. It had gotten more difficult when Goodwill started selling their own donations directly online, but I could still usually score a book or two that I could re-sell online at a marked-up rate. Or else I could pick up some second-hand clothing. My weight shifted so much in both directions that I was constantly in need of wardrobe upgrades.

Mother was no fool. As Dalton liked to say, "She runs her own covert operations." What he meant by that was that Mother really did want to know and understand the world's suffering and she sought reliable ways to sort the useful badinage from the lies, and she didn't shy away, in private, from the footage of children maimed, gassed, displaced, losing everything. It was all there at her fingertips online or on television, and though it existed in her town, she preferred the forms of it that were far away and had to be accessed through devices.

In her mind, the people of America didn't suffer the way people did in poorer less developed countries. She didn't ask or expect to sort prevarications from truth, though she claimed she knew a fib when she smelled it. Her thinking about issues, world problems, topics I brought up with her in conversation, tended to lead her to terrible suffrage. She still wanted to believe in the fairy-tale America she was raised in. Maybe it was a fairy tale, at least in her mind. Maybe not.

But she couldn't believe. She knew this fate, though she still struggled to accept it. Well, denial had its uses. Aunt Jess suffered the same way. I wrote one of many poems about them titled The Nostalgia Sisters. They hadn't seen it. I hadn't even tried to publish it. I most likely never would.

All of what I'm talking about added oxygen to the fires in the blood of my poems as they scorched their way out of me, rising and insisting I wouldn't be one of those mindless whiffs of a woman in the insufferable traffic in, say, Fairfax County, gawking at the exhaust-burnt and dying rhododendrons, defining liberty as turning right at a red light on my way to golf courses, lunch dates, gated condo communities and pet store parking lots full of SUVs.

I was the one who would stop, my flesh heated and margarine soft and I'd think more than twice about the dismal emptiness of existence. Maybe I'd do something about it other than to go shopping and overeat and vomit. I'd certainly scribble down lines from what would eventually become a poem as another shoreline inside of me eroded, another river overflowing to burst a dam within to remind me that in spite of all the misery I'd endured I was still doing fine, still actively trying to understand who I was, who *we* were (meaning the family of humankind), still in the noble fight, though realistic about my chances of winning since I didn't believe anymore that anyone won. There were no victors. We fought or we loved until we died.

I could sit up high like the other suburban women did, behind the wheels of their oversized vehicles in traffic, the AC on, a Satellite radio bringing the latest package of jingoism and cant and over-sold overplayed tunes. I could sip espresso jolts or nurse Macchiatos and try to sooth my nerves and my conscience — but I didn't. I just preferred my tawdry country home off Fodderstack Road in Rappahannock County, where I had a short-haired white tabby, Mini Me, and a big garden, and there were cupboards full of Twinkies and Pop Tarts and Little Debbie cakes, and dry reds and sweet whites from local wineries, along with hiking trails and fishing streams nearby and a canoe out back and my beautiful Shenandoah River not far away and not a lot of people, though tons of deer and some-times bear, and Mother and Aunt Jess not too far away in Helltown, the nickname for Front Royal, where Mother returned in 1991, one year after I finished high school and Papa died. See, I went to college in Virginia with a scholarship, so that I could be nearer to Mother. She purchased a little house in Front Royal so she could be close to

Aunt Jess and the life she'd abandoned out of fealty to Papa and the places his work had compelled us to live in. Without Papa around, we'd remain a family. We'd stay in touch. It suited the three of us.

It wasn't my fault that I sometimes felt overwhelmed by dread, drowning in it, believing we were all trapped in a nightmare, I mean as a race of humans unwilling to really address the cruelty of our behavior toward each other, and the outright inanity of our choices. It wasn't my mother's fault either, and as one part of me told Sigmund Freud that he was full of malarkey, another part of me still insisted that Dr. Murray had been right when she told me I could control more of this existence of mine, even though both my parents could have helped me see my own flaws better and aided me in improving on them. I had to learn how to forgive my parents, but first I had to forgive myself.

I found different ways. I'd get outside of my own neurosis by learning about a world issue through some thoroughly noxious and guilt-inducing PBS broadcast, or maybe, which was closest to the truth, I just didn't care and wanted to keep gorging on cheeseburgers and hush puppies with lots of ketchup while drifting back to high school days, specifically junior year, when I was thin and troubled and lonely and first began to masturbate and understood that I could not only write poems, but that I could read literature and write about it faster and in deeper ways that none of my classmates could.

Correction. Maybe I cared too much. Maybe I thought too excessively. I knew I felt helpless. Who didn't? Which survivor among us wanted everything to be increasingly equitable and wouldn't have minded knowing more about what our taxes really funded and whether or not our nation really was on God's side? I'd say most of them. And what a God He was, "a real ball buster" as my father used to say, tearing us apart, one baby after another from within so many wombs, from behind so many borders.

I wasn't sure about anything. I'd never been sure. But I'd pass on the religion. I found my happiness by following the heat of one word or line of a poem, one after another as they leaked out of the soulful pores in my vagina to help me shape myself as I groped my way back inside the chambers of my being.

Or else I lost my way, and the poem assured me I should be lost. I was just not sure. I didn't even know if I *wanted* to be.

—◦◦◦—

There's a bitterness that sharpens my tongue as I think again of the phrase "war on terror." Yet without it, Dalton wouldn't be half the breadwinner and esteemed professional that he's become. Yes, I'm proud of my gorgeous man, but I have mixed feelings since I benefit from what the pursuit of national security allows me to purchase during my grocery runs to the new Walmart superstore to stock up. I make those runs once a week and I fill two carts, no problem, keeping our two freezers and our massive fridge full to bursting at all times. Life is too short to go hungry. I won't have it any other way. I not only like to cook. I need to.

Part of me, though, doesn't sleep well as I think of hunger out there and how ghosts in the machine wreak vengeance on the working stiffs and the peasantry and the have-nots and the well-heeled alike and that there is no God, there can't be, but if He exists He's a master at a chess game of international arrangements profitable to corporate enterprises and all unseemly investors involved. Thousands killed somewhere. Just another day. Millions forced into refugee status. Floods, famines, fires. Just another week. I shut it all out. I go shopping. I eat with a vengeance. My paying attention will not really change anything.

There may be a poem brewing. There is. I'll just let it happen.

That's the little I can do to offer change. I laugh at my vanity. It's not like anyone's asking for my poems.

Dalton told me yesterday, while promptly rubbing a circle against the landscape of flesh that keeps expanding as it defines my derriere, a lovely bit of petting that I really like, "Do you think there are other stooges out there like me? There must, has to be."

"Sweetheart, no, you're not a stooge. I think you're brilliant."

"Yeah, guess not. But my meaning is, you know — I'm fed up. Nothing I'm doing makes a difference. All this cybercrime, the dark web, there's no end to it."

"You're having doubts," I told him. "It's natural. I'd say you're bewildered, but it's because you're not in retreat from your true self. The real Dalton. The one who knows that it's all just a game for them. And that's why they pay you so much."

"But people get hurt. You have no idea."

He'd looked at me then, just one aching glance and I stopped talking. I shut myself down and waited a minute. Then I began speaking again, because if there's one thing I like more than eatin', it's talkin' face to face with my husband.

I started saying to Dalton that I suspected he might be bewildered because he was married to a woman who felt exactly the same way that he did. That we had become in many ways the same person and merely expressed our shared pain in our own unique ways. Each of us had our own idioms and phrases. In short, separate vernaculars. This was normal. What made him different from me was that he still believed. In God and country and all that piffle. What made me different was that even though I talked a blue streak, I didn't believe in any of it. What made us alike was that we actually listened most of the time, especially when it was inconvenient for us. I loved that about Dalton. Very few souls really listened when they had to.

"Trust me on this one. You know I'm right," I said.

It seemed to help, though he was maudlin throughout dinner and didn't spend any time with Mini Me before brushing his teeth and turning in. I felt tempted to snuggle in beside him, offer some comfort and more counsel, but my day was just beginning and I felt this poem boiling in my craw and I had to get it out.

I decided to lock Mini Me in our bedroom, closing the door, which forced the sluggish cat with all its calico fur to sleep on the bed a while at Dalton's feet. It was a half measure, I know, but Dalton loved Mini Me and I felt, no, I *knew* that on a subconscious level he appreciated my gesture.

I also had other work to do, related to weed money, extra income, my own ongoing business venture — a necessity due to my inability to stop smoking pot. Yes, I must tell you about this obsession.

Not an inability to stop. I just didn't want to. I could still afford it on my less than impressive salary as an English professor at Cameronshire Community College.

I worked as a soldier in what can be called the army of the gig economy, selling online through Amazon and eBay and Etsy. For a long time, I kept and updated lists of movies which hadn't yet made it to DVD. That all ended around the Obama era as streaming technology hit its early stride and nearly put me out of business. For about a dozen years, I was selling ten to fifteen VHS tapes per day, at a significant profit. Later came DVDs, which further boosted profits. I tested them all before sending them out and received very few negative reviews.

Nowadays, it's mostly books, though many of those are going digital or published as E-books, as well. I'm still able to maintain an anemic average of one sale per day to customers all over the globe. Of course, my sales numbers rise significantly during the holiday season, but not like in my glory days. I remember one time I sold a VHS cassette, still shrink-wrapped, of *Conflict*, a Humphrey Bogart and Sydney Greenstreet classic to a woman named Tina Sinatra with a Hollywood address. It made me wonder, but I restrained the urge to pen a polite note asking if she was, indeed, kin to Old Blue Eyes.

I still love the old Sinatra records that my father used to play for me when a girl. I grew up listening to them. I'm fond of Italian men, in general, but they don't thrill me the way black men do. One thing I never told Papa was that I wouldn't want to marry an Italian boy. I saw too many of them in the Catholic churches I attended growing up and I didn't like the way they behaved toward me, especially during my time in high school. I also feared that such a man would never measure up to my father. I didn't compare Dalton to Papa because the two were so very different. I liked this difference. I wanted it.

An Italian-American lover might also be just a tad too much like me. Impulsive, obsessive, hormonal and over-sensitive. He might be too emotional and compulsive and without much of a filter, just as I was, even though I didn't like to think of myself that way. I never knew why I had a thing for African or dark-skinned men, but I did. It wasn't logical. It was emotional. Dalton wasn't my first. He was my third, though I kept the first two secret from my parents. I can admit that I knew the first time we made love that I wanted Dalton's luscious body for myself for the rest of my days and that I'd do anything to get and keep him. It didn't turn out to be as difficult as I'd imagined.

Maybe I had some charms to offer, after all. For one, I was a natural-born genie in the kitchen and thanks to Dalton's family down in Georgia, I'd learned ways to fry up okra and make collards with bacon and to fry chicken the way my man liked it. The way I'd learned to like it too.

I suppose this will sound strange to some, but I liked being

American. You seldom hear anyone share such a sentiment publicly, though I never doubted other people felt it. I reveled in reading and writing about my American poets. Louise Bogan. Gwendolyn Brooks. Anne Sexton. Denise Levertov, who was born in England but became an American. Then there were what I thought of as the mid-century buttoned-down lunatics, such as Lowell and Berryman. There was the peripatetic Langston Hughes. And women such as Maya Angelou and Lucille Clifton, with her poem "Homage To My Hips" that I've been teaching for a long time. There was hermetic Emily Dickinson and ramblin' Walt Whitman. It was a long list of contemporary and modern she-and-he and black-and-white and blue poets. Fugitives and imagists and beatniks. From Marianne Moore to Audre Lorde. From Gary Snyder to, more recently, Gloria Emerson, Rita Dove, and Natasha Tretheway.

All the work of these poets formed inside me a stewing influence that I became more open to and found more appealing as I got older and a bit weary of the tight-knickered TS Eliot, and Mr. Swift and Mr. Keats, and the Brontes and all the English, not just American writers that I soaked myself in as a scholar of the old-school English major curriculum, from the Bible to Milton and everyone else the likes of Harold Bloom and his cronies at Yale and Harvard had decided on as defining the canon.

For me, poetry was about language and its umbilical connection to identity, but I never even heard much Italian, or read Dante or *Orlando Furioso*, or any of the cliché Italian-American Sicilian gangster argot while growing up in the different places we lived in as Papa took contract work with companies connected to the military.

I was born in Houston, the *Port* of Houston, as many people didn't think of it. Lived there until I was about five and don't remember much other than the heat and humidity and Rusty sweating and sitting in her bra next to a fan that was constantly whirring.

After Houston, Papa moved us three times in three years. First, Nevada, where he worked near or maybe on the Nellis Air Force base. I didn't know why. Next, San Antonio, also hot all the time and where I learned that Mexican food and my stomach did not get along. Thirdly, Papa worked on a project connected to Langley Air Force base and this, I remembered, made Mother happy because she wasn't far from Aunt Jess and home, and it was my first taste of Virginia and it just felt like heaven to me.

That was a happy year. I went to the beach often. I was eight years old and Papa's career, though erratic, was taking off. I thought we'd just stay in Virginia and live happily ever after. So did Mother, I think, but little did she know. The following year, Papa was offered a contract with Raytheon that he couldn't pass up. We moved to New England, specifically to Seekonk, Massachusetts, small and crowded and cold in the winter.

I thought, okay, it's just one more temporary address. More new kids to meet at school. Seekonk wasn't too far from the ocean. And I began suspecting we'd move again in a year or two, so I'd give Massachusetts a chance. First, I had to learn how to say the word. Then I had to get used to the cold weather. And the cold people, their brittle attitudes. But this was the state of Longfellow and Louisa May Alcott. Of Thoreau and Emerson. My secret passion for poetry would connect to the outside world. One of my best days ever in high school was when we went on a field trip to Salem to visit the House of Seven Gables.

But maybe, someday, we'd go back to Virginia. I knew Mother hoped we would.

It wasn't in the cards. Little did Rusty and I know that we'd live there in the Bay State until I was finished with high school. What Papa had, and what any man wants when raising a family, was job security and a rising salary. My teen years until Papa's death and my high school graduation, were spent in Seekonk and though I tried to make new friends and I swam often in places like Newport and Cape Cod, my confusion and disorientation and unhappiness mirrored that of Mother's. We tried, but neither of us ever felt at home there.

I couldn't say why. Lots of reasons, I suppose. Damn Yankees, as I heard Mother remark now and then. True, the people were harsher and less patient, with none of the courteous ways of Virginians or Texans. Though for me it wasn't about that. It was more about growing out of childhood and fitting in and experiencing puberty and all the blues that came with it. I wasn't any different than any of the other girls at school in that I envied those who were pretty and popular. I was just lonelier than the others, I guess. There'd been no continuity.

My parents may have noticed, but I didn't make it easier for them. I became secretive, stayed in my room, and read constantly. All of Dumas. All of Jules Verne. Fennimore Cooper. Conan Doyle. Pippi Longstocking. Nancy Drew mysteries. Stephen King. Ursula Le Guin. I brought home stacks from the library and devoured the language, setting myself free to get lost in the romance, the mystery, the faraway lands. I was safe there. I felt thrills and excitement.

Maybe my parents didn't see how maladjusted I was because they'd never had the opportunities that they believed I had. What were those opportunities? I didn't know where to look for them or who to ask. Unlike them both, I was an only child. But at least I had them as my parents. During that time, my dear Mother lost both her parents in the course of one year. She went away to stay with Aunt Jess and didn't come back for six months. All that she'd known other than Aunt Jess was now dead. She'd finished high school at Warren County High when it was still segregated. End of education. She was 20 years old when Papa got her pregnant and he, being raised Catholic and ten years older, having served his time in the Navy at

Newport News, married her. Did he love her? I sometimes wasn't sure. I knew he was loyal, worked all the time, including weekends, and Mother never once questioned him about it.

Mother talked about education and opportunities, but I never really heard anything of a useful nature from her because I came to realize that she didn't really know what to give me. She was a provincial and lacked experience in such matters. Our life in Massachusetts, with all its colleges and sometimes smarmy people, made her feel alienated and ill at ease. I told her often that I wanted to go back to Virginia, and this thrilled her to pieces. We had that in common.

What we didn't share was a lasting back and forth as mother and daughter. No talks about my period or boys or any of those important topics. I learned from girlfriends, awkwardly so, and I learned from books. You could say that throughout those lonely Seekonk years, I learned how to learn through reading. I was, without knowing it, well on my way to becoming an autodidact and one adept and resourceful scholar.

What attracted me to Mary Washington College was that it had once been an all-girl's school and it was in Fredericksburg, Virginia, a town I'd visited and fell in love with as a little girl. With Mother's approval and support, I put my foot to the gas pedal and buried myself in my studies at high school. It helped that Mother was home each afternoon. She didn't work, and she sat and tutored me through Algebra and pushed me to keep studying throughout those high school years and I took solace in that studying and came to really love it.

I found so much comfort in my books, delving early into George Eliot, for example, and feeling much less alienation in her world than I experienced from the one at school among my peers. Lo and behold, one day, after the grief I went through senior year of high school following Papa's death, I had my bachelor's in English from Mary Washington, my MA in English as a scholarship student from Virginia Tech, and my PhD earned online from Old Dominion. I had adopted the Commonwealth of Virginia as home and I felt I had, at last arrived.

Bene educata, from the Italian, as Papa used to share with me. I was Papa's little tiger. Well-bred. Well-educated. I lived to bring out the pride in Rusty's breast. Those were halcyon days for us as mother and daughter. I followed the dictates from Papa's ghost as, over the years, he would come to me in dorm rooms and cheap apartments with his encouraging words. "Stay with it, Tiger. You won't regret it."

I didn't. Not a whit, though I was still paying back loans for my Mary Washington, and my ODU diplomas. The latter one helped me secure my position as a full-timer at Cameronshire, after some not so thrilling stints as an adjunct at General Howe, and the Annandale campus of Northern Commonwealth Community College.

They were each as much Mother's diplomas as they were mine. My father never saw them happen, but he was there. He felt them. I felt his presence. I was 18 when he died, and in the fall approaching my nineteenth year, I started at Mary Washington, determined to please Mother, terrified of the skinny girl with big glasses and pimples in the mirror, but doomed to take way too much solace and comfort in reading alone and drinking beer and feasting on Virginia barbecue and red velvet cake. All of it legal other than the beer.

My weed habit didn't kick in until my third year when, at 22, I could finally convince myself I was over the grieving process regarding Papa, even though I wasn't. I'd never be. I thought of Papa every day and I missed him. He never got beyond high school either, but he knew how to educate himself. I thought he was intimidated by the trappings of formal education, but he was brilliant, self-taught, trained by the military, strict with himself, demanding. All those traits I began to see and respect in myself.

How Papa loved me. Of that, I would always be sure. Half the poems in my first book recounted memories of my time with him as a girl. There's a sadness in those poems, an innocence that I stopped feeling as strongly once I saw the poems between the covers of my book. It was still there within me, but I had thought by writing those poems, letting others see and critique them, I would be able to distance myself slightly from the loss. I had been right about this. Naturally, it helped me to heal. But it wasn't the only reason why I wrote those poems. I wrote them because they kept me up at night, singing and screaming and chanting between my ears. I didn't know how to turn myself quiet, to shut off the tap, so to speak. So I wrote and wrote.

In my adopted Virginia, Mother's native terra firma, I began to feel like I had found a sense of rootedness that Papa never really had come to know. If anything, he had his military contracts. Work was what grounded him. Put him at that desk with his slide rule and he was a happy man. Slide an antipasto plate and a huge bowl of spaghetti in front of him and he'd lose himself, as I did, before coming up for air, his ribcage aching. He had known and developed equations for technologies that during his time were cutting edge and had become, quickly, passe. Maybe he just wasn't meant to stay around a long time.

What did I have? For starters, plenty of library sales, yard sales and swap meets and what Yankees called flea markets to choose from. I tried to get to these libraries on a Wednesday or Thursday usually, depending on my teaching schedule. Sometimes, on a Saturday, Mother would join me if it was a sale not too far from her house. She'd become a more avid reader, perhaps inspired by me, but I couldn't stomach any of the bleak crime novels she gravitated toward. This was fine, really. She had her tastes, I had mine. She even used to follow suggestions from Oprah's book club back when it was a thing. And, like me, she loved a bargain.

Dalton never joined me. I didn't want him to. These sales were my own frolic and business at the same time. I followed the belief that each person in a marriage should have his or her own such concerns. I often drove alone on the first night of as many sales as possible, where I paid to become a member of the library's Friends group if I wasn't already one. It became much easier year by years because many of the sales were advertised online through a web listing devoted solely to library sales nationwide. It was quite the business for some dealers, many of whom I had come to know and swap with and learn from.

My early arrival allowed me to elbow out what I called the vultures. These weren't the kindly book dealers with their erudite and genial spirit of professional camaraderie. These vultures were the new-comers, the bar-code readers who weren't really bibliophiles. They were fierce money-grubbing competitors. Some of the sales, such as the big one that happened twice a year in Charlottesville and ran for a week, prohibited bar-code readers during the first day or two. If I went on a first night, I wouldn't dare ask Mother to come along. It was just too much of a battle and it was where I knew I'd score enough titles to cover the cost of gasoline and, in some cases, a hotel room. It just depended on how far I had to drive.

I'd ride as far south as Columbia or Atlanta, time permitting, and as far north as Pittsburgh, depending on my schedule and what I suspected the sale would offer. One of the best sales I'd ever been to, which was totally worth the trip, was sponsored by Brandeis University but held in Kansas City, Missouri, of all places. Dalton joined me on that visit. He went to Royals baseball games while I shopped for books and ate twice my weight in barbecue each day.

I knew better, too, at which sales I would profit from most, and which might be disappointing. Yet there were always surprises. One day, I realized that I'd been doing this for fifteen years, starting the year Dalton and I married. I'd seen the competition grow and get dumber, and I'd seen many truly learned bibliophiles get disillusioned and leave the business, fed up with the increased usage of barcode readers, a tool I had purchased but tried not to use at sales. I found the practice efficient but odious. Sure, it came in handy when I was in a hurry at home trying to determine fair market-value prices or just needing to unload inventory cheaply. But it also meant a dealer really didn't have to know a fig about books, and I loved my books. They were my borrowed children, cared for until I freed them, at a profit, to a better home. I read them too. I learned. God, how I learned, and I enjoyed it so much.

I preferred to think of myself as a perpetual student of the trade, whether I was buying expensive medical textbooks that still commanded a high price, or I was investing in antiquarian leather editions that might not sell quickly but were so rare that eventually I would sell them for a significant profit.

I wasn't a book hound. It was worse than that, I had what Nicholas A. Basbanes described in his memoir, *A Gentle Madness*. I was a zealously passionate bibliomaniac. Tomes were everywhere in our house, with one room as my library and another room as my work space, the books piled separately, either already listed and organized or else in disarray and waiting for me to get to them. I could procrastinate, believe me, especially when I had enough cannabis to enjoy, a habit that Dalton didn't have any interest in, but one that didn't bother him either.

We both knew that Dalton was subjected to random drug screenings at work, so I didn't ask him to smoke with me. When I indulged, which was often enough, I did so alone in the privacy of my work-space where I kept my paraphernalia and there was a window fan that drew the smoke out into the woods and farmland behind our house. Some nights, I just sat outdoors under the oaks in our back-yard and puffed away, in private, communing with the stars.

I also baked a mean pot brownie and kept stores of them in the freezer at all times. I'd come to use cannabis as a way to calm my nausea and my irritable bowel syndrome. To take the edge off my bouts with anxiety and steep plummets into depression. It also helped me rein in my poetic and sometimes schizophrenic impulses. It had been de-criminalized in so many states, that it had become easier to purchase and I was on the bandwagon to have it legalized one day nationwide. Not that I was losing any sleep over the issue. I had a reliable connection and we had our safe, legal means of doing business.

I wasn't the beer drinker I used to be, though I could down a few pilsners while at a barbecue. Mostly it was wine, often from local vineyards, and on weekend nights, especially, it encouraged a calm in me as I stayed away from my desk and let my mind help me find my way through poems, but mostly it was for after I had finished writing so that I could unwind and escape the dread that invariably set in. This dread had me worrying that my work was third-rate, that I'd never publish again and that, as James Wright penned in his poem about lying on a hammock at Duffy's farm, I had "wasted my life."

Nobody I worked with at Cameronshire had an inkling that I was such a habitual stoner. Or maybe they did and I was so fogged all the time I couldn't read them. I didn't know. I didn't socialize much, if at all, with colleagues. I was online mostly and when other profs saw me I believed they were just looking at another harried absent-minded English professor whose weight kept shifting and, like anyone else, had her bad-hair days along with her good ones.

When it came to preparing my lessons, or evaluating student

work, I did it with a clear head, concentrating fully. My reward when the work was done was to launch myself into a cerebral numbness, pour myself a glass of Pinot Grigio, certain I had enough food in the fridge for when the munchies set in. Dalton saw none of this because he was usually asleep when this happened. It was my time. The house quiet. One or maybe two cars per hour passed by on our road. I had my various perches outdoors, including a large swing chair chained to the low limb of an oak tree.

I'd sit out alone in a bulky sweater during the cold weather months and watch for the lambent eyes of deer now and then, assessing me from the darkness. I'd hear them crashing through groundcover as they leapt off. Dalton's fences were high enough around the property and my garden so the deer couldn't do too much damage, though they still managed. It was all rather bucolic and my only worry, in all honesty, was that I'd get bitten by one of the ticks those deer carried and come down with Lyme disease. It wasn't an unreasonable phobia.

This was why we didn't own a dog. Neither Dalton nor I had the patience for dealing with the amount of deer ticks that we heard our neighbors and folks county-wide contended with. My mother had a dog, a dachshund named Lady and seeing her was enough for me. Mini Me stayed inside, where she wasn't shy about asking for seconds, though she, along with the local snake population, was skilled at keeping the rodents at bay.

So many people, when they heard about where we lived, would tell me how it was so bloody peaceful and quiet in the country. The truth was that country people who didn't drive to work every day were usually working on their farms, orchards, gardens or vineyards, or else repairing buildings on their mini-plantations, and that meant hammers pounding and chainsaws whining, well-diggers and tractors and backhoes and hay bailers and delivery trucks and, for fun or else profit, target practice. In short, gunshots. Lots of them. All hours of the day.

I couldn't just wander off into the woods alone and start crossing the rolling vales and pastures like I was Heathcliff lost on the moors. I had to dress in the appropriate way, seen easily from a distance, usually in an orange hat or vest. I needed to know which hunting season it was. The woods were full of rednecks with weapons looking to kill animals for meat. Many of these hunters knew what they were doing, and I respected them, and their right to hunt, but there was always that one idiot or two, or the inexperienced game seeker from the city who was too jumpy on the trigger. He had a brother or a cousin, so even if he lost his hunting license, someone with the same genetic disposition toward ignorance would still be around to take his place.

Dalton took his guns to a firing range and used them there. He had no use for most of the hunting culture, but having grown up on a farm in Georgia, he could handle firearms and he ate venison and had friends he bought it from and kept it stored in our meat freezer and cooked it for me on different occasions. The care and use of weapons was his business. I had nothing to do with them. No guns for me, even though I was that rare poet who supported the NRA and most, not all, of its mission is about. Yes, you heard me right. I was for the Second Amendment and I thought Ted Nugent was sexy and when I was younger I saw him in concert and he put on a fantastic show.

There was fishing, though. That was the outdoor pursuit I really loved. Dalton and I both fished for trout in the spring. We'd canoe the Shenandoah, too, or the James, or we'd drive south along the Blue Ridge all the way to Roanoke for a weekend, on fishing trips. Dalton, as I told you, didn't fit any stereotype. He knew country people and their ways. He respected them, to a degree, and he'd be the first to say that they weren't all racist. He'd also add, with a wry smile that got me every time, "But you never really know just by looking, do you?"

Another thing about country living that Dalton had a grasp on was maintaining a car. We had three of them and we owned them all outright. Mine was a used Honda CRV and I liked it because it was roomy and reliable and we could fit our canoe on a rack on top of it. Dalton drove a newer vehicle, a hybrid Prius, though it took him a few years to pay off the small loan he took out in order to buy it. We also owned an old Dodge pick-up that spent most of its time in our garage.

We used that old Dodge to haul wood and any furniture, for example, we might pick up on a weekend drive to antique centers or fairs or just to nowhere to see what fate had in store for us. I sometimes used it for visits to book sales that weren't far away, within a three to four hour drive. Anything longer, I took the CRV, which had a large enough storage area for the amount of inventory I tended to purchase.

That inventory could be both the wonder and the bane of my existence. I was constantly online updating it. Along with that came my responsibilities for keeping Mini Me and mice and moths and worms away from delicate old pages, along with the purchase of proper shipping materials, and packaging our products well, and sliding Bounce Dryer Sheets, usually perfect for lint, between pages of books once owned by a smoker. Over time, they absorbed the smoke aroma and allowed me to change my listings to "smoke-free home" which always increased the chance of a sale. I learned lots of little such tricks and never tired of them.

I liked driving to the post office to ship my inventory out on time. Everyone who worked in the post office knew me, and I knew the best times to show up, never having to wait in line or be dealt with begrudgingly. I disliked city driving with a passion and stayed out of Fairfax County traffic, for one, as much as possible. When Dalton and I went to DC for a weekend, he did the driving. These trips were a busman's holiday for him, but he enjoyed the city. I'd sit through baseball games and I came to enjoy those games with him just as he tolerated and came to enjoy our many visits to one of the Smithsonian galleries.

If I went alone to DC it was to visit Summer Rain, or to see a play at a small theatre, or a poetry reading. I'd insist Dalton join me now and then to see a show at the Kennedy Center. And sometimes I just wanted to go out and dine at a posh restaurant. To be waited on. Dalton knew where they were. He also knew affordable hotels where we could spend a night. I never tired of those weekend restaurant visits. I'd eat and drink like a queen, and the hotel sex would be terrific. I knew DC had a lot to offer culturally and I'd begrudgingly admit needing that stimuli, but not all the time, not a chance.

I could never live as Dalton did, coping with traffic, especially on 66 where there were too many maniacs and unmarked police cars and speed traps. Never. Sometimes, usually twice a week, even Dalton gave in and drove to the Culpepper Amtrak Station and took the train. Other times, he'd drive 211 to 66 until the Vienna Metro stop. It depended on his mood. I remained in awe of his unflappable calm. Though my drive to work took less than an hour, and it was on 211, which by most accounts was a country road, I was still a wreck when I showed up to work. Dalton just laughed at this, since my biggest complication usually meant having to wait due to an accident, or getting behind a school bus or a slow tractor or a logging truck and not being able to pass.

That's why I liked to stay home, where I knew more than a thing or two about books although Dalton was a little better than me when it came to contemporary movies, though they really didn't sell any longer. I mean, if I wanted to, I could find nearly anything on torrent sites. Dalton was a little better, too, when it came to music on vinyl, and he helped me in this area, but we didn't store or sell many vinyl albums. When we did, it was usually at a healthy profit to collectors in Japan.

One of our rules was to always buy an lp that was either in mint condition or still unopened in its original wrapper. We rarely broke that rule. I'd read on blogs that vinyl was making a comeback, but they were heavy and, like books, took up a lot of space and I preferred to buy cheap albums to listen to them, as Dalton loved to do on the stereo system he'd set up in our living room. He was something of an audiophile and without neighbors to worry about, we sometimes played our music loudly while we danced naked in the living room before ravishing each other on the floor.

As a bonus, since I'd bought so many movies over the years, most of them for half a dollar, I spent many wee hours stoned alone, Mini Me and a bucket of popcorn on my lap, watching films made during the last five decades and writing reviews in my head as if I was Dixie Whatley, Roger Ebert's old co-host. Now, there's an arcane reference, but I lived for such trivialities. My favorite flicks tended to be from Republic Pictures, or RKO, anything from what were called the Poverty Row studios. I'd savor any story told in black and white featuring lots of shadows and glamorous brunettes like Gene Tierney, for one, or goofy hunky oddballs that have been forgotten such as Steve Cochran.

Back in my most profitable era, every one of my tapes went out clean after being tested on one of my two 4-head RCA players — I still maintained a pair of them at all times — and I'd become a whizz with Goo Gone, cleaning away the gum residue after removing old Blockbuster or Hollywood Video sales stickers from VHS boxes.

I'd been feeling, of late, some nostalgia for those days. It had been particularly trying during the Corona Virus time, which, other than the mask wearing, wasn't all that trying for me. I was used to staying at home. I liked it.

I'd thought we'd see an increase in business during that time, but just the opposite happened. I had to unload far too many of my books by driving them into Culpepper or Front Royal and donating them to thrift stores or Goodwill. I loved my books, I did, every last one, and I wanted them around me, but I couldn't have too many of them and periodically, as I did with my eating, I went desperately into purging mode.

There were valid reasons to purge too. If not mice and worms and too much dampness, a handful of them would get ruined because of a leak in our roof. It was always leaking in the spring, no matter how many local workmen came out to allegedly repair it. Dalton didn't want to replace the whole thing. Neither did I. It wasn't that old, but there were some issues with soffits and gutters that never fully got resolved, not even before I sold the house.

The same risks were involved with the other forms of media. As much as I loved clearing a sticker from the jacket of yet another British J.K. Rowling first edition, it just didn't generate the same thrum of pleasure as mooning over a pristine and rare copy, the box flawless and shiny, of a 1944 copy of Negulesco's *The Conspirators*. I loved his movies, even that droll bit of tedium Mother adored, *Three Coins In The Fountain*.

Based on the many old films I'd seen, the 40s war era and even the 50s brought out a softer more respectful rapport among people, as portrayed in these films of course, showing people as capable of more character and empathy. I went through phases when I felt convinced that in the current era everyone was crass, a slob, proud of their igno-rance, ready to tell you to piss off at the slightest provocation.

What happened to people? Was I wrong about this? I couldn't say and I doubted I'd find an answer. It was just one more reason for me to feel twinges of helplessness and fear and anxiety. Maybe I'd take a stab at writing a poem about it.

—⁂—

A student named Kyle, one of those coy princely entitled under-achieving white boys with wealthy and educated parents who thinks he's above the pedestrian tropes demanded of a community college student, once told me I had it all wrong and that *carpe diem* is not Latin for "seize the day" but rather for "fish god." As much as I chuckled at his tawdry joke, I still couldn't stand the little twerp. There were always a few of them in every class and what got me every time was that I knew that the Kyles would land decent jobs and advance their careers and never really have to worry about money.

Yet, unlike his classmates, most of whom did not come from such privileged backgrounds and could be deemed overachievers, if anything, he'd never worked a crummy job in his life. He got a new car for his high school graduation and in his sparkling and entitled mind, compromising on community college credits was just an expedient way to save money before enrolling in his university of choice. In the Commonwealth, it might be UVA or the University of Richmond. It might be Georgetown in DC. Naturally, Daddy's ability to pay, rather than any track record of excellence, would get our Kyle into his institution of choice.

The California poet Kenneth Rexroth once labeled colleges and universities "fog factories." Rexroth was the sort who liked to bite the hand that fed him, although his name was both an appropriate and accurate one for these institutions, generally. The fog wasn't so much something that spread through the craniums of students, though there was enough of that miasma to go around, it was more in what these institutions did, or didn't do to churn out ill-prepared graduates while cashing in and mismanaging budgets and taking a freewheeling approach to raising tuition rates in order to remain solvent.

I, too, often sounded too fond of biting the hand that fed me, but as automation replaced more and more people in the work force, it was become painfully evident to most thinking people just how expensive and impractical many a diploma really was. I knew that during the time of the Covid-19 pandemic, many institutions lost millions of dollars. Honestly, I'd hoped that more of them would go out of business. There should be fewer of them. It should be much harder to get into them and it should be harder to finish high school, as well, for goodness sake. However, my opinion wasn't really shared by too many colleagues or administrators or students. So be it. Most of the time I kept it to myself.

Everyone got the roll of sheepskin and the trophy and the pat on the back just for having shown up to endure the tribulations of a dull game. The actual trophy itself, in any practical sense, meant very little. Papa used to complain about this because he'd worked with college-educated engineers who he believed knew nothing, had seen nothing, and had skated through their courses on their charm and good looks, ultimately landing high-paid jobs due to their connections.

I used to argue, as if I knew, that this had always been the way of things with people. He'd argue back, "No. Not always, Tiger. You learn by doing. You become valuable through what you know. You get what you want by who you know."

He used to say this to me all the time. I couldn't forget it, but a part of me still disagreed. People liked their cliques, true. They feared mandarins like my father who burned the midnight oil, and demanded excellence from themselves. Why? Because outliers such as my Papa were the people who made a difference, who really added to the whole of any project through sweat and meritorious labor, and by doing so exposed the lies behind so many cliquish companies with all their esteemed intermediaries and lawyers and consultants.

I was not of that world and didn't want to be. It was way back during my early high school years that I knew I wouldn't ever enter it. I was just lucky enough to have found full-time teaching, outside of a high school, a suitable fit. They weren't easy jobs to come by. The majority of my colleagues and fellow grads were not teaching, researching, writing, or pursuing those intellectual interests that had been so much a part of their early career dreams.

When I thought of myself as a poet, my diplomas had nothing to do with how I practiced. They were simply what I had needed to secure an estimable form of employment. I happened to like the social aspect of teaching, even though I wasn't really a social animal. If I hadn't broken into teaching, I'd have likely become a baker or opened a restaurant, some kind of occupation that kept me around food all the time. One favorite poet, the inimitable Wallace Stevens, whose work I liked more than I understood, had nothing to do with teaching. He was an insurance company executive. A suit and tie man in the cops and robbers world of corporate profits by any means.

My point of view on this, which I never professed as anything original, was something I mostly kept to myself. I'd share it on occasion with Summer Rain, who thought much like I did. The two of us were poets because we wrote, and we didn't always publish or garner praise or awards. Much like Flaubert, we didn't care what others thought of our work. We never knew when it was good or not. We understood there was mostly nepotism and trends in publishing.

Lots of political correctness and identity politics. Technological developments had created such horrors as Snapchat poets who wrote banal tropes that a three-year-old could understand at one glance. Emily Dickinson published *nothing* in her lifetime. Don't get me started....

I expended far too much mental anguish thinking about my students. I learned with time how to curb this. What I reveled in and was grateful for was being home each night, having Dalton come into the kitchen and find me shaped like a bowling pin in my red and white checkered apron, fuming and bumbling my way through preparing dinner for us. I liked hearing him telling me about his sister Charleena down in Atlanta and her increasingly hopeless situation with men. Or else he'd tell me how some of his co-workers were still driving him crazy, and then he'd laugh and whack the pot-belly I was growing so fond of seeing him develop and, sounding every bit like my middle-aged husband and sweetie, he'd say, "Enough about work and my crazy sister. What's for dinner? I'm starved."

He wasn't starved. My Dalton ate very well. Too well. We both did, as you know. I'd started making lunches for him in order for us to save money. Two maybe three days a week he brown-bagged it. A pair of sandwiches and fruit and a pastry treat. On other days he ate lunch out with some of the co-workers he liked.

I'd show him whatever soup or sauce I was involved in and remark, "I know what you mean, Love. I asked myself today, am I not growing a little long in the tooth to be chasing down the emulation of tropes by that New England formalist Mr. Longfellow?"

"What are you talking about?"

Then I would laugh and laugh, happy to have confounded him. It was a little game I liked to play as cook and homemaker and quasi-farm wife. He knew so little about my area of expertise and I didn't mind. I grinned at him and told him dinner would be ready soon and I'd watch him shuffle off into his room to change and enjoy a little downtime alone before we sat and feasted together.

As my disorder came under control, and it did for the longest of times, on a typical night, after we'd eaten, Dalton would lean back in one of the easy chairs of our living room. Ours was an old house by some local standards. It reminded me of the apartment house I'd lived in when I was a student at Tech. I was dating Dalton then and I'd see him maybe twice a month, driving all the way up to Fairfax County, where he lived and worked at that time. I lived in Blacksburg alone on the first floor of an old two-story house. The man who lived above me traveled often for his job and so I hardly saw him. What I remembered about that house were its windows. The older heavier kind controlled by lead weights.

Our house had them too. They could be drafty when winter winds blew down out of the hills, but we'd decided not to replace them. Dalton and I worked on repairing them together. We learned how to take them apart and change the ropes that held the lead weights that kept them balanced. Two of the larger panes we took to a professional in Warrenton who replaced them for us. Dalton replaced the smaller ones himself, using a glass cutter and a glazing tool. He was so handy. I really admired that about him.

He was playing the stereo loudly enough to cause a minor trembling in all the shelves that held speakers and compact discs and albums and books, enough to line one wall of our living room. We had a decent Internet and cable connection, but we couldn't rely on it. Trees fell down too often in storms and high winds, or the flooding of local streams that washed away a road that took a telephone pole with it. These weather events didn't even get reported, but they often took out our electricity for days at a time. One more joy of country living, I supposed, but we were prepared for it. We had generators and lanterns and antique hurricane lamps, as well as our analog forms of entertainment. Not to forget books by the hundreds.

Listening to quiet jazz. That was Dalton. He couldn't get enough jazz. After that, came soul. He wasn't a rap or hip-hop maven. He was a romantic. Sometimes it was sultry Dexter Gordon or Ben Webster on saxophone, and other times it was the Braxton Brothers sounding their honks as if reproducing the insanity of serendipitous urban traffic and sudden accidents. There were also many evenings when he wanted only silence in long deep meditative interludes. This wasn't one of them. Though I had a bit of a pre-menstrual headache and would have preferred the silence, I didn't say any- thing. Any lasting marriage is about compromise, after all.

I wasn't always so flexible. Sometimes I just shouted at him to turn it down. And the walls tended to shake when I marched across our wide floorboards from the kitchen into the living room, demanding he help me with the dishes. Sometimes, I'd get screwy as my body reacted to my medication, especially the Zoloft. Sometimes, I needed to increase the dosage, and sometimes I needed a break from it. When I underwent the latter choice, I was prone to fits of anger and headaches as I fought off urges to binge and purge, even though I'd just had dinner. Life just went that way with me. Dalton knew this. He abided by a rule not to take it personally and, because of this, my blowouts and tantrums never wreaked too much havoc between us.

Nor did my wants always meet his, but we managed. I happened to like jazz for the most part, though it wouldn't be my first choice. My first love was classical. What followed next was a singer, a night- ingale like Alison Kraus or Emmy Lou Harris, both of whom I'd seen perform live in concert. Their songs made me feel so sad that I became happy. It was the effect I wanted my poems to have on people, as well. I didn't think we experienced happiness by avoiding our pain. If we burrowed inside of it, took a look around and examined it closely, we might come up for air feeling invigorated.

I was old-school country too, going all the way back to Houston days. Dolly Parton, Tammy Wynette, Crystal Gayle. I didn't know how else to say it, but I idolized such women. I found a little piece of the best of myself whenever I listened to them sing. Sometimes, I felt like they understood me better than my mother ever had. And sometimes I wanted to be one of them.

For Dalton, this music was for white folks. It was just country twang. Fine. Of course. He had his tastes and an esthetic and I gave him credit for it. Yet he listened to it with me sometimes, just as I endured his journeys into outside jazz, not all of which I liked, hardly, to be sure.

I'd been to a library sale recently in Staunton, pronounced Stanton by locals, where I picked up about twenty musical CDs for fifty cents each. I knew a few would sell and I'd listed them, but there were three in particular for myself, classical compositions played by the women of the Eroica Trio. I had a terrible crush on these women, though I'd never admit it to Dalton.

So, on this, which was essentially a typical night, Dalton was listening and shouting to me over the music, "Each man a singer." He shouted over the jazz in his own musical and knowing way, as if talking to himself and to me at the same time, in synch with the music too. He was smooth and rhythmical, so sexy, a joy to watch as he slid and oozed about the room, swooning, prone to harmless outbursts of commentary that didn't always make sense. They didn't bother me in the least. I found them generous and appealing. I would have done the same thing if capable of it, but I wasn't. That's why he was there. He knew how to entertain me. He took joy in hearing me laugh and seeing me forget about my anxieties and disorders. It was night and we were in our home and safe, after all.

"I don't follow," I told him.

"Each man, he doesn't really want to talk. He just wants to shape words in his mouth and hear his own voice. But each woman, now she's a mystery of complexity, independence and certitude."

I smiled. This was going to be fun. "Without equal?"

"Maybe," he said. "And maybe one's a raving confessor that many still try to imitate, and the other's a sepulchral formalist who's been relegated to oblivion."

What was he going on about? Sometimes, his use of language was so startlingly original and articulate and fresh that I wondered if I shouldn't just throw in the towel regarding my poetry obsession.

I had to step out of the kitchen, apron on, a skillet in one hand, a spatula in the other. I couldn't shout anymore. I nodded toward the stereo and Dalton turned down the volume. "What, my love, in the blue blazes are you yakking about?"

"Can I call myself a poet now?" he asked.

"Yes," I told him. "Stop being so insecure. You're a great poet."

"But nobody cares."

"I care!"

I moved back into the kitchen. I heard that Dalton had turned up the stereo, sending one of his signals, one that he knew I would recognize. It was a weeknight, but he wanted to have sex. God, that's all men want. It was what I wanted too. We never had sex on a week night.

I stepped out of the kitchen again, apron still on, and glared at him. Our conversation was over for the time being. My eyes told him everything. If he turned down the stereo, or changed the music to something more accessible and melodic, he'd get what he wanted, even though we were breaking one of our rules.

This was when I knew I'd been married a while, and it was really good. Without a word, he turned down the stereo. Then he remarked, "Think I'll change the album. How about some Roberta Flack?"

And I went back to the kitchen and finished cleaning up and didn't think at all about stuffing my body or vomiting. I thought about how sweet it would feel to have him embrace me.

—✦—

My third collection, *Fog Banks*, had been out about a month from a little press in Indiana. Some of the venerable lit mags, Ploughshares for one, had also accepted recent work. I never really knew what would grab an editor's fancy, just as I could never predict how I'd respond to one more rejection. I had, it seemed, endured thousands of rejections. I was so numb to them that I couldn't even recall when they'd occurred. I used to read them and worry over them, seeking perhaps an inroad into the editor's mind. Now, I just expected them, and since most of them were computer-generated, I deleted them. On occasion, I might get a pat on the back and an encouraging word to send more in the future. I would write down the name of this editor and the magazine in a little notebook titled Future Possible that I kept for myself. I would then pour myself a cup of tea to enjoy with a few hits of weed and some oatmeal raisin cookies, telling myself to be calm, not to overreact, all part of the game and I should be used it now even though I wasn't, even though I would never get used to it and I was out of my mind for still playing.

Like anything else, enduring rejection had been a process for me, one I'd adjusted to and let harden me, but I could never tell myself I had it under control. The dirty truth was that many so-called poets just went to writer's conferences and pressed the flesh, so to speak, and *voila* they were able to bring out a book in a gorgeous edition from an esteemed press. These career poets, and there were plenty of them, kept me away, for the most part, from anything contemporary in the name of poetry. See, I still nurtured the delusional thought that poets, as TS Eliot once said, craved immortality. No, it wasn't a thought. It was a belief. Why bother to write if my work didn't matter long after I was gone? Did my work matter, at all? Not really. It was all such a narcissistic enterprise. Time maybe to break into the cupboards, one fistful at a time, starting with Oreo cookies. No, no, I couldn't do it. I had to breathe, to stay calm, to stop thinking so much.

For a few years, I kept my rejection slips, back when they came in the mail, in a shoe box, but they began to accumulate and I tired of seeing the pile grow, so I just started burning them in a little ritual every Friday night while getting high. Now, with all my submissions electronic, it was easy to hit the delete tab on the canned allegedly supportive and meticulously crafted ways that editors condescended to writers by pretending not to condescend to them, plunging each of us scribes into fugues of regret and self-doubt, no matter how experienced we were.

O, how fragile I was. Too sensitive for this rotten world. I found myself inching back toward the kitchen, quivering, holding on to the counter's edge for balance. There was so much I could eat. So much I could throw out of my body.

It was all in one's name, too. I would look at little magazines. So multi-cultural, so proudly out there, because every heterosexual and bisexual and homosexual Amanda or Ryan or Jenny or Cain or Dirt or Bone in America, in the world, had a rightful claim to seek excellence through language we all shared in and out of translation. Summer Rain called it the freak parade. It had become easier to see, especially behind the scenes, because all those involved were so candid about providing photographs and marketing themselves as if they were dog food. I missed the old early days when as an undergrad I lost sleep over the sending out of an opaque manilla envelope, or having one come back to me in the mail and it was a surprise and a real adventure to see a cover for the first time, to smell the pages, to thumb through and absorb work by other poets, and then to hold the page open to my own little creation. To read it again and again and feel pride of accomplishment and then think: not good enough, time to move on.

No one asked me to become a poet. It wasn't what I did. It was who I saw myself as. Career poets approached it as a way to publish themselves into a high-paying teaching gigs. Not me. I had to write my poems. I couldn't live without the release, the balancing act that kept me from blowing myself up. I could name many of those career poets who were still active and still venerated in the circle that took such pursuits seriously.

I'd quit trying and I'd attempted to, but I simply couldn't be a career poet. I'd never been to a writer's conference. What the hell for? So many angry and puzzled and hungry and ill-at-ease morsels in me needed to keep shaping words into little stanzas — the Italian word for room, by the way — like they were spice containers in a pantry that I could go to at any time when I need sustenance.

Publishing in the *New Yorker*, where lonely and erudite New Englander Ms. Louise Bogan was once poetry editor, had for the longest time been my ultimate goal, a stamp of approval I could show Mother, but I gave up on it, unsure that I had the requisite form of talent for that aesthetic. There were, essentially, the kinds of poems that the *New Yorker* liked, based on length, depth, a type of showy erudition that wasn't erudite at all. And there were the poems I wrote because madness screamed in my blood and if it wasn't freed and left to drip all over the couch like so much spilled wine, then I'd start taking a hatchet to myself. I wasn't born with the skill to pose in any way. Posing was a talent in of itself, one that I wasn't at all good at. I was part of Summer Rain's freak parade, unable to wear a mask, bloated in the face due to all the honest hatred I'd inflicted on myself.

I wasn't sure that I was good at all, frankly, and often not even sure I wanted to keep living. Starting to get the picture here with me? I didn't call myself well-adjusted, carry a pedestal around, wear pearls, or attend an Ivy. Nor was I brown, black, red, yellow, trans, the victim of reprehensible acts or compromised by a physical disability. Well, compromised, but there are millions of bulimics out there.

American poetry and art, in general, worshipped the victim culture. Not the victor one. All bards were supposed to be wounded outsiders who hurt so very badly. No *joie de vivre* allowed in one's work, at all. All must be about suffering. One more poor old bard should mope around the planet feeling sorry for himself.

Not me. I wanted to live. I wrote to live. It was a means to getting there. Publishing and fame and approbation had nothing to do with it.

I was also busy with teaching hours that exhausted my mental, spiritual and physical energy. What recharged me was my zeal for reading, but I had to admit that this passion began to erode as I strained to wade through increasingly puerile and uninspired student essays, most of them a chore, products of cut and paste plagiarism on the Internet, a drag on the time of all teachers everywhere. Proof that literacy, in its most venerable state — not driven by image but by words — was doomed.

I was not only busy but I was sinking deeper into another pit of despair. Inconsolable, worn out, I felt sick-to-death of dealing with insecure male bardic editors and demanding colleagues, cocksuckers all, in the literal sense. Hey now, there was a title for a little poem: *Cocksuckers All*. No one would publish it, but I'd write it just the same, send it to the *New Yorker* the old-fashioned way in a big opaque manila envelope with a Virginia State lottery ticket and a cover letter on Cameronshire stationary. Dedicate the poem to all the Republicans out there in Candy-Corn-Land.

Maybe I'd write one titled *Ode to Maypole Wine*. I'd started thinking about him again, in fact quite often, of late. See, early on, I was fortunate to meet his honor, Mr. A. H. Maypole when he came to Tech to strut his stuff. He wouldn't remember me if I phoned or wrote or pestered him. I'd heard the man was ill. Maybe he needed a boy-toy *a la* Auden and Isherwood to clean his apartment twice a week. I could cut my hair into a pageboy, wear sweatpants and a baggy denim shirt and latex gloves, kowtowing, "Yes, Mr. Maypole. No, Mr. Maypole. Of course, I'll scrub your toilet with a toothbrush. Anything to get published by Penguin and reviewed in the *Times*."

I no longer marveled over anything, certainly not poems by Maypole or anyone else, but I admit I used to. If I was hard on A.H. Maypole it was because I had a personal connection to him, a young African man from Mali, a former student of mine who was a little older than the others in class and seething with a hunger to convert his life experience as a refugee into some form of art. He went by the name of Furlong because, as he told me, he had no legal citizenship "for so long" and he also liked to tell other Americans in his French accent, "Yes, I like it here in your country, but I do not think I am really here for long."

In the 90s, Furlong held three jobs at all times. One was as Maypole's cleaning boy. Furlong and his girlfriend Sam, an actress with a diploma from one of those woodsy campuses in North Carolina, cleaned the apartments of wealthy bohemians in Georgetown.

Bohemians. All the so-called hippies and boho sorts I'd ever met were rich enough to live poor by choice. What a joke. The idea of bohemianism made me alternately want to laugh out loud and to vomit. Ginsburg and Kerouac, both of whom I admired tepidly for quite a while, were Ivy League dropouts. As were most of the hippies that came after them. Please, give me a break, they're all driving Subaru's and Volvos now, eating at Thai restaurants, keeping the CEO of Starbucks rich, and shopping at Whole Foods in tony suburban enclaves.

Poor Furlong would scrub Poet King Maypole's bidet, vacuum his Persian carpets, take out his first-world trash, dust his hand-crafted vintage furniture — the works. Furlong asked me to keep it a secret that Maypole smoked his way through many an ounce baggie of cannabis. As a pothead myself, with dubious self-control, this endeared me to him. Naturally, I didn't tell this to Furlong.

I don't know what it is about weed, but I couldn't get enough of the accommodating removals it brought me. It marred my ability to write, teach or drive a car, but when I wasn't performing those tasks it helped me to push aside suicidal tendencies. A therapist like Dr. Murray would call it self-medication. Who wouldn't? While stoned, I bounded over my prison walls and headed straight to the night kitchen where I could start eating the way I really wanted to, and hold on to the calories and be myself. So often, I refused to allow myself to do this when not under the influence.

It was all in the timing and in moderation and knowing where to spark up. I had my brownies, too, though I didn't worry about smoke fumes that might arouse the ire and curiosity of neighbors. They lived too far away. I had a little crush on Furlong in those days when a dime bag was the thing. Pot was cheaper, though less potent. Furlong told me he liked Maypole's gifted friend, the poet LuAnn Wald. He found her sexy and so did I. I also found her inane and banal at the same time, but that was only when I was judging her by her poems. But I couldn't judge. It wasn't in me. I was likely more of a pathetic lunatic than she'd ever be. I took comfort in knowing this. I also found it comforting to realize that, as with nearly all contemporary poets, in spite of any short-lived fame, she'd soon be neglected. The worst thing about her was that she didn't appear to be aware of this.

Cavafy, Neruda, Seamus Heaney, men all of them, surprisingly, but *there* was a group more suitable to my predilections. We all needed our saints, our mentors.

Sam, Furlong's girlfriend, had a crush on Ms. Wald too, but Sam had a much bigger crush on me. It was the first time I'd ever slept with a woman and I had to admit that the sex with Sam was sublime, especially when I was high. I still couldn't say that I preferred women, but if Dalton were to grow some wild hairs and run off with a chippie (which would lead me to divorce him immediately), I could switch preferences without much of a problem, though I might choose spinsterhood and spend my days reading Henry James by candlelight.

Honestly, I revered everything about Dalton and he surely knew that I'd leave him if he was unfaithful. I adored the female form. I'd never told anyone about my tryst with Sam, but even if I had, I didn't think either Furlong or Dalton would have minded. They revered the female form, as well. Sam, as some boys say, was put together.

Furlong was remarkably open and candid about sexuality. He was more than just a student. He looked up to me as a friend. I probably shouldn't have slept with his Sam, but no one got hurt and I learned a few needed lessons in how to pleasure myself. Dalton, however, wasn't as open. As our years together evolved, he became as loyal as a hound dog, but that could always change. He liked to say he was open, of course, but he was fond of an illusion that he possessed me, and that I needed him. I did need him, but to a degree, and I granted him a certain right of ownership that he was entitled to as my husband and due to his tolerance for my bulimia.

I didn't like it, but I also didn't mind the king-of-the-castle attitude from Dalton, since I knew that standing at six feet tall and with an average fighting weight of around 250 pounds, nobody could own me. I'd hit 200 pounds with ease before I gained my Freshman fifteen at Mary Washington. In those days, I even concerned myself with dress sizes. Not anymore, of course, not since I started wearing an F-cup. I also knew I loved Dalton. We loved each other. No shrinking violet he at somewhere between six-foot-six and six-eight and I've no idea what he weighs, though I'm sure his BMI puts him in the same Class II obesity category that I've been in for most of my adult life.

We couldn't own each other. I couldn't even own myself.

What I got from Dalton is what I needed: empathy, honesty, compassion, concern. He let me be bigger than big, a screw up, prone to dramatic overtures and operatic tears and exultations. He also let me laugh and breathe in all the wrong or politically incorrect ways. He didn't get high with me, but he didn't disapprove. He admired women most would consider as plus-sized, such as Queen Latifah, Oprah Winfrey and Rosie O'Donnell. They didn't intimidate him; they humored him. So did I. He never once called me fat or overweight. He'd been shamed by that language himself when younger, so with sensitivity he'd label me full-figured, or he'd laugh when I described myself as Rubenesque.

Dalton let me feed him constantly and by doing so feed myself vicariously. He didn't criticize the stretch marks on my stomach and hips, and the sudden swelling my body would go through, and then the shrinkage, back and forth, along with the return to problems with my esophagus and my blood pressure. It never ended with me. I'd relapse. I'd blow up to 285 and then back down to 240, and back up again. I bought all my professional clothes at Lane Bryant, or else I wore sweatpants, or jeans, and Triple-X men's flannel shirts.

He listened well, he tried to understand me, and he didn't get defensive when I told him to slow down, to be quiet, to exude an air of calm and to concentrate when he was around me because I was having trouble concentrating and I needed someone to observe and model myself on, and did he understand what I was trying to tell him? *Ma grande taille*, as the French say, and I'd grown up long before any body positive movement helped me understand I just wasn't made to fit into a size 12 or less.

He didn't read or comment on or pretend to be interested in my poems. I think I'd have despised it if he showed such an interest. Our marriage was, like in the mafia, *cosa nostra*, our thing. The excesses of my weight and my bulimia along with my artistic temperament and drive had to remain central to and separate between us at the same time. It wasn't always an easy balance. We could not live in our own private echoes, so to speak.

Summer Rain once told me there was a darkness in Queen Wald's lines that she didn't experience in King Maypole's. Summer was even bigger than I was. She didn't fluctuate either. She used to joke she weighed 150 at birth. She was shorter than I was, too, but with thicker legs and a wider bottom and smaller breasts. We could have been a tag team on the Weight Watchers circuit, posing as Before examples. Not After ones. Not ever.

Summer once explained that this darkness in Ms. Wald's lines had to do with the man-Maypole's belief that "insanity grieves its loss of edges over time" — whatever that meant. Quoting Summer Rain was always a challenge. I never did find out what she'd meant by that, though I used the line in one poem inspired by our conversation.

Summer Rain understood profoundly, in her unique sometimes oblique way, that suffering happened because we are here on earth to understand and mature and deepen. She wrote with flair, improvising on line breaks and pace, sometimes reading with musicians who played exotic wind and percussion instruments I still didn't know the names for. They might have made a tangy series of poems, one for each instrument.

Summer Rain wasn't bad on stage either. She'd thundered across the stage in original plays with a posse of Marxists and Anarchists who'd once called themselves the Bread Is Red Theatre Company. They didn't last long in DC and most of them shipped off to Philadelphia, I think, and some even made it to Manhattan. I had no interest in living in any city, least of all one where I needed to make three ferry connections to journey from home to the maze of rat-infested alleys my job was situated in.

I'd seen Summer Rain do everything for the theatre companies she'd worked for. She had painted sets, managed props, hung lights, played all walk-ons and one-line parts. As she put it, she'd found a home for a while in the theatre. With her stocky, muscular build, so imposing and so mannish, and her ability to transform her body and face, she moved to Los Angeles to try her luck in TV and movies. I think she was inspired by Camryn Manheim and Anna Nicole Smith. I thought it a horrible idea, but she didn't do too badly there, getting into a union and landing work as a crew member in lower-grade action movies and then working as a grip for a female director who took such a liking to her that she put her on the regular crew of a 90s-TV space opera that ran for about five years on a major network. I never saw that program. I can't even remember its name. I was never a fan of most television shows, though I was happy getting cozy with my old tapes of *Columbo* or *Murder, She Wrote*. I would bring them to Mother and Aunt Jess and we'd watch them together quite often.

For a while, Summer Rain was happy in LaLa Land, specifically Huntington Beach. She even lost a little weight. I sent Furlong to her when he'd had enough of living the downside of a nation's capital city where taxation-without-representation really meant not holding your breath when waiting for a city bus, or a pothole to get filled. I knew that Summer Rain had helped him out and that he and Sam got married.

As far as I knew, Sam and Furlong were still out there. Maybe they'd learned to surf. I could look them up on Facebook, but I was like Summer Rain in that regard. I really didn't want to cheat the past and the distances that separated us naturally through time. If it was meant to be, I'd run into Furlong again. He'd appreciate knowing I thought this way. You could call it a faith in kismet, I guess. I liked to imagine him under palm trees with Sam walking to their apartment on the beach, with the sun setting behind them, a steady income keeping their bank account full, and maybe even children of their own.

As the years passed, and as Summer Rain returned to DC and we reunited and grew even closer as friends, and grew fatter together too, so many of my past students folded into blurry memories steaming out of the ethers. I'd wake up often in the middle of the night remembering their names and something they once said that struck me as comical or profound. I remembered their faces, too. It was uncanny. It didn't bother me. Other nights and for months at a time, I didn't remember any of them and this, too, didn't bother me in the least. Just how it went. Not that they'd remember me either.

⸎

Having treated myself to a pair of classic movies, both new for me, they'd brought me back to fantasizing over starting a blog about film. I was old enough to remember Gene Shalit and Pauline Kael, both of whom I'd admired and envied. I mean, what a job. Just watch movies, go to Cannes once a year, write from your own perspective about what you think a particular filmmaker succeeded or failed at trying to say. The problem was that I'd not a lick of talent for that kind of writing. One had to pump it out, I supposed, with a deadline looming, and that was never easy for me. I fell in love with my words. I took my sentences and metaphors out on long dates and I splurged with them, going places we'd never been before. A reviewer with a column, or a blog, couldn't really do this.

The first film, *Pickpocket*, directed by a Frenchman, Robert Bresson, left me numb with a respect for and a trust in simplicity. Bresson never tried to impress. He just told his story. The second one, *Veronika Voss*, a rather disturbing work by a German, Rainer Werner Fassbinder, was about a morphine addict that put me into a cold sweat and I had to keep drinking warm water with lemon slices to get through it because all I wanted to do while watching the incredible Rosel Zech was down bottles of dark beer at room temperature, smoke weed out of a bong, and masturbate, but I didn't, I wouldn't.

I watched these films to affirm an intelligence within me, at least this was what I told myself. Or maybe I watched them because I knew that if they were any good, they would alter my perspective and pull me out of the traps of my provincialism by reminding me of the paltry nature of my own attempts to create lasting art.

This was why I read other poets, wasn't it? One must be constantly reminded that it has all been said before. This used to make me cringe and ache all over until I learned that I had to take small comfort in understanding that any attempt I made at poesy, as such, just added to what's already out there. Nothing more. It might or might not bring a handful of readers some pleasure. Amen to that. The doing of the work had to be enough.

I began thumbing through one of my massive art tomes, engrossing myself in a work by Paul Klee as I listened to ambient music by Brian Eno, to the colors in his music. I was thinking about a poem I would title: *Synesthesia.* A broad title, but one that would allow me to examine smaller pieces of myself in relation to color and food and sound. I wanted to incorporate Klee, as well, and mention how for years I pronounced his name to rhyme with tea, which proved I was little more than a pretentious hick.

This poem might, if I let it, help me share what it was like to go through the worst of my bulimia, to feel so lonely and disoriented and maladjusted in that high school in the southeastern part of Massachusetts, in that town of about 14,000 called Seekonk. I always saw that town as a drive-through suburb divided by three always noisy crowded highways between Providence and Boston, including points east all the way to Provincetown on Cape Cod. The busiest and most dangerous was Route 1-95. I could possibly create three sections in each poem that would stand for or be named after these three busy byways. The one most crowded with mega retail outlets and third-rate restaurants was Route 6. The coziest and most New Englandy, at least for me, was Route 44, which I liked to drive west on sometimes with my mother all the way to Foster and tiny communities such as Harmony where we picked peaches and apples in season.

I'd written a bevy of poems about that so-called hometown where I often felt I didn't belong and never felt at home, starting with my *Three Sisters,* (not to be confused with the Andrews, or the lighthouses in Orleans on Cape Cod). In this threesome of poems, each one was labeled separately as Maize, Beans, and Squash. These were the three basic foods eaten by the Wampanoag Indians who once lived here.

As I saw it, essentially, all lore related to the American tradition of Thanksgiving began and ended with the Wampanoags, who resided in grass and stick round-topped huts known as *wetus* and spoke in the Natick, or Massachusetts language. Their most famous chief, Metacomet, also known as King Philip, began ceremonial feasting at harvest time with the English settlers in the 17th Century, offering to them these three forms of sustenance.

Hence, upon learning all this, mostly on my own, I came to simultaneously like and hate that I was going to high school in a place that could claim itself as the root-home of Thanksgiving. I knew that Americans from all the native tribes despised this holiday and viewed it as a day of mourning. If I enjoyed it, selfishly so, and often I did, it was because I welcomed any excuse to let the demons of my demented relationship with food run wild as I relinquished control and overate until nearing the point of passing out. Often, I did pass out, which kept me away from my purging ritual. It began for me the holiday season, which translated meant that for the next five weeks, all the way into the New Year, I would indulge myself and not to do any purging. I'd add, with ease, a noticeable twenty pounds, tipping the scales at close to 300 and happily putting Aretha Franklin or Mama Cass Elliot to shame.

In my *Synesthesia* poem, I would need to find a way to address in a more than just biographical way, the fact of English settlers inadvertently bringing diseases such as smallpox to the New World. This was the foodstuff they'd provided. Disease, essentially. I'd been thinking, as well, of the animus in people that drove larger issues such as colonialization, a kind of hunger, isn't it? Whether it be the romance of unexplored territory, or the lust for conquest (not too dissimilar to my lust for losing control and binging) as it's explored in works such as Terence Malick's film, *The New World*, and in Warner Herzog's classic, *Aguirre The Wrath of God*. How this urge to super-impose one culture atop another was really a form of dis-ease, especially if I broke the word dis and ease into its two parts and wrote of the conquerors as a restless and unhappy lot, unable to find "ease" in their own native culture, in their identity, yet intent on exporting it and teaching it to others. Humans of a certain kind, ever ill at ease, had been involved in this sort of endeavor for a long time.

I would look at how disease was not just a generic word for a host of medical conditions, but a state of the human soul and mind. Coupled with human aggression, it could lead to motives for one side or another to take what wasn't rightly theirs. In my case, it would be the fighting which started between various tribes and settlers within about a year's time after the first feast. This fight, along with smallpox, decimated the Wampanoag, who once numbered about 12,000 souls.

One drawback to this ambitious project, which could be one long poem and certainly book length, was that I was hardly an expert on the topic, and I'd learned about this history piecemeal through reading one of my heroes, Jill Lepore, and from engaging original sources such as Benjamin Church's, *Diary of King Philip's War, 1675-1676*. While in high school, I went with my mother, begging her to take me, to Church's gravesite in Little Compton, Rhode Island, a place where I couldn't shoot enough close-up pictures of the Edward-Gorey-like etchings on many of the cracked and lichen-patched headstones there.

After publishing my three Wampanoag food poems, thrilled by the sight of my work in print, I followed up with a quartet, each one named after respective Wampanoag leaders, starting with Squanto, then Somerset, and finishing with Metacomet and Massasoit. As a student first at Hurley Middle School, and then a Warrior at the brick edifice on Arcade Avenue known as Seekonk High, where I faked it often in order to bleed true navy-blue and white, I grew up with a few kids who had Wampanoag ancestry, but it wasn't anything we dwelled on much. It never occurred to me to question our school symbol, an Indian spear arrowhead with two feathers that ran through a large letter S. I didn't know that Wampanoag meant "easterners" in Natick. Nor did I know that that the word Seekonk comes from *Seekonket*, a shortened combination of the word *sucki* meaning "black," and *honc* meaning "goose."

How's that for alliteration, poet? The *et* suffix meant "place of" and explained the suffix for Nantucket, among other local New England place names. Our drive-through shopping mall town was where geese migrated to twice a year, enjoying Runnins River, Clear Run Brook, and the five-mile Seekonk River.

Long after I'd accepted and began to cope with my colossal ignorance and a nagging sense of feeling that I didn't belong, I started to dig more and more into history and learned Seekonk became a township in 1812. It was separated from an approximately eight-mile tract of land labelled as Rehoboth by the English settlers, and a domain ruled in relative peace by Chief Massasoit until about 1641. This Wampanoag tract included present-day Attleboro and Rehoboth in Massachusetts, and some of Pawtucket and Cumberland, Rhode Island. It also included an area that was known as Wannamoiset, which had become today's western parcels of Swansea, and Barrington, and the name of a swanky country club in Rumford.

In my day, Seekonk certainly wasn't as racially diverse as nearby Brockton, Fall River or New Bedford, but we weren't as white as our arch rivals the Falcons from Dighton-Rehoboth High. At least, that's how we saw it. I grew up with classmates and friends who had Cape Verdean, Brazilian, Portuguese and all sorts of Asian and African ancestry. Not that, looking back, any of those differences mattered in the world as I saw it. They just didn't. If a boy was cute, I tried to get to know him. I didn't like girls as much, didn't trust them, but they'd win me over if they were smart or bookish.

I wasn't all that shy. I spoke my mind. Ethnicity didn't concern me. I was an ardent student, always did my homework, competed freshman and sophomore years on the swim team, believe it or not, and worked part-time at a Dunkin Donuts on weekends. I ate cream-filled sugar doughnuts the way a nicotine addict chain-smokes. I mean, I pounded them down in private whenever business was slow. Surprisingly, this didn't show on my body.

That all changed junior year when my quitting the swim team combined with my weekend job surrounded by doughnuts, my mother's cooking and my penchant for reading long books in all my free time, made for an alarming change. My Warrior culture was no longer my own. Nor were my hormones. They had taken over. I wasn't really about the wasteland of malls, shopping plazas, box-retail, chain restaurants and humongous mega-stores, or the latest in corporate flummery that could be found pretty much in every version of Anywhere, USA. I was about getting manically depressed when my periods and my cramps lasted, it seemed, longer and longer. That was the last time in my life I felt comfortable in a snug sweater or a button-down blouse.

I grew, and I mean all over, especially my breasts. I lost my virginity, at last, but this led to a fist fight with Elaine Costa, who I learned had also slept with Brady Dunlap on the smelly couch in his parent's damp basement. Lucky for me, I lost that fight, meaning I lost Brady, who one year out of high school got Elaine pregnant and bolted out of town, stranding her. Nothing I wanted. Sex, of course, was an experience that I was after, but as my hormones helped me grow even heavier , I went through a spell that was three years long before I found myself with another boy, a rather homely specimen, in that way.

As much as I accepted that Seekonk never felt like my own, and was known to most visitors to New England as a place to find an inexpensive chain hotel for one night, I didn't really despise it. I felt nothing about it. One drove through it. One shopped there. It was where I learned that I wasn't like the others and never would be. I was too busy eating scones and savoring *Middlemarch* and *The Moonstone* and *Mansfield Park* to worry about making it to the latest beer keg party or pep rally. I never disliked it nearly as much as towns such as Warwick with its nauseating amounts of suburban shopper traffic.

My Seekonk, specifically short Colleen Drive linked by Musket Road on one end and Buckboard Road on the other, was where I first learned to ride a bike, capture a toad, scrape my knee and bring home caterpillars to put in jars hoping they'd become butterflies overnight. This was where Rusty and Papa loved me the best, watching me grow up in all my zany and quirky and uncomfortable glory. I was their little girl and needed to feel close to them. They knew this. They were there for me. That is, until Papa's heart exploded.

All that happened so long ago, yet even then I was writing in my head as I was thinking. Some might think me crazy. Dalton didn't.

He knew how to have the kinds of days he needed for himself, just as he knew how to let me have my days, as well, giving myself permission to enjoy an unfettered interest in what some may deem frivolity. It was the kind of permission I needed in order to think, breathe and eat normally again.

Dalton started to cook for me, but I wouldn't always eat. His kindness brought tears to my eyes. More than once, I broke down sobbing at the dining room table, because I couldn't just sit with him and indulge in my food and enjoy it without worrying what would happen next. All I wanted was to just eat and then sit back, perhaps drink a cup of hot tea, and then sit with him.

I couldn't do it. I knew what would happen. I feared it. I went cold. I would eat and then about an hour later I'd be leaning over the toilet and ramming two fingers down my throat. I was still a mess. Sure, I'd made some progress, but I still had so far to go.

I needed my poems, my art, my music and movies and my weed the way a koi needs to nibble at nutrients on the surface of her pond. I was moving slower, laboring to become less lethargic, taking the extremely expensive Saxenda that Dr. Murray had agreed to write me a prescription for. You see, initially I'd agreed to this prescription because I wanted to lose weight while my BMI was still within a reasonable range. But I couldn't afford it. Insurance didn't cover the Saxenda, either. The worst thing, though, were the side effects. Skin rashes, constipation, dizziness. What the hell was I doing to myself?

I went in another direction entirely. I decided I wanted to hold weight, to add it to my body, to just think of myself as being able to eat like a Sumo wrestler or a lion before going to bed because this was how I behaved, who I was. My goal was to gain five pounds every week, to embrace life as a feast, and to waddle about proud of my avoirdupois, or else stomp though each day like one of those boiler-on-stilts creatures from *War of the Worlds*.

I wanted the fighting to end. Completely. Would I ever learn to loosen the reins?

I'd also been querying editors, sharing dreamed-up projects for blogs, magazine features and sidebars. None of them were ever as appealing to editors as they were to me. When I wasn't reading or writing poems and student essays, or watching movies, I was glued to my computer screen. The idea of actually penning these side projects, all of them freelance, drove me into nervous fits, but I liked knowing that they paid. I liked the idea of earning more money. Who didn't?

I hadn't stopped harboring the notion that I could quit teaching because I'd earn enough writing such pieces full-time. Dalton had supported me on this, saying I should go where the spirit moved me. He knew that we could live on his income and that I didn't really need to work, though we'd have to be frugal and stop making double payments on school loans. In the ethical, moral, spiritual and emotional sense, I was afraid it would kill me not to have a job. Dalton understood this. Adding in my online business, I managed two jobs. They kept me busy and imparted a sense of purpose to my life, and helped me feel grounded when the writing of poems didn't go well.

Per the request of two editors, I'd written and sent out a piece about a new cookware appliance made with a 3-D printer, and another piece about new advances in technology related to how to childproof your kitchen. If they were accepted, and that was not a guarantee, I'd earn about two-hundred dollars. Based on how much time I put into them, because I was such a lover of my own language, I stood to earn about two dollars per hour. Ridiculous, I knew, but it was an addition to who I was, without any purge involved. It was solid, substantial. It was also food, wine and weed money. More importantly, it was a bit of dabbling I simply had to try my hand at. Maybe I'd become skilled at it. As Papa used to say, "You can't know if you don't try."

I didn't think I'd fail. I thought I would succeed. I needed to think along such lines. I needed to keep going, all options open, and believe in possibilities. I'd grown weary of seeing myself as teacher, professor-poet, arbiter of taste, a reader with a laudable sense of discretion, and one unselfish enough to respect any aesthetic not my own. I was afraid that there are too many of us now. The Covid pandemic, for starters, had showed me clearly that we were all replaceable, not really needed. Computers could do all the work.

In the larger world, the one that was on screens everywhere, life was about information related to technology and money. My world, what I brought to it, the cheeky humor and big smile and a loving show of patience for a timid student's first attempt at under-standing and writing about, say, *Lord Of The Flies*, was not going to live on. Margaret Atwood couldn't have dreamed it up any better. Robots would eventually replace cops. These enforcers of law and order would not know race or envy or hatred and therefore make no mistakes. Women would look increasingly more like men, and behave in the same selfish way. The robots would just enforce the law and behavior by the book.

In education, digitized robotic voices known as online English teachers would uphold a rubric that evaluated only the grammar and vocabulary of a student's five-paragraph essay. Plagiarism would become a norm. It would become accepted, much like sampling in rap music, or stealing jokes in stand-up comedy, as part of what would be touted as the cooperative osmotic nature of creating literature in the post-post-human world. Cameras and visual documentation of our lives would become so prevalent that reading for pleasure or to get outside of the saturation of current visual messages and narratives, would be seen as akin to knitting. This was what Grannies did when they had too much time on their hands. All books, of course, would be designed for Grannies too. Grandpa, well, he just don't read.

I wouldn't see this day come. I was already too long in the tooth. But it was coming. Women and men like me wouldn't have to work. The State would keep us happy living on chump-change checks that came once a month, just as all our neighbors earned, and we'd continue making our once a month trips to Mega Konsumer World to buy all our processed vittles. We wouldn't talk to each other, but we'd look and discern the chill in the air, along with the stench, and hurry ourselves along to parking lots and wheel our carts down the shopping aisles and fill them and hurry back to our vehicles which would drive us automatically home. We really wouldn't have to do much of anything other than to program our electronic existence.

I used to think that teaching was noble, about decency, morality, love, desire, self-actualization and critical thinking. Thanks to what I imagined looming as the future, as well as the drudgery of experience, and a generally lousy salary, all that idealistic hooey had filtered through my spleen and evaporated. One day, a hologram would teach the children. Going to school would mean sitting in a circle and pressing little buttons. Helmets on. Nobody would talk to each other. The screens in the helmets would come to life. Six hours per day of it. The alpha and omega of the educational experience.

My idealism was rotting away. It died a little more whenever I learned that the likes of, Helena Elaine Minerva, which is not her real name, had won yet another lucrative award, enough to pay the mortgage on her summer cottage for another couple of years. A Yale grad, Helena Elaine in her glamorous book-cover photos was always luminescent, swan-like about the neck and in pearls. She proved that to be a successful poet, you had to be thin first, and then look successful, entitled and celestial, though not in that order. My pet belief that a poet should be hungry and maybe even dirty was just outdated avant-garde nonsense. Precious Helena Elaine had won so very many awards, showing such dexterity in the Ottava Rima form. She was a genius and upon seeing her, someone like me should drop to my knees and start chanting, "Not worthy, not worthy…."

I'd spent too many years paying too much attention to boors, bitches, throne-sitters, cads, bastards, mediocrities, charlatans and ultra-elites, each able to cleverly craft *vers libre* word-dances in tidy stanzas that dispensed no fumes or tides from the soul or any larger meaning, and mostly just concealed empty vapors behind style while questioning nothing and ultimately saying nothing. Yet all the while sounding and appearing so deep and profound. After all, the most important thing for a poet beyond identity politics was his or her photo. And the politically correct pronoun.

Did *they* look like a poet when reading in public? People say *they* does.

A game. This was the trick, the point of it all. It wasn't about what I had to say, the magic was in the pretense of how I *didn't* say it. This was the primary lesson I'd learned regarding the way to gain esteem in poetry publishing as I'd come to understand it. Remember, I said publishing. Esteem. Reputation. Identity. Not writing. Not ideas. These were all different creatures.

The published proclaimed poets, riding in the saddles of their feigned otherness, knew how to profess without professing. They didn't search or discover, question or doubt. They stood for mostly their own career advancement, disdaining any other candidate for a freakshow soapbox to stand on and bark from. They told the wrinkled rumpled wheezing lumpen masses that people and poetry were all about decorous ambiguity. Not important. And let's not forget, all white people lead to evil and, knowing this, are afraid of themselves and the racism deep, deep within the fibers of their being.

Even the white people proclaimed this from on high, some of them in funded chairs at venerated, untouchable universities with endowments larger than the GDP of many small countries. These endowments allowed such institutions to maintain an incredibly rigorous defense of their mediocrity, their shows of otherness and empathy no matter how vacuous, their mismanagement of funds, their excessive rises in tuition while parading their anointed bards and scientists and resident cretins, keeping them comfortable. From what I had seen, they'd become places where many a fresh mind went to die.

Many of the elite had only one mission: to maintain the elite aesthetic. "To cover their own asses" as Papa used to say. Many celebrated versifiers really were or might be potentially brilliant minds, but the accolades went to those trafficking in palaver, the players, shakers and marketeers, a tiny incestuous lot that I'd become sourly and righteously disillusioned with. This was my professional envy, I knew, due to my fanatical romanticism. I was still a believer in what poetry and the arts, in general, could do for those who weren't spending all their time chasing down awards and attending the apt cocktail mixer and conference, parked in multi-tiered garages with ivy climbing up its walls.

For a while it was Louise Gluck who encouraged my disgust with this realm I'd chosen to inhabit. After her, Carolyn Forché. Both fine award-winning poets for some, I supposed, and living quite well off grants and endowments, but if I removed their names from their poems, I wondered if any reader could say if they were or were not written by the same hand. These two poets and so many others like them, such as Mark Strand and Mark Doty, struck me as tawdry in their work and yet so deft when it came to promoting it and scooping up grant dollars, schmoozing, garnering accolades and awards, setting proudly into motion cadres of tuition-paying imitators. They weren't really about the art. They were about themselves and, of course, in America, where money truly meant everything, they were rewarded for this.

I sometimes talked to Dalton about all these things, asking him if this was status quo in all fields of endeavor. He didn't know. He once said to me, "The maintaining of security is in of itself a form of security."

I thought so too, though I was still not entirely sure what he'd meant by that. One at a time, elites vacuumed up the attention and the money. They spent their hours with other elites and those who could help advance their interests. That was the worst part. Poets, politicians, businessmen — I saw no difference. Humanism was on life support. All practitioners were hermetically sealed inside their professional pods and unwilling to venture anywhere that might put their comfort at risk. Nobody in American academic circles wanted a poor poet. They wanted proof that diplomas from vaunted fog factories made a difference.

I imagined the likes of, say, a Charles Olson or a Charles Bukowski. Those frazzled, flatulent, booze-belching bardic castaways wouldn't stand a chance. Nor would they bother with today's anti-academic scene, all the so-called slam poetry, since they'd see it for the watered-down version of rap music that it was, a kind of Hegelian hacky sack competition that the college-educated and hipster working-class sometimes found becoming. It was like lacrosse, I supposed, meaning one had to attend a private college or prep school to even know it existed.

Nor could I imagine that a lot of the beats would make it today, either. Those *men* — and let's face it, could I name one female beat poet? I couldn't. Well, maybe Diane di Prima, but she went to Swarthmore for a while, didn't she? They had their time in the sun. They wouldn't flourish today. Too many voices. All too fractured. No one individual able to really emerge to make a difference. Neglected beat drifters such as Kerouac, though a product of Columbia, would get lost in the swirling cacophony of plaints, tweets, chats, travel blogs and video diaries. Thank you, Internet. He'd also need to compete with the news feeds that come to one's phone whether wanted or not, or the Rupi Kaurs of the Instagram Universe, with their identity cards raised high, in her case Sikh Canadian, automatically granting them status as poet though they don't really challenge anything with their E-scribbled whining stuck in a greeting-card Starbuck's confession loop lacking any nuance or depth, as if all that essential learning and erudition once required of poets can be dismissed in the post-human age.

I couldn't speak, of course, not a word on such topics. With Bret Weinstein and what happened to him at Evergreen College as an example, I began to shrink and cower, accepting that the cancel culture had so infected educators and intellectuals alike that I couldn't even think about some of the impressions, reactions and responses that I felt. They were simply not expressed. The fascistic thinking engendered by the Politically Correct Machine had metastasized into an absolute straitjacket for anyone willing to look at both if not the many sides of any complex issue. All nuance was dead. This had been coupled with the unearned fearlessness that tweeters, hacks and trolls indulged in online. I viewed these missives alone in the silence of my room, mourning the death of an expansive and once more mature critical standard of any kind in all endeavors, especially those of the humanities.

Hectoring and lancing each other became the norm, as uninformed miscreants biliously slung epithets and unproven accusations, with an unwillingness to listen to reason, no matter if blue, red or purple in the political spectrum. What I saw this leading to politically were dictatorial forms of leadership. Alpha dogs began to abound with their zealotry and tyrannical approaches. Why was I feeling as if I was the only one who saw this? I wasn't. But no one would discuss it. No conference on the topic of this muzzling any time soon. To suggest one had a right-of-center political belief, a traditional approach to once sanctified rituals such as marriage, for one, meant curtains in Academia.

Another day meant another thousand "new voices" as long as they met the new harsh criteria regarding identity politics. They were deemed "new discoveries" as long as they don't bring anything "new" to the table or speak or write of themselves in the third person singular. I had become they. No one could be centered or reasonable. One had to be fractured and unsure. It was a sign of dignity to come across as easily triggered into a breakdown. We were all victims.

From what I saw on campus, there were very few who felt any need or willingness to question the venerated and sick reality of the emerging cancel culture. Overnight, is seemed, the LGBTQ began to act as one mass, as if each letter, each separate form of identifying didn't mean anything different, as if the whole group acted and believed monolithically and interpreted every law and point of view in the same way. Of course, this wasn't so. Not in the least when one took the time to really examine what the various political messages and approaches of these groups really were.

But I couldn't and wouldn't dare bring up such a topic. Nor would I dare argue that queer culture practiced and lived by the very form of one-sided, narrow-minded, chauvinistic control on culture it so decried from those who didn't identify as queer. I saw myself becoming a disaffected liberal thinker. I began to believe that if I said one wrong thing that I would be dead. If I worked hard, I'd still be replaced by a hack or a hologram. In my waning years, I'd need to understand that the government would get most of my retirement money. Clogged up. Sideways. Watching all the greedy blood-suckers keep the class war going as zoom became a verb just as prominent as google, and the bow of Ulysses, the warrior's bow, remained destined to rot in storage.

As this new form of loathing seeped in, I felt it starting to rain inside my body. It rained there every night, torrentially so, and I couldn't open my eyes to all that I'd seen and could remember. I began to feel different, wanting to erase myself, or else blow myself up, each of my memories an object of disdain.

Dalton called it "the prisoner's mind." I wasn't alone or original in thinking of it as a victim culture. I saw myself as a victim. This was not a topic that Dalton and I agreed on fully. How many black men were seen or heard in the mainstream and allowed to discuss this? Very few. Though I wasn't hopeful, he was. I didn't understand him. I thought it would be welcomed news to hear that this prison-mind-victim-culture would die soon and rest in peace. He thought it was simply the new way of being, and that we should get accustomed to it. He believed we were only victims if we saw ourselves that way.

I disagreed, sometimes vehemently, and our discussions would turn into arguments. Sometimes, they became fights. I'd throw things in the kitchen and break them. I'd start seething and eating in a panic, shouting at him stay away, to leave me alone as I stuffed my face and then, of course, later on I purged.

I was thinking too much, letting it all get the best of me, convinced that we, as a couple, were weakening ourselves by talking about a video-generated music culture that had been corporatized to create millionaire "rap emcees" that degraded women. We didn't have to celebrate or even acknowledge the worldwide trend of backward-baseball-cap and bling-wearing poet-puppies cashing in on getting swallowed into the trend babble. We could rise above all that and do our own thing, in our own quiet way. This was Dalton's perspective and it was the right one, but I didn't listen to him often enough.

I was too strident, too earnest, too involved, yelling at my Dalton about the useless junk-in-the-trunk noise broiling its lava at high simmer. The poor and ignorant were cannibalizing each other while those that produced such trash, propagating such a loser's hopeless mentality, got richer and richer along the way. We couldn't just live with that, could we?

Yes, Dalton would say. We could. The man heard me out. He endured me. The saint, God, he somehow knew with time that I would calm down and open my eyes and begin to see better. Before I'd met him, I hadn't known about Coleman Hughes, Thomas Sowell, Candace Owens or Larry Elder. Just to name a few voices in the black community that many of my allegedly open-minded liberal colleagues, in all their arrogance, would never listen to and had probably never heard of. Dalton introduced me to these black thinkers, insisting I keep my mind open and really hear what they were trying to say. They didn't all have to be right of center either. He knew more about John Hope Franklin, Malcolm X and Langston Hughes than I did.

"They don't have all the answers," he told me. "I don't always agree with them either. But they're out there. And others like them, they know that they can see in a different direction. Always truth to power, that's the thing to remember."

Right, Dalton, but what I wanted to know was where did it all end? How would things get better? Where were all the voices of Americans with roots in Mexico, Central America, and South America? Were all of them left-leaning liberals? I doubted it. Yet those who were loudest got plenty of air time. Those who weren't, well, where the hell were they? Not all black or Latino men had to end up in prison, or get killed on the streets. There was nothing heroic in any of the ghetto mind-set. It was a culture and when layered under economic strain, a built-in sense of lack of opportunities, it set in and hardened and became a generational way of thinking and being.

Dalton knew this only too well. He listened patiently. It might take me days to calm down from one of my fits, but eventually I would. For many years, I thought naïvely, fecklessly, sedulously, that I had to be invested in the one, the only issue in America, that of race. Racism writ large. Such a problem in the black community. With Dalton's assistance, I started to see that it was not just a "black community thing," as he put it. He saw it as a problem, of course, but it was something bigger, a problem that existed everywhere among people without hope that their lives might change, that some fairness and egalitarianism would enter in. This was what made whites racist toward blacks in the first place. It was not genetic. It was economic, attitudinal, nurtured.

"They need to begin to accept that it's not gonna happen, that they're not gonna win or lose," said Dalton. "They need to feel hopeless. Then, maybe, they'll get it going. You know how it is. You hit bottom. Then you start looking up."

I remained in disagreement with him. After all, in response to injustice, I had chosen to teach at a community college, where some of my students came from truly impoverished backgrounds. I tried to bring into my teaching, keeping it separate from my poetry, methods that helped me become a voice that questioned not the burning down of illusions but rather sustained a living question about why we were not all paying more attention, not listening better, not wanting to create new ways to make and do and see before we challenged or burned down what already existed. I refused to accept that poetry and education was by and for Volvo-driving suburbanites. That the humanities had lost all relevance, importance or meaning as a way to communicate new ideas and fashion a new vision of what humankind was capable of. Destructive impulses were an easy surrender to our basest impulses. What were we going to build to replace what wasn't working?

If one were to examine causes rather than symptoms, were there any connections between the death of poetry and, say, all the shootings that had happened in our schools? Wasn't rap a primitivist stab at capturing the poetic muse? The young in our culture hungered for Erato, an elusive connection, a chance to free themselves of their muddled feelings, to breathe louder than the rest, to find a rhythm and to understand that others, for a long time now, for thousands of years, had felt similar confusions, joys and desolations.

Give me the critical mind, any day, one like that of my intellectual Mommy figure, Camille Paglia, who I respected not only for her undying seriousness, but for the marketability of her labors and her methods of analyzing and deconstructing text while at the same time invigorating interest from non-academics. Give me Gloria Steinem, Doris Lessing, and Toni Morrison. I loved them all, even though I knew they would not save me, however, from my steady plod toward corpulence and self-immolation. I ate and I ate, whether puddings or potato chips, the unhealthier it was, the more I indulged. Dalton didn't like this in me. For a while, I tipped the scale at nearly 320 and had trouble breathing whenever I walked anywhere. I didn't like this either; I'd lost the ability to respect myself. Maybe I never really could.

For a brief while, I suppose, during the first, say, four or five years of our marriage, I had felt myself glowing. I was a rose in new bloom, as happy as I'd felt during my first years at Mary Washington when I really sank my teeth into my dream of being a professional and how my life as an intellectual would see me thrive in pursuit toward writing poems that would endure as art.

I wasn't looking inside of all that I was doing. Nor was I pulling it apart. I was just dallying and yet advancing my work, sending my poems out, poring over them incessantly. I never tired as I lost track of time, staying up all night reading Spenser, Milton and Donne while snacking on mountains of junk food and re-writing page after page sometimes to come up with as little as one stanza. I could always let it flow freely, open the taps within, but to control the content, to shape it into metaphor, to apply what I was learning about language and to accept that I was not "street" or "ivy" but somewhere much more common and in between — all this took many years, far too many hours of what Dalton sometimes would call "butt scratching."

Such a big butt it was, too! LOL, girlfriends. It was during those years I bloomed physically. I mean, to speak crudely, my bottom spread like a new Midwestern suburb. By the time I graduated, I was seething in a perpetual sweat of panic over the increasing amounts of flab and rolls that defined my figure. I should not be so Rubens fat. Not even so Mary Cassatt rosy. Not me. No way. I couldn't say on what day it began, but it happened. I began to make myself vomit. I had to. This wasn't suffering. It was a duty to myself. I didn't deserve to be so large, not in control, and so uncomfortable. The increasing girth that defined my perimeters didn't reflect who I thought I was. I had to do something about it. I made sure my roommates weren't around and then I found a toilet where I purged and denied, purged and denied….

I didn't like it, but I needed it. I wouldn't be anyone's velvety soft, cushy, or squeezable playmate or diva. My imagined cadaverous angularity would prove I was self-actualizing or, even better, that I wasn't at ease. *No contentment among poets, not in my house.* This was a dynamic I struggled to explain to Dalton many times. Dalton claimed to understand some of my pathology, but he didn't, not really. I knew this simply because I didn't even understand it myself. For example, why hadn't I started to purge while in high school? Had it been due to the feelings of safety I felt with my mother so nearby? I carried many such questions within, and few were ever answered.

I preferred Dalton as a cheerleader, a cook, a doofus gummy bear, bedrock, a wailing wall, a sofa and a tree, anything I could fall against, squeeze, rest on, take succor from or rely upon. Dalton knew I tried to understand him, myself, and life in general. He wanted me to feel happiness. He believed I needed to change some of my ways. That I was too extreme. I generally agreed with him on this, of course. Bruises covered my body. I seldom had any energy. Indeed, I'd gone too far. I wasn't sure I could make adjustments.

Did I want to change? I wasn't certain. A poet should be ravenous and desperate and confused. I was passionate, to be sure, obsessed with a desire to end my life as I saw it, and this was linked as I viewed it with Dr. Murray's help, to my depressions, which passed over me like clouds, those lake-sized ones that blot out all the sunshine.

At times, it was as if nothing remained of my body to draw from to keep going. Yet, to be frank, I wanted to change, I knew this, but I was so afraid of swelling again, of being seen as not pudgy or chubby, I could live with that, but of being a whale or a walrus, one of those obese ladies in church that others feel sorry for when she walks up the aisle for communion, her ankles swollen, her thighs wobbling as they rub together, out of breath, sweating, none of her clothes fitting her well. I'd be happy to have my Papa pinch my cheeks like I was his little girl again — oh God, I was still his little girl, I'd always be.

I felt hopeless and it didn't push me or make me want to get better. I felt as if standing on soil that was eroding underfoot, giving way, and at the same time erupting within only to release all this bile and frustration I'd gathered and stored inside and sometimes shared with Summer Rain and wouldn't share with Dalton.

I didn't fully comprehend what Summer Rain did for me, but she was medicine, my saving angel. Nor did I know what she did at the PR and marketing firm that she worked for. I believed she did more than edit copy while snacking at her desk. She didn't like to talk about it, so I didn't ask. I didn't blame her. What we talked about was poetry and body acceptance issues, and love. Yes, love. She was the one I felt most comfortable with talking to about such a big abstract topic. When Dalton and I talked love, it was in frag-ments while we touched each other and cheered each other up. With Summer Rain, it was more of a clinical discussion and this made her a kind of second therapist for me to lean on. She never seemed to mind.

We had lots in common. I knew she'd had problems in the past with accepting her body, as well as her sexual orientation, but she'd come to terms with both of them. The last time I saw her she was easily twenty pounds heavier, but she was smiling and aglow. How I envied the way she'd turned indifference into a form of self-confidence that allowed her to do more. She was neither bitter nor nasty. She was so unapologetically masculine, too, and yet kind and not aggressive in many of the commonly seen ways, fully outré, and each time I saw her I gave her the biggest hug I could muster. I'll admit that I was fond of large men. Dalton, for one, especially. The bigger, the better, and this was how I saw Summer. She was a big man in a woman's body.

Dalton had been beefy, especially around his mid-section, but not too large and ungainly of a man when I married him, but the potential and a family history of diabetes had been there, and he'd been right to be concerned about his health, so I didn't push too hard, though his body, over time, changed considerably. He widened across his backside and sternum, and his legs got thicker. I didn't mind. I enjoyed seeing him in our kitchen, and I crafted clever ways to encourage him to stay there and to keep cooking for me.

As with Dalton, I never failed to tell Summer how much I loved her. I missed her and appreciated the e-mails, letters, cards and occasional books she sent. She liked to say, in return, that I did not have to be a size two and would never be, so why the hell was I killing myself? Even when I had a clever comeback, I wouldn't share it. Maybe I liked imagining myself a size two. Or at least a twelve. And maybe I just liked being difficult.

❧

A steady mist was arousing humidity and a wormy smell that mingled with the fumes of rancid food from a garbage Dumpster at the end of an alley next to Summer Rain's building in her Washington DC neighborhood. The city was having its usual effect on me, a creeping fear of the apocalyptic, some form of a biblical end times that gnawed at my insides and made me paranoid. Having come to visit for the weekend, I'd been stoned and eating and drinking non-stop, salaciously giving into a gluttony that had begun to soothe my fears starting with my Friday night arrival in turgid and sometimes hazardous traffic.

Saturday night was looming. I'd gone 24 hours without a moment of clarity and without purging. I wasn't sure what we would do next, though I was certain food would be involved. We were getting high again. I couldn't remember the last time when my belly had felt so painfully full for so long, my senses so lethargic. It was a zombi-fied state of being that I'd forgotten I was capable of maintaining, and as more time passed I began to fear it less and less. I was, at last, embracing my wanton self, resting, in weekend vacation mode, relying on Summer Rain to take care of the noxious details.

She was drinking beer. Draining them two at a time. That woman could drink, but she never came across as sloppy or out of control. If I was following her correctly, which was sometimes tricky to do since she spoke breathlessly in large abstract chunks, she was saying that putting together my *Synesthesia* manuscript was a brilliant idea and I should take my time, really push the bound-aries for about a year and get it all out, and only after that should I start concerning myself with it being polished and professional.

We had been talking about music. I was seated on the floor in her living room. She was on the couch, a can of beer in one hand, another one next to her on an end table. Two at a time, that was how she downed 'em. I'd never even bothered trying to keep up. She didn't mind. She never had. I didn't know anyone who drank like she did.

What could one tell from someone else's taste in music? This was our question. With my legs stretched out, feeling dazed and sedate, my stomach still swollen, and my breathing difficult due to the massive of amount of comfort food I'd crammed inside of it at a nearby buffet. How I loved comfort food. Why had I been *denying* myself this love?

As I listened to Summer, I dawdled through the titles of her CDs, many of them spread like playing cards on the floor in front of me. Yes, she still used this old form of technology. I did, as well. So did Dalton. I guess we all liked choosing randomly from what we could see in front of us. We couldn't always do that with electronic sources, especially when the music choices that came our way were determined by an algorithm, not by fickle on-the-spot impulses. I also liked thinking of the music experience as one separate from the laptop or computer. This was why I wrote in long-hand, as well. I saw technological devices as delivery tools, nothing more. For me, it was about the feel that I liked when selecting a book from a shelf or a CD from a rack, or of the pencil in my hand when writing, and the way that hand moved across a page. How I liked the smell of vinyl, and the opening of a CD case to remove its insert. I sat there and drew on memories of opening double-fold albums and getting lost in the pictures and information there. Why on earth did my entire life have to be linked and synched to my phone? Ah, better to track you with, my dear. According to Dalton, who I trusted on such issues, it was really that simple.

Scattered on the floor in no particular order, I picked up a few discs at a time and I listened as Summer Rain said she was going to buy a storage unit for them made of wood through mail order, a proper library case with deep doors that swung open and shut, and maybe spun like a Lazy Susan, but for the time being it was impro-vised stacks around her laptop and underfoot for me to cull through and to consider as I thought freely about color and mind and music and synesthesia and how they were all blended together.

In spite of all the music at my fingertips and what it promised, I kept returning to one stirring and consistent thought that Summer Rain had this slightly demonic influence on me. She allowed me to find it easy to loosen up and splurge on whatever I craved at any moment. It was like she enjoyed seeing me do this as much as I enjoyed doing it for her. I'd be lying if I said there wasn't sexual tension between us. There always had been, but I was too loyal, too much in love with Dalton. Summer, knowing this, would never force me into anything physical that would be awkward, but if I gave in to my curiosity, and reached out with my lips to kiss hers, I knew she'd take them in and we'd kiss and hold each other and find our way into her bedroom and, well, it would most likely be wonderful. Would it last? No. Would it ultimately destroy my marriage and our friendship? I didn't want to find out, but I had a solid hunch it would.

It also occurred to me that, regarding music, I could say nothing about it any critical way. Many of these artists I liked. They were once cutting edge, but had now become tape-loop choices for the aisles at Walmart, which made me wonder if in the future whether bovine women with tattoos shopping for diapers in Costco would be subjected to the likes of Biggie Smalls, and System of a Down.

I knew these pop artists and I appreciated that Summer liked them, but they spoke of a gone era. Of yesterday. If I understood Summer correctly, she thought my *Synesthesia* manuscript should be a disturbing cutting-edge social statement. How could that be that if the music tracks that I explored, and that influenced my thinking were from The Pretenders, The Doors, Aimee Mann, Renaissance, Elton John, Billy Joel, The Beatles, and Joni Mitchell? Lots and lots of Joni, who I still adored, but who I'd also grown a tad weary of back in the 80s.

"See anything you like?" Summer had grown heavier since I'd last seen her and she was wearing a loose flannel shirt over sweatpants. Her laptop was on her lap, open in front of her, though she sipped her beer without any concern that she might spill some into her keyboard. It was like she was stuck in 1977, or 87, or 97 — I didn't know.

She flashed me a devilish yet warm and enchanting smile. We were friends and I was so glad to be with her again; I shouldn't judge her harshly. I respected her. I didn't think DC was a cozy place to live in and I adored the way she helped me feel safe and brought out my willingness to be playful. With Dalton I felt wanted and revered, which I loved of course, but with Summer Rain I felt as if I had permission to misbehave and do naughty things to myself.

The apartment living room was small enough so that we spoke place to each other without any need to raise our voices beyond any volume that would be deemed normal. It wasn't intimate or sexy or anything like that, just relaxed, insouciant, without formality or an edge. Summer's desk was in one corner. A small empty loveseat along one wall. Her sofa along the opposite wall. No television. Only music for Summer. And her books. They were in her bedroom, from floor to ceiling. We both loved a good book the way we loved a wedge of frosted carrot cake.

The longer I stayed there on that floor, the more I enjoyed the way I was letting myself breathe. I could feel my breathing return to a more normal pace, though I could also feel my thighs spreading as if tubes of gelatin. My stomach erupted in slow occasional languid measures and I belched now and then and this made Summer smile and it was all so cerebral.

"Such the Joni fan," I told her. "Her *Mingus,* that's still my favorite. But you don't have that one. Do you know it?"

"I like *Blue.* It's over there. I like *Hissing of Summer Lawns* too."

"Oh, love that one," I said. "I'd forgotten about it. She wrote so much." I find her copy of it. "Here it is. But it's so 70s, don't you think?"

"Maybe it can be a part of a flashback in one of your poems, or in your thinking, or connected to a memory," she said. "Music can be used in so many ways."

"I think tone's the thing," I said. What was I saying? I was so stoned. It made no sense. I sucked another hit from the joint that I'd forgotten had been smoldering between my fingers. I couldn't remember what we'd just been talking about. I felt infantile, staring, and as the little gastric eruptions continued inside, giving me warm jolts of delicious pleasure, I realized that I'd been drooling, as well. I wiped the drool off my lips, too stoned to speak at the moment. As I coughed, I passed Sumer Rain the joint. I wanted to eat again. Lots of food. Why? I didn't know. But it was a pleasantly intriguing idea. I blew a sigh and imagined mountains of coffee ice cream with sprinkles on top. It would all go down so effortlessly.

I beamed at my dear friend. She beamed back and at her urging I searched further through her CDs: The Waitresses. B52s, Barry Manilow, Perry Como, Andy Williams, Judy Garland, Peggy Lee, Bette Midler, and Johnny Mathis. To me, all of these suggested that Summer was a lesbian living in her past. I couldn't prove this. Nor would I want to. It served no purpose. Nor was her sexual orientation relevant. This music simply reflected her taste. It had nothing to do with mine, even though our tastes sometimes overlapped. So what was the point of doing this? There was no point.

"Think of the music as my colors," she said. "Then think of your own colors."

Now we were getting somewhere. My head lolled to one side. Bette Midler. My hero. I could be that kind of woman. In charge. Volatile. And Johnny Mathis. My Dalton, though bigger of course, had similar eyes and skin tone. Oh, my dreamy Dalton, my African prince.

I heard my voice as if from a distance. "We're getting older, for sure."

"Not that old." She snorted out a laugh then and I didn't know why. Her laugh sounded swinish from a woman of such girth, but it was endearing.

I was stoned enough to risk asking her for a sip of her beer. As if she'd read my mind, she gave me the can on her end table. I popped it open and drank off my cotton mouth and when I stopped, I felt suddenly gassy and I sounded a large and rather disgusting belch. I liked the way the belch tickled my nose. Summer began laughing at me as if I were a child she found entertaining.

Maybe I was. Maybe I liked being that child.

"The joint," I said. "I need."

"No you don't."

I swiped it out of her hand, startling her, but knocking the lit ash to the wooden floor. I put out the ash with my shoe and then lit the joint again before sucking down another few hits. I wanted to get really blasted. Beyond catatonic. I knew it would allow me to float away, and at the very worst I might vomit, fall down or pass out and force Summer to lug me to bed. It was the thrill of losing control that felt so enticing. I had started to get more than a little moist over it and no doubt Summer Rain could feel this.

"Got any suggestions?" she asked.

I looked at her. Really saw her. So butch with her short ginger hair. Her yes to life so open, as blue as the broad seas in her smile. Benevolent, generous, gregarious, beatific incorrigible Summer Rain. She knew the dizzy heights that I was climbing to. Or maybe not climbing. Maybe just being swept up into the clouds, going wherever the jolts took me. I flashed her a little smile in return.

"I think," she said, "you should write a collection of poems that's as outrageously over the top as a Baz Luhrmann spectacle."

I sipped my beer. I felt like all my limits and edges had melted away. I was one with her, another boy in a girl's body. She had such a liberating effect on me and I wasn't about to fight it. "But I want to think about colors that are born out of sounds," I told her. "I'll give you an example. One song that I know you know. It's 'Wichita Lineman' by Glenn Campbell. I love that song. I want every one of my poems to create the colors it brings. I don't want to write about that song, but I want to borrow and share its effect on me. Let my poems be about where I've been when I've heard it, and what it helped me see and feel."

"That's it." She clapped her hands together once. "Love that song. Don't just use it or explain it. Explore it. Say how much you love it. But don't use the word love."

"I know what you mean," I said. "I need time to ponder."

"Of course you do."

So, I looked inside as if craning my neck to look down a well. My mind started to open various cages. Little tarts and pies started to float about in the darkness and I saw myself reaching for them one at a time and shoving them into my mouth and chewing and seething with pleasure as I found Boy George, Annie Lennox, Barry White, Kate Smith, Robbie Williams, and Rick Springfield.

"Kate Smith, really?"

"I know." Summer looked apologetic. "Guilty pleasure. I can't help myself. I'm even starting to look like her."

This had been true for a while, but who cared. We're not about our bodies, really, are we? How wrong, me of all people, Queen Bulimia, I was. Okay, permit me to be delusional. What harm was there in thinking we humans are about spirit and light and energy. I wanted to tell my Summer Rain that she was adorable, but that might send too forward a sexual message, so I toasted her instead and guzzled my beer, showing off that I could drink with the best of them.

She watched me and sounded a dim chuckle, not all that impressed but perhaps pleased that I was trying. As I caught my breath, dizzied a bit by the quantity I'd consumed, Summer, still watching, said simply, "This is how it's done."

With ease, one long voluminous swallow at a time, she emptied her can of beer. Then she crushed the can in her fist and let rip a gargantuan belch.

Rabelaisian, that's what she was. In awe, I fell back to my hands and gawked at her. I was really damp now and the warm jolts were expanding into slow-moving shifts. I could do that. I could drink like a mad sailor on shore leave. Why didn't I? Why was I holding back all the time?

Summer then struggled to lift her Falstaffian bulk from her chair. I didn't believe it was possible, but I found myself wondering if I could become even larger than she was. Not at all beyond possible. Wouldn't it be an endless joy to just indulge? Dr. Murray had encouraged such imaginings more than once, telling me I should embrace my fears because actually my fears were my desires. What a thought! Goodness, I was so high.

I watched Summer wheeze and limp, one heavy tread at a time, off to her bedroom. She took a long time or maybe it just seemed that way because I had lost all sense of time. All I knew was that I'd been able to finish the beer she'd given me. This was an achievement. I was usually a wine drinker, and a slow one, though two bottles of rosé in one night was not unusual. I'd polished off my beer in about twenty minutes.

Returning red-faced, panting, Summer held a cardboard box full of record albums up to her waist with both hands. "Look at these," she said. "Vinyl. Can't you smell them? I love that smell. You have here a wily old sage of a woman living in this collection. I'm talking about you. I can feel her vibe. These may help you find it.."

"The mother figure," I said. "Just find her. No playlist."

"Exactly."

She set the box of record albums down in front of me. She then left me alone, padding off to the kitchen and returning with two beers for her and one for me. I offered her the joint in my hand. "It's almost done."

"No. You finish it. Take some more hits. And have a long look," she said. "You need your eyes to be sharp for this . I think you're starting to feel the color thing."

"But shouldn't we go easy?" I said. "Isn't this stuff expensive?"

"You mean the weed? Don't worry. I have more in the freezer."

"You do? How nice." I grinned at her.

She sat, not without clumsiness, and she sighed. Then she nodded, looking down at me from the couch. "Just enjoy yourself, my sister."

How I delighted in the smell of her old records, and as I thumbed through them recalling Papa's collection, I really did feel like a little girl seated there, and Summer wasn't unlike my Papa looking down on me and nodding his approval. There were more than a few Wayne Newton albums that once belonged to Summer's mother, along with Dean Martin, and Don Ho albums. My parents had owned albums by these artists, as well.

"Why albums?" I asked. Such a large box of them struck me as a sad sight since Summer didn't even own a turntable. "Why are you keeping them?"

"Mother, I guess." She shrugged. "And love. Different reasons. One, her character. My love for her. For the past. For what we can't have any longer. The poems I'm writing these days are about her and her generation. Not so much about her native bloodlines, but how she became a kind of Sophie Tucker clone, in a way. How I'm becoming one too. Brassy. Not afraid of who I am. Though I don't think it was easy for her.   She was a closet singer. Never did much with her voice. These crooners were her idols. Especially Wayne Newton."

I melted there, for a moment, unable to speak. How much love Summer Rain must have felt for her mother. How alike we were. I hadn't yet read any of her newer poems about the woman, but I was sure, with time, that I would. I knew I wanted to, just as I'd always wanted to meet her mother, though I never had and never would. But I was meeting a form of myself, through her, through Summer too, wasn't I?

"What was she like?" I asked. "Tell me more about her."

Summer paused a moment before answering. "I think I knew her, just as I think I know who Ethel Merman was, but I can't be sure. So I write my poems. Mother had medicine woman blood in her too. She was a complex spirit. Sometimes, I fake it. You know, I just write as if I understand. I get so high on the work, without any weed, that even if I ask myself who she was, I can't remember. But maybe that's why I still keep writing my poems."

"I know what you mean. It's like you can't help yourself. That you have to give up control. I struggle with that."

"But you're getting better. You came to see me. You're here, right?"

I nodded and grinned.

Summer said, "I'll ask myself again tomorrow or after you've gone and I'm clear-headed and alone, who she is. Who I am. It's not like I can look us up online. Honestly, I don't know who she was. I never knew. But I sense her. The music she liked, these record albums, they bring me back to her. Like I said, there's no playlist. No order. Just impressions. I think I see her colors. That's what really gets me."

I was thrilled with all this. "Wait. Say that again. When you listen to her music, you think you see the same colors that she saw. You mean like a kind of shared synesthesia?"

"You could say so. My big mistake was that I thought I did understand her. But the more I learn, the more I realize I don't. That's why I keep these. She *wanted* me to have them. Maybe she knew they'd teach me something. Of course, just looking at them, smelling them, they conjure some of her emotional mood swings and attachments. But who she is, or was, I look in the mirror and I don't see her. I see myself. And then I see her again. In the end, I see both of us. It's remarkable, really, I can't get enough of it."

"Wow. That's what I feel sometimes when I think about my Papa."

"Maybe it's natural. Part of the process. I know I can take pieces of my mother out of my body. I do it all the time. I examine them before I put them back. It's like that."

The room grew silent. I knew exactly what Summer Rain was getting at. It astonished me to think that a new manuscript, a refreshed mission in my poetry was gaining traction and growing within. I could spend the coming year just plunging the depths of my taste in music, my relationship to my father, to my sense of alienation during high school years, those three roads back there in Seekonk, my love for Dalton, my complicated love for Rusty, and how each of these parts displayed a different color when linked to music. And a different texture when linked to food.

What was happening to me? I was becoming someone else. I disliked myself at that moment because I felt I knew nothing about emotional attachments and yet I thought I could write poems about them. Yet I'd never really thought I knew my subject in any of the poems that had bled out of me. My poems just happened. I shaped them. I chased them down and forced them to behave. All the pieces of the puzzle that had made me who I was up until that moment, and anything I wrote about these pieces or synesthesia would sound most likely maudlin and not empathetic enough. Amen. Just the same, it was no reason to stop writing.

I felt overwhelmed and a little lost. Nothing new there. A journey with all its possibilities was opening itself to me, yet it was intimidating. To go deep inside, to take my time and follow through and make one poem after another, recreating some of the language from within my shared experiences, well, it was never an easy task. It drained me. It made me feel sad and lonely, but when I looked at Summer Rain, I saw someone who looked even worse, seated there, her beer can in one hand resting across the top of her voluminous belly. She was still breathing hard too, her cheeks pink and puffy, winded after such a short walk to her bedroom and the kitchen.

She was a sullen constant drinker, had always been, and there was no consoling her. No consoling me either. It had been different when we'd been younger, but her youthful looks had long ago faded and she was middle-aged now, missing her mother, her old life, coping with failed dreams, impending health issues, trying to write great poems, of all things, as if that would change the trajectory of her existence.

I sighed. I wasn't all that different. We wouldn't live long lives, expiring serenely in our sleep. We'd burst and send asteroids and fountains of starlight into the stratosphere. I didn't know how to find the greatness in my work that I wanted to achieve. Great in the sense of scale, of an unquestionable power and force. All poems that lasted, no matter how long they were, possessed this sense of scale that resonated once a person had finished reading it. Could I write such poems? Hadn't everything I'd written up to this very moment been an attempt, nothing more, and otherwise fraudulent, juvenile, an exercise in learning how to write?

It had. Yet in accepting this, I felt as if I were justified. I began floating. I'd been too ponderous and restricted by unwritten codes of excellence that were the products of my imagination. I wanted to grow, to get out of the shell I'd been living in. I also wanted to walk outdoors where I could let the city air at night sink into my bones while I was high. Too bad it was still misty outside and so grimy. Maybe it would taper off soon. I hoped so.

I slid the box of albums out of the way, unable to look at them any longer. I thought of the Summer Rain fourteen years ago when I first met her. She'd worn her hair longer then, with tints of carmine dyed into it to brighten its natural chestnut color. She was a little thinner then. She took up less space in the world. When she spoke, not very many people other than myself paid much attention.

I remembered her first reading, the one where we'd met, and how small the audience had been that had come to hear her and maybe buy one of her books. Now looking at her, I was reminded of the bloated version of Orson Welles, not the one who starred in *Citizen Kane*. I wasn't comfortable with this thought and association. Should I tell Summer that she should take better care of her health? Shouldn't I be telling that to myself? Letting go was one thing, but alcoholism and steady slow suicide was quite another.

The room grew silent again. Just the sound of rain. It had picked up and was louder, splatting as gusts threw it against window panes. The metallic pop of Summer opening another beer can. We each were lost in our various ruminations. The music that had been playing, a spritely bit of classical she'd put on for me, had stopped. Did Summer understand that her lifestyle wouldn't allow her to live much longer? Did she care? Did I? She was bored, wasn't she? She was old and alone. She knew she had a drinking problem, but she didn't see it as such. She'd told me that she could function as an alcoholic. Her father had been able to, though he'd died young. She'd do the same and I thought she found it annoying to ruminate on what she considered such trivialities.

If anything, maybe I helped by being there because my presence made her feel she had a purpose for living. Otherwise, life was a farce and her work, no matter how good, would in the end amount to nothing. I realized, too, as I looked at her, just how maliciously loving and controlling she could be, but I could never get angry with her for this. I was strong enough to think for myself, to turn Summer away if I had to and quit all this debauchery. It would not be difficult. All I'd need do was to purge as I conjured a picture of how sotted with beer she appeared, and what kind of state her body was in.

Hopeless. I felt everything collapse within me. I had to remain seated there on that floor a while longer and to steady my breathing. I watched the rain streak Summer's third floor window. Cities were best at such a time, when the darkness was coming on and everything looked slick with rain. Maybe I'd use such a tawdry thought in a poem.

Summer Rain was in for a big fall. Did I have the strength to catch her? Was it really my responsibility? I felt sick. Wasn't I falling too? I needed to lie down. I asked her and she said I could go to her bedroom and shut the door behind me. She said it in a grumpy and disappointed way. I thanked her and, struggling to stand, belching again, I excused myself.

A poem was taking over. I grabbed my purse, knowing my poem notebook was inside of it, and I took it with me to Summer's bed. Once I lay down, I found it a pleasure to listen and be enveloped by the now steady downpour. It was blessed music. The colors came. First indigo, then shale, then a deep jade. Some words come. They made no sense. They blended with the rain and the colors. The room began to spin.

—∞—

Our bodies were stenciled cuneiform shadows on our bedroom's walls. That night, on a stage somewhere, a lover was begging for proof that her passions would not expire in vain. At first, with Dalton, it was every bit love at first sight. We'd both changed over the years, but he was still hearty and bumptious and a little sly. I was comely and naïve when he'd met me, not looking nearly as ungainly, swollen and creased and worn out. He'd thought of me as a New England girl, which I wasn't and told him, but he'd never really accepted me as a woman from the South. Not that it had ever mattered. I met him and shared my ambitions to publish poetry and to teach literature. I still had those ambitions, along with the same slightly olive-toned skin, though more dimple in places, and raven flames of black hair and a passion for oversized denim shirts, and long leather jackets, high-test marijuana, and any kind of chocolate or gluten.

Early on, I started turning him on to all sorts of books by poets. He'd liked a few, but, unfortunately, most of them had made him start disliking poetry generally, leading me to give up that practice. One poet, surprisingly, that Dalton liked and was still reading now and then was Anne Sexton and all of her sometimes onerous, sometimes herculean and peevish confessions. I liked hearing what he had to say about her work, just as he too, liked hearing how I wrote poems because it was like plunging my nose into the crushing isolation that I felt. One of my favorite Sexton poems was *The Addict.* Her opening, "Deathmonger, sleepmonger…" spoke to my own cloying inclinations to feel liberated enough to write cheerless dispassionate sometimes deranged confessions of my own without skimping on my small-boat-on-a-big-ocean stabs at lyrical examinations of existence.

My life had not been one drunken-boat vision of hell, but rather a conventional affair. I suffered for my art, by my own choice, which was what poets, what all artists should do. Dalton liked this about me. He thought me noble if not horribly impractical. What I'd liked most about the moment when he'd gone to one knee and proposed, was that he'd said so matter of factly, "We're talking true love here, Stella Luna."

During those first years of marriage, with lots of sex, my buli-mia went into hiding. It was all the physical attention. We went to Florence and Rome for our honeymoon. I get chills thinking how happy a time we had, and the meals we enjoyed there. I looked like a delicious bowl of apples packed into my wedding dress, and my curves radiated in everything I wore that I bought in Italy, and there was so much genuine youth in me except for the deep black hollows under my eyes. Except for those frightening honeymoon pictures of me in a one-piece bathing suit, flowing and fawning in ridiculous poses like an overfed version of a Mucha maiden with cellulite, none of my ribs visible and my jaw protruding like that of a raptor's waiting to audition for the next Jurassic Park sequel. A jaw that wanted to snap open and shut and just keep on consuming. It's an understatement to say that I didn't eat much during those early years of our marriage. And I was miserable because of it. I starved myself and may have even slipped into a borderline tem-porary anorexia, but I was already so naturally *zaftig* that the sight of me didn't raise any eyebrows. It was after I was certain we would not have children, that I began to loosen up. Thank God, for Spanx. I kept the illusion of an hourglass figure going for a while, choosing long dresses and scarves, anything that flowed to help me look as if rendered more by Maxfield Parrish rather than Botero or Renoir. By the time we reached our seven year itch, I began caving in to the bulimia completely, dipping and swelling from between 220 to 270, wearing anything I could find that didn't cut off circulation.

I'd learned to adapt and change. I was still learning. I could lick this thing. The visit to Summer Rain had really borne this out. I couldn't look at my body any longer. It wasn't *my* body. It belonged to another woman, a dorky dweebish book nerd loner in the halls at Seekonk High who couldn't stand trying to make sense of her afflictions. I craved some meat on my bones for my Dalton to grab on to. He craved it too. I'd started making love to him with the lights turned off. I kept myself wrapped in my pajamas. He didn't say anything. Men seldom do. We must coax it out of them. I tried to be diplomatic and respectful. I didn't tell him that I, too, looked forward to seeing my flesh fully roseate again, making warm love to him, the cuddly sweetheart I married.

In high school, I had both a healthy, some might say monstrous appetite and what now appears obvious as a body inclined toward curves. This maybe was the problem and where it all began. Somebody somewhere told me I didn't count if I wasn't wearing a size ten dress. I couldn't show cleavage or sumptuous lines. The lines of my body couldn't babble like a river or spread like a tree. I should look more like a pole or a stick. Sharp clean lines. None of those fleshy undulations or muffin tops.

Didn't I want to keep changing and to level off once and for all, convinced I'd gotten better? I often heard myself saying that I did, but I still didn't know if I could believe in myself. Would it be that I'd never know?

⚬⚬⚬

Dalton and I were in the kitchen, always sunny there, its windows facing east, with lots of food around, the best place we'd found to discuss my eating disorder. I'd learned to never discuss it in the bedroom; it was like dipping Dalton in ice-water.

"Do I need to tell you I love you more?" he asked. He was at the gas stove and pan-frying two large steaks. Potatoes were baking in the oven. He'd already made us a salad. All rather conventional fare, which suited him on a weeknight especially.

"More than what?" I asked.

"More *often*. Do I tell you enough?"

I had to chuckle. "You're so sweet. No, honey, it's nothing like that. Don't you understand that it's all about me and how I see myself? Don't overthink it, really, it's not your problem."

"But it is. You're all I've got. I can't lose you. A couple, you know, that's us. And we need to make love now and then. I'm a man. I have needs."

How on earth was I to respond to that? It wasn't as if he'd been insincere or controlling. He was trying to share his concerns with me and he'd meant every word and they weren't easy for him to bring out of himself.

It wasn't as if I was perfect. I, too, could be introverted with a tendency to clam-up due to stress. I was also prone to bouts of dramatic nervousness. I gnawed at myself from the inside out, justified by all sorts of illogical reasons which only I could explain. That was the problem. I couldn't explain them. Not to Dalton. Not to myself. It was this other Stella Luna, the one I saw in the mirror, she had to do the explaining, but I didn't know how to reach her and open her up and give her permission to share.

Sometimes, I wondered what it was I'd been saving myself for. Was it another man? Not at all. I wasn't unhappy with Dalton. I wanted to love him better, more consistently, to go wild on his body at night. I'd once been able to do this, but I was weaker and, with time, had lost stamina. I was growing dryer and colder and more wrinkly too. Not that I wanted to, mind you. Not in the least. On the contrary. I wanted to return to the old Stella I imagined myself to be, saucy vixen poetess who'd do dirty little things to Dalton while he was driving in the car, depending on the road of course.

I just couldn't pinpoint where this hatred of myself was coming from. Was it pointing to another woman for Dalton? Or was it a desire on my part for another man? I felt so baffled by it all and maybe I was dreaming up these possible scenarios because it was a convenient way for me to rationalize my difficult and erratic condition.

"You eat, Dalton. If you want to help me. You do want to help, don't you?"

He flipped over the meat with a sizzle of steam that smelled of onions and a touch of barbecue sauce. "Of course, I do."

"So, to please, you, if I bring home some doughnuts, you'll eat them?"

"I love doughnuts."

"And you'll help me eat them too, even if I resist at first?"

He nodded. Then he shook a little of the juice in the skillet, sounding another sizzling explosion of steam.

"Homer Simpson? Is that what you want me to become?" he asked.

"I like Homer." I worked up a little smile. "I ravish you, Dalton. You are aware of that, *n'est ce pas*?"

"Stop talking like a poet. You need to understand that I keep thinking the next time I get on top I'm going to crush you."

That, of course, would never happen. I had to laugh. I shook my head and lurched backward, falling into a kitchen chair. "No. Right now, there's a little girl inside me who needs to be crushed. It's an obverse form of support. Truth be told, I'm frightened. I feel secure when I'm with you. I want to watch you eating doughnuts. I like that you're such a big man. Is that perverted?"

"Yeah, kind of weird." He smiled at me. "I suppose you want to film it, too?"

I had to smile back. I felt my shoulders dropping. "That's not a bad idea."

He laughed and I laughed and I tilted my head sideways and stared at him and then I pretended to grab a doughnut, rushed toward him and forced my fist against his lips. I knew I smelled of strawberries — all of it in my damp hair, recently washed. I knew Dalton would like this scent. And this joking around. While he started seething a little, playing along, I kept up the act and pretended to shove the doughnut into his mouth as I said, "Dr. Murray tells me we can't let what frightens us take over. You show me it's okay. This is what I need. Show me it's okay."

He looked at me and he withered a little as he saw that a smile had spread across my face. I was feeling radiant, turned on. I assumed I looked both satisfied and hungry for more. I collapsed in a slight daze away from him, back into my chair. I began breathing calmly but quickly and there was a bizarre sexual feel that I really liked.

"See, I can admit it now."

"The fear?" he asked.

I nodded with an apologetic look. "It's Friday night. Things will get better. I'm so glad you're home for the weekend. You know I'm always glad about that, don't you?"

"I'm glad you're glad."

The sex that night was better than it had been in quite a while. In the morning, still asleep, I heard him going out and I whispered to him, "Don't forget my doughnuts." I went back to sleep and took my sweet time getting out of bed and facing the day.

When Dalton returned, having done some shopping, he told me he planned on staying home all day to cook me a big meal. It would be so delicious that I wouldn't be able to resist. I thanked him for not shying away from talking about my disorder, for being honest with me.

"You know I'm all in," he said. "I want you to get better."

It was exactly what I needed to hear and I told him so. Then I asked if he could cook me some waffles for breakfast. "Let me try," he said.

"Cook me a bunch of them. With lots of butter and syrup. And some toast too. And some eggs. Wait, why don't we just go for a drive to Culpepper? There's that little breakfast place there you like. He said no. He was sick of driving. He needed to stay home.

I did too. I planned to do nothing but decompress and maybe read the Washington *Post* newspaper he'd brought me last Sunday, the one that was still there where he'd left it ever so casually without saying a word. The news would depress me, but I could do the crossword puzzle and then get really stoned on a fresh batch of weed that I I'd bought. While getting stoned before breakfast, I kept myself busy cleaning the apartment, labor I knew Dalton would appreciate. I put in a load of laundry. I ironed one of his shirts and a pair of his slacks so they'd be ready for him on Monday. I'd do the rest later. I saw this housework as needed exercise, a way to lose weight. I was too damn fat. But I was a hefty woman. Always would be. I had to somehow grow thinner, yet more muscular, but without purging.

During a break, feeling fatigued, I went to the kitchen and found Dalton there cooking not breakfast but some kind of lunch or dinner. My breakfast, which I had smelled from the living room, was ready. He made me sit and he poured me a fresh cup of coffee and then he uncovered a plate stacked with waffles drenched in butter. There was another plate of potatoes, one of bacon and a third one with toast and eggs. It was enough food for three people, easily.

"I can't eat all this."

"Yes you can. I'm not eating doughnuts for you if you won't even eat breakfast. Now go on. Try, at least. In the meantime, I'll play some music."

So, with quiet jazz piano music playing, maybe some Bill Evans, I did my best. First, I took about three big hits from my pot pipe. Then I began mindlessly and rapturously eating all the food in front of me.

Dalton, in his apron, looking so cute, kept working on what looked like a roast and he was peeling potatoes and carrots and onions to go with it. He made a point of keeping away from me, not making me feel pressured. Seeing this, I began to feel looser and since I'd ironed his Monday clothes and started laundry, I allowed myself to relax.

I had to labor to chew and chew again, and to keep stabbing my fork into those waffles, keeping an imaginary door open inside of myself, letting myself see that there was still room inside this ribcage of mine as I struggled to inhale and exhale and swallow. Struggle was the appropriate word. Dalton's breakfast was delicious, and more than enough, frankly too much, but I couldn't think about that. I couldn't imagine limitations. I just had to scoop and slide spoon and fork, shoving them into my mouth while letting syrup drip down my chin.

I didn't how much time had passed before I'd realized I'd eaten nearly all he'd prepared for me over the course of an hour. A sugar rush came on, I felt groggy and yet, as I tried to stand, which was awkward, I also still felt hungry. Now, wasn't this strange? But rather than eat, I decided to light up my pipe and refresh my buzz.

I just had to get out of that kitchen. I took long strides toward the bathroom, where I knew what I'd do, both fingers ready, but Dalton, without a word, stopped me. He led me to the sofa and helped me lie down. He told me to rest, to breathe easy, to fall asleep if I had to.

When I awoke, it was late in the afternoon. The house was so quiet. I could feel heat coming from the kitchen. The stove was still on. Dalton's roast was cooking. Its smell nearly knocked me over. Scrumptious. I went looking for him. He was gone. He'd left a note taped to the fridge. He was out buying some dessert and he'd be back soon.

His roast smelled heavenly.

My debate began. I had my Ipecac solution and my fingers. I had wine or I could start smoking again and I thought about my status in life and told myself I didn't really have it all that bad. I had, in fact, too much of everything. Perhaps I'd always had too much and maybe that was why I'd never felt I fit in anywhere. It seemed others, not me, didn't have enough. I mused on an apt French word I had claimed for self-definition: *déracinés*. The uprooted ones.

I felt a poem coming on. There was my answer. It was time to work. I poured myself a glass of water and went to my desk and began to write.

We are here and I am one of them and when I look at you, I'm looking down inside the rings of a dream city where I become a woman sparkling with the towers of Ilium and Babel and I think of Emerson's quotation which I wrote in one of my journals during a time when I needed daily affirmations. Ralph Waldo's directive was to "Make much of your own place."

I was hoping to use some of this because it had flowed so effortlessly out of me, but as I read it over, I suspected I wouldn't use any of it because — well, I didn't know why. It just didn't feel right or relevant to anything. Just warm-up language, really. A way to fire up the rapport between mind and pencil. So much of my writing of poems was intuitive. Certainly, the average person would never grasp the gist of it. I wasn't even sure that I did. Still, I needed to free a certain amount of cerebral residue from my head and the best way to do that was to keep writing, to keep pushing it out. As always, I believed that with time, enough of the detritus would get cleaned out to allow the real gems to emerge.

Yet I wasn't sure. I was never sure. This made me feel jittery, ill-prepared and untalented. I liked playing with words, but did that make me a poet? I started thumbing through my notebook, a dilatory pleasure I indulged in when I needed a moment to recharge at the desk. I found that, about a month back, I had penned an entry quoted from Henry James describing America as a "huge queer country." This had cracked me up and I was sure it would make Summer Rain laugh when I shared it with her. My visit had helped solidify something in me. I couldn't pinpoint what it was, but I felt it vaguely as a little more confidence in myself. Nor was it lost on me that those three words, "huge queer country" described Summer Rain in a nutshell. She was a country I liked to visit, and when there I felt loved.

I brought that love into my home and it spread to Dalton as I found it effortless again and a joy to talk to him, to explain my pathological concerns both to him and myself. I would continue to love myself in new ways, some of which I didn't recognize. I took comfort in this. Just as it comforted me to know I'd been eating significant meals too. Four days straight of hearty eating without forcing myself to vomit, and I felt proud of this. I saw it as an accomplishment. With that in mind, I began writing again with a renewed sense of vigor and all sorts of fireworks began to spark and crackle.

⚬⚬⚬

I sat up in bed and looked at my alarm clock. It was around seven a.m.. It was Sunday, wasn't it? I expected to see Dalton lying next to me. It wasn't Sunday. The weekend had passed. I remembered my breakfast on Saturday, my writing session, but nothing beyond that except for the first bottle of red wine I'd opened. That explained it. Blame it on the Cabernet. Was that a Sondheim number?

There had been blurry walks bumping into furniture and eating so much of Dalton's roast that my sides ached. I'd made love to him more than once, and then drinking and smoking all day on Sunday and eating yet another big meal in front of the television while watching football with him. He'd spent the whole weekend with me.

Fully there. Cooking and cleaning and fighting me off each time I tried to sneak to the bathroom for a purge. My man. My keeper.

I sat up in bed and saw the impression of his head in the pillow next to mine. Immediately, I began scribbling down a description of it in the notebook I kept next to a pile of books on my nightstand.

I didn't like how I was feeling, so dazed and light-headed. I hurried out of bed, compelling myself to keep moving, not knowing why, nauseated, dizzy, washing my face in the bathroom, gargling and brushing my teeth. Now, I was ready for bed.

Of course, I didn't sleep. I couldn't. I was up and it was time to start chasing the foxes sprinting through the grey meadows in my brain.

After getting out of my pajamas and into one of my house robes, the terrycloth one Dalton had given me for Christmas, I nestled into my favorite chair, a high-backed wicker with two quilted cushions to pad its bottom. It looked out on the pastureland beyond my window, which faced west, which meant the sun, as it rose, was lancing spears of light away from me, as if I was shooting them. They spread in softly liquid bands of gold.

I warmed myself in the tangerine glow from the trees that cut a serrated line across the horizon. I heard the first car of the day moving down our road. Someone was going to work. I heard, too, as I sank into my chair and continued to absorb the silence, the faint whisking of traffic from one of the county roads quite far away. I felt so lucky that on a Monday I didn't have any reason to break this contemplative hour of morning by thinking of the day as a work day. My earliest class started at two p.m. and was online, which meant a big part of my day would be spent snuggled in my robe with a cup of tea and inside my home with my cat purring on my lap, with my books, my pencil and paper and the silence.

Didn't I realize how fortunate I was? I should celebrate. I should have breakfast again. A big one. Three days in a row. And not purge it either. There were leftovers, I was sure of it. Yes, I would eat again today and I would think, do some seriously deep recollecting from my past, and I would take notes and maybe I'd come up with more stanzas for a poem. Maybe I'd even discover a complete one.

I never knew. The point was to stew and brood and contemplate, to wait and listen and then write and revise. I would go through all of these steps over and over again and I would not move my body. I would try to eat a lot and to keep the food down. I would not vomit. I would live. I would be well. God help me.

I left my chair not feeling satisfied, but also feeling glad I hadn't given up on myself. Once in the kitchen, having taken off my robe in favor of sweatpants and a T-shirt and an apron, I made coffee. I sat and stirred in some sugar and started to consider whether I could eat a slice of toast.

I sipped my coffee. Some music would help me loosen up. I took my coffee with me from the kitchen to our living room. I turned on Dalton's stereo system and guided the tuning knob until I found a classical station. I didn't know the music, mostly jaunty strings, but it felt soothing and I kept listening as I returned to the kitchen where I sat again after refilling my coffee cup. It was while there seated alone, with my cat asleep on the windowsill, I realized that there was a reason I needed this. Some hunger in me for reflection needed to be sated, and much of it had to do with how I'd surrendered to my own private hope campaign as one who'd been sick for too long. Hope, I'd learned, led me to feel disappointed, frozen into a mode of wanting to recede, take cover and not believe in anything.

I started with doughnuts. Dalton had never bought any for us. Then it came back to me. What he had bought one Sunday morning after coming home from church, were muffins. I saw them atop the refrigerator. Two big blueberry muffins still in their box. I began to savor the thought of eating one with coffee, and so I cut it in half and put it in our toaster oven and buttered it once it was heated.

Each mouthful went down easier than the one before it. Washed down with hot coffee. This was a victory for me. I didn't feel panic. I felt sleepy and sated. I thought of how hope had led me to read the likes of Noam Chomsky, Christopher Hitchens and Chris Hedges. Authors I'd devoured insatiably during the first seven years or so after 9-11. What had all that reading on my part amounted to? Perhaps some insight, but, in general, nothing but misery. Politics, once a passion, as my poetry still was, had flourished when President Obama came along, and of course I embraced everything he appeared to represent. I thought he would bring real hope and change, just as his slogan promised. Now that he, as President-As-Savior, was gone, not having really changed anything for the better, with nobody in echelons of power being held accountable for the colossal messes they made, we had a populist tycoon, a business-man, a real red-blooded American. I thought it perfect that he bore the same initials as Delirium Tremens.

Of course, I was dismayed. I was still a liberal, however disaf-fected and disillusioned but I couldn't get on the Biden train. The old coot didn't inspire or uplift. He was just more politics. Each time I saw him on television, I worried his medication would wear off and he'd start babbling nonsensically.

To quote Dalton: "Who the hell is this Harris lady, anyway? Just another uncle-Tom opportunist." I'd thought those toxic and unfair words, ones I'd never dare utter, but I'd kept the thought to myself. As one so disaffected, this was the best I could do: stay quiet, be wary of the Woke police, learn to eat properly again.

I didn't exactly love Hillary, never had, but I still wanted in my lifetime to see a woman hold that office. But not Harris. Sorry, girls. She inspired nothing in Dalton and nothing in me. This, too, I wouldn't dare express to just anyone. Not even to Mother, no, who couldn't stomach Hillary, thought her an out-and-out thieving liar.

As part of the zeitgeist, as I saw it, all these political musings were not irrelevant. They were part of an understanding of the era that I was living in, and in various ways that understanding would seep its way subtly into some of my poems. Amen to that.

I'd reached the last piece of the muffin. All this time I'd been thinking, I'd also been eating. Yet I didn't feel nauseated. I didn't want to rush to purge. Nor did I want to keep on living in this state of dismal acceptance, but I saw for the time being that I had no choice. I would have to ground myself deeper into recalcitrance, living in opposition and argument with any forms of status quo that I might not like, knowing that I could not alter or discuss them openly, least of all with my liberal colleagues.

When I thought of 9-11, for example, and how some said we deserved that, had it coming, while others said it was a conspiracy masterminded by our own leaders. Two decades later, did I still believe what happened that day as it was reported? I still didn't know, but I hadn't talked about it to anyone. I saw no point. None of my students knew much about the event. They needed aging teachers like me to explain what it felt like to know that for about a month every television in the country was glued to a news feed, each of us shocked, entranced, befuddled and angry. I had been. Maybe I still was.

The muffin. I'd finished it. As I sat there, I began to feel it settling in. I wanted to smile knowing what this meant to me as an accomplishment that I'd never share because no one would consider it interesting. This was how I lived: keeping my secrets sealed off from others, seldom visiting public spaces. Besides, what would I shout even if anyone cared to hear me?

This disease called hope. These ongoing wars on terror and drugs. The many psychic, economic and physical wounds inflicted on people around the world during the first two decades of the twenty-first century. Though I really should have, I couldn't stop thinking about these issues. But I had an answer now. Dalton had provided it. He'd told me, and he was right, "Comic books. Men in tights. Women in capes. Extraordinary powers. That's what the people want. That's what you should indulge in."

I felt afraid that I'd end up like one of those elitist mandarins such as Gore Vidal, sadly gone now, laboring to address wrongs, wounds, a prevailing disinterest, a malaise, all the wars, weaponry and the sheer tonnage of waste filling our oceans. They weren't really ours. We, needing them to survive, belonged to those oceans, but who in power thought of it that way? None of them.

I found myself brimming with a need to do research, take notes, frantically analyze ideas such as the rise of a persistent mediocrity and anti-intellectualism in all aspects of the popular culture. The increasing number of boy bands, the mainstream nature of gangster rap, tweener pop girl singers, hyper-individuality, to name a few. What I saw developing was a demand in the culture for anything that refused to question our ways or deepen our empathy.

How degenerate we'd become. I would stay safe in my cocoon. Someone as critical and accurate as the comedian Bill Hicks, who I couldn't get enough of, had been reduced to a puny shout. No surprise he'd been a hit in the UK, but a mere outlier in the States.

I moved as if in a trance. I was starting to understand that it was easy to buy muffins. It got easier to eat two of them each morning with my coffee, and I wanted them heated with lots of butter and maybe some toast and eggs and bacon and a cup of orange juice.

It was warm in that kitchen. I liked being alone there. I kept it well stocked for Dalton and for my changing habits. Kill or be killed seemed okay again.

There was nothing to feel really happy or sure about. Maybe there never had been. If, like Dalton, I was a true patriot — and I didn't like to think of myself as one — then I could admit that along with my fellow citizens I wasn't learning any lessons because I wasn't testing or applying any enlightened new ideas. Ecclesiastes. Nothing new under the sun. I had doubts about wanting to stay alive, lots of them, too many, and what I felt most consistently was despair.

A good war makes sacred every cause. When in my life had the nation I lived in not been involved in a war? Why? So I could sit with both a blueberry and a bran muffin and weep over how I couldn't control desperate urges? Me and my first-world problem.

I'd begun to make a pilgrimage every other morning, buying muffins half a dozen at a time in a paper box tied with string. They were heavy, substantial. They warmed my insides. They stayed down as I sipped tea or coffee and told myself I had to learn to breathe, to be substantial like the muffins. This was not a crime. I was giving my body fuel, sustenance, pleasure.

Certainly, I had my reading, and listening to debates and absorbing insightful cultural commentary and criticism from various online voices, but what did these exercises in intellectual examination do other than to aggravate me and make more distant from what I imagined was out there? Those two words: *out there.*

All my thoughts would change nothing. They might open me and keep me raw, exposed to the philistines and manipulators, but they weren't even my thoughts. They were the products of an intelligentsia industry, represented through digital portals, whether television or the Internet. Was I really getting a whole representation of such a large country? No, of course not. I knew I was being lied to, but what troubled me most was my willingness to accept this, compounded by a feeling of helplessness that I could do nothing about it.

Muffins, however, didn't rattle me in the same way. They brought immediate assurances. So did lots and lots of butter. I told myself I'd walk off the calories later, though I never did. The opposite occurred. I found more calories. I spent more time in the kitchen. I kept my apron on. I made spoonbread and ate it all myself. There was always dinner on the table for Dalton each night when he came home.

As I continued to explore synesthesia in my work, and those three highways from my Seekonk years, I also began to dabble with more theoretical and political ideas in my poems. Personal narrative and the confessional felt played out. I found it empty and self-serving to start and end with imitating Whitman or Dickinson whenever I thought of myself as an American poet. I'd also begun feeling sick of thinking gender identification was any kind of issue, at all.

This simmering disgust with identity led me back to what I'd always revered in the works of Mary Oliver, Joy Harjo, and Maxine Kumin. These were my lady friends. My pals. There were others too, such as Anais Nin and Marguerite Yourcenar , but they didn't observe and capture nature in the way Mary did. Or the way Leslie Silko, Jamake Highwater and Scott Momaday did. They learned from it, though. As Frost or Wendell Berry had. They understood it would always be larger than any sense of self we imagined that we might inhabit. Humility, in a word. There wasn't enough of that, especially in academic circles.

I hungered for poets who could look outside of themselves. Loren Eiseley was another one of them. Though perhaps a better essayist than a poet, the man sought to understand that science, mathematics and chemistry were what shaped the way we often thought of ourselves, but not who we were. That we're essentially a passive lot, clinging to our religions and totems, waiting for our next reassuring nod from whatever Godhead we deem significant.

Warner Heisenberg understood that the more precisely the position of a particle is determined, the less precisely its momentum can be known, and vice versa. What did that mean to me in terms of empathizing with a commuter riding the Metro in DC, for example, fearing that the train might be blown up by either a White Supremacist with grenades and a semi-automatic rifle, or one radicalized Muslim with a bomb strapped to his chest? Nothing really, other than it brought solace during my drives along country roads to pick up groceries. Anything was possible at all times, no matter how quickly or slowly I was moving, and no matter the movement or lack of it around me.

This was why I sought out hills, hiking trails and rivers. The James, Shenandoah, and Rappahannock. The York and the Potomac, as well, both of which I revered, though I tended to visit more often lonely local hideaways such as Old Rag Mountain, or the Rose River where it flowed into Syria, or else I'd just dawdle about in Sharp Rock not too far from the vineyard there, or walk the trail at Little Devil's Stairs. Like anyone else, maybe more than others, (I didn't know, couldn't say) I needed to feel at one with motion within and without, and by doing so I created order among those many mountains still moving within me. I began to dissolve from the inside out. I saw how each morning my face was hardening into a reptilian civility. I still fit the way Summer Rain liked to describe me as Eliot's "hollow man" stuffed with straw and ready for nothingness.

Cocoon Mother, welcome me with open arms. In Latin, *cuius regio eius religio* refers to the meaning of a treaty that states that the ruling Monarch of a country possesses the right to determine the religion of those that she rules. In my opinion, this relates to the Treaty of Westphalia of 1648, which set the stage for France's revolution and was helping me design my own insurrection, specifically from harm done to me by others, and from the memories and myths that advanced their campaigns in my imagination.

I needed to protect myself. I was no longer anybody's cutie pie, though Dalton, such a dear, still treated me that way. Aging was starting to morph my face into a pudding flecked with the suggestions of bone, with tension in my chin collapsing, and a bleak puffiness under my eyes that no matter how much make-up I used, I could not conceal. Cringing, tongue out, I studied myself in the mirror. I looked like one of those gargoyles, chin in hand, atop the Notre Dame cathedral in Paris. I cried when I watched the newsfeed of that gorgeous building in flames. It made me feel like I'd been sentenced to an eternity of watching ugliness sentenced upon us from above.

How did I cope? You want a recipe? I wrote my poems and starting with that first morning I dared to eat not a peach but rather one muffin, I found myself learning how to accept losing control. Still benefiting from my visit to Summer Rain, I saw better how it was right for me to live far from any large city and to visit now and then. I felt invisible and I didn't mind it. I liked trying to force myself to put aside all worries about my figure as I indulged in a slab of cake or pie for dessert after dinner.

I began to cook a lot, encouraging Dalton to eat, which he did passionately, enjoying my spoonbread and macaroni and cheese, potato salad, and fried chicken — lots of comfort food that I could still serve up but had forgotten how to enjoy. With breakfast becoming a regular event again, lunch came next. I began making Monte Christo sandwiches. After lunch, when I wasn't teaching, I took long walks alone and these kept me feeling healthy. Once home, I began to prepare dinner. I worked on my poems. The smell of food began to become part of my desire to think and write, and to feel I had something to offer the world. It was all positive.

On those days when I had a tad more free time and no desire to take a walk, I'd drive to Sperryville where there were a couple of family-run cozy eateries where I could always get a table on a weekday. Lots of healthy farm-raised food there. I might arrive stoned, having indulged along the way with the car window down. Often, I was the only car on the road.

I liked all the local people I met in those places, and they appeared to like seeing me. As time passed, I was treated with the politeness and courtesy afforded a regular. I sat alone and I ordered soup, a sandwich, any kind of salad with mayonnaise in it, and then dessert. On the drive home, I'd smoke a little more, or else I'd eat a pot-brownie and the more I indulged in these splurges, the more joyful they became. I suffered the usual amount of paranoia while driving, but I knew the roads and they were seldom busy, and the views throughout the region were to die for.

Much to my delight, too, the sex improved with Dalton. He found my body as not the usual turf and, like his, a little fuller and softer, his hands were more active in their caressing. I was writing more fearlessly, too, the poems spilling out of me, my notebooks filling up.

The purges had, in essence, stopped. I'd reached my goal. I could accept that I really wasn't fat but rather big-boned, taller than average, of a certain body type. Dare I say mulish rather than a mermaid? I should be a diva. Hecuba or Miranda. A goddess. Extraordinary. In fact, I'd need to add at least ten more pounds to feel relatively normal, weighing in at about 260 I wasn't scientific about it. Ten just felt like a good number. I could go as high as 275 without feeling winded all the time. I wasn't sure I could do this either, but I'd turned a corner and was trying and, frankly, enjoying myself.

I had my beloved poets and hours to read and write, and to watch old movies. Occasionally, I'd lose myself in long phone chats with Summer Rain, or with Rusty or my colleague Dr. Nicky Soren. My rapport with Dalton was improving too. I felt more relaxed around him and because of this I listened better and didn't interrupt him when he was struggling to make a point he wanted to share. This habit had started to irritate him and I was glad to see myself getting rid of it.

On exceptional days, I suffered the illusion that I had the love and maybe the respect of my students. This was, I think, mostly due to the increase in the dosages of Prozac that Dr. Murray had prescribed. In my Composition class, forced to read one personal essay after another, some of them about a student's romance with video games or mind-altering substances, I was always shocked to discover a student *without* ADHD or identity issues. It was as if a whole generation had been taught that one didn't count unless one was flawed, easily triggered, injured and disappointed and could show it.

I had my TV programs on Netflix, too, such as *Orange Is The New Black*, which I binged on while burning up buds of high-test cannabis that came to me through a connection who always had plenty in stock. I had my cooking and my online retail business, as well. I felt confident enough to really assess what I had, rather than what I lacked. I found myself feeling tiny precocious thrums of excited contentment. Was it possible that I could accept living with a certain amount of inner peace?

Steady then, Stella Luna. Don't lose your grip. But I liked losing it, I needed to now and then. Most of my problems had begun when I'd tried to control or deny my many sensual impulses. Life, in the end,

might not be a screwball comedy about the antics between gat-tot-
ing armies of AARP field-trippers chartering buses to a new casino.
It might be a Busby Berkeley musical celebrating the sly manipulations of gold diggers. It might also be about a lone gunmen in
a basement somewhere hoarding freeze-dried food packets, flash-
lights, batteries, ammo, lasers, blankets, Tasers, semi-automatic
shotguns, phase regulators and security cameras. I had to remember that the seeds of compassion and perseverance tended to smart
when the winds of chance blew them free.

I didn't have the answers, but did I need them? I had notebooks
full of poems in which I tried to discover such answers, to understand them better. To what end? Life didn't have to be a riddle. Why
shouldn't I just sing of it all in its complex vagaries?

⁓

I continued working on a poem called, tentatively, The Beast. For
a while, I toyed with using a French title, *La Bête*, but with some
research I learned that had been done in film back in the 70's.
Knowing the poem and its title would continue to develop and
change, I labored on and saw that it began to take shape as a *cri de
coeur* about the loss of control one must accept when in motion.
We simply cannot control everything. In the poem, my narrator is
a cross between Summer Rain and a woman's strange face I once
saw on the DC Metro, a face I'd never forgotten because it looked
so suspended in doubt and mordant confusion. This woman finds
herself racing toward the future, losing traction, unable to comprehend or slow down the images that lash at her in lurid dreams.
She feels as if her body is out of control. She speaks about riding
through the "desert of unknowing" as if she's a "dehydrated missile that's been fired toward an invisible oasis." I didn't know if
these were distinguished or tawdry lines, but I liked the way the

narrator's voice kept developing. She sounded frantic and that was what I wanted.

When I thought of this poem, working on it every day, I was reminded of the Rashomon Effect, another cerebral delicacy that obsessed me. I was reminded, too, of the squeals I'd often heard from train cars and how long they lasted and how those cars sometimes shuddered on their rails like they were living creatures. My imagined trains stopped, doors slid open and out jumped thoughts of all my friends and their parents and how we'd sped through our lives and missed one another and longed for days we couldn't have again. Nobody had enough time, it seemed, for each other, for what they really desired, not in that faraway time that never really existed, and not in the present. We lived an endless struggle with loneliness that compounded our feelings of having never reached the promise we believed we felt and were certain of in our childhood.

Which brought me back to Rashomon. In 1951, Akira Kurosawa brought out his film of that title and in it, as I saw it, he investigated philosophies related to the very idea of who we are, always seeking abstractions such as justice. Is there such a thing when our communication is as garbled as the end result of any game of telephone? In the film, four different people recount versions of the story of a man's murder and the rape of his wife. Four people, four versions, four different results in a court of law. Who was telling the truth? They all were, of course, but it was their individual truth, had to be, because there really doesn't exist one truth behind any act.

I thought, too, of a song that had begun to feel old for me, *O Superman*, by Laurie Anderson, in which a ghostly repetitive breath sounded short bursts of laughter in the background while Laurie intoned the words "Mom and Dad…Oh…Mom and Dad…."

In that song, short expulsions of small stylized laughter continued repeating to establish a rhythm. A heartbeat. It was a slightly comical, clever and sometimes haunting sound, and it struck me as genius when I'd first heard it so many years ago, with its eerily critical and spooky effect. Sometimes while writing, I heard it in my head, couldn't get it out. It reminded me that nothing I'd done should be praised or exalted, that I was a vulnerable child, always would be, missing Mom, Dad and blessed moments of innocence and exultation that I could not return to because perhaps I'd never had them.

A Thursday. I'd written copiously and while still writing, still in motion, I'd felt reborn, as if I'd been riding my imagined DC subway. I was seated, waiting to get off at the Smithsonian stop and I turned and looked at a man next to me and I worked up a grin for him. The man looked away with a twinge of bitterness. I felt sure he was old enough to remember when Yanks called them H-bombs, and red suspenders at the upright GE radio were fashionable and the *Ed Sullivan Show* meant escapist laughter inside one's own cold-water flat. I was sure he was a decade older than Papa would have been if he were still living, and that he'd mined the quest-soaked eyes of broken daughters in after-dinner rooms with padded leather doors closed.

I observed that strange man's imagined face and I saw that it was remarkably much like my own, only faded, buffed smooth by time, the button-like protrusions in his cheeks polished like pebbles found on a beach strand. He was hairier and fleshier than me, but we both had big longing in our eyes. I wanted to tell this man to trust any peace he could find. I didn't. This was how it stood with me in public. I didn't know how to connect. I dove deep within even as I was looking across the train car as if staring at nothingness, the void.

For a moment, I caught my face reflected in one of the train car's windows. My cheeks were sucked in. They made my eyes look larger than they really should have. My chin projected out like a wharf into the sea. I looked starved. I disliked when this happened because I realized that this was what people looked at when they saw me. I was no longer young, no longer attractive.

The roaring that filled each Metro tunnel filled my head. My senses hadn't left me, not yet, but after that moment, after all of them, I would never be the same. I could smell my own stink on my fingers — what a thought. Would I recover from this eating disorder? I didn't know. I want to, there's no longer any doubt about that. My bones ached. I felt the weight of time inside of me. Was God watching me?

If only I were invisible and bulletproof. What saved me from myself, I supposed, were my releases into a passion for learning. Many of those innate instincts were nurtured outside of the classroom during sun-kissed afternoons spent reading. I had always lived near the sea, so I'd spent lots of time roaming beaches with either Rusty, Papa or one of the few friends I'd make who I knew I wouldn't keep in touch with once we moved again. Would I end up like my mother's mother, who lived alone as a nut-hard and shriveled widow for about forty years.

The Indians came to me. I felt their ghosts. In high school I'd read about Metacomet, Massasoit's second son, later named King Philip. He warred against the colonials at the Great Swamp near Usquepaug and Pettaquamscutt Rock. Every September, Narragansett Indians danced around those places to honor their living dead. Papa had taken me one time to see them dance and, soaked in wonder, I'd asked myself then what it must have been like to have been one of a tribe and to have met those bearded Dutch, English and Germans with their bibles and sextants? Did Praying Indians of Natick, if there were any left, or Algonquian, Nipmuc and Mohawk (among many others), hear the same ghosts that once visited me? Did they listen and mourn? Was I a lunatic to ponder such thoughts? I didn't think so. I'd come to learn that there was too much blood oozing from each rock and tree, more than any soul could claim to understand. We were all so incomplete, so meagre.

My history wasn't grounded in dates, arrivals, conquests or wars, but in emotional groundswells and needs. It was an autodidact's private means of expressing revolt. Each one stemmed from within. They endured there, too.

As a lonely girl always on the outside, part of a family that had moved into town, I'd found ways to counter rages and fears. I'd come to a fondness for the benign study of anything other than money and status. Watching a butterfly, for example, acted as a balm against the endless tedium of cliquish gossip, paranoia, insecurity and self-promotion that defined so much of my high school experience. I didn't learn to enrich my life by seeking my identity. I did just the opposite, frittering away my sense of self in daily fevers, without mourning losses, finding that I could always feast on myself from the inside out. This was perhaps where the bulimia began. I didn't want to fit in. I wanted to snap myself out of the crowd, to reject it all, and then to sob in the darkness, to stay there, withering.

The Observer Effect. I learned that what I had been doing, convinced I was so original, had already been studied and codified by scientists. Measurements of certain systems could not be made without affecting the systems themselves, that is, without changing a component in a system. Consider terrorism. How stop it in the name of freedom without becoming a terrorist or else limiting that freedom? Within this Observer Effect, the Uncertainty Principle existed inherently, as it did in the properties of all wave-like systems.

It arose, riding the waves, seen most clearly in quantum mechanics due to the matter wave nature of all quantum objects. I had to thank Papa for all my curiosity about science and physics.

That was right, Stella: Matter Wave Nature. It's what I was, what we all were, and those three words might well be the title of my next collection of poems. It was either them or *The Beast.* Or, most likely of all, *Synesthesia.* I was still on the fence. Not always a bad place to be. Though any fence had to be a strong one to support me.

⸺∾⸺

Night hadn't sent invitations. It had welcomed me as a sidewalk salamander who had undressed, removed make-up and then showered. Night had concealed the corruptions in me, extinguishing their mistaken suppositions. Snoring, restoring myself, blinds drawn, I watched the whores wipe salt from their eyes and remove their hair pieces before sponging off their make-up. Those whores of the night swelled to arouse the loins in my imagination, smoke rings expanding within my solar plexus, pulsing in time to neon blurs and the heartbeats of speeding colors that erased memories of day-hours spent on auto-pilot, humping it to pay for bed, heat, grub and the kinds of fabric that look best on me when I'm in a dark mood or having my period.

I awoke with the thought that I was chasing windmills. I was a failure, a dreamer. I'd wasted too many years. They were gone, couldn't get them back.

As I began to prepare breakfast, determined to make it jumbo-sized to suit the need for placating the vapidity I felt within, I told myself that I should not give up, that I'd never been a quitter. I was Papa's girl and she didn't roll that way. Then again, maybe I should quit. Ridiculous, all this pretentious agonizing over poetry. I didn't want to force myself to do it. My purges had resumed and the five pounds I'd added had fallen off me again and my throat was sore and my face was bloated. I didn't recognize the pumpkin on a stick that I saw in the mirror. I couldn't bear to look at myself.

Was it because as a teacher I felt disrespected and didn't earn enough? I told myself that my students appreciated me, though one never really knew. With teaching, I'd found it was the granular moments, the sparks of connection between myself and various students, on their terms, that had shown me I was getting through. It hadn't ever come from peers or colleagues. I'd never really known if I was succeeding.

My lunges toward poetry and, I supposed, my budding reputation could probably have helped me land a better teaching gig at one of the more esteemed four-year colleges in the area. , I preferred, however, to work with non-traditional students, those outcasts and alleged misfits and poorer children of immigrants a community college appealed to.

Two Decembers ago, before the Covid-19 virus hit, career concerns had been going well. I'd brought out a new book that had merited a pair of excellent reviews. If an author gets one review she should be happy. I'd gotten two, both of them online. My happiness had showed in my body. I'd begun to eat and to keep it on my frame again. At first, I'd thought it was because of the Christmas season, but then I'd accepted the notion that it was simply because I'd felt happy. I was also nominated for a Pushcart Prize. I didn't win, but I didn't care. It was such a feather in my cap. Positive reinforcement. What anyone needed.

Something had to change. There was too much nervous quibbling in my body. I should make the changes happen rather than let the changes happen to me, but I couldn't because I didn't know how. I was part of a couple. I should never forget that Dalton and I rode the waves together. When we made love, we were two waves fusing into one. Maybe he could help, but I shouldn't lean on him too much. Back and forth I went, volleying all these thoughts in my head.

After my breakfast, which included poached eggs on toast, bacon, oatmeal, I indulged in a few tokes and felt myself glowing within. This day, like all the others, was just another start. Many of them had been false. I couldn't remember how long it had been since I'd said *hasta luego* to fears and absurdly cinematic bouts of paranoia.

I nodded off in my easy chair and had a dream that I was in New York City with Summer Rain and we were walking along 23rd street and I was sharing thoughts with her about writing a poem titled Touchpad And Maxi-Pad Century as an homage to the ghost of one forgotten American poet that I still really liked, Kenneth Patchen. When Dalton and I were dating, he'd lie in bed while I'd get high and I'd read Patchen's love poems aloud to him while walking around the bedroom naked.

What I'd always admired about Patchen was that he'd proved to me it was possible to write about love without sounding archaic and sentimental. He wasn't cynical either. My favorite poem of his, *23rd Street Leads Into Heaven*, was one I never tired of.

So, I dreamt of walking on 23rd Street. By Manhattan standards, it was still quite early. I was fat in my dream and wearing a beret and a jean jacket and feeling chipper with Summer Rain on my arm. I felt pleasingly obsessed with Patchen's poetic vibes and my own hunger for anything that would stir in me the art that bred a reverence and appreciation for feelings of freedom, love, vulnerability, fear and joy.

Stoned, happy on foot with Summer Rain in Gotham, I leaned a moment against a parking meter and caught my breath. I was missing something. I wanted the old Stella Luna, the one with a sultry curiosity in her limpid eyes, who didn't feel lonely while self-medicating. I was in the grip of a nocturnal fugue of despair. I felt that old self inside of me wishing someone was there to hold me upright.

I woke up in my chair. Was I fat? Was the bulimia my fault? Where was my beret? Yes, it was all my fault. No, it was just a dream. I should be different. I should be all here. I wasn't. I was invisible. I heard Dalton tell me: *Shut off your mind, Stella, take a chill, shut down the fever.*

Why couldn't I just relax and eat a tub of buttery popcorn and watch Jimmy Stewart in Technicolor while Doris Day sang *Que Sera Sera* ? Why did I have to struggle and squirm and suffer and think so much? Was it really true that I only ate and became a more fluidly natural person when stoned? How had I allowed this to happen?

 I lit up my bong and sucked a couple of long bubbly draws that staggered me as I exhaled. Then I sagged, slowing down, feeling sweetly doltish as I lolled about like the second coming of Garfield the cat, my eyes bloodshot. Giggling and fumbling about, I shed nervous tension and zeroed in, began scribbling in my notebook, getting lost in silence and all the music and movies and windows it offered. I went, then, to my desk and I wrote without thinking, unsure of what I was writing and not regarding it as a problem. The point was to release.

After a few hours, I stopped, drew a few more hits from my bong and found myself in the kitchen where I began inhaling large helpings of cold leftovers. Just shoving a spoon into my mouth, gorging. I had flipped the switch and there was no getting in my way. When Dalton was cooking, I stayed out of the kitchen until he was finished. But Dalton wasn't there and I didn't feel like cooking, so I just emptied the leftover containers and then went straight into junk food snacks from the cupboards. Any bag or box that I found was ripped open and all mine.

—◦◦◦—

One Saturday morning at a library sale in Warrenton I found a vintage first edition of an Edith Wharton novel, *Hudson River*

Bracketed. It had a weak spine and dog-eared pages and some water stains, but I didn't care. It was also one of her later works, not her best, but not her worst either. I had begun, at last, to read it, and I relished her graceful prose and she became again for me a favorite among all the classical women authors from the States. I'd told Dalton earlier in the week that I'd decided that I was just going to sit and read and learn to concentrate better. This, I hoped, would help me stop feeling so prickly and on edge. At least, that was the plan.

I didn't find it difficult to force myself to be docile. When he was there, Dalton did everything around the house. I asked him to cook extra-large dinners so that I could eat the leftovers the next day. Beyond the work required for me to keep my job, I did as little as possible. After two weeks of this, I began to see that it was working. There began to emerge in me a new voice, one that slapped me on the cheek each morning as it remarked at my reflection in the mirror: *Look at you! Look at this vision of what you've become, where you've been, what you're going to make of yourself. Get on with it, Girl.*

The size of my body didn't matter. The one I loved most, Dalton, loved me just as I was. He adored me, but I had to learn to adore myself. How happy it made me feel knowing I could tell this to myself without any guilt or need to apologize. Had I reached a new sense of ego? If I had, it might be a comfortable place. I could get used to not giving a hoot about life outside of my home and my tiny daily agenda. Let Dalton do his own thing. I liked the promise of such a comfortable place and I wanted to claim it.

As more weeks passed and winter and the holiday season set in, I felt myself growing ever more serene. Dalton, on the other hand, had returned to some of the outspoken fire-breathing character he'd shown when we'd first met. He didn't seem to mind how lazy I'd become. I mean, I did absolutely zilch. Not even laundry. He did all of that. I puttered around in the same pink robe, slippers and sweatpants day after day, and were it not for my job, those days would have blurred together as they'd done during the Covid lockdown. Actually, even with my job, I seldom knew what day or time it was.

Yet all about me felt more controllable, familiar, steadier. My poems were starting to blaze again. I knew this because I didn't understand any of them, but while I read them I felt surges of enthusiasm and even sexual titillation. Summer Rain wrote to me that she did too. She was wont to respond openly, honestly, and she saw that the porchlights in me were again starting to come back on. I thanked her in my emails over and over again.

I found myself wanting to hold Dalton and squeeze him, and I did. I was pawing at him constantly, especially while stoned, telling him that I was destined to get my forehead nicked by cyber-kinetic zephyrs and crosswinds. Laboring over explanations that it appeared a soul-searching operative like myself would never find any consoling, challenging, heart-wrenching voices to help make sense of what it meant to be a woman, to be childless, to go down with the crew at the bow of the Not So Good Ship 21st Century post Covid-19. Dalton, ever resourceful, would just look at me in his baleful and sometimes puzzled way, a deep crease running above the bridge of his nose.

"What is it?" he often asked.

"I can't do it," I'd tell him. "I can't find any words. I'm stuck." "Is that bad?"

"I don't know. I think so."

One night after dinner I led him toward our sofa and coaxed him to sit. The weather was getting frosty, we had our tree up and our mistletoe and strings of colored lights around our windows, making the interior rooms crimson and putting me in a balmy mood, perfect for such a moment. "I have to ask you this," I said. "Are you or were you, or have you been cheating on me?"

"What?"

"You heard me. I mean it. I can't believe I'm telling you this, but it's true. For the longest time, not lately, but for the last year or so, especially when my bulimia was flaring up really badly, I thought you were cheating on me. It's a stupendous allegation, I know, but I need to know if it's true or not."

He didn't scowl, but he looked a bit angry as he faced me and said, point blank, "Not in the least."

"I had to ask. Dalton, please. Look, just tell me the truth."

"I told you N and O," he said. "It spells no. Do you want me to say it again?"

"I just thought, you know, that you were feeling guilty because, you know, I got back to the purging thing."

"The eating disorder? That's about you. Not me."

I looked at him, pleading for an answer. "If you want the truth, if I understood it, I could control it. But I am getting better."

"I know. It's been at least a month. Unless you've been hiding it from me."

"I haven't been hiding anything. I can feel it. I know how I feel. You have to trust me on that."

"I'm trying the best I can. But you have to trust me too."

"So, there was never any affair?"

" Nobody else. When would I even have the time?"

I backed down. I blushed, ashamed. But secretly I felt glad that I'd gotten it out. "That's what I thought, but the way I was seeing it, I was thinking maybe you got bored with me. I mean, we've been together a while."

"Our normal isn't normal," he said. "Just understand that. And no, there has never been anyone else."

"Only me?"

"Would you want me to cheat on you? Would that justify your behavior?"

"I had to ask."

"Jesus, Stella. I can't believe you sometimes. The things that get into your head."

"We'll work it out, won't we? I can get my old body back. Firm and proud and a lot of it. Stella Luna Mountain. That would show you something, wouldn't it?"

"Be careful what you wish for."

"Now you sound like me." I had to laugh. It felt good to let it out. "By the way, this new medication I'm on, it does have side effects. Weight gain being one of them."

"You seem the same to me."

"But it's holiday season. I'm just warning you." I didn't tell him that I'd do better, be better. I'd be his friend, trusting, a lover, a loyal wife, one who believed completely in him. Maybe I should have, or at least shared a bit more, but I wasn't sure what was appropriate. I settled on, "Let's get something to eat."

"You're hungry?"

"Not a lot. But you are. I can tell. You have that puckish look."

I offered my arm. He took it and helped me off the sofa and I pressed myself against his body. We were together as one again. My silly fearful totally insane question had been answered. I felt much better. The fit against him was right as we made our way to the bedroom. We didn't bother to eat. In my post-coitus sleep, I walked in a somnolent daze through a dream of frosted lanes atop a gigantic cake, sampling every marzipan tree branch and shrub that I laid eyes on.

⁓

Eyes closed, my head against Dalton's shoulder, I heard lines echoing from Delmore Schwartz's poem "The Heavy Bear Who Goes With Me." Bears. They thrived nosing about the shadowy forests within me, seeking Schwartz's *central ton of every place*. Day by day, one of them *trembles to think that his quivering meat must finally wince to nothing at all.* I knew this trembling only too well and it showed as I remained fixed to the sofa, propped against my hubby, listening to holiday music, Burl Ives singing "Silver Bells," one big bearish singer and me one bear statue frozen in time, I suppose.

I found other poems in my sleep, and paintings too, for some reason by Basquiat who made me think each time I looked at his work that he apparently liked people enough to capture their happiness for his own enjoyment. If only I could do that in my own poems, but I was afraid I wasn't able to like people enough, not really, and while studying them I was often reminded of an Edith Sitwell quote that poetry was the "deification of reality."

I couldn't imagine framing the images that I saw whenever I looked at people. I didn't see them. I saw what they might be trying to hide, what they'd lost to the call to keep noble in the good moral fight. Sagging people. Banal souls. I preferred to look at flowers, or the kind of eye-popping colors in, say, a Georgia O'Keefe rendering, all to remind me of a quotation from E.E. Cummings that poetry was "being not doing."

What I did like knowing was that if told Dalton that I didn't want to glorify people, and that many of them wouldn't even deserve to suffer a hanging at the gallows, he wouldn't be insulted. He respected my sour quirkiness, my inclinations and tastes, and I thought sometimes he enjoyed them more than his own. Lately, he'd been withdrawn, over-compensating for his dourness by being extra generous in the kitchen, making overtures to pamper me with three-course meals.

I felt astonished. I kid you not. Salads and hearty soups and clever vegetable dishes before stunning me with an entrée such as steak au poivre, going out of his way to make sure I ate seconds at dinner and, of course, dessert. Lots of dessert. And I did my best to keep up with him as he shoveled it down and said how yummy it all was.

I knew something was wrong. He wasn't seeing another woman. We'd been down that road. It had something to do with his job. An issue, I assumed, he couldn't discuss. It had me worried, but, in a way, that was a positive development, because when I worried, I tended to stress eat. I was already eating a lot, but I ate even more. I'd gained about three pounds in a week. Dalton had gained too. I tried to keep up with him, wanting to gain about thirty and to keep it, to call it my own. I'd be huge and I didn't care.

When I begged Dalton, at last, one night in bed, to tell me what was bothering him, there was such a look of agony on his face, but he opened up slowly, cryptically, in his fashion. He told me that he was dealing with his aspirations and expectations and some new hires and new protocols and new pressures on the job.

"I wish I could tell you more, but I can't," he said. "You know that. But please just know it isn't you. Okay?"

I kissed him and said, of course, it was fine. I didn't want to force anything out of him. He said that he hoped things in his department would return back to normal soon, so that he could feel like he lived a more regular and predictable life with me. Though I didn't show it, this saddened me. I'd always thought our life was reasonably dull and normal. Was I missing something?

As we made love that night, I tried to show my concern, to make it clear to him I was fully on his side. Afterwards, as we talked a little more, I told him that I was on a path toward change, that I'd figured out some of the issues that had been plaguing me. Naturally, I said it in the heat of the moment, but I meant what I said. I expressed that I desired to continue to change my habits, to put the food disorder behind me once and for all. I didn't say how I would go about doing it, but I reminded him that I was a patient sort, and so was he, and part of this change toward a more lasting self-acceptance would have to be more than just enjoying third helpings of sweet potatoes.

I told Dalton that I'd decided to make the best of my time alone, since I had plenty of it, almost as much as I'd had during the Corona lockdown. I wanted to continue to support what I saw as a consoling maturity that was developing between us as a couple, especially during times when I couldn't write. I would do more research and accumulate life stories and scenes from Rappahannock County that I might be able to use in a future book. By doing this, I told him, I would seldom feel stuck and wouldn't suffer writer's block. I'd be taking the advice I often gave to my students, which was to read when I couldn't find the inspiration to put my thoughts on to a page. Enough reading, and one stores up an arsenal and in the quiet hours as they pass, all the complications have a way of working themselves out. Naturally, once inspired, I would return to my poems.

Somehow, I would manage to get my teaching work done, but in all honesty, it had never been a priority for me. It tended to lean toward drudgery, though I had to admit that each semester I took pleasure in getting to know the kinds of students that our community college tended to attract, whether a divorced middle-aged woman with three children who'd taken the plunge to earn a diploma, or veterans who'd seen action, or a black man who, in his fifties, after years of loyalty to one employer had been dumped for someone younger and still had four children to raise. The job put me in touch with people of all ages, and races, each one invested in coping with the consequences of issues such as a dwindling middle class, wage disparity, and a growing lack of gainful employment. It also paid for my psychotropic medications and all the food in the fridge that I was day by day learning how to enjoy again.

"Just keep learning," is what my teaching colleague Nicky Soren often told me. "That's when you know you're a good teacher. When you're learning in front of them."

I appreciated any time with Nicky, older than me by nine years, usually cheerful and always straightforward and outspoken — everything I wasn't. Our friendship had grown over the years, though I'd never been to her house or met her husband, nor had she visited with me either. It was unlikely that would happen. She had three kids of her own and a husband who'd been laid off. He, not unlike some of my students, was re-inventing himself, in the hunt at middle age for a regular paycheck and an illusion of security.

If I was to believe Nicky, the man didn't drink, wouldn't dare smoke weed, and treated her like she was royalty. She didn't want to leave him. He was the Soccer Dad. Their oldest child worked at Subway making sandwiches and they didn't like taking the girl's paycheck each week, but that's how lean their situation had become.

Nicky and I were work pals, bosomy together, and this was how we liked it. We knew we could talk to each other about anything, though I tended to keep it about teaching and I avoided occasional impulses to foray into the subject of healthy eating. I admired and envied her because she wasn't a slender woman by any means. For a couple of years, though she lunched out often and would invite me to join her, I'd refused. I knew I'd risk a purging bout mid-day, which would mean I'd look and feel horrid in front of my students during my later afternoon classes.

I was on a different trajectory and I knew this when I accepted her offer one day. I hoped to be able to relax at lunch with her. I would order a salad and skip dessert. Nicky didn't know this, but joining her was a major step for me. Most importantly, I had to keep my promise to myself not to purge later.

We sat together in a franchise place, a Chili's, and she didn't know that I was tearing myself apart inside, asking myself how I could get comfortable adding to my frame when I believed I wasn't worthy of taking up more space in the world, that I should be erased and the one who should do the erasing was myself. I couldn't discuss this, of course, but I didn't mind. I was happy to have some company.

That first lunch date had gone well. So well, in fact, we met for lunch at least once a week for most of November and December. When I'd first met Nicky at a department Christmas party, she was a little thinner but no less sociable. . For a while I'd been stuck in a corner, one of the wallflowers until she showed some *savoir faire* and brought me a cup of egg nog and since I was a new teacher on staff at the time, she introduced me to other professors and helped me fit in. She also asked if I knew one of the staff members, a woman I'd heard about but hadn't met.

I must tell you about this woman, Joyce Brenda Lawson Malquist, because she'd become for me a cautionary tale, an unfortunate light to guide choices by. Mrs. Malquist, as she preferred to be called, had committed the cardinal sin of discussing gender and language with a male student who identified as a female. An iron horse of an educator with a few decades under her belt, she'd written a couple of sentences on her white board, each one taken from said student's most recent essay assignment. She'd done so as a way to critique grammar, specifically the student's lack of pronoun agreement.

As the story was told to me, according to Mrs. Malquist, if a writer began a sentence with the third person singular male pronoun, that writer should continue, in proper textbook fashion, to use that same singular male pronoun throughout the sentence, and throughout the essay. Simple pronoun agreement.

Not so fast. Not in this era. Her student, shocked by this humiliation, outraged for having been called out and dressed down in front of peers for identifying as more than one gender, went straight to the dean with his complaint. He later told a committee that he was made to squirm and suffer under the disapproving wrath of the evil Dr. Malquist, who was clearly homophobic, insensitive and didn't understand the challenges that a woman in a man's body must face every day.

Poor Malquist was put on trial and had to argue in front of the same committee that she was only suggesting that the outraged student be more aware of grammar and how sometimes a subject could be pluralized, especially if one was making a blanket statement, therefore omitting the need to agree with a singular third person pronoun. This was considered a reasonable argument, but when Mrs. Malquist then suggested that the student was perhaps overreacting, and that she'd never intended to hurt feelings or criticize gender preferences, she all but sealed her fate as a pariah at Cameronshire.

To further destroy her career, Joyce Malquist explained to the committee that she'd been trying to help the student grasp the concept that any writer of estimable value wants readers to understand the language used, rather than create prose meant to confuse readers in an already confusing world.

The committee, many of them Malquist's colleagues, were for the most part younger and more inclined to accept the forms of chaos propagated by queer theory when put into practice. They may have had misgivings, but they couldn't accept any of what dinosaur Malquist deemed relevant in order to support her defense. The whole affair became painfully trite and disturbing because it effectively ended the career of an upstanding well-intentioned professional.

As Nicky had commented with a snarl when we'd first discussed the case, "She was railroaded. So be careful who you consider your friends."

The student threatened to press charges, to take any legal action necessary to have Joyce Malquist removed from her position. Rather than be fired, Mrs. Malquist resigned in shame. I never learned whether she was able to collect on any of her state pension or not. I asked Nicky about this. She didn't know either.

"Can you believe it, the pettiness," Nicky had said.

Apparently, this girl in a boy's body was not one of those from our stable of poorer more resilient students rebuilding their lives. Daddy was well-to-do, employed as a white-collar consultant and lobbyist in one of those needless and grossly overfunded government agencies that speckle the Northern Virginia landscape like so many mold spores. In the spirit of American pragmatism, our student was taking community college classes to get high marks to compensate for some goofing off in high school. Maybe he'd earn an Associate's while securing entry into one of the tonier four-year institutions.

Whatever was said to the woman who was dean at the time must have been really convincing, because, as I'd heard it, lawyers were prepared to press charges related to abuse of a minor and defamation of character, as well as public slander. Threats were made that media outlets would be alerted. As a state institution, there would be much attention paid to this issue, and all sorts of negative publicity. A year after the incident, the dean took a job elsewhere.

As Nicky related it to me, Mrs. Malquist vanished, no doubt with the fear of eternal damnation striking death knells in her heart. There was not to be any expounding on any issue, not just English grammar, from the lips of any teachers. We, as a faculty, no matter our disciplines, shared this restriction in common. It was time to shut-up or get out. Nobody talked about this, of course. Muzzles stayed on, as masks had stayed on during the Covid pandemic.

Nicky, in private talked to me about this many times. It made her furious. Joyce Malquist had been a friend and confidante for a long time. All that Nicky knew was that Malquist had left not only the region but the state and the profession. Nicky believed that Joyce "had some real *cojones* and she really cared about her students and the college and where did it get her? Nowhere. Dumped as if she were garbage."

We drank lots of eggnog at that first Christmas party and many others after it. What fun we had as we talked about music and how nothing any of the young people listened to was remotely tolerable. Where had the free-love spirit of rock and roll or even punk gone to? We talked about the gentrification of most American cities, and the high cost of living. She talked lit, of course, and she dated herself, not caring about it, as she sang the praises of author George Plimpton, a man she'd worked for once as an intern at the Paris Review, a little biographical nugget that I found fascinating.

At another party, this one at the end of a spring semester, Nicky and I were joined by Fergus Calvin, the only male professor on the staff who I'd gotten to know beyond the usual formalities. Fergus, having since retired, had been terribly fond of Nicky, and at that party he was raving about George Plimpton's book, *The Man In The Flying Lawn Chair*. I told him I hadn't known Plimpton other than as a rather waspish erudite sort of editor. A man's man and all that.

Fergus had insisted he wasn't that way at all, that according to Nicky, he had been a lot of fun to work with, and very kind. Nicky had then joined our conversation, chiming in. She'd expounded on how Plimpton had taken to her since she'd once been an athlete, a basketball and tennis player during her collegiate days. Fergus insisted then that I should read the book, *Paper Lion,* about the time when Plimpton, the nerdy journalist, took a chance on playing professional football in Detroit.

I didn't know anything about sports. Fergus knew a few things, but Nicky was just the opposite, a dyed-in-the-wool DC football, baseball, hockey, soccer and basketball fan, many of the teams that Dalton tended to follow. She beamed at me at that party and said brashly, still going on about Plimpton, "That man really lived. Not like these limp noodles we have for men nowadays."

Fergus had roared laughing at Nicky's statement and it was at that moment I knew that I would stay at Cameronshire, that I could, in Nicky, and in Fergus, find enough camaraderie and fellowship and humor to keep myself sane. I really wasn't the peripatetic type. I'd hoped, knowing the odds were slim, to find one good job and to keep it until retirement. At that party, in that moment, I knew it would happen.

On Fergus's recommendation I'd begun reading Joseph Conrad. I'd started with *The Secret Agent*. I still had mixed feelings about the man. I found the racism in his *Heart of Darkness* impossible to stomach, but I had to admit his maudlin prose could be finely tuned, elegant, and visual. It was Nicky, of all people, who suggested I read *Lord Jim*. She loved the character Stein and his butterfly collection. Though I taught English 241, and 251, which were slanted toward American literature, and interpretation, it wasn't exactly a boast to admit I'd read so little of Conrad, and of Twain, as well. What I appreciated was that neither Nicky or Fergus ever made me feel that my reading, though inadequate, should be a source of embarrassment. Their reading, in all its omnivorous expansiveness, never ceased to amaze me.

Everyone in the English department had to teach at least one section of English 111 or 112, basic composition, and with guidance from Fergus, I learned to use Conrad's preface to *The Nigger of The Narcissus* in some of those classes. I confessed to Fergus that the clarity in the language of that preface — when it was clear, which wasn't always, as in the case of *Under Western Eyes* — helped me when I was taking a scalpel and lantern to the polishing required in my own work. I wrote a number of poems inspired by Fergus, and he was never jealous whenever I published a book. On the contrary, he was one of the first to boast he'd bought a copy, and he brought them to me to sign, and he came to my occasional readings.

I missed him so much that first semester after he retired. He moved to Florida, where he and his wife lived in a small condo near Fort Myers. For a while, whenever I saw Nicky, I asked her about him and she'd have a little something to say. Eventually, that stopped. We never heard from him. Then, one summer day, far from teaching and work, I got an email from Nicky that told me he'd died. He was cremated. There'd been no ceremony. His wife lived alone in Fort Myers in an assisted living center for seniors who could afford it. We were all getting old.

God, Nicky and Fergus and I were such geeky book worms, but we were never boring at a party. Nicky was one of those chameleons who changed herself to accommodate whoever she happened to be with at any given moment. Truly politic, and my opposite, and maybe because of this I'd managed to keep her as a friend. There was one time when Fergus told her how disappointed he was to learn that neither she nor I had read *The Secret Agent*. Conrad again. I'd had my fill. Not Nicky. She finished that novel in a weekend. She called me on a Sunday night to tell me that, boasting how she planned to tell Fergus where to shove it. We talked a long time and I remember her saying "One man with a bomb on his chest. And all these weapons everywhere in the world. Yet what's a few thousand lives in a maze of warrens like DC? Millions of them. They scurry in and out of their cubicles, exhumed, extinguished. I swear, not all the technology in the world can stop a single lunatic willing to sacrifice his life for the sake of an ideology."

Nobody spoke to me in such a way, only Nicky, and I loved her for it.

Our latest point of discussion, in private of course, was an understanding that our families had to come first. Nicky long ago had come to the realization that everything she did and said and wrote was for her family's well-being. Her health came first, of course, then her children's, then her parents, and lastly her husband. She called it her "four-chess-moves rule." She had to be at least four moves ahead of any listener. She was doing well if she kept her audience, no matter who it was, guessing perpetually.

I told her I understood this rule. When I was writing poems, I had to understand, as Carl Sandburg once wrote, that I was making an art form akin to "an echo asking a shadow to dance."

Nicky loved that I'd said this to her. She'd tittered and sighed and later that week we'd enjoyed lunch together and reminisced about Fergus and how much we missed the old boy. She told me how under-appreciated I was, and that she couldn't wait to read my next book.

For hours after lunching with her, I walked on air, no lie. I didn't even think about purging. She just had that kind of effect on me.

—◦◦◦—

I was starting to fill out. Getting fatter and getting happy. Now, there was a surprise. I wanted someone to pinch me, to grab a big ol' chunk or blob. Body-surfing the day's lambent tides I asked: *Where did I go? Am I back?*

I was, perhaps, too ignorant of the way I feared and despised strangers. The looks I got must have, indeed, mirrored the looks I gave. They were making me start to think that I was becoming one rather coarsely complexioned she-goat of a woman. A battle axe. A broad. A bullish female. So be it. I was real. I was doing so much better, taking regular meals and smiling and breathing and making corny puns in my conversations.

Dalton had, of late, been saucier too, less morose, pinching me more often, of all things. He was coming out of the low-grade gloom he'd carried through the holidays. His situation at work must have changed. Or else he was seeing how I was changing. We'd had an uneventful Christmas, always the best kind. We'd visited Rusty. We hadn't visited his family, since we'd seen them during Thanksgiving.

It wasn't like I'd added too much weight, maybe twenty pounds, but I had more confidence now whenever I went shopping and whenever I ate. I enjoyed three whole meals a day, too, just like a normal person, and I snacked in between. It had been almost three months since I'd done any purging.

Was my succumbing to self-acceptance really making me happy or was it that I felt afraid to go back to who I was? What a jumble of conflicting impulses I'd become. I hated to think of those razor-souled days outside of my own wants, minting myself along tedious homogenized lines because that was what a good girl did. Where was crude and original? That's what I wanted. Well, I'd find her in the mirror, of course. If I couldn't find her there, where else would she be?

The last time I spoke with Rusty about all of this self-identification, the journey I was on, she listened, didn't say a word. When I was finished and nearly begging her for a response, she told me I needed more of a sense of a mission. That most women had children because by being a mother they felt able to fully self-actualize. I wasn't certain I agreed with this completely, but it felt swell to be able to talk freely with my mother about such a topic, though I was definitely sure there were many women who believed, and rightly so, that they were born to bring children into the world and to nurture and raise them.

The raising of children was out and we knew this. I did like her idea of a mission. I wanted to link it to a research project. Call me a doofus, but I loved doing research. Learning made me happy. I forgot myself fathoms deep under the interwoven layers of history and literature in all its forms.

One thought had been plaguing me: where had all this new-found courage come from? With my bones, and standing so tall, I had really thickened well beyond looking more pudgy or plumpish. I'd also stopped weighing myself, so if I had gained any more pounds. I didn't know how many. I didn't want to know. I had wanted to see a difference and there was one, more than a few horizontal folds and love handles developing along my lower backside. I took up space in a small room, and I didn't fit as well into many of my clothes either. This was fine, because I relished any excuse to go shopping.

I closed my eyes and saw an image of myself as a domineering and rangy full-figured woman in a robe, really saw what I looked like and I asked myself if I liked what I saw. Yes, I did. Dalton, I think because of this, wouldn't keep his hands off my body. It was as if he'd re-discovered me along with his sexual appetite. I felt as if I was being opened. From the inside out, though, as if I were allowing it.

I liked this feeling. When I stopped my work each day, I felt elated in the sense of satisfaction that often came after sipping a glass of white wine with a meal, or shedding some tears during a movie. I wanted to talk about it a little, to share my gut-level reactions, bounce them off my friends. When Dalton wasn't around as much, I usually phoned Rusty.

Our relationship had changed. She'd become less willing to hear me speak, no matter how frantically emotional I could get sometimes. She didn't share my enthusiasm for feeling healthy and accepting myself at any size. I told her that was my mission. That she'd been right about needing one. It was really very simple. Yet this began pushing us, I thought, farther apart.

"It's worth it, isn't it?" I said to her on the phone.

"Life is good, Stella." She sounded cold. "Your father always used to say that."

"It's not like I'm doing anything different. Not taking any medicine," I said. "But I feel different. Like it just happened. Like I know where I am now."

We finished our conversation with her saying, matter of factly, "Well you just keep on feeling that way."

This saddened me, so I turned to my relationship with Dalton, who argued with me less often, not nearly as much as he'd used to. He continued to cook passionately. Maybe it was all the love he put into the food. I knew it wasn't my medication, because I hadn't increased my dosage, but I could feel my eyes shining as I chewed and emptied my plate and watched myself as I went for a third helping and admitted to Dalton that each bite tasted better than the last. I watched him watch me and saw how the warmth had returned to his complexion and something had changed in him, as well, had shifted and found its way.

There had to be an explanation. Outside of my misgivings about my mother, I was feeling just a little too darn happy. As a test, I wanted to go a full week without my medication. I told Dr. Murray about this and she encouraged me to try it, to see what might happen, but to be careful.

I found I could still eat and I didn't feel anything I would describe as withdrawal. Dalton no longer had to coax me into the kitchen. I spent a lot of time with him there, helping him out until he chased me away because I was distracting him. At night, he'd pull down my underwear and tip me over into our bed and climb on top, as well. He felt heavier than ever, but I didn't mind at least for an occasional night, though it was too hard on my ribs for it to become our customary position again. I would be the one on top, where I belonged. He hadn't been on top for a long time, going back to our early and really fiery sexed-up days together.

He began to say such sweet things to me in bed. "You're starting to love yourself again. You're working things out, aren't you?"

I began to coo and to shiver and to just lose myself in his arms. I'd tell him he could talk that way to me all he wanted, whenever he wanted, that I couldn't get enough of it.

When we sat at dinner or breakfast, how could I not beam at the sight of him across from me at the table, practically glowing? Why did I ever think he was having an affair? Had I really been that aloof and out of touch? Apparently, so.

When he spoke to me, I listened with more care, with courtesy, putting my own concerns and responses aside. One thing I noticed was the lack of any pain in his face, no worry lines, no shortened breathing. Like me, he moved more gracefully, though more slowly, as well, and if the movie that was our marital relationship had a pop music theme, it could have been titled: "Nobody Likes Me Unless I'm With You."

All of this was helping me come to understand how a handsome Hollywood icon such as Richard Widmark, one of my favorite old-school actors, managed to stay married for 55 years. When asked the secret, Widmark replied, "I happen to like my wife."

Still, in spite of my more consistent happiness, I got stoned more and more often. I got behind in my work. I became careless. I went back on my meds, mostly the Saxenda, and this kept me from gaining even as I ate well and consistently. I still rambled on, drinking wine, sloppy, and I'd succumb to the munchies and polish off a bag of chips while I yammered about how the American dream was dead and it was all one big world market and the Internet was full of nothing but lies and sidebars and agenda-driven platforms.

Dalton, surprisingly, endured these bouts. He told me how people had no idea what went on in that cyber world he was so familiar with, the dark web. Bless his heart, my Dalton, he just listened as I babbled and babbled. No matter how stoned I was, how lost in the ethers, I shared plenty of my own fuzzy and ill-informed opinions, having my say, trying to forget my pain and my confused sense of self.

I would hazard a daring opinion and I'd wait for a dispute from him. None would come. By dint of fatigue perhaps, he seldom contested anything I said. Maybe he'd stopped listening. I didn't always listen either, or agree with him, and I didn't have to be right. Nor did he. That was how marriages went. They were uneven. They yo-yoed much like my weight. I might have to take his side on many issues, and he'd have to take mine on many others. We still thought alike. We often anticipated and finished each other's thoughts.

I'd taken to using him on the sofa as if he was a big pillow. I'd also gotten into the habit of scooping each night with a soup spoon from a rather large bowl of ice cream. First a few hits of the ganga, and then into the quart of Edy's or Turkey Hill as if it were my right, and no matter what I'd already eaten for dessert.

Wasn't I still bony, still so little? No, I wasn't. I'd never been. Who was I kidding? Myself, of course. I loved lying to the baby Stella Luna within me. I knew she felt a little warmer and softer in places, but she was starting to believe and trust again in herself. I mean, myself. And in us. We not only loved each other, but we understood each other. We had a deep lasting trust and friendship to share. The same could be said of my relationship with Dalton.

So, I could eat all the ice cream I pleased. I gave myself permission. It was all so wonderful. It felt like a kind of death and resurrection, and it was proven by how the two of us, Dalton and me, were coming alive again. I thought I'd found something new beyond the sexual in our relationship. A confirmation, I supposed, that I'd needed.

This is the thing Dalton understood about me. When we spent time together, there were always three people present. Myself, the tiny yet oversized voice within me, and Dalton, of course.

I shared these thoughts with Dalton along with any other memories that all the pot in my head was allowing me to spill out in wobbly surges. He listened and encouraged me to write them down, saying often that it was probably okay if I wanted to use some factual events in my poems. To be honest about my voice within. I loved talking to him, feeling that I was finally beginning to understand that one's life changed quickly. It confirmed how temporal our existence was and how challenged we were to believe in anything that was solely physical.

In my twenties, inspired by music, I'd rather liked suspecting that very little lasted for long. Now, having lived, knowing how this reality tended to dump me into gloomy depressive moods, I could turn to Dalton and we could turn to each other and I, for one, felt gratitude knowing that we wouldn't last that long. Who needed an eternity anyway, when the universe was on a screen in front of us, or in my pocket and I could watch movies on the Metro train — didn't even have to look out the window or talk to a soul. I could drop out entirely, content with the knowledge that I had all the connectivity that digitized light provided, a rocket ship to that constellated universe known as cyberspace, where at any moment I was either at a library or in someone's bedroom, forcing myself on their consciousness one hypertext digit at a time.

In the past, I'd worried that I was starting to sound like a nagging wife. I didn't worry about that any longer. I didn't argue. If I was wrong, I didn't act proud of it. I'd learn. I believed it was my right to be a different person, better than the one I'd been when I'd first met Dalton and was so eager to please him. I still wanted to give him pleasure. I never tired of that. Yet my mind, like my body, wasn't the same. It stored more memories. It trusted that love was real and lasting. It was tired. It glowed. It knew defeats as well as triumphs.

Yet it's the struggle that completes us, isn't it? Why had it taken me so long to accept this? If I didn't make adjustments consciously, the struggle forced me to. There had to be new comforts to find. I shouldn't *fear* laughing, being the loudest in any room, my eyes brimming with light and charity.

I went to the scale. I'd gained another fifteen pounds. Shocking. Yet not shocking. My clothes had been sending messages all along. I was proud of each one, on my way to becoming more than just a shapely vessel. The thought of myself as a continent delighted and intrigued and inspired.

Then the happiness ended. I supposed I'd been stupid to hope she would beat the cancer. She'd died mere weeks after it was diagnosed as Stage Four, bless her heart. Dalton didn't fall apart. I loved him so dearly. He remained doggedly consistent and sanguine. He was the manager, his thumb on the pulse. I told him I couldn't live without him. I was just one more snail walking the razor's edge. Not him, no, he was steadfast, a real brick.

"Everybody," he said. "Does everything they do. Why? Just because they need the money. My Momma, she's in a better place. I don't like that she's gone. But it has got to be better there. It's just got to be."

I told him it was. He didn't press me to say anything more. We spent a lot of quiet time together and for his sake I laid off the weed. I wanted to be pure for him, clean, alert. His new boss had been riding him hard, making him work longer days, including Saturdays. It didn't matter that his mother had died recently, or that he had a lot of time in the system and knew the right, the reliable people. His work situation had changed and he had to ride it out. He told me he didn't like it, but he didn't want to quit, not a chance. Nobody quit a government job. The pensions were just too good.

I penned my lines each day so as not to inform or insult but to befuddle God just enough so that each poem sounded like a work of art. Even though I was on hiatus from Queen Cannabis, I continued forgetting the location of my keys and my eyeglasses and my phone. One day I forgot to turn off the coffeemaker when I left the house. On another day, it was the iron. Luckily on that day I made only a short trip away from home. These absent-minded errors might burn our house down. I made them all the time in front of my students, as well, though it never really hurt our lessons. Thing was, I just didn't function as sharply as I once had, and to tell you the truth, it bothered me. I thought often of Mrs. Joyce Malquist, sharper than sharp until one day she'd made one fatal slip and where had that gotten her?

Wisely, I kept my lips sealed, my head down and tried to listen without showing anyone what I really thought. That was the key. I had to bury myself alive and get used to breathing through the layers spreading around my middle and weighing down my chest.

Something had to give. I needed release. I needed an occasional respite from Dalton. Sometimes, I couldn't face the pain in him, that loss any boy must feel when he loses his mother. That was when the buffets began with Nicky, who appeared to be facing her own mid-life issues, particularly regarding her oldest daughter's raging sexual desires and her lack of common sense when it came to choosing boyfriends. Nicky, too, just needed someone to sit with and talk to. She started taking me to Shoney's or else Golden Corral for lunch. These all you-can-eat-until-bursting palaces had never been Dalton's style, but they suited me. Buffets with Nicky were more than solace mid-day; they were an inexpensive adventure and a splurge, but I had to do them in the right way, so I began to meet

Nicky at them on the days I didn't have to teach. I'd started to get high again, and I'd smoke before going and arrive stoned out of my mind, beaming when I saw Nicky's face, and she knew I was stoned, but she didn't care, it was game-on, because no matter how many calories we stowed away, neither of us appeared to ever came close to the others, those strange and sometimes humungous hard-working salt of the earth people around us who we tried not to stare at.

I couldn't say when it started to happen. Partly it was my holding on, my stubborn refusal not to purge. I also think that the death of Dalton's mother fired off a switch inside of me. I had felt it lighting up when I was in the airplane with him flying back north from Atlanta after the funeral. I'd felt radiant, at ease, and reveled in the feeling. It was as if my breathing apparatus had changed. I no longer twitched each time I sat and began to read. I wrote in peace, sedately, and the calm I felt when doing so was exhilarating.

As I got better on one hand, I got worse on the other. I began going to the buffets alone, but only during the days when I taught online. Neither Dalton nor Nicky were at my side. I found buffets I'd never been to, shocked to learn they even existed. I marveled at all the food and discussed it with myself in private conversations as if I'd cooked it alone and had been in the kitchen for hours. I imagined Dalton was with me and we were supportive and gentle with each other. We didn't talk much about his mother or his family and how strangely one of his cousins had behaved during the funeral ceremony. The sale of his mother's house was now in process and there was no telling how long it would take. What I'd learned was that it was expensive to die with dignity, especially if that's what you worked for all your life. It left an aching wound inside. It made the buffet more appealing.

At home, Dalton was still often weeping in his sleep, waking up at odd hours, struggling to get traction, groping for me in the dark

— which I really enjoyed and was learning to appreciate in a new way. He held on to me and our bed became an open sea and I was his life preserver. It was so gratifying to feel wanted in such a way and to be there for him, to do my part.

Days and weeks continued to pass. Snow fell. Snow melted. It never stayed on the ground for long in that part of Virginia, though in the higher reaches of the hills it glistened with a sugary sparkle when the sun was at its zenith. I went for walks and drives and remained my sleepy, drowsy, oblivious self, couldn't always say which day, hour or year it was, and I was getting to be fine with that as long as I had my forays into gluttony to take solace in. So what if I was a ditzy absent-minded poet and professor, after all? I wasn't looking forward to being anyone else other than myself.

That was my new secret. Like all my colleagues, I paid the higher parking fees and learned the updated MLA regulations and got tired of the grinding performance art that was so often teaching. I continued my buffet lunches with Nicky. My days were about meals and everything else fit in around them except my clothes. It had been a long time since I'd stepped on a scale, but I knew, and others knew, and now and then I'd hear the whispered comment about how I was putting on alarming amounts of weight. So be it. I was making my way, never in a hurry to walk the dead air of corridors between classrooms, avoiding eye contact from students who got younger each year.

As much as possible, I tried not to think about the hive of partitioned cubicles that I shared with six other underpaid, overworked and overeducated instructors, all of whom I knew fairly well. I got fresh air each day, and this helped my appetite and helped my body, though filling out, to stay firm, especially my legs. I enjoyed trails or just strolling along our road during times when I knew there would be sparse traffic. I'd linger under oaks and evergreens and get lost in the sway of their branches against the sky. I watched cardinals, the birds Virginia was known for, alight on pine boughs that still held snow. They'd peck about and chirp, and as I stood there, entranced, I told myself it was a thrill to be alive. I'd get home and I'd hurry into some Keats, losing myself in an orgy of bliss.

Each ordeal passed. This was what I told Dalton. He would claim and understand this better soon enough, but he needed time. He'd been telling me for weeks that he hadn't thought for a moment about his job. He was doing it, of course, showing up, but his mind and heart weren't in it. The funeral had cost him a lot of money, but he'd get it back with his share of the sale of his mother's house. Our online business had slowed considerably post-holiday season, but still brought in enough to keep me in Mint Chocolate Chip, and marijuana. Dalton started talking about putting away enough for a trip maybe to the Caribbean, or a cruise. In another year, he'd have the last of his school loans paid off.

Was he really getting that old? We'd need a few more years to pay off mine. I was getting that old too, but I didn't feel old. I felt younger, oddly, than I'd ever felt.

I thought that for a couple in mourning, we'd been remarkably upbeat. What I liked was that he was home every night and I loved *knowing* the kitchen would smell like braised beef or his latest version of a sauce. We ate as if it was the only task that mattered each day. We did so quietly, steadily, with gusto and certainty. We took our time, as well. I was no longer purging or even thinking about it. I was planning and following through. First, breakfast. Lunch either a private affair at home or else I'd hit the road to a buffet, driving sometimes all the way to greater DC, looking them up online ahead of time and making sure they were worth the trip.

I could no longer just eat a small meal. I had to eat until sated beyond comfort in that nether realm where I felt myself suspended as if underwater. A low-grade food coma. It was often a struggle to get in behind the wheel to drive home, but I believed it was what I needed, and I got home in time to make sure that I could nap, finish some work, maybe smoke a bong or two, and before I knew it I was eating dinner, a big one, just hubby and me, feeding until I was suspended underwater again, slipping back into coma, but in our home where I knew I could soon lie down and just hold my sides and think of myself as filled in heaven.

Since Dalton had begun working Saturdays, we had to go to restaurants on Sunday, either a Mexican, Italian or Asian place. What I didn't like was that we had to drive pretty far and I liked to get stoned before we left. By the time we arrived, my buzz had usually worn off and Dalton never allowed me to smoke in the car with him. Sometimes, even with the munchies I felt too tired to eat. I just wanted to lie down and sleep, though the cuddling was often sweet once we had eaten and were riding home.

I struggled at first as I began to continue to upgrade my wardrobe, opting for elasticized waistbands whenever possible, and looser tops and larger panties and bras. I'll say it again: thank God for Spanx. Forget about jeans. I just gave up on them. Dalton didn't seem to mind. Frankly, I'm not sure he even noticed. As I looked in the mirror and argued over whether I should scale back and start weighing myself, or else just start purging again, I told myself I was adjusting, coming around, maybe overdoing at first, but letting myself relax, *at all times*, enjoying the freedom that for years I wouldn't allow myself to have. I ate the kinds of spicy entrees Dalton sometimes savored. He'd added more weight too, was struggling to squeeze into a size 42 trousers, but I shouldn't be too judgmental. The mirror didn't lie. It was obvious I was keeping pace if not outdoing him.

Was it hopeless? No. I came to like my jowls and chin. We

talked, we laughed. I told him funny stories about my students while I sipped a glass of wine. If home, I would finish the bottle by myself. He tended to prefer beer. If we were out on a Sunday, I drank at restaurants knowing I wasn't going to drive and could fall asleep in the car on the way home.

We were both becoming increasingly docile and domesticated. I approved. I donated to charity bags upon bags of clothes I'd outgrown. When we had dinner at home, which were events now, planned out, shopped for, our menu was comprised of experiments and recipes learned from some of the cooking shows we liked to watch together. I liked Nigella Lawson, and Jacques Pepin. He liked Mario Batali and Marcus Samuelsson. The two of us enjoyed taking pains to plan and prepare, and with exquisite concern. It felt like something we were good at and this consoled us.

There was a deep calm that developed between us in the kitchen, with no need for words. I was never sure that Dalton knew just how much I revered it. He'd never been adept at reading my signals, probably because I didn't always send them that clearly. Instead, I had chosen to start trying to *show* him what I was feeling by my actions. I wasn't afraid to sound little sighs of delight and to roll my eyes and sigh again when a morsel tasted surprisingly piquant. He didn't have to make me go for seconds, or create mounds of food on my plate. I was doing this on my very own, proud at last that I was leveling out emotionally, not fighting a war with that tiny voice inside and perceived horror images of my body.

I started to tell him I loved it when he prepared dessert, so he just kept doing it and obliged me every night. I knew I was in for it when he brought home a second-hand copy of *The Joy Of Cooking*. On the days I went to an afternoon buffet, and then had his desserts for dinner, whether it was tiramisu, cheesecake or coffee ice cream with chocolate sauce — the calories, oh, the calories, and even my therapist had said she saw how more relaxed I looked — but maybe I should consider the negative consequences of letting myself go too far in another direction. This was code, of course, for telling me politely that a second new moon had started to develop below my chin.

But I liked that darling little moon there. I liked being the alarmingly big body in small public gatherings. Remarkably, much of what I felt could be called joy. Indeed, my days with Dalton started and ended with terms of endearment and many a sweet kiss among the culinary accoutrements. It was like we'd just gotten married and because of this I didn't mind the numbness I felt sometimes in my shoulders. I tingled all over. I sometimes struggled to breathe. I felt weird chest pains, and a constant achiness in my knees. I told this to Dr. Klein and he told me that it was typical due to the weight I'd gained. So I should lose some weight. How I wished he hadn't said that.

I'd have to make adjustments again. I went back on the Saxenda. I'd get used to them, those side effects. I'd probably start losing the weight.

Sometimes, Dalton would join me to go shopping. We began cooking to slim ourselves down. Dalton joined a gym in the city and came home a little later on Friday nights. While shopping, some of the pop music of my teenage years, the really sickening stuff that was piped in, reminded me that I was of that age now, of that demographic, that I should be a parent, a consumer, a church-goer, a fan of daytime TV. I was none of these, never would be. Dalton was, to a degree. When he was home on weekends, he kept the TV on all day, whether he was watching it or not. It was like he didn't trust the silence.

Dalton would tell me about a song playing in a store and ask if I knew it. He wouldn't complain that he'd heard it too many times. I did this. I complained. I bitched. More and more, a lot of bitching as a side effect due to my meds. I lost control and launched into diatribes. I needed Dalton to be my sounding wall and I needed to vent. I bitched and relaxed and leveled off. I wasn't as hungry as often and I began to eat much less, but when I did eat, I enjoyed my food. I mean, I really dug in.

Then I began to purge. There was more of me now, and that meant longer sessions on my knees. It wasn't pretty, mind you.

Naturally, I lost many pounds and all in a rather short amount of time. No one could convince me this was healthy. I began feeling tired and depressed. I turned to my poems. My girls. Heather McHugh. Amy Lowell. Lisel Mueller. Rita Dove.

The other down side of these shopping excursions was that some of the muzak ditties would remind Dalton of a certain time with his mother, or when he and I were younger, more limber, fresher and more energetic. He'd tell me these things later, never when they were happening. They brought out a profound sadness in him, one I knew I'd never be able to wipe away.

I was, frankly, stymied by the constant changes my body was going through, their severity, and the lack of discipline I'd shown by returning to my purge habit, even while taking Saxenda. I told myself I would not continue. Nor would I accept it, not any of it, not one bit. I had myself and I had Dalton. He was my teddy bear, my rock-candy mountain. He wasn't perfect, but he was mine, and I was nothing if not difficult. God, was I a wreck, and the fondness I felt for him was, at times, impossible to express. As a poet, you'd think this would have been easy for me. It wasn't. I kept telling myself that one day, I'd find the language. I'd find steadiness. I'd dedicate a whole book to him. All the poems, from all the notes I'd been keeping since our marriage, would be about him.

I think in the wake of his mother's passing that all of Dalton's sense of adventure and how he once defined it, began to appear to him as a one-way trip to Nowhere. He didn't talk about good old days as we wandered the aisles and filled our shopping cart at Costco or Target, grabbing bargains on family-sized portions of toilet paper, 32 rolls at a time, or laundry detergent and the occasional kitchen appliance. Tawdry, that's what we were and I could get used to it.

Some of our favorite destinations were the Dollar General stores that had popped up all over. I bought jams and crackers and snack cakes and all sorts of unhealthy desserts, knowing I'd get stoned and binge on them and then vomit them all up. It was while shopping, getting lost in the aisles, overwhelmed by so many choices that I began to remind myself that I had punished myself with my eating disorder because I'd wanted to murder the tiny voice within, and also to become and remain invisible. I could no longer be that way. I needed to be present, fully, for my husband. I loved being his voluptuous wife, just as I loved running into former students now and then while out shopping. None of my students ever passed remarks behind my back concerning how large I was. I only *imagined* they did. To them, I was Ms. Stella, as I liked to be called. I was the one who explained to them what the word predicate meant when used as a noun, or the difference between an active versus a passive sentence.

Why couldn't I follow through on such a simple task? Why couldn't I just love myself? Dalton was such a big part of my life, whether in the kitchen or the living room, in our bed: my heavy wounded bear, scarred but diligently keeping himself alive. I hung on his big arms. I'd do whatever it took to keep him at my side for as long as possible, till death separated us, though not even death could do that. There was an eternity brewing between and within us. I felt myself carrying it inside.

I knew so much more about myself than I had when we'd married. I really didn't care to do or to be more of anything else. Or did I? Together, we'd tend to the issues which would improve our domestic life and keep us comfortable. Little else mattered. There might come a day when I'd get over this eating disorder and these body issues once and for all, not need a single med, and then look out, because by then I'd probably be sporting a pair of hips that wouldn't let me fit in the candy aisle.

I became increasingly obsessed with my figure and how it sagged in places as I saw the purging was helping me to shed pounds, leaving stretch marks, but I wanted to feel peace. I just didn't have it in me to fret and punish myself any longer. The purges left me spent, babbling my way into a shower where I'd sob and let it all out, remembering the sight of Dalton's mother lying there so emaciated in her coffin, and thinking one day I would be seeing Rusty there too, in a similar coffin, all sealed up. As I'd seen my father at his wake so many years ago in his suit and tie with his flesh so sallow and his cheeks caved in.

I was coming to understand that I needed to evolve beyond a teenager's obsession with how I viewed myself. *Slay that tiny bitch within.* Maybe I was finally growing up. Though I had to be honest. On my best nights, I didn't purge. Getting stoned, losing myself in poems and then collapsing to sleep at Dalton's side was still the kind of day many a woman would look forward to.

In the bedroom, ever since his mother's death, we hadn't been making love as often. Not exactly the same amount of fire. He'd been dazzled and inconsolable, so had I, both of us unable to speak beyond the required minimum to fuel a conversation, struggling to feel a sense of belonging. He was worse than me, so lonely and motherless. I was worse in that I didn't come to bed. After my sob sessions, I'd self-medicate with a bong hit and listen to music with headphones on and the cat on my lap, or else I'd bundle up and go for a walk behind the house with my flashlight. Dalton had lost his anchor to everything. Afloat. Unmoored. Dripping with self-pity, crushed by an inability to pretend everything would be okay. I'd never found my anchor. Yet we were fluid and as content to be together, knowing we needed each other, as we'd ever been.

Many of our nights still ended with him lying still and trying not to burst into tears. He just couldn't help himself. I knew it had not been weeks but months; there's no time logic to the emotions that come with experiencing death. One of the qualities I so admired in him, his sensitivity, fueled his suffering. His emotions overwhelmed, took over his body. I was proud of the way he could just let the tears out. Most men can't, or won't.

I lived to be there for him. Some nights I lay by his side. I read while in bed. I'd stopped snacking in bed too, though I still scribbled little notes. I was snacking less and less, no more potato chips and little cakes and cookies and all the high calorie junk that had set into motion eating habits that I no longer wanted to enjoy. I'd also begun to stop going to the buffets. I was such a mess, setting goals for myself with the help of Dr. Murray. Could I last a year without sneaking Ipecac? Could I make eating a regular choice without any drama attached to it? This was a realistic achievable goal. I was in a much better place than I'd been six months ago. I'd gotten back on the scales and the numbers proved it too. Rusty noticed the change during my last visit to Front Royal, and she didn't warn me to be careful, to lay off the ice cream, because she saw that I was thinner. Don't get me wrong. I weighed about 235 and was nobody's definition of a waif. She didn't say I looked better, though, that was the thing with Rusty. Always tight-lipped when I needed some words of comfort the most. We'd spent many a long Saturday shopping for blouses, sweaters and slacks.

One night, Dalton asked me what was wrong with him. "I can't stop bawling."

"Honey, there's nothing wrong with you. It's all very natural," I said. "You hear me bawling in the shower, don't you?"

"But why does life have to be so hard for us? Why do people like us have to suffer so much? My mother did everything she could for us."

"Don't think about that now. Let time heal all wounds. Just close your eyes and try to rest."

Many nights passed like this, marked by Dalton's inconsistent ability to pull himself out of emotional distress. I assumed this period would last two to three years. I wanted him there, needed him, and I had him. I should have been content with this. I was. Yet something was missing. He needed me, of course, but on most nights all he could muster was enough energy to lie still and breathe while I curled against him and lay my arm across his chest.

What was it? What was missing? Not a child, no, something *within* us, a flaw, an incompleteness that marked who we were.

❧

Just this nagging sense of incompleteness — *we're not worthy of a child and he now without his mother and maybe I never really had my mother's love* — saddens us both in its various manifestations and at one point with Dalton I could do nothing but watch while he broke down and sobbed over a photograph of himself and his mother together. A black and white 5 by 7, curled and with a little water stain in one corner, he'd found it inside one of his mother's bible, the only book she'd left for him, having made sure everyone in the family knew that he was to have it upon her death. The photo pictured Dalton in his Sunday best, a little dark suit jacket and bow tie, Dalton just a tall meaty kid from Georgia with a few crooked teeth in his big smile. To his left stands his Ma, looking fatigued, bosomy, overweight, squinting into the sun while holding a small bouquet of flowers.

Looking at the photo, seeing himself as once so innocent, so happy — I mean he's really grinning — Dalton couldn't control his grief. He covered his head with two hands and lowered it as if trying to push his forehead into his stomach, balling himself up, attempting to shield himself from the world. I put on a brave face, acting like I trusted my resolve and steadiness, which I didn't . I told him he didn't have to control anything. I was linked to Dalton in subtle ways, many of which I hadn't realized until finding them in that moment. I would have to take on the mantle of consoler and guide. Usually, it was the other way around. He consoled me. Could I do this? I was grieving too, after all.

Of course I could do it. As I petted my man's broad shoulders, I felt myself growing stronger, more resilient, tolerant and aware of my shortcomings. Maybe it had just taken this event, this loss shared between us, to notice what I was capable of. I did not, *would not* criticize him. My love was unconditional, an act of surrender; I was fully there for him. This was my weakness and my strength. I couldn't feel or express any emotions in a half-hearted, lukewarm fashion. I was with Dylan Thomas, raging against the dying of the light. We both were. This togetherness — and I knew Dalton felt it — defined success in a marriage. It lived in the words of our vow: for better or worse, in sickness and in health. If I had anything that was certain, it was this commitment from him, and within me. Nothing to sneeze at, as Nicky would say.

—⁂—

In an ever-quickening yet increasingly remote sense of the present, I took another bite, head down, bilious with doubt, fork at the ready for more, my jaw throbbing as I chewed and remembered there was a time when I loved my job, never thought of it as work, not really, it was my way of paying for my pursuit of poetry. What had it become? I didn't know.

Just thinking about our upcoming trip to Staunton to see one of Shakespeare's plays at the American Shakespeare Theatre had put me in a saucy mood. I loved their theatre, a wonderfully authentic reconstruction of the Blackfriar's Playhouse. Throughout the Covid pandemic, I'd been jonesing for live theatre, but those days were coming to an end, at last. I was moving away from a perpetually wine-soaked torpor, having become the proud owner of a body that was starting to look more like a Harley than a Mack truck.

I loved my body's changes. I was down to a size 18 dress size , slowly returning toward an albeit full but more defined curvature to my shape. I had never been an apple or a pear. More of a picnic basket or a stack of watermelons. I hardly recognized the thought that I wanted to be seen again. I felt nourished by the attention of strangers. I needed it as a form of compensation for the wretched forms of repulsion I felt toward myself.

I wanted to quit my job, too. I could happily stay home and do nothing but write and memorize and read poems all day. I still had my online retail business, and I could also write as a freelancer, publish some articles, start a fat-girl blog, write about surviving bulimia and significant yo-yo gains and losses, the kinds of topics that Oprah Winfrey had once helped make some authors famous for exploring. At least for the time being, I was allowing my imagination to embrace not only myself but the electronic landscape, what it offered, and all the forms of commercial work that my quill and my experiences might accommodate.

When I asked Dalton about his opinion on this, he proved again how committed he was to trying to love and understand me. "Will it make you happier?"

It would, Dalton. It would.

"Then do it," he said.

⁓

I had returned from my visit to Dr. Murray and was feeling downright chipper. Once I closed the front door and felt, at last, home for the day, I heard music. They were harp strings tinkling in ever so lush and somnolent strains. I was transfixed at once. It was coming from Dalton's room and I stood outside his closed door and I listened, transported. I didn't know the music. It sounded elaborate and yet exceedingly simple and gentle at the same time. There was a suggestion of a melody, but there wasn't one recognizable through-line, more of a series of impressionistic tones that rained out of that harp.

Inside of me, I felt this giving way, an erosion of all tension. I closed my eyes and I waited, letting the music sink in and wash over me. I felt such a sublime relaxation, such relief, as if each note was directed toward some pressure point in me that needed to be fingered, unlatched and opened.

I began to flow, carried off, back to one of my rivers, one current blending with another, though this time I was floating downstream and the water was percolating around me, sounding little slaps. It smelled crisp and fishy, perfumed by cedars, and I saw sunlight passing through their green boughs. I saw the rays dapple and sparkle off the water, blinding me for an instant as I bubbled along.

The door opened. There he stood. My Dalton. I wanted him. "That music, what is it? Sounds like Satie."

"It is French. You're right there. But it's Debussy. I found it by accident online."

"What are you doing home so early?"

He paused a moment as if making sure he was clear-headed and perhaps doubting he could trust me. I knew the look. It blended uncertainty with restlessness writ large.

"What is it? What's wrong?"

It burst out of him, panic-stricken, and he didn't to take a breath as he poured it on. "I think they're after me. I don't know who they are, but I see them in the city following me, and they follow me in the car too, and I don't know who they work for or what they want, but they are definitely gunning for me. And today, I just had enough. I had to get out of there. I'm tired of it, Stell, I had to get out of there."

"Honey, Sweety, slow down." This wasn't like him. He was rattled.

"I know too much. I figured I'd just come home and goof off and try not to think about it. I'm sick of it, you have no idea. They figure I'm dangerous or something."

"Who is they? You sound like a paranoid lunatic."

"I'm not, believe me. You have no idea. It's this project I've been working on."

"Spying on the Russians?"

"No, nothing like that. I can't talk about it. For all I know they're listening through my phone."

Was this my Dalton talking? His upper lip was twitching. "But who is *they*?" I asked. "You keep saying they. My God, you're sweating."

"Do you like this music? It's harp. I need something to calm me down."

"C'mon Honey, don't dodge the subject. What's going on at work?"

"You know I can't talk about it." He stood taller. He made a move toward me, a suggestive one. Sex was definitely on. He cleared his throat. "Just forget I said anything. A minor lapse, that's all. There's nothing to worry about."

I didn't believe him. "Are you sure?"

"Dead to rights."

We shared a tense moment of silence. I decided not to push him. It wouldn't get us anywhere. He was too well trained. He'd never tell me anything. "What's it called?"

"The operation? I told you I can't say."

"No. The music. I like it."

"My French is terrible. I'll show you."

I read it on one of the three screens on his long desk. *Deux Arabesques.* "Two Arabesques."

"I figured that out," he said. "It's just hard to say it in French."

"Two Arabesques. Two Arabs. Me and you."

"Two Arabs?"

"Spinning 'round and 'round. Think I'll write a poem."

"I downloaded it. I'll send it to your phone. How was your session, by the way?"

"Productive, I think. I may indulge in a big dinner to celebrate."

He moved closer and gave my bottom a squeeze. "That would be nice."

"Happy wife, happy life."

"Are you making dinner?" he asked.

"You really hungry?" I asked. I raised one eyebrow. "I'm hungry now. But not for food."

This wasn't typical with us on a weekday and at such an early hour, but there was nothing I'd have preferred to do at that moment. Besides, in the heat of passion, Dalton might calm down and forget about his absurd paranoia regarding whatever covert operation he was part of.

I asked him to play the Debussy again, to turn up the volume. As he did this, turning his back to me, I giggled. It was me, all right. Giggling again. And then I seethed and lunged toward him as he began to tear off my clothes. It was splendid, symphonic, absolute rapture, but it would be the last time ever that we made love.

—⌇⌇—

Dalton, that's why I cry. It hurts too much.

Nothing felt right. I hadn't seen him for three nights in a row. I'd started to worry, had called down to Atlanta, had even called Nicky to ask her what I should do. When the requisite amount of time had passed, I filed a missing person's claim.

I blew a long sigh and my body weakened under a burden of sorrow, but I wouldn't weep any longer. I'd let the rain weep for me. It was a line for a poem. I wrote it down, changing its tense to *I'm letting the rain weep for me.*

It was raining the morning they came with the news. It had been raining three days straight and there was bad flooding out Manassas way along Highway 17 and in some other areas, a real gulley-washer, as they say, and it was only going to get worse, but I stopped worrying about that when those two black vehicles with tinted windows pulled into my driveway, one a sedan, the other an SUV, one of those huge rigs that drug dealers often use in cheesy action movies.

These were no drug dealers, and they were polite as they rapped on my door and asked if they could come in. They flashed their badges, though they hadn't needed to. One was a black man, the other an Asian woman. They entered first, both of them in civilian clothes but wearing guns. They were followed by two armed uniformed state police officers, both white men, solid Virginia stock, who'd stepped out of the SUV.

I let them in and I knew, I just knew, and when they told me, well, the floodgates opened. I collapsed and started bawling, howling and tearing at my hair. The Asian woman, I never learned her name, was with the FBI. A real pro, sympathetic and gentle, she knew just how to soothe and manipulate me so that before I knew it we were seated on my couch side by side and I was trying to under-stand the meaning behind her words. Something about "bad actors" and "compromised national security" and "a federal issue" and that Dalton had died during the night in a terrible car accident.

While that kind Asian woman with her silken voice tried to con-sole me, the other FBI agent and the two state troopers confiscated all the electronic equipment in Dalton's office, as well as his binders and notes and boxes of file folders. They left nothing there except cords and empty furniture and dusty shelves. While removing all of it from my house, they didn't ask permission. They did it as if it were their right. I was too stunned and confused to say anything.

This didn't take them long. When they were finished, one of the troopers told me they had a search and seizure warrant and that because this was a federal case, certain allowances were permissible under law and, unfortunately, had to be made. He offered to show me the warrant. I just waved him away. I didn't want to see it.

Dazed, numb, weeping, I was unable to believe and accept that these strangers had just shown up and could in such a matter of fact way share such tragic news and empty out my husband's office. This wasn't happening to me. I'd eaten some spoiled Chinese food. It was a surreal nightmare and I'd wake up and realize nothing had changed. Any minute now, Dalton would walk in through the front door.

I couldn't stop sobbing. I felt my throat burning as I coughed and gagged on my own tears. They asked me about the other rooms and I did my best to explain that all of Dalton's work-related effects were in his office. Not in our bedroom, not in any of the others. During a brief moment of clarity, I realized the last thing I wanted was for them to find my bong, or Dalton's guns, or my stash which, lucky for me, was depleted. There was also the little box in which I kept other forms of smoking paraphernalia. I must have looked guilty, though I think I sounded sincere, but it didn't matter. They searched everywhere. They confiscated Dalton's guns. My bong. All the drug paraphernalia. Turned the house upside down, but in a controlled and all too efficient way. I thought for sure they'd arrest me for the bong. They didn't. Like the other paraphernalia, they boxed it up, wrote it down on an inventory list attached to a clipboard, and didn't even say anything about it. *Dalton where are you?* One of them asked for my car keys and went outside in the rain and made short work of my car and our old truck. *This isn't happening.* I didn't know what he was looking for. *This can't be happening.* I didn't care. Not about them. Or law. Or government operations. I cared about Dalton, who was gone. Who wasn't coming back.

How polite they were, how professional, as they ripped my soul from my body.

Other than the torrents of rain, the slick washed-out roads, and the flooding throughout the region, I never got a complete explanation as to what happened. Not from them anyway. They were there for all of an hour, ending my three-day ordeal of miserable limbo wondering what had happened to my saint of a husband.

I contacted our lawyer, Roger Smythe, who had been an alum with Dalton at VMI and was a junior partner at his father's firm, Allen, Powers and Smythe based in Warrenton. Roger took the bad news graciously and agreed to help me in any way possible. Dalton and I had already made out a will with him, so he had all our paperwork and followed through on our wishes, which were to have us both cremated when the time came, and for the surviving spouse to inherit all assets belonging to the deceased. Roger, with time, would work out all the details regarding Dalton leaving me the house, his municipal bonds, IRA and military pension and other fund pay-outs, all a tidy sum of hard-earned wealth, that I would have coming to me. The only thing I had to do was to follow through on Dalton's wish to scatter his ashes at a special place we both had chosen together in the town of Shenandoah, along the river there, our hidden spot that required about a ninety-minute drive and then a mile of tracking through brambles and dense ground-cover where the river widened and pooled and the bottom was sandy.

There would not be a funeral. As days passed, I stayed in contact with Roger and he, in turn, spoke with the VA and learned all the details regarding what I had coming to me. It seemed fair enough, but what I really wanted was my husband. I didn't want a military funeral for him, or anything so showy as a burial at Arlington. I regained some composure, and I had an obit posted online. I didn't set up a fund or ask for donations. He and I, as a couple, had never been all that religious. On his own, he had read his bible often enough and never hesitated to talk about Jesus or God in a respectfully pious way. But he'd never been a churchgoer, not even during Christmas. Oddly, I never learned why, since his family was a devout lot, fully invested in the Baptist traditions.

It was only fair, and the right thing to do, so I began to painstakingly phone each of Dalton's brothers and sisters to tell them the news. These were calls I dreaded, but I made them, tried to keep a stiff upper lip, though I burst into tears, just the same, over the phone. It was hard telling them there'd be no funeral service or memorial. Though I didn't have to, I asked them all to pray for Dalton. Each of them, in their unselfish way, said they would pray for me, as well. Their compassion, frankly, floored me. I felt I didn't deserve it.

I learned from Roger that Dalton's vehicle had been a total loss, confiscated as evidence by the FBI. His body had been removed using the Jaws of Life, which pretty much explained why no one except a mortician had ever seen his corpse. It's all a blur now as I look back. I don't know how I did it. I phoned Rusty at one point during the ordeal, telling her "Dalton's dead, Momma. I wanted you to know."

It wasn't her fault, of course, but I didn't want to deal with her until I felt more stable and had some distance from the bouts of sobbing that interrupted my sleep night after night. I was doped up, of course, stoned all the time and drinking up bottle after bottle of red wine and on all sorts of meds, including the Seconal and Valium that Doctor Klein had prescribed for me.

I had Dalton's ashes in an urn, and during the second week of July, I hit the road to Shenandoah at about three in the morning, with the hope of arriving to our spot — it was never mine or his, always *ours* — at about sunrise. I was not in the best shape, having somehow managed to stop purging, but not having been able to stop eating and drinking to ungodly excess. None of my hiking clothes fit me as I'd hoped they would. I struggled into a pair of jeans I'd bought, foolishly so, for the occasion. Lastly, I settled on wearing Dalton's cherished and roomy Number 17, an old maroon foot-ball jersey from the days when they were the Washington *Redskins*, the number of one of his sports idols, Doug Williams. It hid the considerable bulging of my stomach over the top of my tight jeans. As if my weight mattered. As if how I looked mattered. It didn't. It appeared to me that I understood this, and that I was coping, taking care of business, keeping my chin up, but on another level I felt cheated. It had done me no bit of good to have heard from so many that my Dalton was "in a better place." Though maybe he was, he and his mother side by side in heaven. It was a childishly appealing thought, but I didn't believe it. I wasn't an atheist, I mean there had to be more, something spiritual, but I couldn't accept such an overly simple fantasy that he and his mother were at last re-united in the clouds and looking down on me and touching me daily with their angelic grace.

When I scattered his ashes on the river's surface, I teared up, but I hardened too. This was our final step in our journey together.

I understood just alone I was, had always been, would always be. How we're all so completely alone. For comfort, I had brought a thermos of coffee and some sandwiches with me, and I sat on a stone and I ate those sandwiches, chicken salad on rye, Dalton's favorite, as I watched the continued rising of light in the east, as I drank in the scent of honeysuckle, swatting away gnats and midges, listening to the darling little chirps and canticles from tiny birds, the gentle purling of the river, the air so brisk and clean, and so many questions, none of them to be answered.

There was no such thing as moving on. Dalton was not replace-able. I prayed that I had the fortitude and courage to keep him forever in my heart and to keep strong all my connections to him. I loved him and I would miss him. I would keep all the pictures, all the souvenirs and mementos, and I would tell no one how much I would honor my undying love for him. To quote Jane Hirshfield: *Let her have time and silence, enough paper to make mistakes and go on.*

⸎

Summer Rain's first comment was that I looked heavier and, indeed, delectable. "It's about time," she remarked.

I thought of Anne Carson's line "Girls are cruelest to themselves." I asked Summer if she intended to eat me. She said it wasn't beyond the realm of possibility, but only if I was interested. I thought of another Anne Carson line, "Give and take were just words to me at the time. I had not been in love before."

Summer asked me how I was dealing with my job. When I explained that I'd taken an extended amount of time off, a form of bereavement leave without pay that I'd agreed upon with the dean of humanities, and that I might quit, that I was miserable, she quoted a Woody Allen line about academia, stipulating one must be careful in that world because the stakes were so very small.

I close the fridge door. Bluish dusk fills the room like a sea slid back. More Anne Carson. I'd been binging on her. *Husband and wife may erase a boundary, creating a white page.* We went out on the town in DC, feasting at a Korean barbecue, paying homage to Bacchus by polishing off two bottles of red wine and Summer all night long staring with lust at my body, pawing at my extra flesh, telling me in little whispered secrets how much she'd like to feel my softness against her own. I didn't like needing to fight off her erotic urges, but I did so, even though I was turned on by thinking how much of her was there for the world to see and how much I still wanted to let go and allow myself to look that way, too, not caring about how others saw my body.

I wanted to exude her devil-may-care confidence, but I wasn't ready yet. Maybe one day in the future. I'd need at least a year, maybe two, before I could even think of sharing my body with anyone. It was banal for me to admit that I missed Dalton, but I told this to Summer anyway, and she was sincerely empathetic and didn't judge me. She reminded me, more than once, that she'd always be there for me, to never forget that we were such close friends.

She asked if I was still seeing Dr. Murray or if I'd found a grief counselor, instead. We both knew I'd always be seeing one counselor or another. I told her I was still with Dr. Murray, a woman who had my full trust, and that we were discussing and experimenting with different meds.

"One for each finger on each hand: Klonopin, Ativan, Xanax, Zoloft and Prozac. I haven't tried them all, not yet, but I will eventually."

"You look so much better."

"You said that already. Do I, really? I think you're the only one who thinks that. I'm terrified of what my mother will say when she sees me."

"You haven't visited her yet? You really should."

"Not ready. You have no idea, the binging, the collapsing, I mean the Zyprexa is helping, it really is, though it gives me cotton mouth and makes me constipated sometimes, but it levels me out, slows me down. It's not as extreme as the Saxenda was. I get this fuzzy stoned feeling to the point where I just want to float around through space and laugh while I eat and drink without any worries. But I can't. I can't do anything, not yet. It was all I could do to come here and see you."

"And I'm so glad you did."

We chattered on like this throughout the weekend, though Summer did most of the talking. She even talked about doing a reading together. She had lots of new poems. I did too. She wanted to share. I didn't. Eventually, maybe, but not yet.

"I've been invited to read in New York City, at the KGB bar. Come with me."

"Nope." I hadn't needed to think about it. I just knew I wasn't going anywhere, not for a long, long time. Judging by the look on her face, this had disappointed her. "Sorry. Got my hands full."

It was awkward, and maybe I was too cold, but that's how we left it. Not the goodbye, perhaps, that either of us had envisioned, but I knew she was my dear friend and so I'd given her the honesty that I thought she deserved.

After I returned from DC, I sank deeper into the mire, the fugue of melancholy, bitterness and grievous befuddlement I was getting used to living in. I hadn't expected this. I'd expected that I'd feel energized, livelier, perhaps more willing to continue to be social. I couldn't stand the sight of Dalton's emptied-out room, all his clothes and belongings still there. I just shut the door and kept it shut. I threw away all his belongings in the bathroom. This was my house now, my home, more than just a kitchen, and

I would have it for myself and enjoy it. I didn't want to go anywhere or see anyone.

I digressed into supine hours in my bedroom, keeping it dark. I bought a new bong and pipe and smoked my weed, and drank my wine, hoping to remain permanently removed from reality as if it would help. I wasn't sure. I hadn't been on Zyprexa for long, and I still didn't know if it would work long-term, but the early signs showed that my weight was increasing. Fine. I didn't care. No more Saxenda either. Nor was I forcing myself to vomit after each meal. I was happy with these small consolations. What I really wanted was to go off the deep end, to prove that I could swing as far in any direction that I cared to. I liked extremes. I always had. This was my way. It sometimes felt as if my mind was too strong for drugs, that I invited them in and then once I got a sense of how effective they'd be, I pushed them into working either more or less effectively. Or else my system rejected them.

The only thing worse than an artist who claims she's original is one who believes that claim. I took much solace in endless days of reading the works of masters, of forgotten geniuses, neglected mediocrities — their biographies unimportant to me, even though they were often fascinating. These works helped me put myself into perspective. I was just one more color blending on the wheel. I had my palette and my five senses. The rest was tedium and patience and prolonged bouts of waiting.

It would be an understatement to remark that I was swamped in mixed feelings when it came to my so-called career. I didn't want to be teach any longer. I felt weary of being on display, even on a computer screen, and answering questions, telling young aspirants what and how to cherish literature in order to get a grade. All the punishment and reward that teaching, at its worst, boiled down to. The idea of grades and school felt increasingly like the controlling of young hungry minds and I didn't want any part of it. Let them fail and learn and fail better on somebody else's time, not mine. They weren't interested, in the main, in the written word. They couldn't concentrate. I tried to imagine one of them laboring through *Middlemarch*, or *The Olde Curiosity Shoppe*. This would not happen. Most of them were generally incapable of concentrating on anything for more than ninety seconds. Then it was time for a commercial, or another IMS bleep, or another pop-up intrusion to slide them into another web page.

I recalled the many times I had harped on this with Dalton, lamenting how Big Electronica was destroying their minds and their ability to reason and argue and concentrate. It was destroying my own, as well. I had days when I did nothing but piddle in front of the Internet, letting click bait take me from one page to the next, feeling like a slug. To counter this, I told myself that I did, truly, want to keep following my muse. That I couldn't help myself. I had to write poems, more so now than ever. No other pursuit put me in such a desirable trance state and maybe that was all there was to it.

I felt this cloying hunger to be outside of reality, adrift inside consciousness, channeling language and echoes and sounds, but when I looked with care at the landscape for poets, I continued to observe what I had seen since graduate school — cliques of celebrated bards, a well-heeled bunch of banana-heads and misfits and self-promoters, most of whom taught at upper-tier universities or the Ivies or else slept with the right career promoters, no matter their gender. I thought, perhaps, that it had always been this way, but this hadn't made witnessing and accepting it any easier to take.

Gissing's *New Grub Street* was the novel that brought me back to my desk in earnest. I felt Dalton's weight on my shoulders and I liked it there. Dalton would have to start putting up with me now as *poète maudite* again, boozier and crabbier and more hairy each day, eating and drinking like a regular Sir Toby Belch and I even asked the ghost of Dalton to start baking for me and this surprised him, but, sounding delighted, he said "you do it." So, I began baking and eating fresh whole wheat bread and cookies basically 'round the clock. They were the big ones, my own homemade confections, some of them from Dalton's recipes. I continued to let go, and I believed that was what I needed to keep moving away from purge cycles and toward a healthier sense of myself.

What I told Dr. Murray was that I wanted to feel fully warm and safe. She believed that visiting my mother would be a big first step, and a help. I needed to begin to stop looking at myself as having failed her. It was with Rusty that all my self-loathing began. I'd never felt like I lived up to her expectations.

Well, Dr. Murray was entitled to her opinions, but I wasn't prepared yet for Rusty face to face. I needed to write more poems. They helped. They filled and emptied me at the same time. This was a puzzling dynamic but one I'd grown accustomed to, really the only process I trusted. I was no artist. I wasn't even a swimmer. I was just trying to keep myself from drowning, and I used writing as therapy.

Every person was a poet. They all had an ear, a sense of rhythm, and some of them just listened better and used it with more felicity. And some had too much to share. A good measurement of genius, as I saw it, was in the holding back of how much one said. Understanding the act of it. The show. It wasn't about marketing culture or the web. Just look at the word. Web. What kind of spider did I want to be? A trapped one?

I didn't exist. I lived to read, mostly poems and a lot of C.S. Lewis and Marianne Williamson. *It is our light, not our darkness that most frightens us.* Angered and flummoxed behind my mask, my many layers and faces concealed, I was one more stranger out there, increasingly agoraphobic, immersed in my own demons more than I probably should have been. I returned each day to the same tattered punch-drunk question: How did this life happen?

I existed in scenes that filled the darkness of my empty Virginia-Woolf cavern, not really a room where I meditated or fretted and sometimes forced myself to pig out on so much junk food that I had to lie down and close my eyes and fight off shooting pains in my ribcage. *I am Stella Luna. I am substantial.* I could only be a falling star once.

I wept and wept, my body shaking like a candle flame in my arms. I was slaughtering myself. This would be the title of a new poem. Slaughter was a subject I'd begun researching, having started with the Albigensians, about one million strong, all of them vanquished. Next, about 200,000 Teutons and Cimri, and after them another 70,000 Saxons. Between Jews, Slavs and Gypsies about 20 million, along with Protestants from France who numbered about 75,000 and I was only including representatives of the Europeans' own kind, leaving out Africans, Native Americans, and other non-Europeans all debased and erased genocidally by the millions.

I started to toy with a belief that I could not support or research enough to convince anyone it was true. This belief was an idea, not truth, that came from reading about slaughter, in general. My silly belief linked the word *slaughter* to a Native American word, *Mátchi*. There is no proof of their linkage, no linguistic history, it was merely a capricious notion that inspired me to seek a unifying metaphor in the new poems that were spilling out of me. The word *Mátchi* comes from the Massachusetts Indians, and from the Cree, the Powhatan, Delaware and the Ojibwe, as well, suggesting an evilness in mind, speech that is evil, as well as actions. This *Mátchi* can take a benign form or else an extremely violent one, rife with psychosis. It was the very energy that drove most humans. It also drove me, though I turned it inward and wreaked genocide on myself. So, you see, the link is not to anything universal as much as it is a link I found to the way I'd been behaving toward myself for so long. Basically, slaughtering myself through food.

In one of my new poems, I asked that as a child of God, by dint of being born, if I am a sinner. I didn't think my answer would be yes, because it made me a typical Christian, of course. I wasn't typical anything. But the poem, surging out of me, wasn't about dogma. It was an examination of my ideas and emotions and how I saw myself through the prism of my senses. Like all poems, essentially. For example, if I was born a sinner then why not continue to sin? It seems an appropriate choice. If there was such a force of evil as Satan, then I faced Satan daily in the mirror, because She — why must Satan or God be male? — lived inside me, within and without every choice I made.

Did anyone really want to read such poems? I didn't think so.

Guilt, fear, condemnation of my soul into some form of daily mundane purgatory were all part of accepting who I was. One might achieve salvation without the help of a supreme being. One might not. I didn't know. I believed I was still alive because I had to examine these questions. Dogma was tedious. It was my lot, pre-destined, that I followed through to a realization that born a sinner one dies a sinner. One acted through one's sense of grace, finding either a savior or a form of evil as an accomplice. One of my poems was titled *Love/Evil*. Could one exist without the other? The essence of life existed in the tension between them.

What did it mean to fear evil when I, daughter of murderous Western mankind in all its imperialistic hubris, had been raised in a tradition of justifying both fear of my own kind and The Other? I looked at the record of my kind — the sadomasochism, pogroms, slavery, ethnic purges, abuses of women and the exquisitely nuanced attention to detail when it came to constructing and maintaining toxic warfare and prisons. This was the mantle draped over my shoulders at birth. Not just me but millions of others. How many individuals had my ancestors wiped out because of skin color, and different beliefs in what none of us really knew? These Others were labelled savages, brutalized, systematically exterminated. Yet I was hardly a natural born killer; I was a child of the moon and stars, the conflicting harmonies between light and my own death extinct. All my inclinations were bent toward understanding that my impulses as a daughter, a wife, a *materna pura* to ideas and the life of the mind, were ultimately destructive ones, in spite of having been loved. I turned these impulses inward toward myself. I fed them and then forced their ejection out of my body.

Dear Rusty, dear Momma, I am a child of your mercy and tolerance, but those are mere words compared to the history I'm learning. What I see each day inside my heart, tells me that if I'm to thrive I must follow the Western tradition and extinguish discomforting annoying and disturbing life forces. Otherwise, I will permit myself to be enslaved to them and to wallow in helpless inaction.

I waited. I listened. I felt Dalton there with me as I controlled my self-destructive death impulse by writing about slaughter and genocide.

～∾～

I was in the kitchen yet again, surprise-surprise, but I wasn't trembling. *Do I dare to eat a peach?* I'd been shopping earlier in the week, so I knew I wouldn't be disappointed when I opened the refrigerator. I felt a sharp pang in my bowels. My breath shortened. I couldn't remember the last time I actually smelled Dalton. I moved my hands over bowls and containers of leftovers. I didn't want to cook. I didn't want to eat. Or did I? I began to swoon thinking about the act of eating. I knew there was milk and cereal. I wanted some. Wasn't this a good sign? I wanted and wanted and wanted.

I took the first container, a Pyrex glass bowl with a Rubbermaid lid that sealed tightly. At one time, all Rubbermaid products had been manufactured in nearby Winchester. Most Americans didn't know this. Joe Bageant did. One of my favorite Virginia writers, his book *Deer Hunting With Jesus* should be required reading in every high school curriculum. I remembered how Dalton liked these containers because he could bring his lunch, hot or cold, to work with him.

I pulled the container close to my stomach, held it there and liked feeling how cold it was. I moved slowly, sitting on the floor in front of the fridge, keeping the door open, letting the smell and the bright light and cooler temperature soothe me. It was summer, after all, and humid.

I then opened the container and imagined myself when a little girl at Christmas opening one of my presents from Santa. I didn't even look at what was inside. I just dug my fingers in, scooping out a cold gelid leftover salad or maybe it was a casserole, not caring what it was that I had prepared a few days back. I just shoved it into my mouth one fistful at a time, chewing and swallowing and letting myself breathe through my nose and tingle all over until the container was empty and I set it aside.

I hurried to my knees and started searching. This was working for me. I found another container. It was full of chicken wings I'd made the day before and I ate each one of them and dropped the bones to the floor, indifferent to the mess I was making. I found milk to wash them down, letting the milk spill down my chin as I drained the carton. I shooed my cat away as I found a two-liter bottle of soda and sipped on what was left of it as I kept poking around, taking two more containers, one of rice, one of cold macaroni. I found some bread, some cold cuts, and I made sandwiches while on that floor, using my index finger as a knife to spread mustard and mayo. I ate three sandwiches. Was I finished, at last?

I stood, with some difficulty, and began drifting toward the bathroom. "No, no" I shouted. "No I won't."

Silence bloomed as I waited for an echo to my shout. Some fruit, some crackers, some dry cereal out of a box, that's what I'd take. "No," I shouted again. "No, Stella, don't. Don't."

I waited. I felt like there was nothing left in me, yet I felt so full that it was a struggle to stay on my feet and lean back as a flaring pain shot through my ribcage. I smacked my lips. I bumped against the sink countertop, feeling so dirty and dizzy and capricious as I swung open the freezer door, sounding a gasp of delight, indulging in my happiness as I discovered the gallon of Turkey Hill that I had hoped would be there. I took it with me along with a spoon and a roll of paper towels into the living room where I sat on the floor by a window that soaked in tree shade all afternoon long. One slow spoonful at a time I played the empress of ice cream. *Let be be the finale of seem.* Yes, Mr. Stevens, more comfort. I needed to read more of him. I stared out the window at the trees, lost in soft afternoon sunshine imprinting long amber rectangular patterns. I would miss who I had been, but I could not be her any longer.

〜

Butter, milk and cheese. That sometimes oleaginous flesh-sweetening trifecta of bovine and caprine byproducts has become my most enduring love. As friend and comforter, I talked to the butter as I layered it in wide smears across two heated poppy seed muffins. I spread pimento cheese across two slices of wheat toast before scooping grated cheddar into my steaming bowl of spoon bread. For complementary sides, I had two wedges of ham, a bowl of mac and Velveeta, a mound of fried potatoes and chicken livers along with my entrée, a full plate of steaming biscuits and gravy.

It was a small breakfast. I'd known that my mother, ever so

vinegary, wasn't going to eat, so I figured I'd eat for the both of us. I offered to share, but, seated across from me, she said no by providing a host of disapproving scowls which I was free to interpret in any way I pleased. I wasn't surprised that she looked so shocked. I'd hoped for and expected it.

"Stella, what happened?"

I shrugged. Wasn't it obvious? Her baby girl was blooming, at last, out of her misery.

"Let's go clothes shopping today," I said, "at that discount place, you know, near the Big Lots store, the one you like so much. I need a few things."

"Bigger sizes, you mean," she said. "Much bigger."

I kept chewing as a smile stretched across my face. I sounded little moans of delight, swooning as a toboggan of buttery goodness slid down my esophagus. I washed down my spoonbread with hot coffee and cream. What Mother didn't yet know was that I'd be going back for seconds. Maybe thirds. We were at a buffet and I was on a mission. I intended to get my money's worth.

She had no idea what I'd been through. She could assume, of course, but no clue, not really. I'd coped with my unhappiness by avoiding her. I saw no point in trying to play nice or to explain what I was feeling.

I hadn't told her yet about my fantasy. I decided, in that moment, that I wouldn't. Maybe I'd tell Summer or Nicky. They'd understand it. But not Rusty, no, she'd never understand me.

In my fantasy, I sold the house for a handsome profit and gave Mother a third of those profits. Having left my job too, I legally changed my name, having processed the correct documents and gotten them approved. I then bought a tiny place where no one knew me and where I'd likely never be found. Shreveport, Louisiana. Its obesity rate ranked second nationwide. I'd eat fried alligator and catfish for breakfast there. A town in Texas was rated first for obesity and I'd considered it, but as much as I loved the idea of visiting Texas and feasting on porterhouse steaks grilled over mesquite coals, I couldn't see myself putting down a grubstake there. Shreveport sounded like an easier place to hide.

If my fantasy went smoothly, Rusty and I would never see each other again. Not while alive, anyway. This choice had nothing to do with her. Then again, according to Dr. Murray, maybe it had everything to do with her.

Nicky and Summer Rain would be the two women I'd miss most, and it hurt to think about them. I hadn't said any proper goodbyes. They'd both been trying to call me until I'd changed my number. Good thing it was just a fantasy. I'd hate not having those two in my life.

I was venturing into new territory, with confidence and drive. I intended to show myself off for all to see, the old Stella vanishing, the new one emerging.

Who ever said it was wrong to bury the heartache of one's past?

I flounced my tresses of hair. It had grown longer. More importantly, it was thick again.

"Like my do?" I asked. I'd always worn it long even though for years it had thinned prematurely as a side effect to all my binge-and-purge cycles.

Rusty continued to scowl. "You're not a blonde. You never were. Lord help me, Stella, what's got into you?"

"I'm a blonde now," I said. "Gonna be a real big one too." I shoved a forkful of ham into my mouth. "And it's not falling out."

I felt a pang of regret realizing how much this was hurting Rusty, but she'd get used to the new me. I was on a new path. *My* path. I'd get used to it, too, and one day in the future, someone might find me living my fantasy down in Shreveport. I'd be unrecognizable.

Maybe I'd remarry. He'd have to be a bigger man than Dalton and so much heavier than I planned to become. Of course, if I kept my current splurge going full-throttle, I'd burst open of coronary failure in front of a burbling chocolate fountain at a casino buffet long before Rusty shriveled up and went, at last, to her own salvation.

Naughty, naughty Stella.

About the Author

John Michael Flynn has been Writer in Residence at Carl Sandburg's Connemara in North Carolina, and an English Language Fellow through the US State Department in Khabarovsk, Russia. He also writes as Basil Rosa. Previous shot story collections are *Something Grand, Dreaming Rodin*, and *Off To The Next Wherever*. Poetry collections include *Restless Vanishings, Moments Between Cities*, and *Second Nature Third Eye Fifth Wheel*. His book of essays, *How The Quiet Breathes*, was published in 2021 by New Meridian Arts. Visit him at https://jmfbr1.blogspot.com/.

Fomite

Write a review...

Writing a review on social media sites for readers will help the progress of independent publishing. To submit a review, go to the book page on any of the sites and follow the links for reviews. Books from independent presses rely on reader-to-reader communications.

For more information or to order any of our books, visit fomitepress.com

More story collections from Fomite...

Joshua Amses — *How They Became Birds*
MaryEllen Beveridge — *After the Hunger*
MaryEllen Beveridge — *Permeable Boundaries*
Jay Boyer — *Flight*
L. M Brown — *Treading the Uneven Road*
L. M Brown — *Were We Awake*
Michael Cocchiarale — *Here Is Ware*
Michael Cocchiarale — *Still Time*
Neil Connelly — *In the Wake of Our Vows*
Catherine Zobal Dent — *Unfinished Stories of Girls*
Zdravka Evtimova — *Carts and Other Stories*
Kevin Fitton — *Auras*
John Michael Flynn — *Off to the Next Wherever*
Derek Furr — *Semitones*
Derek Furr — *Suite for Three Voices*
Elizabeth Genovise — *Where There Are Two or More*
Andrei Guriuanu — *Body of Work*
Zeke Jarvis — *In A Family Way*
Arya Jenkins — *Blue Songs in an Open Key*
Bobby Johnston — *The Saint I Ain't*
Jan English Leary — *Skating on the Vertical*
Larry Lefkowitz — *Enigmatic Tales*
Larry Lefkowitz — *Lefkowitz Unbound*
Julia MacDonnell— *The Topography of Hidden Stories*
Marjorie Maddox — *What She Was Saying*
William Marquess — *Badtime Stories*
William Marquess — *Because Because Because Because Because*
William Marquess — *Boom-shacka-lacka*
William Marquess — *Things I Want You to Do*
Gary Miller — *Museum of the Americas*
Jennifer Anne Moses — *Visiting Hours*

Fomite